P9-CDY-577

Praise for Joan Johnston

"Joan Johnston does short contemporary Westerns to perfection."
—*Publishers Weekly*

"Like LaVyrle Spencer, Ms. Johnston writes of intense emotions and tender passions that seem so real that the readers will feel each one of them."
—*Rave Reviews*

"Johnston warms your heart and tickles your fancy."
—*New York Daily News*

"Joan Johnston continually gives us everything we want . . . fabulous details and atmosphere, memorable characters, a story that you wish would never end, and lots of tension and sensuality."
—*Romantic Times*

"Joan Johnston [creates] unforgettable subplots and characters who make every fine thread weave into a touching tapestry."
—*Affaire de Coeur*

DELL BOOKS BY JOAN JOHNSTON

Mail-Order Brides Series
Texas Bride
Wyoming Bride

Bitter Creek Series
The Cowboy
The Texan
The Loner

Captive Hearts Series
Captive
After the Kiss
The Bodyguard
The Bridegroom

Sisters of the Lone Star Series
Frontier Woman
Comanche Woman
Texas Woman

Connected Books
The Barefoot Bride
Outlaw's Bride
The Inheritance
Maverick Heart

and don't miss . . .
Sweetwater Seduction
Kid Calhoun

Books published by The Random House Publishing Group are available at quantity discounts on bulk purchases for premium, educational, fund-raising, and special sales use. For details, please call 1-800-733-3000.

Wyoming Bride

Joan Johnston

DELL

NEW YORK

Sale of this book without a front cover may be unauthorized. If this book is coverless, it may have been reported to the publisher as "unsold or destroyed" and neither the author nor the publisher may have received payment for it.

Wyoming Bride is a work of fiction. Names, characters, places, and incidents are the products of the author's imagination or are used fictitiously. Any resemblance to actual events, locales, or persons, living or dead, is entirely coincidental.

A Dell Mass Market Original

Copyright © 2013 by Joan Mertens Johnston, Inc.
Excerpt from *Montana Bride* by Joan Mertens Johnston copyright © 2013 by Joan Mertens Johnston, Inc.

All rights reserved.

Published in the United States by Dell, an imprint of The Random House Publishing Group, a division of Random House, Inc., New York.

DELL is a registered trademark of Random House, Inc., and the colophon is a trademark of Random House, Inc.

This book contains an excerpt from the forthcoming book *Montana Bride* by Joan Johnston. This excerpt has been set for this edition only and may not reflect the final content of the forthcoming edition.

ISBN 978-0-345-52746-2
eBook ISBN 978-0-345-52747-9

Printed in the United States of America

www.bantamdell.com

9 8 7 6 5 4 3 2 1

Cover design: Lynn Andreozzi
Cover illustration: Alan Ayers

Dell mass market edition: January 2013

This book is dedicated to
LAUREN LINGUANTI
and her family

Chapter One

Hannah had never been so scared in her life, but running wasn't an option. If she didn't go through with her part of the marriage bargain, Mr. McMurtry might not go through with his. Her husband had left her alone in their room at the Palmer House Hotel to ready herself for bed. It had taken less than no time to strip out of her gray wool dress and put on the white flannel nightgown that was all she'd brought with her. She paced the outlines of the elegant canopied bed without ever going near it.

The room was luxurious enough to remind Hannah of the life she and her sisters and brothers had lost three years ago, when their parents were killed in the Great Chicago Fire. The six Wentworth children had ended up in the Chicago Institute for Orphaned Children, at the mercy of the cruel headmistress, Miss Iris Birch.

Hannah caught herself staring longingly at the fire escape through the fourth-floor window. The view blurred as tears of anger—*terrible* anger—and regret—*enormous* regret—filled her eyes.

Hannah felt trapped. Trapped by a moment of generosity she rued with her entire being. Why, oh why, had she listened to her tormented sister Josie's plea?

Two months ago, their eldest sister Miranda had left the orphanage in the middle of the night with ten-year-old Nick and four-year-old Harry to become a mail-order bride in faraway Texas. Hannah, her twin sister Hetty, and Josie had been left behind to await news of whether Miranda's new husband might have room for all of them.

They'd waited . . . and waited . . . and waited for a letter from Miranda. Weeks had turned into months with no news that she'd even arrived safely. No news that she was now a wife. No news about whether there might be a place for the three who'd been left behind.

Hannah and Hetty had been prepared to wait until they turned eighteen in December and were forced to leave the orphanage, if it took that long, for Miranda to send word to come. Josie had not.

Hannah tried to remember exactly what tactic her youngest sister had employed to convince her to answer that advertisement in the Chicago *Daily Herald* seeking a bride willing to travel west to the Wyoming Territory.

"We should wait for Miranda to contact us," Hannah remembered arguing.

"That's easy for you to say," Josie had replied. "You only have eight more months of beatings from Miss Birch to endure. I'll be stuck here for two endless years. You know she's been meaner than ever since Miranda stole away with Nick and Harry. I can't stand two more years here. I can't stand two more days!"

Hannah had taken one look at the desperation in Josie's blue eyes, owlish behind wire-rimmed spectacles, and agreed to marry a man sight unseen.

At least she'd had the foresight to get a commitment from Mr. McMurtry that he would bring her two sisters along on the journey, which entailed three arduous months traveling by Conestoga wagon along the Oregon Trail. The trip could have been made in sixteen hours by rail, but as a child in Ireland, Mr. McMurtry had been on a train that derailed, killing the rest of his family. He refused to travel on another train.

They would all probably die of cholera or drown crossing a river or be scalped by Indians or trampled by a herd of buffalo long before they got to Cheyenne, where Mr. McMurtry planned to open a dry goods store.

Even if they made it all the way to Wyoming, she and Hetty and Josie were headed *away* from Miranda and Nick and Harry, with little chance of ever seeing them again. Agreeing to marry a total stranger headed into the wilderness was seeming more harebrained by the moment.

What on earth had possessed her to do something so very . . . unselfish?

Hannah was used to thinking of herself first. That had never been a problem when she was the spoiled and pampered daughter of wealthy parents. It had even served her well at the orphanage, where food and blankets were scarce. Before Miranda had left to become a mail-order bride, Hannah had been perfectly willing to let her eldest sister consider the needs of everyone else before her own.

Now Hannah was the eldest, at least, of the three who'd been left behind. Now it was her turn to sacrifice. Although marrying a perfect stranger seemed a pretty big leap from giving up food or blankets.

She was lucky the groom hadn't turned out to be seventy-two and bald. In fact, he was only middle-aged. Was thirty-six middle-aged? To a girl of seventeen, it seemed ancient.

Her brand-new husband had a thick Irish brogue and an entire head of the curliest red hair she'd ever see on man or woman. His nose was a once-broken beak, but it gave character to an otherwise plain face. His eyes twinkled, like two dark blue stars caught in a spiderweb of wrinkles caused by years of smiling broadly—or too many hours spent working in the sun. Oh, yes, she felt very lucky.

And very, very sad.

Her tall, rail-thin groom was not the man of her dreams. He wasn't even close.

Hannah was trying to decide how difficult it would be to open the window and retreat down the fire escape when she heard a firm—but quiet—knock at the door.

She scurried away from the window as though her presence there might reveal her desperate hope of avoiding the wedding night before her. There was no escape. She was DOOMED. She'd been well and truly caught in the trap Josie's agonized eyes had set for her.

Her husband had arrived to make her his wife.

Hannah's heart was jumping like a speckle-legged frog in a dry lake. Even knowing who must be at the door, she called out, "Who is it?" Her voice was hoarse and breathy. Fear had constricted her throat. She cleared it and said, "Who's there?"

"It's Mr. McMurtry," a quiet—but firm—Irish voice replied. "May I come in?"

Hannah realized her husband expected to find her in bed. She stared at the gold brocade spread that still covered the sheets. She needed to pull it back and get into bed. But she couldn't do it. She couldn't!

To hell with being unselfish. She *hated* what she was being forced to do. She should have let Hetty do it. After all, Hetty was only *two minutes* younger! Hannah should have insisted they wait until Miranda contacted them. She should have told Josie *No!* in no uncertain terms. She should have run when she had the chance.

But she was married now, like it or not. And her husband was at the door.

Hannah curled her hands into angry fists and fought the tears that blurred her eyes and burned her nose. She hoped the coming journey was as dangerous as it was touted to be. Maybe her husband would die and leave her a widow and—

She brought herself up short and looked guiltily toward the door, behind which stood the man she was wishing dead. Wishing for freedom was one thing. Wishing another person *dead* to earn that freedom was something else entirely. That wasn't how she'd been raised by her parents. Hannah was ashamed of having harbored such an unworthy thought.

No one had forced her to marry Mr. McMurtry. She'd volunteered to do it. She had to GROW UP. She had to put away childish hopes and dreams. This was her life, like it or not.

Hannah stared at the bed. She tried to imagine herself in Mr. McMurtry's arms. She tried to imagine kissing his thin lips. She tried to imagine coupling with him. She couldn't. She just couldn't!

She groaned like a dying animal.

"Are you all right in there?"

Once again, Josie's agonized gaze appeared in her mind's eye. Hannah choked back a sob of resignation, then yanked down the covers and scrambled into bed, bracing her back against the headboard before pulling the covers up to her chin.

"Come in," she croaked.

"Mrs. McMurtry? Are you there?"

Hannah cleared her throat and said, "You can come in, Mr. McMurtry."

The door slowly opened. Mr. McMurtry stepped inside and closed the door behind him, but he didn't move farther into the room.

Too late, Hannah realized she'd left the lamp lit, and that Mr. McMurtry would have to remove his wide-brimmed hat, string tie, chambray shirt, jeans, belt, socks, and hobnail boots—and perhaps even his unmentionables—with her watching. Unless she took the coward's way out and ducked her head beneath the covers . . . or he had the foresight to put out the lamp.

Her new husband swallowed so hard his Adam's apple bobbed, and said, "I had a cup of coffee downstairs."

"Coffee will keep you awake." Again, too late, Hannah realized there was a good reason why Mr. McMurtry might not want to go right to sleep.

Neither of them said anything for an awkward moment.

Then he said. "I'd better . . ."

Hannah watched as Mr. McMurtry blushed. His throat turned rosy, and then the blood filled his face, turning a hundred freckles into red blots on his cheeks.

He stammered, "I've dreamed about this . . . My whole life I . . . You are so beautiful."

Hannah found herself staring back into her husband's very blue eyes with astonishment. She'd known she was pretty, but this was the first time a grown man had remarked on the beauty of her blond curls and wide-spaced, sky-blue eyes, her full lips and peaches-and-cream complexion. It was surprisingly gratifying to hear such words from her husband.

Despite Mr. McMurtry's speech, he remained backed up to the door.

Why, he's scared, too! Hannah realized.

Her fear returned and multiplied. The situation was already mortifying in the extreme, but if *he* was inexperienced, who was going to tell *her* what to do?

"I'm really tired," she blurted. Hannah dropped the sheet and put her hands to her cheeks as they flamed with embarrassment. "I don't believe I said that."

He chuckled.

She glanced sharply in his direction. "Are you laughing at me?"

"No, Mrs. McMurtry," he said. "I was laughing at myself."

She narrowed her eyes suspiciously.

He continued, "I've just married the most beautiful woman I've ever seen, and I'm standing rooted to the

floor a half a room away from her." His smile turned
lopsided as he admitted, "You see, I've never undressed a woman before . . . or undressed before a
woman."

Hannah swallowed hard and whispered, "Never?
Not even a . . ." She couldn't say the word *prostitute*
or *soiled dove* or even *lady of the night*. Ladies did
not speak of such things.

He shook his head. "I'm Catholic. Fornication is
a sin."

"Oh." Hannah couldn't breathe. It felt like all the
air had been sucked from the room. He was thirty-
six, and he'd never been with a woman? This was
going to be a disaster.

Chapter Two

"Shall I turn down the lamp?" Hannah asked.

"No!"

She froze with her hand halfway to the lamp and turned toward Mr. McMurtry, her eyes wide.

He shook his head and smiled. "I didn't mean to sound sharp." He hesitated, met her gaze with serious blue eyes, and said, "I want to see you."

It wasn't often that Hannah found herself speechless, but she had no idea how to reply to a comment like that. He wanted to see her? *Naked?* "Are you sure?" she replied in a small voice.

He chuckled again and for the first time since he'd come into the room, he took a step toward the bed. "I've never been more sure about anything in my life."

Hannah felt her heartbeat ratchet up. She sat even farther upright and once again pulled the covers to her chin. She'd been intimidated by the prospect of allowing Mr. McMurtry the rights of a husband. The thought of baring herself before this stranger sent a shiver—really more of a shudder—down her spine.

She watched with disbelief as Mr. McMurtry pulled his black string tie loose and tugged it free of his white collar, then yanked the collar free of his shirt at the back of his neck. He tossed collar and tie onto a nearby upholstered wing chair, then let his black suit coat slide down his arms. He folded it in half lengthwise and laid it carefully across the top of the chair.

He gave a little sigh as he released the top button of his striped cotton shirt, and she realized it must have been a little tight. He pulled the shirt free of his trousers, unbuttoned a few more buttons, then reached around to the back of his neck and pulled the whole thing forward over his head, leaving his unruly red curls even more wayward than before.

He was still wearing a long john shirt, but he looked positively skinny without the striped shirt and suit coat. He paused with the striped shirt in hand, and said, "You look like my sister did every time she saw a snarling dog on the road."

"What?"

"Brigit was afraid of dogs. She always expected them to bite." He shot her a crooked smile and said, "I promise not to bite, Mrs. McMurtry."

Hannah wanted to believe he was harmless, but when the half-naked stranger took another step toward the bed, she heard herself whimper with fear.

He held up a hand and said in a soothing voice, "I'm not going to hurt you." He grimaced and added, "At least, not any more than is necessary."

Hannah swallowed noisily. "I know."

"You know?" He frowned. "What do you know?"

He looked so formidable, Hannah regretted opening her mouth to say anything. "I mean, I know you won't hurt me any more than you must."

The frown was still on his face, so she continued, "I've only known you for a day, Mr. McMurtry, but you've been more than fair in your treatment of me and my sisters. I trust you not to hurt me."

"Any more than is necessary," he added.

Hannah lowered her gaze to her knees, which were knocking under the covers. She knew more than she should about what was to come. One of the girls at the orphanage had enjoyed marital relations with a man to whom she was definitely *not* married, and she'd shared that experience with Hannah and Hetty.

Hannah knew the first time would hurt, perhaps more than a little. She wasn't sure whether to trust that things would be better the second time, and perhaps even pleasurable by the third, as her friend had promised. Would Mr. McMurtry want to do it three times tonight?

Hannah managed not to flinch when Mr. McMurtry sat down on the bed beside her. He reached out a hand to brush a stray curl from her cheek. She'd confined her blond hair in a braid that ran halfway down her back. She bit her lip to keep from protesting when he tugged the covers from her hands and let them fall to her lap. She stared into his somber blue eyes as he pulled the heavy braid forward over her shoulder, so it rested on the front of her nightgown.

She kept herself very still as he released the frayed ribbon on the end of the braid and unraveled it. His focus shifted to her blond curls as his fingers sifted through them. She shivered involuntarily, which caused him to look up and meet her gaze.

There was something about his half-lidded eyes that held her spellbound. He met her gaze with an intensity—and a depth of feeling—she'd never experienced. It left her breathless. She began to pant as if she'd run a race, even though she hadn't moved an inch.

Neither had he.

He slowly leaned toward her, and Hannah realized he was going to kiss her. She held herself very still, but the closer he got, the more difficult it was to breathe. She put a flat hand against his chest to stop him, to give her a chance to catch her breath, but he moved inexorably closer, forcing her to cede him the space.

She could feel the heat of his body through his long john shirt. She could see the beat of his heart in the pulse at his throat and the dark auburn whiskers that were already sprouting on his cheeks and chin. He was so close she went almost cross-eyed trying to look at him, so she closed her eyes. And waited. It was her first kiss. Ever. And she wanted it to be perfect.

Her heart pounded in her ears, and she felt her cheeks flushing with heat. She wanted to like Mr. McMurtry's kiss, but his lips were dry and cracked, and he pressed them against her own hard enough to mash her lips against her teeth.

Hannah felt suffocated and shoved hard with both hands against his chest, turning her head to break free. "Stop! Don't!"

He jerked back as though she'd slapped him. Which she had, with words. She stared at him aghast. He was her husband. It was his right to do with her as he willed. He held her life in his hands. The safety of her sisters—their escape from the despicable Miss Birch—depended on her pleasing him tonight.

Hannah blinked back the tears that brimmed in her eyes and tried to smile. "Could you . . . Would it be possible . . . to go more slowly, Mr. McMurtry? More gently?"

He looked disappointed. And frustrated. And worst of all, embarrassed.

Hannah felt bad about chastising her inexperienced husband. She should be glad he was a morally upright man. They would be learning together. That is, if they could get through this first night.

When her husband started to rise, Hannah put her fingertips on his wrist to stop him. She took his hand in hers and lifted it to her cheek, pressing it softly against her warm flesh. His hand was rough and callused and hard. He was no gentleman, nothing like the sort of man she would have married if the Great Fire had never happened. Her father would never even have allowed her to speak to such a coarse, low-born person.

But that life was gone, and she had to make the best of the one she had now. She forced herself to continue, leaning toward her new husband, afraid that, at any moment, he might reject her advances.

He sat still as a post, waiting to see what she would do.

Hannah pouted her lips out, as she'd practiced in front of the mirror with Hetty, when they'd imagined someday kissing the handsome prince who would arrive to carry them away to his castle. When her mouth finally touched Mr. McMurtry's, she pushed her lips against his tenderly, softly. She felt his lips give under the pressure of hers, felt the surrender as his mouth conformed to her own . . . and something totally unexpected. A surge of desire.

Hannah backed away suddenly and stared with awe into dark blue eyes covered by eyelids lowered in a way that told her he wanted her, too. They were both breathing erratically.

She realized something else. She felt like prey, pursued by something savage that was capable of devouring her. She resisted the urge to flee, controlling her panic as she had many times at the orphanage, while waiting for Miss Birch to give her three hard strokes of the rod. Three only. That was the limit. Anything could be endured if one only freed one's mind from what was happening.

This, too, would pass.

She lifted her gaze to the dark blue eyes staring intently back into her own. Instead of easing, the strange feelings inside got worse. Her breasts felt swollen, her throat felt raw and tight, and her womb contracted. Her body seemed not to be her own, out of her control, headed on a course toward something frightening and unknown.

Hannah didn't resist when Mr. McMurtry reached for the bow holding her nightgown together at her neck and pulled it free. He eased the fabric off her shoulders, but before it fell all the way down, she caught it and held it in a knot against her breasts.

She could do this. She had to do this.

"I want to see you."

His voice was so low and guttural she almost didn't

recognize it. The fierce, feral sound of it sent goose bumps of fear skittering along her arms. She swallowed hard, trying to clear the thickness in her throat so she could speak. She wanted to say, *All right*.

Nothing came out.

She loosened her grip on the front of the gown, leaving it in a crumpled ball at the top of her breasts. And held her breath. And waited.

At last, he shoved it down, pinning her arms against her sides, making her a prisoner, and revealing to his avid gaze her soft breasts, including the nipples that had turned to hard buds against her will.

He froze and stared. "You're perfect," he grated out.

Hannah was staring down, so she saw his hands cup her breasts—too hard, too tight—and lift them. Saw his head lower and felt his lips, unutterably soft and gentle, kiss first one breast and then the other.

Her body stirred and hummed and begged her to do something. She tugged her hands free of the sleeves that were pinning them and threaded her fingers into his hair, surprised to find the curls so soft. When he lifted his head to look into her eyes, her hands were still caught there.

She held his head close, wishing him to be gentle. Wishing him to be kind. Wishing him to be the prince that he was not.

He leaned forward and kissed her lips again. He was gentle at first, but that didn't last long. His hands tightened painfully on her breasts as his mouth pressed harder against hers, crushing her lips painfully against her teeth.

She couldn't catch her breath. She couldn't breathe. She felt as though she were going to suffocate. She tried to draw breath, but everything was happening too fast.

He grabbed her hips and pulled her down in the bed so she was lying flat, then shoved up the bottom of her nightgown.

"Wait!" she cried.

She pushed against him, but he grabbed both her hands in one of his. His hold was gentle, but inexorable. Suddenly, she was fighting him, as a drowning swimmer fights the water that threatens to swallow her, scratching and clawing.

"Easy, girl," he soothed. "This is what happens between a man and a woman."

Hannah felt reassured by his voice and fought her panic. But it was a losing battle. She didn't want to be here. She didn't want to be doing this. She reminded herself, *He is my husband. I am his wife.*

She took a deep breath and let it out, forcing herself to lie still as Mr. McMurtry unbuttoned the front of his trousers and forced her legs wide with his knees. She could feel him hard and unforgiving against her innocent flesh.

She bucked once to be free, but he answered with that same "Easy, girl," and added, "It will all be over soon," then lifted her bottom with his free hand and impaled her.

Hannah felt as though she'd been stabbed with a human knife. The pain was excruciating.

He pumped into her. Once. Twice. Three times. Then he groaned like a dying animal and sagged onto her with his full weight before sliding onto the bed beside her.

Was he done? Was it over?

Hannah sobbed once, but it was grief she felt, not physical pain. She was truly married now. There was no going back.

"I'm sorry." The apology was muffled, since Mr. McMurtry's mouth was mashed against her throat. He levered himself up onto his arms and stared down at her.

She saw the regret in his eyes and wondered at it. He had what he'd wanted. Why was he sorry?

He pushed himself away from her and slid the awful, limp pink thing that looked not at all like the knife she'd felt impale her, back into his trousers. "I wish I'd been able to make it hurt less, but . . ."

But he'd had no experience with women. Hannah's heart went out to this plain man who had kept himself chaste for marriage. In that moment of understanding, she forgave her husband for the physical pain he'd caused. Nevertheless, she instinctively recoiled when he reached across her to turn out the lamp.

Hannah saw another look of remorse cross his face before it was lost in the darkness. He *was* a kind man. He *hadn't* meant to hurt her. She felt the urge to offer her new husband comfort, but she was afraid it might make him want to do it again. Instead, she held herself perfectly still.

"Get some sleep, Mrs. McMurtry," he said. "We have a long day ahead of us tomorrow."

Hannah let out a silent breath of relief. It was not a

wedding night to warm a young bride's heart, but at least it was over and done. She took a deep breath, then exhaled long and slow, letting go of all the fear she'd felt of the unknown. Now she knew what to expect. She hoped her friend was right. She hoped it wouldn't hurt as much the next time, and that someday it might even be pleasurable.

But as far as she was concerned, she wouldn't be sorry if they never did it again.

Chapter Three

Hannah was pregnant. She'd missed the courses that should have come two weeks after her wedding night, but several days had passed before she'd realized that fact. Even though her period had come as regular as clockwork since she was fourteen, Hannah had thought the excitement of starting on such a fabulous journey might have caused the lapse. Four weeks later, when the bleeding didn't start for the second month in a row, she was no longer able to deny the truth.

Now, here she was two months pregnant, and she still hadn't told her husband or her sisters about the baby. Hannah didn't know why she was waiting. Or maybe she did. Announcing she was pregnant meant acknowledging to herself that sober, hardworking, and considerate—as well as placid, wooden, and untalkative—Mr. McMurtry would be her partner for the rest of her life.

At the beginning of the journey, Hannah had sidestepped Mr. McMurtry as much as possible, hoping to avoid her wifely duties. It wasn't until they'd been on the trail for almost a month that she'd realized *he* was also avoiding *her*! It seemed he was shy around women, and her, in particular. That might have been endearing, except whenever she tried holding a conversation with him, he answered in as few words as possible, never sharing his thoughts or feelings.

Hannah had tried harder, choosing subjects she thought might interest her husband, with no success. She'd tried making Mr. McMurtry angry, but he refused to be drawn. She'd even tried—she cringed at the memory—flirting with him. That had caused him to visibly blush and sent him stumbling away from the campfire.

She'd given up. Marriage, she was discovering, was more about two people sharing the work than much of anything else. Maybe it would have been different if she and Mr. McMurtry were sleeping together in the same bed. But they weren't.

It wasn't a case of her husband not desiring her. Hannah saw the yearning, almost wistful look in her husband's dark blue eyes in the firelight before he took his bedroll and went to sleep by himself, while she joined her two sisters on a pallet laid out under their Conestoga wagon.

It seemed Mr. McMurtry was too fastidious to couple with her unless they had complete privacy, and he wouldn't take the risk of leaving the safe circle of wagons with her at night to get it. Hannah knew this hiatus was only a reprieve, not a release from her dreaded wifely duty. However, she had some hope her pregnancy might delay their next coupling until after the child was delivered, instead of resuming in another month, when they reached Cheyenne.

Hannah set down the long wooden spoon she'd

been using to stir the venison stew she was cooking over the evening campfire, stood upright, and placed her hands gently against her still-flat abdomen. She was amazed by how much love she felt for her unborn child. And disheartened by her lack of similar strong feelings for her husband.

How did one fall in love? Hannah wondered. Could it be done on purpose? What did "being in love" feel like? Considering who she'd married, she might never experience that emotion toward her husband. Was liking enough? She already liked Mr. McMurtry, but she felt lonely imagining a future with a man incapable of holding a conversation.

Hannah sighed. That was bad enough, but it was impossible to feel close to someone she was still calling *Mr. McMurtry* after two months of marriage. Would there ever be a day when he would call her anything except *Mrs. McMurtry*? Or a day when they would call each other something more familiar, like *dear* or *darling* or *sweetheart*? It was heartbreaking to realize that the only time she'd heard her husband's first name spoken aloud was during the wedding ceremony. *Roland.*

Hannah mouthed the name but didn't say it aloud. She stood alone at the campfire, but someone from the circle of wagons might walk past and hear her. She glanced around and saw everyone going about their business, unhitching mules or oxen, making repairs on their wagons, or tending their evening fires.

No one seemed to notice the roiling tension she felt inside as she cooked supper for her husband and sisters. She felt too many things at once, all of them mixed up together. The excitement of having a child of her own to love. The despair of knowing she would likely never see Miranda or Nick or Harry again. The sadness of lost dreams of love. And the growing acceptance of what must be.

She mouthed, *Roland and Hannah*.

Hannah wanted Mr. McMurtry to say her first name. To whisper it in her ear. To speak it with devotion. She wanted the intimacy it implied. But it was hard to imagine her plain, practical husband ever doing something so tender. So romantic.

Mr. McMurtry might not be the man of her dreams, but for her child's sake, she had to see the good in him and make the best of her marriage. And there was a great deal of good in Roland McMurtry. He never spoke harshly to her. He shaved every day and bathed when he could. He never blasphemed, even to his stubborn oxen. And he was tolerant of her sisters, who caused him endless trouble with the wagon master.

It was time to put her girlhood dreams away. There was no handsome, dashing Prince Charming in her future, only solemn, honest, hardworking Mr. McMurtry.

She felt tears well in her eyes and brushed them angrily away. Would she ever stop dreaming and hoping and wishing for something she could never have?

Hannah had spent the entire day as she walked beside Mr. McMurtry's wagon in the choking dust and pounding heat from the sun, pondering her life. That is, when she could hear herself think over the jangle of the traces and the rattle of pails tied beneath the wagon and the crack of the whip and the lowing of footsore oxen.

She rubbed the same hand she'd smoothed over her flat belly against the ache in the small of her back. The work on a wagon train never ended. There was always something that needed to be done—above and beyond walking on blistered feet every endless mile of the way. Luckily, she hadn't experienced any sickness from her pregnancy, but she was more and more exhausted at the end of every day.

It was Hannah's job to grease the axles, to milk the cow that was tied behind the wagon, to feed a ration of corn to the four oxen that pulled the wagon, to fill pails of water whenever they crossed a creek or a stream or a river and dump them in the enormous barrel tied to the side of the wagon, to cook morning and evening with the other wives on the wagon train, and to wash dishes and silverware and pots and pans and pack everything away afterward.

Last, but not at all least, it was her job to keep Josie, and especially Hetty, out of trouble. Both girls were making Hannah's life difficult, but in different ways.

Josie's only job was to fill a sling under the wagon with sticks and dried cow patties she collected along the trail, so they would have enough fuel for the evening fire. Instead, she spent every day walking along with her face stuck in a book. More than once they'd needed to share the fire of another family, because they didn't have enough wood or cow chips for their own.

Still, it was hard to be angry with Josie. Her youngest sister had made friends with a former teacher, Thomas Stanfield, and his sixteen-year-old son, Micah, who'd brought two big boxes of books on the trip

West. Josie was trying to get through as many of their precious tomes as she could read before they parted ways at Cheyenne, since the Stanfields were headed all the way to Oregon.

Josie seemed oblivious to the fact that Micah was romantically interested in her. Hannah knew her sister was in love with Micah's books, rather than the tall, good-looking boy who spent every day at her side with stars in his eyes.

Hetty was another matter altogether. Hetty's love life was creating havoc, and she was not the least bit repentant about it.

Hannah glanced sideways from the evening cook fire and saw her twin flirting with Joe Barnett, while the man Hetty had been favoring for most of the trip, Clive Hamm, scowled at them.

Hannah could hardly blame her sister for wanting to be admired by not one, but two attractive men. After all, Hetty was the prettiest unmarried woman on the train.

But Hannah saw what Hetty did not. Though both suitors were young, they weren't boys. And here in the West, arguments between men were settled not with words, but with fists . . . and guns.

Last week, the two men had engaged in a bout of fisticuffs that the wagon master, Captain Hattigan, had broken up. The captain had warned Mr. Mc-Murtry, "Control your ward, or you will no longer be welcome to travel with the train!"

After everything Hannah had seen during their two months on the trail, that threat was terrifying. The wilderness was vast, and dangerous beyond belief. She'd watched people die from stupid accidents, from drowning, from disease, from the simple act of birthing a child. Every time she'd watched families grieve, it had reminded her of the family she'd lost and left her with a terrible ache in her chest.

Hannah couldn't imagine what it would be like for their lone wagon to travel without the support of the others. What if an axle broke? Who would help Mr. McMurtry repair it? What if one of their oxen died? How would they travel on with only three? What if Josie didn't gather enough fuel for an evening fire and they were forced to do without one? What if they ran out of water?

Hannah had endless nightmares about what might happen. Yesterday, she'd finally shared them with her twin, hoping it would make a difference in her behavior.

"Captain Hattigan would never make us leave the train," Hetty had said, laughing at her fears.

"Please, Hetty. I'm begging you. Don't flirt with *both* men."

"I know what I'm doing," Hetty said defiantly. "Clive has hinted that he's going to propose, but he wants to wait until the end of the journey. I don't. I'm just flirting with Mr. Barnett to make Clive declare himself."

"It's only a matter of weeks before we reach Cheyenne," Hannah argued. "That's not so long to wait. And since when do you call Mr. Hamm *Clive*?"

Hetty flipped her blond curls back over her shoulder, grinned, and said, "I don't call him that—to his face. He's still Mr. Hamm. But Joe—"

"*Joe?*" Hannah interrupted, appalled at such familiarity.

"Mr. Barnett told me I could call him Joe." Hetty smiled, revealing the dimples in her cheeks. Hannah knew her own dimples hadn't seen the light of day since before she was married.

"Do you like Mr. Barnett better than Mr. Hamm?" Hannah asked.

"Of course not! I'm only using Joe to make Clive realize I won't wait forever."

"Hetty, you're playing with fire," Hannah warned. "Mr. Hamm won't stand still for another man poaching game he thinks is his."

Hetty's eyes narrowed and her nostrils flared. "So now I'm a bird in the hand, is that it? Clive doesn't own me. No man owns me. Yet."

"No man will want to own you if you keep flirting so outrageously," Hannah snapped.

"We'll see about that!" Hetty had flounced away, chin uptilted, a disaster waiting to happen.

Hannah stirred the pot of stew again and watched with disgust and disappointment as Hetty smiled up at Joe Barnett. She saw her sister take a surreptitious glance in Clive Hamm's direction, then reach out and briefly touch Mr. Barnett's sleeve.

At that moment, Josie plopped down on a stone near the fire, tilting an open book toward the flames in an effort to see the words in the meager light.

"You'll ruin your eyes reading in the dark," Hannah said.

"I was almost done when the sun began to set," Josie replied, pushing her spectacles up toward the bridge of her nose. "I hoped there would be enough light from the fire to finish. But there isn't," she said as she snapped the book closed.

"What are you reading?" Hannah asked.

"It's a good one. *Pride and Prejudice*. About a family of girls in England. About falling in love. About failing at love. About the foibles of love."

It sounded like something Hannah might like, but before she could say so, she heard Clive Hamm shout, "Get away from her!"

Hannah took one look at Hetty, standing with her mouth open and her eyes wide with fright, dropped the spoon she was using to stir the stew, picked up her skirts, and ran.

"I told you to keep your distance," Clive snarled at Joe.

"Please, Mr. Hamm—" Hetty said, her hands raised in supplication.

Hetty's paramour shoved her aside.

Hannah heard her sister cry out as her shoulder landed hard against the large back wheel of Joe Barnett's wagon.

"Clive, please don't!" Hetty babbled. "I love *you*!"

Mr. Hamm didn't hear her. Or didn't care. He was totally focused on his rival. "I told you what would happen if you went near her again."

"You don't own her," Joe Barnett shot back.

"Get the captain!" Hannah shouted as she passed Mr. McMurtry. He looked startled, but he took off in the direction of the captain's wagon.

Hannah reached her sister in time to grab her arm and keep her from flinging herself between the two men, who were faced off against each other.

"I have to stop them," Hetty cried as she yanked at Hannah's grasp on her arm, trying to break free.

Hannah tightened her hold and said, "There's nothing you can do now, Hetty. It's too late."

"He'll be killed!"

"If he is, you'll have no one to blame but yourself," Hannah snapped back.

"Please," Hetty begged. "Let me go!"

Hannah only held on tighter. She felt a sinking sensation. This was not going to end well. She wasn't thinking of the two men. They deserved whatever they got from each other. She'd sent for the captain, because she hoped to avoid bloodshed. But Hannah knew, as sure as God made little green apples, that even if neither man was injured, Mr. and Mrs. McMurtry and the Wentworth girls would not be moving on with the wagon train.

"Oh, Hetty, you fool!" she said bitterly.

"I didn't mean for this to happen," Hetty retorted.

Hannah was riveted as Clive closed the distance between himself and Joe Barnett. "Shh," she hissed at Hetty. She didn't want to distract either of the men.

"We're going to settle this once and for all," Clive said through bared teeth. He pulled a knife from the sheath at his waist and menacingly sliced it through the air.

Joe pulled a gun.

Clive turned the knife in his hand and threw it hard and fast just as Joe pulled the trigger.

The gunshot reverberated in the night air.

The knife landed with a sickening *thunk*!

Neither man made a sound, and for a moment Hannah thought both of them had missed their marks. But then Joe put a hand to his chest, where the knife was buried to the hilt. And Clive put a hand to his chest, where a dark stain was blossoming on his muslin shirt. The two men exchanged looks of disbelief. And their legs stopped holding them upright.

There was nothing dramatic about it. Clive's knees crumpled, and he fell forward onto his face. Joe dropped to his knees and fell onto his side, the Colt .45 still gripped in his hand.

Hannah was so shocked, she loosened her hold on Hetty. Her twin ripped free and raced toward the fallen men.

"Clive!" Hetty cried. "Clive!" She dropped to her knees beside the man she'd professed to love and reached down to lift his head into her lap.

Hannah could see Clive's lips moving and watched as her sister leaned close to hear what he was saying. Tears filled Hetty's eyes and began streaming down her cheeks. She sobbed once as she pressed her cheek against Clive's.

Captain Hattigan was tight-lipped when he finally arrived and surveyed the mayhem. "What happened here?"

"They was fightin' over her, Captain," one of the nearby men said, gesturing toward Hetty.

The wagon master turned to Mr. McMurtry and said, "When we leave tomorrow, you won't be going with us."

Hannah met her husband's gaze and saw frustration. And disappointment. And despair.

Those emotions she'd expected. What surprised her was what she saw next.

Understanding. And acceptance. And forgiveness.

Hannah's throat tightened with emotion, and her nose stung with unshed tears. She might never love

Mr. McMurtry, but in that moment, Hannah knew she would always be grateful to him.

Marriage was no fairy-tale romance. It was supporting your partner and accepting the bad with the good. Fortunately for her and her wayward sisters, Mr. McMurtry was a very tolerant man. Because, during their very brief marriage, there had been far more bad than good.

Chapter Four

Hannah stopped walking abruptly as Mr. McMurtry bolted off the wagon bench and stumbled to the dusty ground. She took a step toward him and then had to back up as he bent over and vomited.

They'd survived alone on the trail for four weeks and five days. They hadn't made as good time alone as they had with the wagon train, but at least nothing had gone wrong that Mr. McMurtry couldn't fix.

It seemed their luck had come to an end.

Mr. McMurtry slowly lifted his head and reached into his back pocket for a red kerchief, which he used to wipe his mouth.

Hannah met his gaze and saw the same despair she'd been feeling ever since he'd gotten sick. "You should rest," she said.

"We have to keep going." He turned, lifted a booted foot to climb back onto the wagon bench, then dropped it, gripped his belly and bent as though curling his body around the pain. "Goddamn it to hell!" he muttered.

A feeling of foreboding slithered down Hannah's

spine. For Mr. McMurtry to take the Lord's name in vain, he must be in agony. "What can I do to help?"

He looked up at the sun, which was at its zenith, then shook his head and said, "We'll have to stop here for today. I can't—" He rubbed at his belly with knotted fists, met her gaze, and said, "Oh, God, Hannah."

Hannah stared at her husband with horrified eyes. Finally, at long last, he'd used her first name. *Hannah.* But there was nothing soft or sentimental in its utterance. It had sounded like . . . a death knell.

He brushed past her, running to the back of the wagon, yanking the braces off his shoulders and unbuttoning his pants. Hannah turned her eyes away, but she knew what was happening behind her. To her horror, she heard him vomiting again as well.

Hannah had been watching her husband with worried eyes for the past two days, ever since they'd left the last place they'd stopped, a collection of shanties and tents where folks had given up traveling west and decided to try and farm.

Surviving on the trail alone as long as they had was a miracle, as far as Hannah was concerned. They'd stayed close behind the wagon train for two weeks, but had fallen steadily behind ever since. Hannah had no idea where the other wagons were now.

She watched Josie clamber up onto the wagon bench seat and take up the reins Mr. NcMurtry had dropped.

Josie looked down at her and whispered, "He's really sick, Hannah. He didn't even bother to put on the brake." She pulled on the leather straps he'd dropped until the oxen stopped again.

"Can you set the brake, Josie?" Hannah asked.

"Sure. I've seen Mr. McMurtry do it plenty of times."

"Then do it." Hannah turned and strode toward the back of the wagon, where Mr. McMurtry was lying on the ground, curled into a tight ball.

Hannah looked around for Hetty, but she was far behind. Her twin had hardly spoken since they'd left the train. Or eaten, for that matter. If Hetty wasn't careful, she'd get sick, too.

In that moment, Hannah hated her sister. Fervently. If not for Hetty, they wouldn't be all alone out here in the middle of nowhere.

She reached Mr. McMurtry and crouched down beside him. The wind was blowing more than one foul smell toward her, and she put the back of her hand against her nose to keep from losing the contents of her stomach.

Mr. McMurtry batted lethargically at the hand she reached out to him and said, "Go away." His skin looked shriveled. His eyes were sunk deep in purple sockets.

Hannah felt unaccountably hurt that he'd rejected her offer of help. She couldn't count the times Mr. McMurtry had assisted her with some job. Now that their roles were reversed, he was acting like she was some stranger to whom he'd owe a debt. She'd been the best wife she could be, done her share of the work and never shirked. His refusal to allow her to minister to him seemed like a rejection of her as his wife.

She wanted to shout, *You're not perfect, either!* But he was sick, and she owed him the respect he'd earned during their marriage. So she swallowed over the wretched lump in her throat and asked, "How are you feeling?"

"How the hell do you think I feel?"

The irritability, and especially the profanity, were frightening because they were additional signs Mr. McMurtry was not himself. Hannah felt a rising panic and shoved it back down.

He tried to get up but grabbed his stomach, groaned, and lay back down. "I need a little time to rest."

"I'll wait here with you," Hannah said as she settled onto a tuft of buffalo grass beside him. She watched as his eyes slowly closed.

She tried to hold the fear at bay, but her body began to tremble. They were out here in the middle of nowhere with no one to turn to for rescue. Maybe if Mr. McMurtry got some sleep his illness would pass. Maybe someone traveling behind would catch up to them and help. She thought of every possible scenario where someone—some stranger—saved the day.

Hannah felt a hand on her shoulder. She lifted her head and saw it belonged to Hetty. How long had they been stopped?

"Come with me," Hetty said. She reached down and took Hannah's hands and pulled her to her feet and led her several steps away from the supine man.

"He's got cholera," Hetty said in a soft voice.

Hannah shook her head in denial. Cholera could kill in a matter of days. Mr. McMurtry had been sick for at least forty-eight hours. That would mean he didn't have long to live. "What makes you think it's cholera?" she demanded.

"There was an outbreak in those shantys we passed," Hetty said. "I heard some folks talking about it. He must have come in contact with someone who was infected."

"Then why aren't the rest of us sick?" Hannah challenged. "We went everywhere he did."

"He visited those folks camped in tents away from the others. None of us went there with him."

"He can't have cholera." If Mr. McMurtry died, who would yoke and unyoke the oxen? Who would tell them which way to go? Who would protect them from strangers on the trail?

"He's been in the bushes on and off for two days," Hetty said. "We need to camp here, Hannah, so he can rest and maybe get better."

"*Maybe* get better?"

Hetty shrugged.

"We're getting farther behind the wagon train every moment we stand still."

"I know, Hannah. But we don't have a choice. Look at him."

Hannah stared at her husband. His eyes were closed, his breathing shallow, and he lay motionless. She looked for a pulse at his throat but couldn't see it. Her heart was pounding in her chest as she knelt beside him and pressed her fingertips to the spot where his blood should be pumping strongest. And found a thready pulse.

She looked up at Hetty and said in a shaky voice, "He's going to get well," as though the spoken words could make it true.

"Sure he will," Hetty said.

Hannah could tell her twin didn't believe what she was saying. Surely not everyone died of cholera. But

Hannah had heard stories of enormous death tolls in places struck by cholera.

Josie climbed down from the wagon and joined them. She'd been sulking as well, angered by the loss of that cherished wagonload of books. However, with nothing but the trail to look at, the tarp slung under the wagon was full of grass for tinder, dried wood, and cow dung. "What's going on?" she asked.

"We're stopping," Hannah said. "Until Mr. Mc-Murtry gets better."

"We're getting farther behind—"

"There's no help for it," Hannah interrupted. "We can't go on with him as sick as he is."

"We could put him in the wagon and keep traveling," Josie said practically.

The suggestion made a great deal of sense to Hannah. And it would move them closer to their destination and help. "All right," she said, getting to her feet. "Let's do it."

"We're going to have to unload a bunch of stuff and leave it behind to get him in there," Hetty pointed out.

"What other choice do we have?" Hannah asked.

"We could wait here," Hetty suggested.

"Until what?" Hannah said.

Until he dies.

Hannah heard the words, even though Hetty didn't speak them. Instead, Hetty said, "Maybe the last place we stopped has a doctor who could help him."

Hannah didn't believe that any more than Hetty probably did.

"We'd be better off finishing the journey," Josie said. "We can't be too far from Cheyenne."

"The problem is, we don't have any idea exactly how far it is," Hannah said.

"It can't be more than a couple of days farther on," Josie said. "Unless we're lost."

"Don't even *think* that!" Hannah said. Although she'd thought exactly that herself when they hadn't reached Cheyenne after four full weeks of travel. Mr. McMurtry had looked worried after their stop at the collection of shantys. She wished now that she'd asked what was wrong.

"Going back to a place we can find sounds safer than going forward to a place we've never been," Hetty said.

"If the last place we left is infected with cholera, I'd rather steer clear of it," Josie said.

That made sense to Hannah, too.

"I say we keep going," Josie argued.

"How will we find the trail by ourselves?" Hetty asked.

Josie pointed to shallow ruts the width of wagon wheels that led across the prairie. "We follow those."

Hetty stuck her hands on her hips. "Who's going to drive those stubborn oxen?"

"I will," Josie said. "I've been watching Mr. McMurtry snap that bullwhip every step of the way. How hard can it be?"

Hannah looked from one sister's face to the other's. They didn't look nearly as afraid as she felt. There was no sense reminding them of the difficulties that lay ahead. "All right. Let's get the wagon unloaded. Josie, give the oxen some water, but don't unyoke them. We'll have to take a good look before we do that tonight to make sure we can figure out how to yoke them up again tomorrow morning."

They'd started out with a wagon filled to the two-thousand-pound limit with supplies, everything from hammers and hatchets to snowshoes, from dried fruit and beans to pickles and vinegar, from a butter mold and churn to a coffee grinder. Even after nearly three months of travel, the wagon bed was still packed so full that there was barely space for Hannah and Hetty to stand.

"You're going to miss having this rocker on your front porch," Hetty said as she dumped it out the back of the wagon.

Hannah picked up a chair and threw it onto the patchy grass in the center of the wagon tracks they'd been following. The chest under it was too heavy to move by herself. "Help me with this chest, Hetty."

"Maybe we should unpack it first, so it's lighter," Hetty suggested.

Hannah opened the chest and saw a beautiful quilt. "We can cover him with this, once we get him in the wagon." She threw the quilt aside and found sheets. "We might need these, too. They're wrapped around something."

Hannah unwound the sheets and found a beautiful framed mirror.

Hetty took it from her and studied her dirty, sunburned face and windblown blond curls. "I don't think any man would be attracted to me the way I look now." Then she tossed the mirror onto the ground, where it splintered into a thousand tiny pieces.

Josie looked up at Hetty and said, "You shouldn't have done that."

"Why not?"

"When you break a mirror, you get seven years of bad luck."

Hetty sneered. "Our luck couldn't get much worse than it already is."

"Keep working," Hannah said. "We're losing daylight."

They threw out furniture, mostly, but also got rid of fifty-pound sacks of rice, beans, and flour, which Hannah knew they were going to miss when they reached Cheyenne.

She spread Mr. McMurtry's sleeping pallet on the space they'd cleared, then put a sheet and quilt nearby. She took out a bowl to use in case he had to vomit and filled another one with water to wipe his fevered forehead. She tore one of the sheets into rags to clean him if he fouled himself while traveling in the wagon.

When Hannah was done, she left the wagon and crossed to where Mr. McMurtry lay. Josie had draped a sheet over a couple of chairs they'd discarded to make shade for him while her sisters worked. "Mr. McMurtry?" Hannah laid a tentative hand on his shoulder, expecting him to knock it away again.

He mumbled something incoherent, but he didn't move.

"Mr. McMurtry?" she repeated. She dared far enough to put a hand on his forehead. It was burning hot.

He muttered something that made no sense.

"He's delirious," Hetty said matter-of-factly.

"We don't know that!" Hannah snapped.

"He's babbling nonsense. What would you call it?" Hetty retorted.

"Let's get him in the wagon," Josie said. "So we can go."

Hetty put her hands on her hips again and said, "How do you propose we do that? He's out of his senses."

Josie knelt down and took one of Mr. McMurtry's hands. "You get the other one, Hannah, and we'll sit him upright."

Hannah did as her youngest sister ordered. Once they had him upright, his eyes opened.

"Where am I?" he asked.

"Can you stand?" Hannah asked.

Hetty removed the sheet that had kept the sun off him and balled it up in her arms.

He started to get up but fell down again. Hannah and Josie helped him to his feet. Hetty hurried to the wagon and climbed up into it, ready to help pull him in. After several tries, the three of them managed to get him onto the pallet in the wagon. Almost immediately, he started retching.

Hannah grabbed the bowl she had ready and caught most of the vomit. Hetty choked and then threw up over the back of the wagon. Josie wrinkled her nose at the smell and said, "I'll go get us moving."

"If you're both going to ride, I'm riding, too," Hetty said to her twin, as she searched for a place to sit in the back of the wagon.

"Fine," Hannah said. "You can help me wipe Mr. McMurtry when the time comes."

"On second thought, I'll walk," Hetty said, throwing a leg over the tailgate.

"Please, Hetty, stay!" Hannah met her sister's gaze and said, "I don't want to be alone with him."

Hetty made a face but stepped back inside the wagon.

Up front, Josie cracked the bullwhip and yelled at the oxen, "Get your butts moving, you lazy sons of bitches!"

Hannah met Hetty's startled gaze with one of her own, and the two sisters burst out laughing. A moment later, Hannah was sobbing. A moment after that, Hetty was hugging her hard, crying just as loudly.

"What's going on?" Josie called from the bench seat. "Did he die?"

"Not yet," Hetty called back.

She looked at Hannah, and they burst into hysterical laughter again, followed by more hysterical sobs.

"I'm sorry," Hetty said between choking sobs, as she stared into her twin's tear-filled eyes. "I'm so sorry, Hannah. If I could take it all back, I would. I never imagined this would happen. I'm so sorry."

Hannah pulled herself free. She wasn't ready to forgive Hetty. Not yet. Maybe never. They'd probably end up dead anyway, so forgiveness wouldn't matter. She took a piece of torn sheet, dipped it in the sloshing bowl of water, and used it to wipe Mr. McMurtry's forehead.

His eyes opened almost immediately. He looked up at her and said in a soft, tender voice, "Hannah?"

Hannah's heart hurt. She stared down into Mr. McMurtry's eyes, wondering if she should call him Roland, wondering if she should tell him he was going to be a father. Before she could do either of those things, his eyes closed again. And he sighed.

Only, it wasn't a sigh, exactly. It was longer and deeper and . . . he didn't take another breath.

Hannah felt her hands trembling, felt her body shivering, felt her whole world splintering. "Nooooooooooo!" she wailed. "Please, God. Please, God. Please, God."

"Hannah, stop," Hetty said. "You're scaring me. What's wrong?"

"He's dead!" Hannah snarled. "Can't you see? He's dead! And it's *all your fault*."

"That's not fair!" Hetty cried. "I didn't give him cholera."

"We'd still be with the wagon train if you hadn't gotten hot britches."

"You're just jealous because I found a handsome man to love me, and you were stuck with *him*."

"He was a better man than either of those two fools who killed each other over you, you stupid cow!"

"Who's stupid? You're the one who married him."

"I did it to save you and Josie," Hannah shot back.

"Fat lot of good you did us. Look where we are now."

"We're here now because of *you*," Hannah retorted.

"Both of you shut up!" Josie hissed at them through the opening in the canvas wagon cover. "Someone's coming. And they don't look friendly."

Hannah bent her head around the edge of the canvas to look in the direction Josie was pointing. She felt her blood run cold. It was a band of half-naked men on horseback. Clearly not settlers. Clearly not white men.

They'd traded with a lot of friendly Indians on the trail. But there were no women or children with these riders. The colorful cotton shirts worn by the friendly redskins were missing. The oncoming horde wore buckskin breechclouts and had feathers in their long black hair. These savages carried bows and arrows and rifles, and they had menacing designs painted on their faces.

War paint, Hannah thought. *It's more colorful than I imagined.*

Chapter Five

"Congratulations, Ransom." Flint Creed grasped his younger brother's hand and pulled him close for a hug. "Emaline chose the better man."

"Thanks, Flint. No hard feelings?"

"None." Flint still couldn't believe Miss Emaline Simmons, the prettiest girl in the Wyoming Territory, had chosen his brother over him. But once Ransom had flashed her that lady-charming smile of his, Emaline had never looked at Flint the same way again. He should have known better than to give the woman his heart before he'd won her hand.

Emaline's father, Lieutenant Colonel Simmons, the commander at Fort Laramie, gestured for Ransom to join him near the fireplace in the parlor of his two-story residence. Even though it was the twenty-sixth of July, they'd woken up to a freakishly cold day, so the fireplace was the only warm spot in the room.

The Sunday afternoon gathering was a celebration of Emaline and Ransom's engagement. Flint felt sick at the thought of living in the same house with Emaline after she became his brother's wife.

"Excuse me, Flint," Ransom said. "Duty calls."

"By all means, go."

Ransom grinned. "I love Emaline. The fact that my future father-in-law is the one making the decision about who gets the contract to supply beef to the fort over the next year is icing on the cake."

Flint watched as his brother joined the small group of military officers, ranchers, and tradesmen, who'd gathered at the colonel's home with their wives after Sunday service at the chapel. Most of the women had their hands held out to the warmth of the fire as they chattered with one another.

The commander put a friendly arm around Ransom's shoulder and the two of them engaged in conversation with Emaline. Ransom reached out a large, work-worn hand, and Emaline daintily put her small hand in his.

Flint felt his gut wrench.

What had Emaline Simmons seen in his brother that she hadn't found in him? Was it something about his looks? He was taller by two inches, a full six foot three, and at twenty-six, a year older. Ransom was lean, top to bottom, while Flint's own shoulders were broader, heavier with muscle. They both had blue eyes, although, to be honest, his were more of a flinty gray—what had given him his name, in fact.

Why Ransom and not him? Was it something as frivolous as the fact that Ransom's black hair curled at his brow, while his own lay straight as a crow's wing down his nape? He didn't smile as often as Ransom, but he was the one who bore the weight of responsibility for his younger brother. Always had and always would.

Flint and Ransom had come to the Territory nine years ago, after the War Between the States, from their home in Texas. They'd left because there was no longer a place for them at their late father's cotton plantation, Lion's Dare. By the time they'd gotten home from the war, it wasn't even called Lion's Dare anymore.

Their mother, Creighton Stewart Creed, had remarried after their father Jarrett's death at Gettysburg. Her new husband, an Englishman named Alexander Blackthorne, had renamed the land Bitter Creek and turned the plantation into a cattle ranch. Not just a ranch, an empire. The bastard had bought—or stolen—so much land that it took three days to ride from one side of Bitter Creek to the other.

Blackthorne had made it plain that if Flint and his brother stayed around, they would be taking orders from him. Flint and Ransom had been only eighteen and seventeen at the time, but they'd gone to war at fifteen and fourteen, and after three years of fighting and killing and living off the land, they were no longer willing to be treated like boys.

So they'd left, driving a small herd of mavericks north to a place where they could be their own bosses. When they'd arrived in the Territory, they'd spent the summer building a sturdy two-story, wood-frame house with covered porches front and back, similar to what they'd grown up in at Lion's Dare.

A staircase split the lower floor in half, with a parlor on one side of a central hallway and a combination library and office on the other. The dining room, kitchen, and pantry took up the back of the house.

They'd built two large bedrooms upstairs that could later be divided as their families grew, with fireplaces that warmed both stories at either end of the house.

They'd located the ranch house on 320 acres of land—160 acres each—they'd filed on under the Homestead Act of 1862. It was a day's ride southwest of the fort along the Laramie River. Most of the land on which they ran their cattle belonged to the government, but they'd set their boundaries as far beyond the ranch house as they could control with a couple of Winchesters.

Flint and his brother were partners in everything, and more important, best friends. They'd suffered through and survived the war together, which had bonded them as tightly as any two men could be. Without Ransom's support, Flint might not have made the decision to try his luck in the Wyoming Territory.

And yet, the thought of Ransom touching Emaline made him want to put his hands around his brother's throat and— Flint cut off the thought. When he looked down, his hands were clenched into white-knuckled fists.

He didn't know what to do with the dark, savage, selfish feelings roiling inside him. Lately, all he thought about were ways he could win—or steal—Emaline from Ransom before the wedding, which was scheduled for the last Sunday in August.

He knew Emaline liked him. If not for Ransom, she might very well have chosen him. Ransom had survived the war because of him, had survived the trail from Texas because of him, had survived the first miserable winter because of him, had survived an accident in the fourth year they'd been here because of him.

Flint found himself wondering whether Emaline might not be with him now if he hadn't saved his brother's life over and over again. There were a lot of ways to die here in the Territory. Renegade Sioux, horse and cattle thieves, and squatters with shotguns were all constant threats. Even more dangerous were the elements—the ever-present, relentlessly howling wind that tormented a man until he thought he might go mad, and the frigid isolation during endless months of sleet, snow, and below-zero temperatures.

Simply staying alive was a constant struggle. And yet, they'd not only survived, they'd thrived.

Flint watched Emaline's and Ransom's eyes meet. When his brother raised Emaline's hand to his lips, Flint felt a surge of murderous rage. And swallowed it down.

There's nothing you can do, he warned himself. *You better learn to live with the situation, because it isn't going to change.*

He felt nauseated. How could he love his brother and yet feel so much anger toward him?

Flint exercised iron control over the jealousy that threatened to spill out and spoil the day. He'd never experienced it before, and he didn't much care for it. Jealousy truly was a green-eyed monster.

The hardest thing to handle was knowing that when he'd lost Emaline, he'd lost something more valuable than all the money and power and land he might possess after a lifetime of work.

Emaline is the love of my life. She's my soul mate.

If I can't have her, I will wither like an unwatered plant and die.

Flint snorted in disgust. *Soul mate?* No man died because he was forced to live without the love of a woman. Otherwise, he and Ransom would have been under the ground a long time ago. But he ached with longing, and he felt a powerful sense of loss.

It wouldn't have been so bad, he thought, if Emaline and Ransom were planning to live in a home of their own. That wasn't the case. Every morning he was going to have to sit down across the breakfast table from Emaline and watch his brother kiss her and laugh with her, watch them touch, and see the love for Ransom grow in her dark brown eyes.

It was going to be pure torture. Maybe he'd round up some cattle and head south before winter came.

The instant he had that thought, Flint knew he couldn't leave Ransom alone through the winter. It was dangerous enough with two of them working the ranch. One man alone would find himself spread too thin to supervise everything that needed to be done, even with the help of a couple of cowhands.

Even worse, they were facing a threat to their survival. Plain and simple, they were losing cattle. Someone was rustling them. Flint had a pretty good idea who it was, but he wasn't going to make any accusations until he could prove it. He couldn't leave Ransom to face that danger alone. He had to stay.

All his life, Flint had kept his brother safe. He couldn't stop now.

He pressed his lips together in determination. He had to get over the feeling that life was no longer worth living if he couldn't marry a woman who was as good as lost to him.

Emaline had chosen Ransom. He was going to have to live with that choice.

"I can't believe the fair Emaline is choosing to marry your brother."

Flint was startled to hear his own thoughts spoken aloud. And disturbed to realize that the speaker was Ashley Patton, a man who'd become the second-richest, second-most-powerful man in the Territory over the past year, using both fair means and foul. Flint knew for a fact that Patton had employed hired guns to move squatters out and paid his cowhands to file on 160 acres each under the recent Timber Culture Act of 1873, which he'd promptly purchased from them at rock-bottom prices.

It was some comfort to know that Patton hadn't been able to win Emaline's favor, either, although Ashley had made a serious effort to attach her.

He supposed Patton would be attractive to a woman. He was always nattily dressed in a tailored suit, his blond hair parted in the middle and slicked down. He had a neatly trimmed mustache several shades darker than his hair and flashy, very white teeth. He was short and stocky, but not fat. He had mud-brown eyes that reminded Flint of most of the cows he'd seen.

Patton had attended some fancy college back East and had inherited lots of money, but he seemed determined to make even more. Flint couldn't help wondering whether it was Emaline or the yearly contract to provide beef for the army that Patton was more interested in procuring.

"Miss Simmons would have done far better to marry

me," Patton said. "She would have made a good senator's wife."

"Wyoming isn't even a state yet," Flint pointed out.

"It will be. And I'll be one of its first senators. What will your brother be? Some two-bit cowhand living in a two-bedroom shack."

Flint found Patton's description of the home he and Ransom had built offensive. The furnishings might be crudely made, and after nine years of Wyoming winters, the house might need another coat of whitewash and a few repairs. But he'd be willing to bet it would still be standing in a hundred and fifty years.

He let the attack on his home go to address the insult to his brother. Which was how Flint found himself in the awkward position of defending Emaline's choice.

"Ransom is a good man," he said.

"I can offer her a more comfortable life," Patton replied.

"Maybe money doesn't interest her," Flint said. "Maybe she's looking for someone with honor and integrity."

Patton's lips curled in a contemptuous sneer. "I guess that explains why she chose your brother over a yellow belly like you."

Flint's face went white. "You son of a bitch!" His right hand was already fisted to throw a punch when he found himself facing a Colt .45 held by Patton's hired gunslinger, Sam Tucker.

"Bad idea," Tucker said.

"Put it away, Sam," Patton said, frowning at his hired gun. "This is a social gathering, not a saloon. Besides, I can handle this."

"Just makin' sure there's no trouble, Boss," Tucker said as he holstered his weapon.

"Get yourself some punch," Patton told the gunman.

Tucker smirked at Flint, then turned and headed for the punch bowl that had been set up on a table across the room.

Flint shot a glance toward the group by the fire, but none of them seemed to have an inkling of what had just happened.

"Be careful who you're calling names," Flint warned. "Words like that can get a man killed."

"I heard a rumor about you," Patton said. "If it turns out to be true, I don't think the colonel's going to give you that beef contract even if you're related by marriage."

Flint barely managed not to wince. During the Battle of Cedar Creek, the final skirmish in the Shenandoah Valley in late '64, the Union counterattack had resulted in panic among the Confederate troops, who fled the battlefield. Left with his flanks undefended, Flint had been left with no other choice than to retreat with his men as well.

Flint had fought bravely in other battles with his company both before and after that incident, but the words *yellow belly* and *craven* and *chickenheart* and *coward* had followed him until the end of the war.

Most of the men he'd fought with were dead, or living a long way from here. There was no way for Patton to have found out that he had so notoriously retreated with his company. Flint didn't lack courage, he was simply a man willing to allow himself to back down rather than die. Maybe that was shaving hairs, but there it was.

However, if he was ever branded a coward in Wyoming, he would have to leave. No man would work for him. No man would ride the river with him. No man would have anything to do with him.

Oh, God. Was that why Emaline had rejected him? Had she heard rumors of what had happened during the war? No, if that were true, he and his brother wouldn't even have been allowed over the colonel's threshold, let alone have a chance at that all-important beef contract.

"I hear the musicians tuning up," Patton said. "I intend to have a dance with the prettiest lady in the room before I leave."

"Just remember she's already promised to my brother," Flint warned.

Patton smiled. "There's many a slip twixt the cup and the lip."

Flint stepped in front of Patton and said, "What does that mean?"

"There are a lot of dangers in a land like this. And lots of reasons to change one's mind about marriage. I'd be very surprised if your brother is still around when it comes time to wed the beautiful Miss Simmons."

"Just so you know," Flint said, "if anything happens to Ransom, you won't be around long enough to become a groom, either."

Patton laughed. "I enjoy a good contest. May the best man win."

Chapter Six

"May I have this dance?"

"Why, yes. Of course."

Flint thought Emaline looked endearingly startled by his request for a dance. He held out his hand and felt the warmth and softness of her hand as she placed it in his. He realized he was nervous as he rested his palm against her back and took the first steps of the waltz the violinist was playing. Her eyes were lowered, so all he saw was the shiny twist of dark brown hair on the top of her head.

He watched the pulse in her throat above the high, frilly collar of her dress. He was aware of the stiff corset she must be wearing, which kept her back so straight. He wondered what it would be like to undress her a layer at a time, whether her skin would be as soft as it looked, whether it would be the same translucent ivory everywhere.

Flint knew he should be making small talk, or she should, but neither of them spoke. He thought he could feel her trembling, but maybe that was him. He knew what was keeping him silent. He wondered why she didn't speak. But he didn't ask.

They danced on, the silence increasingly uncomfortable, at least for him. Finally, Flint cleared his throat and said, "How are plans coming for the wedding?"

She looked up then, her dark brown eyes bright and excited, and said, "Sadly, I don't have a mother to help me organize things, but Captain Harvey's wife, Jean, and the sutler's wife, Phileda, and several of the ranchers' wives have volunteered to help. I'm so looking forward to the picnic after the wedding!"

He watched her mouth as she spoke, imagined kissing it, imagined pulling her close and never letting her go.

"Mr. Creed?"

"What?"

She smiled endearingly at him. "The music has stopped."

"Oh." He let her go and took a step back and bowed awkwardly. "Thank you for the dance, Miss Simmons."

She put her hand through his arm as he walked her back to his brother, leaning so close he imagined he could feel the weight of her breast against his sleeve.

"We're going to be family," she said, looking earnestly up at him. "I've always wanted a big brother, and now I'll have one. I hope you'll call me Emaline, as Ransom does."

He managed a smile as he handed her over to his brother. "I'll do that. Emaline."

She laughed with delight, a sound so velvety and feminine it made his throat ache.

"I'm heading back to the ranch," he told Ransom.

"So soon? The party's just getting started."

Flint forced a grin. "I've already danced with the prettiest girl in the room. It would all be downhill from here."

He saw Emaline blush and watched as Ransom proudly and possessively put his arm around his future bride's waist.

"Thanks for giving me the time off to go to Denver to shop with Emaline," Ransom said, meeting his gaze. "I know it's going to mean a lot of extra work for you."

"I'm glad to do it," Flint said.

"I thank you, too," Emaline said, laying a hand on his forearm. "I'll be glad to have Ransom's opinion when I spend the money my mother left to me. I want our home—which is also your home, of course—to be filled with beautiful things."

He managed not to jerk away, but he freed himself, nonetheless. "With you there, it certainly will be."

Her smile was enchanting. And heartbreaking.

"See you when you get back from Denver," Flint managed to say. He couldn't get out of the colonel's house fast enough. Acid had backed up in his throat.

Our home—which is also your home.

That was the nightmare Flint dreaded. Unfortunately, Ransom had sprung this engagement party and the late-August wedding on him only a few days ago. If he'd had the time, Flint would have built himself another house. But in Wyoming there was only July, August, and winter, and once in a while, even July and August saw snow.

Building another house was out of the question.

He was going to be stuck living with the two of

them. Stuck like a bull buffalo in mud, bellowing in despair, helpless to escape.

Several of the local ranchers attempted to engage him in conversation, including the biggest rancher in the Territory, John Holloway, and his wife, Kinyan, but Flint managed to stave them off and make it out the front door onto the porch. He took the steps two at a time, freed the reins that were tied to a rail in front of the colonel's house, mounted up, and spurred his buckskin into a lope, heading across the length of the military post.

Fort Laramie had been established forty years ago, dead center at the junction of the Sioux, Crow, and Arapaho lands. The fort no longer had any protective walls but was rather a collection of clapboard buildings arranged in a rectangle around an immense parade ground that was more dirt than grass, with a flagpole stuck in the center.

Flint rode past the Second Cavalry officers' quarters and officers' stables and the barracks for the soldiers and noncoms, placed on either side of the quadrangle. Once he was beyond the parade ground, he rode past the bakery, sutler's store, workshops, stable, laundry, and smithy, all of which had been built from sunbaked clay bricks. He continued across a series of grassy, rolling hills until the fort disappeared from view.

Flint turned in the opposite direction from home and crossed the Laramie River, which ran past the fort. He couldn't go home. He never wanted to go home again.

If only Emaline had chosen him! Did he dare, at this point, try to win her away? Ransom would be devastated if he succeeded. More to the point, could he make himself happy at the expense of his brother?

He could not.

Flint galloped his horse until the animal was breathing hard and lathered with sweat. When he stopped at last, his mount stood with his head down, trembling with exhaustion.

"I am one sorry son of a bitch," he said aloud.

He couldn't outrun the truth. Emaline was lost to him. She loved Ransom. They were going to be married a month from today, and they would all be living together. He was going to have to hide his feelings. He was going to have to endure.

The most practical—and most honorable—solution to his dilemma was obvious. He needed to meet and marry someone else. The problem was, there were no single women to be had. Females who made it all the way to the Territory were either too young, too old, or already married.

"Swear to God I'm going to marry the next single woman I meet," he muttered. Fat or skinny, ugly or pretty, good-tempered or bad, any wife would be better than none. "Just let her turn up where I can find her." He laughed bitterly. Fat chance of that.

"Come on, Buck," he said to his horse, sighing in resignation. "Let's go home."

Flint was turning his mount when he spied a splash of sunshine yellow showing at the edge of a gully. Plenty of flowers bloomed on the prairie, but with the lack of rain over the summer, most of them were long gone. Whatever he'd seen wasn't part of nature. Better to be safe than sorry. He hadn't lived this long without being cautious.

He took out the makings for a smoke, while he loosened his rifle in the leather boot on his saddle. He quickly rolled the smoke and cupped his hands around the match to light the tobacco, taking the opportunity to surreptitiously check out his surroundings from beneath the flat brim of his hat.

What he'd seen might be a scrap of cloth blown by the wind that had caught on sagebrush or cactus. Or it could be a renegade Sioux in a shirt he'd stolen from some settler. Or one Sioux in a yellow shirt along with an entire band of renegades that were hidden from view.

Miners had invaded lands in the Black Hills promised by treaty to the Indians. Small bands of angry Oglala Sioux had begun attacking isolated travelers. In addition, the Brulé Sioux had been known to stray from the nearby reservation, where rations were short because they'd been stolen by dishonest Indian agents, and prey on the helpless and the hapless.

Flint deeply regretted pushing Buck so hard. His horse wouldn't last long if he needed to make a run for it. Flint kept his eyes on the scrap of cloth as he eased his Winchester out and leaned it across his forearm. He still hadn't seen any movement, but the scrap of fabric remained visible.

Flint didn't want to turn his back, in case it was savages, so he rode parallel to the hill. His heart was beating hard in his chest as he waited for the whoop that would announce an assault. He kept the spot of color in sight from the corner of his eye.

So he saw the hand that rose above the hill, waved, then dropped back down.

Flint hunched, waiting for an arrow in his flesh. He

was about to put spurs to his mount when the hand
appeared again, waved again, and dropped again.

Curiosity held him motionless.

Was what he'd seen some clever ploy to get him to
come closer, so he could be shot more easily? But why
would anyone planning an ambush reveal his position? Besides, the hand he'd seen looked like it belonged to a child. Maybe some Sioux kid had left the
reservation and gotten himself into trouble. Flint
couldn't ride away without knowing for sure.

"Who's there?" he said. "Come on out where I can
see you."

"Help me. Please."

Flint frowned. It sounded like a woman, but the
voice was so faint and hoarse he could barely hear it.
Maybe this was a trick after all. "Who's there?" he
repeated.

"Help."

Flint took his time closing the space between himself
and the splotch of color, rifle in hand. He tensed when
his horse snorted and sidestepped as they mounted the
hill above the gully.

Flint was shocked at what he found.

The young woman was alone. Her sunshine yellow
dress looked the worse for wear. So did she. Blond
curls rioted around a sunburned face. Her lips were
cracked and dry. Her nose and cheeks were smudged
with dirt. Her eyes were closed, and he wondered
whether she was merely exhausted, had fallen unconscious, or had succumbed and died from exposure.

With his luck, it was the latter.

Flint was off his horse a second later and on one
knee beside her. He lifted the young woman into his

arms, searching for signs of life. Surely God hadn't put this female in his way without some purpose. Here she was. His salvation. She had to be alive.

"Miss?"

Her eyes fluttered open. They were as bright a blue as the sky above them. They closed again, but she croaked, "Water."

He settled her on the ground and ran to retrieve the canteen tied to his saddle. He brought it back, lifted her up again, and put it against her closed lips. "Open your mouth. Drink."

She lifted her arms but dropped them again, too weak even to hold the canteen. He held it for her, and she gulped water so fast it dribbled down her chin.

"Easy. Slow down. How long since you had a drink?"

"I don't know," she said in a frail voice.

"How did you get here?"

"I don't know."

"What's your name?"

For a moment he thought she would say she didn't know that either. She opened her eyes, looked up at him, and said, "I'm Hannah McMurtry. Mrs. Hannah McMurtry."

Son of a bitch. She was married.

"Where's your husband, Mrs. McMurtry?"

Her lower lip trembled and tears welled in her eyes. "He's dead. Cholera."

Flint let out a breath he hadn't realized he'd been holding. He needed a wife. And a woman—a widow— had been placed in his path. He knew he should have her treated by the doctor at the fort, but he wasn't willing to take the chance that some other man would step up and win her favor while he was working the ranch in Ransom's absence.

He decided then and there to take her home. He could care for her himself until she was well. He had plenty of time to woo her before Ransom and Emaline returned from Denver. If he played his cards right, he just might persuade the widow to marry him.

Mrs. McMurtry had provided the first ray of hope Flint had felt since his brother announced he was planning to marry Emaline. If he could convince this woman to marry him, he wouldn't have to spend the winter alone with Ransom and his lovely bride. He would have a wife to distract him from the woman he loved.

Chapter Seven

Hannah dreamed she was home in her bed in the three-story town house in Chicago where she'd grown up. It was Christmas morning and the air in the large bedroom was crisp and cold enough that she could see her breath. Susan, the maid, hadn't come yet to light the fire.

Then she remembered that Susan had gone to be with her family for Christmas. Father had reminded her at bedtime that the fireplace had been readied, and all that was needed in the morning was a match to light it.

Hannah knew she should get up and start the fire, but she was too warm and cozy. The bed was so comfortable and the blanket was soft and fuzzy and always smelled so good.

Hannah inhaled, expecting the scent of rosewater. Instead, she smelled bacon cooking. That was strange. She couldn't usually smell food being cooked in the downstairs kitchen all the way up in her bedroom on the second floor.

The dream ended abruptly as Hannah woke. She couldn't be in her home because it had burned down on the third day after Mrs. O'Leary's cow had kicked over a lantern and started the Great Chicago Fire.

But the lovely feelings hadn't quite faded, so she kept her eyes closed. The air in the room was actually cold, and her fingers closed around the blanket and pulled it all the way up to her chin. Which was when she realized it wasn't at all soft. It was scratchy. And it smelled nothing like rosewater. The pungent smell was not unpleasant, just not what she'd expected.

Hannah tensed. She was in a soft bed. *A soft bed.* How was that possible?

The last thing she remembered was struggling across endless miles of prairie, her stomach empty, her throat parched with agonizing thirst, her body shivering from the bitter cold, completely lost.

She opened her eyes and looked around. She was in a room with whitewashed wooden walls. A stone fireplace took up most of the wall opposite her. A rectangular window was cut into the wall to her right. No curtains covered the four dirty windowpanes. The door opposite the window was closed. She pushed back the panic that rose as she realized she didn't recognize this place.

Where was she? How had she gotten here?

Hannah felt weak and woozy as she pushed herself upright to look more keenly at her surroundings. She closed her eyes until the spinning stopped, then opened them again.

She was lying in a bed large enough for two, with a roughly carved footboard. She turned and saw the headboard was also carved with a rugged leaf design. A plain wooden clothes chest stood beside the door with a small oval mirror above it. There was nothing soft about the room, nothing to temper the rough edges. Nothing feminine.

I've been rescued. I'm safe.

Hannah realized the second half of that sentence might not be true. At least she hadn't found herself in a brothel somewhere, in bed with some man. Or lying exposed out on the prairie dying of thirst, her tongue thick and her throat raw. But there was nothing in this room that suggested a woman lived here. Which meant she might yet find herself at the mercy of some coarse stranger.

She caught a glimpse of her badly sunburned arm and realized she was no longer dressed in her sunshine yellow dress with the square neck and short, puffy sleeves. She shoved the rough wool blanket back and discovered her feet were warm because she had on a pair of too-large gray wool socks. She was also wearing a man's red-and-black plaid flannel shirt that covered her all the way to her knees. But nothing else.

What had happened to her dress and underclothes? More importantly, who had undressed her? Hannah's thoughts skittered away, unwilling to consider the probable answer to that question.

Mr. McMurtry had bought the frilly party dress for her before they'd left Chicago as a wedding gift. It was the nicest thing she owned. She'd put it on because . . . She couldn't imagine why she'd put it on. What kind of party had she planned to attend? And since Mr. McMurtry was dead, with whom? She'd left their wagon . . . Why had she left it?

She remembered donning a light shawl to protect her from the brutal effects of the scorching sun on her fair skin and walking away from the wagon. She searched her mind to discover what else she knew about why she might have left the wagon, but it was surprisingly blank.

That was frightening.

Hannah didn't know when she'd lost the shawl, either. All she knew was that she'd had nothing to wrap around herself when the wind began to wail and blow icy cold. She'd stopped and curled up in a ball and pulled her skirt up over her arms and prayed for death to take her quickly so she would no longer suffer.

Something was niggling at the edge of Hannah's memory, something awful, but she didn't want to remember it. She focused on the present. On the here and now. Whatever that awful thing was, she could worry about it later.

The door suddenly swung open. Hannah gasped and grabbed for the blanket to cover herself.

A tall, narrow-hipped, broad-shouldered man stood in the doorway. His eyes reminded Hannah of a wolf, silvery gray and piercing and dangerous. He had cheekbones sharp enough to cut glass, a straight nose, and a shadow of beard that was as dark as the black hair that hung over the collar of a plaid wool shirt similar to the one she was wearing.

He didn't move an inch, and Hannah wondered whether he was stalling until someone else—perhaps his wife, or whatever female had undressed her—arrived. She waited for him to speak, to explain how she'd gotten there, to tell her where she was.

He said nothing, simply stared with eyes that probed deep inside her, searching out the shadows.

Hannah lowered her gaze to shield her thoughts,

then shied away from the darkness that loomed. She looked up and met his gaze again seeking solace.

He remained aloof, his jaw and shoulders square, his stance wide, waiting patiently, relentlessly, like a wild animal stalking its prey, for her to make the first move.

Hannah resisted the urge to run. There was no escape with him blocking the door. She could see nothing outside the window except cloudless blue sky, which suggested she was in an upstairs room, so there was no escape through the window.

She looked at the pillow beside her in the large bed, wondering if perhaps he'd spent the night there, but she saw no impression where his head might have been. Perhaps he had a wife who'd taken care of her. Maybe his wife was cooking breakfast in the kitchen right now.

Hannah knew it was wishful thinking, but she didn't want to consider the possibility that she was alone in the house with this frightening stranger. She looked up at him and said, "I want to thank your wife for taking such good care of me."

"I'm not married."

"Oh. Then your sister or mother or—"

"I undressed you," he said baldly.

Hannah felt herself begin to tremble and lifted her chin to show him she wasn't afraid. She searched his features and realized they were familiar. She had a faint memory of his face hovering above her, of being held close in a warm embrace. Then she remembered.

"You found me."

He nodded.

"Where are we?"

"The Double C Ranch."

That didn't tell her much more than she'd known before. "Are we near Cheyenne?"

"Cheyenne is sixty-five miles south of here."

"South?"

He nodded.

Hannah wondered how many miles she'd walked. How close had she been to Cheyenne when— She cut off the dark thought that threatened to make itself known. Instead she asked, "Do you live here alone?"

"My brother and I share the house and the ranch, but he's not here right now. Which is why I can't take you to Cheyenne. I need to be here to manage the ranch while he's gone."

"So I'm stuck here."

She saw the smallest hint of a smile before he replied, "I suppose you could say that, ma'am."

Hannah realized how ungrateful she'd sounded. "I'm sorry. It's just . . . We were on the trail for months and months trying to reach Cheyenne."

"You were traveling with your husband." He made it a statement.

"Yes. My husband and—" Hannah cut herself off and put a hand to her forehead. It hurt.

"How did you get separated?"

"Mr. McMurtry died of cholera."

"You told me that. How did you get separated from whoever you were traveling with?"

Hannah frowned. "I don't remember." Her brow furrowed as she concentrated, searching for memories that would tell her how she had come to be here. A swirling black hole appeared. It felt like, if she got too close, she'd be sucked down into it, never to be seen again. She wrenched herself away from the menacing blackness and said, "I can't remember."

"It'll come back when you're ready," he said.

"Ready for what?" she said anxiously. "What do you know?" Hannah's chest ached, and her throat had swollen closed, cutting off speech. Something terrible must have happened. If only she could remember!

"I know you need to get some food in that empty stomach of yours."

"And I need to get dressed." She shoved the covers aside, slid her stocking feet onto the planked wooden floor, and stood upright. Hannah felt her knees buckle, but before she could fall, strong arms caught her and lifted her. She instinctively grasped the stranger around the neck, surprised at the softness of the hair at his nape.

"You're weak as a day-old kitten," he said.

To her surprise, instead of putting her back in bed, he lifted her completely into his arms and headed for the door to the room.

"Where are you taking me?"

"Breakfast's in the kitchen."

"Stop! I need to get dressed first."

He paused at the door but then continued walking. "In what? It's cold outside. That dress you had on is a summer concoction."

"You must have something."

He snorted. "I've got Levi's and wool shirts."

"Jeans with this shirt will be fine."

He carried her all the way downstairs, through a hallway that led to the back of the house, and set her in one of the four chairs around a small, square table.

Then he eyed her up and down and said, "My brother's thinner than me. A pair of his Levi's might work if you roll up the legs. I washed up your underthings."

Hannah blushed at the thought of this man handling her unmentionables. "Would you get them for me? I want to get dressed."

"Breakfast first. You need to eat."

"I'm not hungry."

His lips twisted. "You were half-starved when I found you three days ago. I've been pouring a little soup down your throat, but you need some solid food."

She stared at him, shocked. "Three days ago? I've been here *three days*?" Hannah could hear the hysteria in her voice. She put her hands to her head, which throbbed with pain.

"What's the problem?" he asked.

"No no no no no." There was something she had to remember. Something she had to *do*. The thought was just beyond her grasp.

"Take it easy, Mrs. McMurtry."

She turned on him and snarled, "Don't call me that! I'm not a wife. Not anymore. I was never any good at it. I never wanted to be married. I only did it to save—" Hannah's head felt like it was going to split in two. There was something she should remember. Something she didn't want to remember. She could see Mr. McMurtry lying in the wagon, his face pale in death. Now who would be a father to her baby?

Her baby.

"Oh, my God."

"What's wrong?"

Hannah closed her eyes and swallowed hard. What

an odd thing to remember, when she could recall nothing of the events that had led her to the godforsaken place where she'd been found. How strange that the only things she knew for sure were her name, the fact that she was a widow, the fact that she'd been headed to Cheyenne, and the fact that she was going to be a mother.

Or was she? Had she lost the baby? She instinctively put her hands to her belly under the table. If she'd miscarried, the stranger would have said something, wouldn't he? She wasn't about to ask him about something so personal. She wasn't bleeding, as one of the women on the wagon train had when she'd miscarried, so she must still be pregnant.

"You need to eat to get well," he said, dishing up a plate full of scrambled eggs and crisp bacon and surprisingly fluffy biscuits and setting it in front of her.

Hannah stared at the food. She wasn't hungry. But she had to eat for her baby. The dire truth of her situation hit her hard. She had no husband. Her child would have no father. And . . . And . . .

Hannah felt tears well in her eyes. Something terrible had happened. Something awful. Something she needed to remember.

Whatever it was, she couldn't bring it to mind. Worse, the harder she tried to remember, the larger the black hole loomed. She would have to do as the stranger suggested. She would have to wait until she was ready to remember.

Hannah picked up the fork beside the plate and filled it with eggs. She took a bite and chewed and swallowed. When she looked up, the stranger was watching her from a spot near the black, four-top iron stove.

"Will you join me?" she asked.

"I ate when the sun came up, ma'am."

"Please, sit," she said, gesturing to the chair across from her.

Clearly reluctantly, he crossed to the table and sat down.

"My name is Hannah," she said. "I prefer that to ma'am. What shall I call you?"

"Flint."

"I'm glad to meet you, Flint." She reached across the table and took the hand he offered. It felt warm and strong. "How can I ever repay you for saving my life?"

He took a deep breath, grasped her hand more firmly, and said, "You can marry me."

Chapter Eight

Flint saw the incredulity on Hannah McMurtry's face. She laughed, a lovely birdlike trill, as she pulled her hand free.

The captivating dimples that had appeared on both cheeks disappeared as she sobered. "I must have misheard," she said. "Did you ask me to marry you?"

Flint couldn't believe he'd blurted it out like that. But he didn't have much time before his brother returned to live here with Emaline. He'd thought a lot about how to approach the beautiful woman in his bed. He'd held out small hope of locating a woman to wed in time to avoid the agony of living here as a single man with the newlywed couple. He'd never dreamed that the woman he found would be so fair.

With her blond curls and sky-blue eyes, Mrs. McMurtry would be barraged by single men, once they discovered she was a widow. It had seemed best not to beat around the bush, to simply say what he wanted.

"Yes, I asked you to marry me."

She frowned as she asked, "Why?"

"I need a wife."

"I don't know you."

"Most brides don't know their husbands before they marry them. Not out here anyway. There's not much time for courting. Every moment of every day is spent doing whatever it takes to survive."

"I'm a new-made widow."

"Which means you're free to marry."

Her eyes looked troubled. "You *need* a wife? Or you *want* one?"

"Same difference."

"No, it isn't," she said.

"We don't get many eligible women here in the Territory. A man wants a wife to keep him company during the long winter nights. He needs a woman to take care of his house and give him sons to carry on after he's gone. I could have advertised for a mail-order bride from back East, but . . ."

"You didn't want to take a pig in a poke," she finished for him.

"Exactly."

"And I fit your scrupulous requirements?" she asked with a brow arched in disdain.

"You must know you're beautiful. More importantly, you're young and healthy—or will be, once you've recovered. And you've been a wife, so you know what's involved."

She blushed furiously, and he realized she'd gotten the wrong idea from what he'd said. "I mean, you understand what a husband needs from a wife."

She put her hands up to cover her cheeks, which had turned a fiery red.

"Hellfire and damnation! I wasn't talking about sex."

She stared at him, shocked, and he realized he never

should have mentioned that word in mixed company. Or used profanity. Both had been mistakes, but she seemed surprisingly naive for a woman who'd been a wife.

"How long were you married?" he asked.

She hesitated, looked up at him forlornly, and said, "I don't exactly know."

He swore under his breath. She was too young to have been married for long. Besides, he didn't really care about the circumstances of her first marriage. What mattered was that her husband was dead.

"I'm sorry for your loss," he said. "But life has to go on. And I need a wife."

"So you said."

She didn't seem impressed by anything he'd offered so far, so he continued, "My brother Ransom is getting married and bringing his wife here to live. You'd have another woman for company if you married me. You wouldn't be alone at the house during the day, and you'd have someone to share the work."

He searched her features, hoping for some sign that he was making headway. The embarrassed color had faded from her cheeks, but she had a crease between her finely arched brows that told him she wasn't interested in buying what he had to sell.

"If women are so scarce, it sounds like I could choose any man I wanted," she said. "Why should I marry you? What makes you so special?"

He was surprised by the question. He would have thought she'd be grateful to have somewhere to live, someone to care for her. "I own half this ranch. My brother and I run thirteen hundred head of cattle, and we're about to get the contract to supply beef for the fort."

"You seem pretty sure of that."

His lips twisted. "My brother's fiancée, Miss Emaline Simmons, is the fort commander's only child."

Her lips twisted with a cynicism equal to his own. "I see."

"Besides, we grow the best beef around. We have good water from the Laramie River and plenty of tall needlegrass and bluestem and even more short grasses like blue grama and wheatgrass to fatten our stock. Even so, last year we started growing hay for feed over the winter."

She still didn't seem impressed, but he figured that was because she didn't understand the difficulty of growing quality beef on land more suited to roaming buffalo.

He and Ransom were among the first to grow hay to supplement winter grass for their cattle. They'd hired men to plow and plant. They'd decided the cost was worth it, because the Wyoming winter was so unpredictable. The extra labor and seed had cut into their profit, but they'd figured that more of their cattle would survive the perilous cold, and they'd make back their investment in the long run.

Their gamble had paid off last winter. Most of their neighbors had lost stock that couldn't forage for grass under the deep drifts of snow. He and Ransom had put out hay for their animals to eat. They'd still lost cattle in the hellacious winter of '73, because sometimes the weather was too bad even to drop hay, but not as many as everyone else.

"I'm not interested in your ranch," she said at last. "I'm interested in you. What makes *you* so special?"

Flint was stumped by the question. His experience with women had barely begun when he'd gone off to war. The only ones he'd known during the war were camp followers. The lack of women in the Territory necessarily meant his relationships with them— even the soiled doves in Denver, and more lately in Cheyenne—had been few and far between.

He smiled ruefully. "I'm not sure what qualities you're looking for, ma'am. I'm not used to tooting my own horn."

"It's Hannah," she reminded him. "And the usual ones, I expect. Honesty, reliability, kindness, a willingness to compromise—"

"Whoa!" he said, putting up his hands.

She cocked her head like a curious kitten and observed him. "Am I asking too much?"

"No man survives out here long if he's not honest and reliable. As for kindness and compromise . . ." He shrugged. "Haven't had much need for either over the past nine years."

"Not even with your brother?"

"Ransom has always followed my lead."

"Your word is law?"

He nodded.

Her face was neutral when she said, "So you'd expect your wife to do as she's told without argument."

Flint sensed a trap. He wasn't sure how to stay out of it without lying. "I'm used to calling the shots," he said at last.

"I see," she said, in a way that made it plain she didn't like what she saw.

Flint realized he was going to lose her if he left that statement all alone on the table. "However," he began, "I've never had a wife. I suppose she would be entitled to her say."

"That's very generous of you."

He heard the sarcasm in her voice and added, "Any sensible person would defer to someone with greater knowledge and experience here in this wilderness. My wife would be depending on me to keep her safe, to give her a good life."

"You don't think she might have a right to define what that 'good life' entails?"

Flint rubbed his jaw and realized from the feel of the bristles that he hadn't shaved while she'd been in bed recovering. He knew women put great store by that sort of thing. It simply hadn't been necessary to shave every day when it was only him and Ransom around. He realized that would probably change when Emaline showed up. He felt a stab of irritation that he was going to have to adjust his life for a woman who wasn't even his wife.

Which made him even more determined to convince Hannah McMurtry to marry him and more frustrated by the hoops it seemed he'd have to jump through to get what he wanted.

"Sounds to me like you want a man dancing on a string," he muttered.

"Sounds to me like you want a woman without a mind of her own," she shot back.

She was sitting so straight she might have had a steel rod down her backbone, and her chin jutted so far forward she could have poked a hole in the wall. He'd only seen her unconscious or sick in bed. This was a different woman altogether. Stubborn. Defiant. Willful.

Hannah McMurtry was way more trouble than he'd bargained for, if her questioning so far was any indication of what she'd be like as a wife. She reminded him of his mother.

Flint hadn't realized it until that moment, but he'd measured every woman he'd ever met against Creighton Creed Blackthorne and found them wanting. His mother was capable, shrewd, and spirited. Most females, he'd discovered, were soft, silly things, easily led, easily cajoled, and in the case of soiled doves, easily bedded.

He took another look at Hannah. Physically, she was nothing like his mother, who was taller than most men, with almond-shaped gray eyes, straight auburn hair, and a face that had suffered through sun and wind and trouble. Hannah barely came to his shoulder. Her blue eyes were direct, and her hair was a mass of wild blond curls around what he suspected was going to be a peaches-and-cream complexion once the effects of sunburn had gone away.

Hannah's hard questioning reminded him of nothing so much as his mother in an argument with his father, in the years before Jarrett Creed had died at Gettysburg. From what little Flint had seen, his mother, whose nickname was Cricket, was equally stubborn with her second husband, that son of a bitch Alexander Blackthorne.

Having found one positive similarity to his mother, he looked for others. Was Hannah as hardy as his mother? She was smaller, slighter, but she'd survived in the elements when a lesser woman might have succumbed. He knew from having undressed her and washed her and taken care of her bodily needs that she was very much a woman, with generous breasts and a narrow waist and good, child-bearing hips.

And she was beautiful.

If he had to have a wife—and he did—she fit his needs perfectly. He wished he knew what appeal would work with her.

Flint glanced at Hannah and saw that, instead of finishing her breakfast, her arms were folded defensively across her breasts. "You need to eat," he said.

She stared at the eggs on her plate. "There are more important things for us to discuss than food."

"I promise to answer whatever questions you ask if you'll finish your breakfast."

She eyed him, then picked up her fork and took a mouthful of eggs. She watched him while she chewed and swallowed, then said, "I want to be courted."

He laughed in surprise. "I have no idea how to court a woman."

"Then you'd better figure it out, because that's my price for considering your offer of marriage."

"You mean you'll consider it?" he said, surprised by her seeming acquiescence.

"I'm not agreeing to marry you. I'm agreeing to be courted by you."

"I hear you," he said. "If you agree to marry me, I want us to be married on the same day as my brother's wedding. That's a month off. Will that be enough time for you to make up your mind?"

"I think I can take your measure by then. But I want your assurance that if I decide we don't suit, you won't do anything to try and force me into marriage."

"Done."

"And I want you to introduce me to other eligible men in the neighborhood who might be prospective husbands."

"I can't do that."

"Can't? Or won't?"

"I told you, I have to stay close to the house while my brother's gone." He wasn't afraid of the competition, except maybe for his neighbor, Ashley Patton, who had more money and a finer house to offer a wife. However, Flint wasn't going to allow Hannah to be tempted by a wealthy husband before he'd had the chance to win her for himself.

"You'll have to make up your mind to take me or leave me without seeing what else is out there," he said.

Hannah smiled.

He felt his heart jump when her dimples reappeared.

"I suppose if I choose you, at least I won't be getting a pig in a poke," she said.

Flint laughed and told himself his heart had jumped like that because he wasn't used to talking with a pretty woman across the breakfast table. "Eat, Hannah. Get strong. You may not have realized it, but you'll also be giving me a chance to see what sort of wife you'll make."

"What do you mean?"

"I was speaking of your ability to sew and cook and make this house a home."

She blushed and lowered her eyes.

Flint found himself feeling . . . enchanted. He attributed the feeling to the oddity of the situation. Still, it couldn't hurt, he thought. He should appreciate his wife, even if he never loved her.

"Very well," she said. "I like the idea of a marriage where both parties are satisfied with the bargain they've made." She reached a hand across the table, and he put his out to shake hers.

"One month," he said.

"One month," she agreed.

Flint shook her hand, aware as he did so that he was going to do whatever it took—short of lying, cheating, or stealing—to convince Hannah McMurtry to marry him. Being married, even to a woman he didn't love, was his best defense against doing something dishonorable where Ransom and Emaline were concerned.

Because he knew no way to stop coveting—or loving—his brother's bride.

Chapter Nine

"I don't understand," Ransom said. "I thought every woman wanted children."

"I don't," Emaline said.

They were riding side by side ahead of the wagon that carried Emaline's aunt Betsy, who'd come along on the journey from Fort Laramie to Denver as chaperon. They planned to leave the wagon at a livery in Cheyenne and take the Denver Pacific Railroad to their destination. They'd need the wagon on the way home from the depot in Cheyenne to haul the trousseau and furniture Emaline intended to purchase in Denver.

Although he'd been courting Emaline for six months, they'd never discussed the topic of children. Ransom had simply assumed they would have a large family, like most folks did. Today, in passing, he'd asked how many children Emaline hoped they'd have. He'd been shocked by her answer: "None."

"One of the reasons I'm marrying you is to have children to inherit the ranching empire I'm working so hard to build," Ransom said.

"I know I should have mentioned my feelings sooner, but—"

"You're damn right you should have said something!" he interrupted. "You didn't think it would make a difference to me?"

Emaline glanced at him from beneath lowered lids, her big brown eyes liquid with tears, then focused her gaze on her hands, which were knotted tightly on the reins. "I thought you loved me for myself, not for my potential as a brood mare."

If she'd sounded angry, instead of hurt, he might have been able to continue his rant. He'd fallen head over heels in love with Emaline Simmons the first time he'd laid eyes on her, and he'd believed there was nothing he wouldn't do to make her happy.

But he'd never considered the possibility that loving Emaline would mean giving up the hope of ever having children of his own. He decided to point out the flaw he saw in her position.

"You must have known it would matter," he said. "I've talked about working on the ranch with my sons and about you working in the house with our daughters. Why didn't you say something then?"

She shot a guilty look at him. "I just . . . didn't."

Because she'd known he would care, he realized. Because she'd known any man would care. Because she'd suspected she might lose him if she admitted the truth. What man would marry a woman knowing she didn't want to bear his children?

He had another thought and voiced it aloud, although he spoke quietly, aware of the pointed look Emaline's aunt Betsy had given the two of them after his outburst. "Emaline, sweetheart, I don't know any way to avoid having children if we have marital relations."

"Do we have to do that?" she asked.

Ransom gaped at her. "Are you suggesting we don't?"

She glanced back at her aunt, then kneed her horse closer and put a hand on his forearm. "I love your kisses, Ransom. They're enough for me."

"You're not being realistic," he said, jerking himself free. "I've stopped with kisses out of respect for you. A fiancée is not the same thing as a wife. A man wants to hold his wife and touch her and . . ." *Put himself inside her.* He finished the thought in his head, because she was already cringing away from him.

Dear God. Was she saying she wanted to remain a virgin after they were married?

"You know I'll be as gentle as I can be," he said. "Can you tell me what you're afraid of?"

"Dying."

"What?" He didn't think he'd heard her right.

She met his gaze and said, "Can you promise me I won't die in childbirth?"

"No husband can promise that, but the risk is worth the reward."

She snorted inelegantly. "It isn't your life at risk. It's mine."

She had a point. But there was no future without babies. "What has you so scared of childbirth?" he asked at last.

"My mother died birthing me. In great agony."

"Who told you that?"

"Aunt Betsy. It was ghastly. At least, that's what my aunt said."

Ransom shot Emaline's aunt a nasty glance, startling her.

"But that isn't all," Emaline continued. "Friends and acquaintances have died far too often trying to bring new life into the world."

"You're young. You're healthy. There's no reason you couldn't easily bear healthy children. I'm not saying there's no pain involved."

"How much pain?" she asked.

"How the hell would I know that?"

"Please don't use that language."

Ransom flattened his lips. He'd known there would be changes when he brought a woman into the house, language being one of them. But he'd figured anything would be worth holding Emaline in his arms through the night and making love to her. He wasn't sure how willing he was to turn his life upside down for a woman who had no intention of performing one of the primary duties of a wife.

As far as giving birth was concerned, the only experience he had was with horses and cattle, who bore their offspring without fuss. More often, it was the foal or calf that died, rather than the mare or cow. But he wasn't about to tell her that their child was more likely to die in childbirth than she was.

She was right about the danger. It existed. Especially because there would be no doctor to attend her, unless he brought her back to the fort to deliver the child. There was always the chance the child would come early, or that there would be some complication long before the babe was ready to be born.

"There are no guarantees in life," he admitted.

"But if you won't take that risk, we'll never have sons and daughters to hold and to love."

A look of pain flashed across her face, replaced by the mulish tilt of her chin. "You're not going to cajole me, Ransom. I've been thinking about this ever since I became a woman capable of bearing children. I don't want to get pregnant. If that means not doing anything after we're married, so be it."

Ransom pulled his horse to a stop. "I wish you'd said something about this sooner, Emaline. I really do."

"What would you have done, Ransom?"

I wouldn't have proposed. Was that true? Even though she'd said she wouldn't make love with him, he believed he could convince her to do so. She had no idea how powerful passion could be. He'd had enough arguments with her—and lost enough arguments with her—to know she had a fiery temper. But this wasn't a disagreement about whether they should go out for a horseback ride in threatening weather. This was a disagreement about the rest of their lives.

"Is something wrong?" an elderly female voice interjected from behind them.

"Nothing," they both said at the same time.

Ransom kicked his horse into a trot to increase their distance from the wagon, and Emaline followed after him. When she caught up, he turned to her and said, "I'm not sure I can marry you if you aren't willing to be a wife. In fact, I doubt our marriage would be legal if it's not consummated."

He watched her face blanch as she asked, "Are you sure about that?"

"Ask your father," he said flatly.

Color flooded her face. "I could never talk to him about this."

"Because he wouldn't agree with you?"

"Because the pain of my mother's death is with him still," she replied. "I don't believe he lets himself think about what it will mean for me to become a wife."

"There might be ways for us to lie together but avoid pregnancy," he said. "Would that be all right with you?"

"How certain are you I wouldn't get pregnant?"

He swore under his breath. "The only certain way not to get pregnant is abstinence. That isn't a reasonable choice, Emaline, and you know it."

"Why is it so unreasonable?" she argued. "I love you, Ransom. I want to spend my life with you, with the emphasis on *life*. Why isn't that enough for you?"

"It just isn't. You're asking me to give up too much, Emaline. I want more from marriage than you're offering."

She stopped her horse. "Then maybe we should turn around and go home."

"Is there any chance you'll change your mind?"

"No."

Ransom had already opened his mouth to put an end to things when she said, "I have a suggestion, though."

"I'm all ears."

She glanced at her aunt, then at him, and said, "We won't go to Cheyenne. We'll go back to your ranch."

"I don't want to marry you if—"

"Hear me out," she interrupted. "We'll send Aunt Betsy on to Denver to shop for us while we spend the next two weeks together at your ranch."

"Where are you going with this?"

She took a deep breath and said, "I want us to try living together as husband and wife—on my terms."

"What's the point of that?"

"I want you to see how nice it could be for us, even without the physical aspect of marriage."

"You'll be ruined if we don't get married."

"Your ranch is a long way off the beaten path."

"You think your aunt will go along with this?"

Emaline met his gaze briefly, then lowered her eyes. "She loves me. And she knows how scared I am of dying in childbirth. So yes, I think she will. If things don't work out . . ." Her voice faltered. She swallowed hard and said, "If we separate later, I know Aunt Betsy will protect my reputation. So what do you think?"

"I think you're crazy."

Her eyes glistened with tears that wrung his heart. She was wrong. This wasn't going to work. And he had a feeling it wasn't going to be as easy as she thought for the two of them to separate after she'd been living under the same roof with two bachelors. Then he had a brilliant idea.

"All right," he said. "I agree."

"Oh, thank you, Ransom. You won't be sorry!"

"With one stipulation."

She swiped at a tear that had fallen on her cheek and asked, "What's that?"

"I want the freedom to treat you as my wife. To hold you in my arms at night and to touch you and kiss you whenever the mood strikes me."

"I can't imagine that will be too often. You'll be out working on the range during the day."

"The nights are plenty long."

She eyed him suspiciously. "Touching and kissing are fine," she said. "So long as you agree it goes no further than that."

"I won't do more unless you're willing," he said.

"I won't be."

"But if you are—"

"I won't be," she repeated.

He opened his mouth to argue, but before he could speak she said, "Very well. If I do agree and there are consequences, I won't hold you responsible."

"That sounds fair to me." He held out his hand. "Deal?"

She shook it once. "Deal."

He laughed, feeling alive and excited and hopeful. "One more thing," he said.

"What's that?"

"I'll have to tell Flint what's going on. He's going to think we're both out of our minds. He'll need to hear from you that this is all your idea."

She smiled. "I've always found your brother easy to get along with. I'm sure Flint will be happy to go along with our pretend marriage."

Chapter Ten

"Not just no, but hell, no!" Flint said. "Emaline is the fort commander's daughter. If she doesn't show up when and where she should, he'll have the entire Second Cavalry out looking for her."

"It's already done," Ransom replied. "Emaline's aunt is on her way to Denver alone. I dropped Emaline at the house before I came hunting you."

Flint's heartbeat ratcheted up as he realized how complicated the situation had gotten. An *unmarried* Emaline living under the same roof? Before he'd committed himself to another woman? There was a hell, and he was about to descend into it.

"When you left Emaline at the house, did you go inside with her?" he asked his brother.

"I guess I should have, but I didn't want to be alone with her. I stopped by the bunkhouse to ask where you were working." He shot Flint a chagrined look and said, "I thought it might be easier in the beginning with both of us there."

Flint laughed, but it was a sound without humor. "You're in for a hell of a surprise, little brother. Because there won't be only three of us in the house. There will be four."

"Four?"

"After I left your engagement party, I found a woman alone and dying on the prairie. I brought her back to the house to mend. She's there now."

"Holy shit."

"No shit."

"We'd better get back to the house," Ransom said, turning his horse for home. "What are you doing this close to Patton's ranch, anyway?"

"One of the cowhands riding fence reported that more cattle are missing."

"Missing? You mean stolen?"

"Slim said, 'Missing.' He didn't speculate where they'd gone. They weren't where they were supposed to be."

"Is there fence down somewhere?" Ransom asked.

"I sent Slim to find out. Pete's hunting in some of the hollows and gulleys where the cattle go to escape the wind when it starts blowing."

"How many head are we talking about?"

"A hundred."

Ransom whistled. "That's a good chunk of the herd. That many cattle didn't wander off on their own, Flint. They must have been taken."

"We don't know that."

"You know as well as I do who probably took them," Ransom said, his lips flattened in anger.

"Ashley Patton doesn't need our beef," Flint said. "He's got plenty of his own."

"True, but he also knows we'll need those missing

cattle to fulfill the contract with the fort, assuming we get it."

Flint eyed his brother. "You have any doubt we're going to get it?"

"Assuming we have twelve hundred head of cattle, I see no reason why the colonel would give it to anyone else, everything considered."

"You mean, if you marry his daughter. What if you don't?"

Ransom looked stricken. "I never thought of that. Surely the colonel would understand—"

Flint snickered. "Sure. You tell him you don't want to marry his daughter because she's determined not to die in childbirth and see how far you get."

"Are you saying I *have* to marry her, no matter what?" Ransom demanded.

"One of us has to marry her. It doesn't have to be you."

Ransom's jaw dropped. "What is that supposed to mean?"

"If you don't want Emaline, I'll be glad to step up and marry her, no matter what conditions she sets."

"Emaline is mine," Ransom said, his jaw taut.

"Yes, she is," Flint agreed. Outwardly he might have looked calm, but his heart was thundering in his chest. He'd never have taken Emaline from his brother, but all bets were off if Ransom decided not to marry her. "I'm not going to jump your claim, little brother. All I'm saying is that if you abandon it, I'm willing and able to step in."

"What about your dying woman?" Ransom asked.

"She's a recent widow. Her name is Hannah Mc-Murtry."

Ransom raised a brow. "Is there some reason you didn't take her straight to the doctor at the fort?"

"I figured since I found her, I should have the first chance to court her."

"I suppose that means she's pretty," Ransom said.

"She is, but that's beside the point."

"A pretty wife is nothing to sneer at," Ransom said. "How did Mrs. McMurtry react when you told her you wanted to court her?"

"I didn't tell her I wanted to court her. I told her I wanted to marry her." Flint saw the look of disbelief—almost awe—on his brother's face.

"Where did you get the nerve?"

He felt himself flush. Desperation had provided a sharp prod, but he couldn't say that to Ransom. He got as close to the truth as he could. "Why beat around the bush? I figured you were going to be bringing home a wife, so I should have one, too."

"What did Mrs. McMurtry say?"

"She's considering my proposal." He shot Ransom an admonishing look. "You were supposed to be in Denver helping your wife buy her trousseau while I convinced her to marry me. If Hannah said yes, I figured we'd marry the same day as you and Emaline."

"Looks like we both have our work cut out for us," Ransom said. "You can woo Mrs. McMurtry while I convince Emaline that having children doesn't have to be a death sentence."

Flint tugged his flat-brimmed hat lower to shade his eyes against the setting sun. "The way it stands, neither of us is going to have much privacy to do any courting. And I'm not sure it's such a good idea to put the two women together. What if they don't get along?"

"Better to find that out now, don't you think?" Ransom said. "I mean, if they're going to be living in the same house as sisters-in-law."

"I figured I'd build another house for me and Hannah once we get married."

"You'll have to wait at least until spring for that," Ransom pointed out.

"I don't suppose you'd consider heading back to Denver after all," Flint said morosely.

"I love Emaline, but I'm not sure I can marry her if she doesn't get over this crazy idea she has that pregnancy is going to kill her."

"It's not so crazy when you think about it," Flint pointed out.

"If every woman thought that way, it would mean the end of mankind. I want sons to carry on after me. Don't you?"

"There's no guarantee you'll get sons."

"Daughters would be a blessing, too. Besides, a daughter might mean grandsons."

"Building a dynasty, are we?" Flint said sardonically.

"Why are we working so hard to build a life here if it all ends with us?" Ransom asked.

"Why, indeed?" Flint mused. "How about to provide a good life for ourselves and earn some peace and contentment in our old age."

Ransom scoffed. "What a waste!"

Flint shook his head. "Not to me. What's the plan if Emaline doesn't change her mind and then wants nothing to do with me, either? Especially after she's spent time under the same roof with us?"

"Emaline will return to the fort along with her aunt, with no one the wiser. We'll either marry then, or we won't."

"What makes you think you can change her mind?"

Ransom shot him a sideways look. "The truth is, she's hoping to change mine."

Flint chuckled. "Good for her."

"You can't possibly agree with her," Ransom said.

"No, I don't, but she's entitled to her opinion."

"Hey," Ransom said. "Maybe I can talk that Mrs. McMurtry into helping me change Emaline's mind."

"You keep your charm to yourself. Mrs. McMurtry is mine." Flint was surprised by his feelings of possessiveness toward the woman, especially considering the comments he'd made about his willingness to take Emaline if Ransom threw her back into the pond, like a too-small fish. He simply couldn't take the chance of ending up without a wife in the event Ransom ended up marrying Emaline.

"I was only thinking Mrs. McMurtry might be able to help me convince Emaline that childbearing isn't so bad," Ransom said.

"Apparently, Hannah was barely a bride before she was a widow," Flint replied. "I don't think you're going to get much support from her about how safe life is out here in the West."

"How do you know? Have you asked her how she feels about having your children?"

"No, I haven't. We've barely had time to exchange names." He eyed his brother askance, hardly believing that Ransom would actually give up the woman he loved because she wouldn't bear him children.

"What if Emaline *couldn't* bear children?" Flint asked. "I mean, if later on you discovered there was something wrong inside her, and she wasn't able to conceive?"

Ransom pondered the question for a moment, then said, "I suppose I'd have to live without kids."

"Or adopt some," Flint suggested.

Ransom's lips flattened. "I want a chance at having children of my own before I do anything like that."

"I'd like to have kids," Flint admitted. "But that's not the only use I have for a wife."

Ransom opened his mouth to speak, then closed it again, obviously struggling with whether he should say what was on his mind.

"Spit it out," Flint said.

"Some things are better left between me and Emaline," Ransom said at last. "But I suggest you have that talk with Mrs. McMurtry before you get yourself committed, in case she feels the same way Emaline does."

Flint shook his head. "You're asking me to borrow trouble where there isn't any. Besides, I suspect that by the time we get back to the house, the two of them will have thoroughly discussed the matter."

"You think so?" Ransom asked.

"What I think is that the two of us are going to end up bunking together in your room, while the two of them sleep in mine. And I doubt either of us is going to get a word in edgewise with two women in the house."

"Are you telling me I should give up before I even try?"

That's exactly what Flint wanted to tell his brother. *Give up and give me a chance. I'll take Emaline barefoot and pregnant or with no children at all. I'll take her any way I can get her.*

What he said was, "That's up to you."

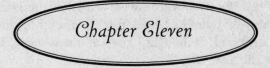

Chapter Eleven

Hannah looked up in surprise when the kitchen door opened. Instead of Flint, returning after a day spent on the range, she found herself facing a young woman, who looked equally amazed to see her standing there. Hannah had always believed her blond hair and blue eyes were attractive, but she almost gasped at the dark-haired, dark-eyed beauty of the other woman.

"Oh, my goodness. Who are you?" the young woman asked, as she stepped inside and closed the door behind her.

"Hannah McMurtry. Who are you?"

"I'm Ransom's fiancée, Emaline Simmons. What are you doing here?"

"I could ask you the same question. I thought you and Flint's brother were supposed to be in Denver."

Emaline glanced over her shoulder toward the closed door, frowned, then turned back to Hannah. "Our plans changed. Does Ransom know you're here?"

"Why don't you take off your wrap and let me get you a cup of coffee to warm you up. Then we can sit down and figure out what's going on."

Hannah was relieved when Emaline smiled, began untying her white-fur-trimmed red wool cape, and said, "That sounds like a good idea."

When the two women were settled at the kitchen table with a cup of coffee in front of each of them, Emaline said, "I thought I knew all the women living near the fort. Why haven't I met you?"

"Because I didn't arrive until a few days ago. To be honest, Flint found me languishing on the prairie, all alone, and brought me here to nurse me back to health."

The other woman reached out and took Hannah's hand. "Oh, how awful! What happened?"

Hannah took a deep breath to answer and found her throat swollen with emotion. When she started to explain, she faced a high stone wall past which she could see nothing. "I don't really know," she admitted. "When I try to remember, everything is blank."

"Oh, my goodness," Emaline said. "If you don't mind my asking, why are you still here? I mean, why didn't Flint bring you to the fort? We have a very good doctor there."

Hannah debated whether to tell Emaline the truth but could see no reason why she shouldn't, especially since there was a chance they might end up as close relations. "Flint said he wanted to court me while you and his brother were gone. If we suit, we'll be married on the same day as you and Ransom."

"Oh, my goodness," Emaline said for the third time, putting her hands to her cheeks. "That would mean we'd be sisters-in-law. We'd be spending the rest of our lives as family. We'd be—"

"Why are you here instead of in Denver?" Hannah interrupted. "Where is Ransom?"

Emaline blushed. "Ransom and I have a difference of opinion, and we agreed to try and work it out before we marry. He went to find Flint. I don't think he wanted to be here alone with me."

Hannah arched a brow. "But you were going to stay here alone with two single men?"

Emaline's blush deepened, and she lowered her gaze. "My aunt Betsy is in Denver buying my trousseau, supposedly chaperoning me. If things don't work out with Ransom, I'll go home with her when she returns with no one the wiser."

She lifted her gaze and focused her striking, dark brown eyes on Hannah. "At least, that was the plan before I knew you were here. You'll keep my secret, won't you?"

Hannah smiled. "If you'll keep mine."

Emaline laughed, and Hannah found herself smiling back at her. "It sounds as though there's some question as to whether you'll be marrying Ransom. Do you mind if I ask what's causing the problem between the two of you?"

"Not at all," Emaline said. "So long as you don't try to change my mind. It's absolutely made up."

"I wouldn't dream of it," Hannah said.

Emaline took a deep breath and said, "I don't want to have children."

Hannah's jaw dropped. "You don't? Why not?"

Emaline met Hannah's gaze and said, "I don't want to die in childbirth."

"Why are you so sure you'll die?" Hannah asked.

"Because my mother died birthing me."

"My mother had six healthy children." Hannah was startled by what she'd blurted. Before this moment, she hadn't been able to recall any information about her distant past.

Was her memory returning? Could she remember anything else about her family? Hannah searched her brain, trying to picture those children in her mind's eye. Instead, she felt a blinding pain in the center of her forehead.

There were no faces to go with the knowledge that she had five siblings.

"You're lucky to have such a big family," Emaline said. "I'm an only child. Where are they all now?"

Hannah opened her mouth to speak, but nothing came out. Her head felt as though it was going to burst open like a ripe melon. She put a hand to her splitting forehead. When the painful bursts of light in her eyes were finally gone, she groaned and said, "I don't know where my family is. I can't remember!"

"Oh, my goodness. You really have amnesia? Then how do you know your name is Hannah McMurtry?"

Hannah rubbed her brow. "My memory loss seems to be related to whatever happened to cause me to end up alone. I suppose something happened that I don't want to remember. I do know my husband died of cholera."

"You're a widow? But you look so young!"

Hannah looked at Emaline's youthful face and her flawless alabaster skin and said, "So do you. I'm seventeen. How about you?"

"Eighteen," Emaline admitted. "Old enough to be a bride. Too young to die."

"You won't necessarily die in childbirth," Hannah chided.

"Can you guarantee I won't?"

"No one can guarantee that."

"Then I'm not taking the chance."

"I don't see how you're going to avoid getting pregnant if you become a wife." Hannah didn't say aloud that a wife would be bound to have sex with her husband. She'd obviously done the deed herself, since she was pregnant.

She opened her mouth to tell Emaline she was expecting a child and closed it again. She wasn't sure she wanted Flint to know about the baby, and she couldn't trust Emaline not to tell Ransom, who would certainly tell his brother.

"I can avoid getting pregnant if I never consummate the marriage," Emaline said softly.

"Oh." Hannah could see why the two young people had interrupted their trip to Denver. "So who's trying to convince whom of what?"

Emaline laughed. "You're funny."

Hannah had never considered herself to have much of a sense of humor, but maybe that was something else she'd forgotten. "You're avoiding the question."

"I want to convince Ransom that we can have a wonderful marriage and live happily ever after without the intimate part of marriage."

"You mean you expect your husband never to make love to you?" Hannah asked bluntly.

Emaline laughed again. "You call a shovel a spade, don't you?"

"Well, do you, or don't you?"

Emaline sobered. "I don't think what I'm asking is so terrible."

"How can you know you won't miss it unless you've tried it?" Hannah asked.

"I presume you have," Emaline retorted.

"Yes."

"Was it wonderful?"

Hannah had a sudden flash of memory—of dry lips and mashed teeth, of awkwardness, of excruciating pain—and realized it was another memory of her husband. She had no idea why thoughts of Mr. Mc-Murtry did not produce the same pain—and pit of darkness—she experienced whenever she tried to recall anything about her family. "What was true for me might not be true for you," she said at last. "Surely it must be different for each person."

"But was it wonderful for you?" Emaline insisted.

Hannah sighed. "Not that I can recall. But that doesn't mean it won't be for you and Ransom, especially if you care deeply for each other. I presume you've known each other long enough to fall in love?"

"I came to join my father at Fort Laramie six months ago," Emaline said. "I think I was introduced to every bachelor between here and Cheyenne. I met Flint first, and I really liked him. Then I met Ransom. He smiled at me and . . ." She shrugged. "I knew I wanted him to smile at me like that for the rest of my life."

"I doubt Ransom is going to keep smiling if you keep him at arm's length in bed," Hannah said.

"That's frank speaking. But I think you're wrong.

In fact, that's why I'm here. To prove that you and Ransom are wrong, and I'm right."

"How do you plan to do that?"

"Until my aunt returns from Denver, I'll be living here with Ransom as man and wife, even sleeping together, but without . . . you know. I'm hoping to prove that being together, having a life together without . . . you know . . . can be just as satisfying, and a lot safer, than the alternative."

"Hmm. That sounds surprisingly like what Flint and I are doing. Including the lack of a physical relationship. He and I were planning to sleep in separate bedrooms, since Ransom was gone. I suppose now Flint will have to sleep somewhere else, since you and Ransom will be in his bedroom."

"Maybe Flint can sleep on the sofa in the parlor," Emaline suggested.

"That won't be very comfortable, but I suppose he'll have to manage."

"Or you could do what I'm doing."

It took Hannah a moment to realize what Emaline was suggesting. She gasped. "Sleep in the same bed with Flint? When we're not married?"

Emaline grinned. "You've been married before, so there's no question of losing your virtue. It would be entirely up to you whether you wanted to do anything more than *sleep* in the same bed. And you could find out whether he snores."

"Now who's being funny?" Hannah said.

"I wish you'd consider it," Emaline said earnestly. "It was hard to talk Ransom into trying this experiment. When he finds out you're here, he might want to forget the whole thing."

"To be honest, it doesn't sound like a very good idea to me, either," Hannah said. "Have you thought about how hard it will be for Ransom to sleep next to you and not be allowed to touch?"

"Oh. Didn't I tell you? It's all right for him to kiss and touch. We just won't . . . do it."

Hannah shook her head in disbelief. "Ransom agreed to that?"

Emaline made a face. "He thinks he can convince me to give in."

"So you're determined not to give in, but he's allowed to try and change your mind?"

"That's about it," Emaline said.

"I think you're both crazy."

Emaline's jaw jutted. "Maybe it is crazy for me to have so much fear of childbirth. But my fear is real, Hannah. I love Ransom so much I think I might die if I can't spend my life with him. But I'm not willing to give up my life for a little pleasure in bed, or even the joy of holding a child of my own in my arms."

"Those two things—an intimate relationship with his wife and a child of his own blood—are a great deal for any man to give up," Hannah said. "Ransom must be very much in love with you to even consider it."

Emaline's dark eyes swam with tears. "I don't think he's willing to give up those things. I don't think he'll marry me if I don't change my mind."

"So you're betting that you can change his?"

Emaline nodded.

Hannah stared at the young woman, wondering how Emaline could let the fear of anything at all make her give up the man she loved. Hannah made up her mind, then and there, to do what she could to help the couple. Which meant she was probably going to have to share a bedroom with Flint.

Hannah shivered. The thought of sleeping in the same bed as Flint left her feeling a little anxious and, if she was perfectly honest, a little breathless with anticipation.

Chapter Twelve

"You're suggesting we *what*?" Flint said to Hannah.

"You heard me," Hannah said. "And I can hear you fine, so you don't have to shout."

After the four of them had eaten supper, Hannah had brought Flint into his bedroom and closed the door so they could have a private conversation. Emaline had taken Ransom into his bedroom to have a similar discussion.

"Ransom might be crazy enough to try sleeping with a woman without bedding her, but I'm not," Flint said.

Hannah felt her cheeks go pink at such blunt speaking. "Not even to help your brother?"

Flint stared at her in disbelief. "What you're suggesting goes a long way past courting. What happens if you decide we don't suit?"

"As Emaline pointed out, you can hardly steal my virtue. Besides, nobody knows I'm here. When she returns from Denver, Emaline's aunt Betsy will escort Emaline—or Emaline and me—to the fort with no one the wiser. I'll be a friend of Emaline's from back East that she met up with in Denver."

He looked wary, Hannah thought, as though she were trying to trick him.

"I can see why Emaline proposed this setup. I don't see why you're willing to go along."

"I'm doing it to help your brother and his fiancée," Hannah said.

"How is the two of us sleeping in the same bed going to help them?"

"For one thing, you won't be spending your nights on that too-short sofa in the parlor, or on the floor somewhere, so Ransom won't feel guilty. And you'll be less grumpy in the mornings," Hannah said with a smile meant to cajole. "It won't be so bad sleeping in the same bed, will it?"

"I don't know," he said. "Do you snore?"

Hannah laughed. "I don't think so. Do you?"

"Haven't had any complaints."

The answer suggested he'd spent the night with other women. Hannah took another look at the man who'd saved her life. Certainly he would be attractive to other women. She fought a shiver—of anticipation?—every time she looked directly into his gray eyes. She felt *aware* of him with her whole being.

Hannah wondered if she'd felt this way about her late husband, but the only memory she had was that single harsh image that had flashed into her head during her talk with Emaline. She certainly couldn't recall wanting to be held by Mr. McMurtry or kissed by him, two things she found herself imagining with Flint.

She met Flint's gaze and felt a thrill of danger as she asked, "Well, what do you think?"

"I'd rather sleep on the floor."

Hannah frowned. "Really?"

"I think this whole house of cards is going to fall in on itself," he said. "Those two have their own problems. I don't think we should take them on our shoulders."

"You do want to help your brother, don't you?"

A look Hannah couldn't fathom—guilt? chagrin? despair?—crossed Flint's face. He hesitated, then said, "I suppose."

"Then this is what I think we have to do. Besides, kissing and touching is part of courting, and since I only have a short while to make up my mind about whether to marry you, I think this might help me, too. Aren't you even the least bit curious to see whether we would suit that way?"

Hannah's cheeks felt rosy with heat. She'd had more intimate conversations with strangers in the past few days than ever before in her life. At least, it felt like she had.

Flint didn't answer right away. He put a hand to the back of his neck, rubbed it once, then said, "Yeah. Sure. All right."

"You'll do it?"

"I said I would. What else do you want from me?"

He was agreeing, but he didn't sound happy about it.

"Is there something wrong with Emaline that makes her a bad match for your brother?" Hannah asked.

"No! Emaline is perfect."

Hannah stared with wondering eyes at the man who'd proposed to her, aware of the sudden tension in the room. She fixated on his one-word description of Emaline because it seemed so odd to describe any woman in those terms, but especially one who belonged to another man. "Perfect?"

He threw up his hands. "You know what I mean."

"Perfect how?" Hannah persisted.

"She's beautiful, for one thing."

Hannah felt a twinge of jealousy and told herself not to be stupid. She couldn't quibble with his description of Emaline as beautiful. She'd thought the same thing. Besides, Emaline was engaged to Flint's brother. He could admire Emaline all he wanted, but that wasn't going to change the fact that she'd chosen Ransom.

"Gentle. Sweet. A true lady," Flint continued, listing more qualities he admired. "Any man would be proud to have her to wife. My brother is a very, very lucky man."

Emaline smothered a gasp. It was the second *very* she found alarming. Did he wish Emaline had chosen him? Did he secretly hope Emaline and Ransom would split up so he could have Emaline for himself?

Hannah reined in her vivid imagination. That was a pretty big assumption to make when she knew nothing about the parties involved. Besides, the fact that Flint had proposed to her was proof he wasn't in love with the other woman. Wasn't it?

"I suppose we should get ready for bed," she said.

"You want me to leave so you can get undressed?" he asked.

"I don't know. I would plead modesty, but you've already seen everything of me there is to see. Seems to me, turn about is fair play," she said, smiling up at him. "What do you think?"

"I think this is looking and sounding more and more like the real thing," he said, eyeing her askance.

"Isn't that the whole point?" Hannah said, her hands on her hips. "Ordinarily neither of us would have this opportunity to get to know each other so well before we're committed to living together for the rest of our lives. Why not take advantage of it?"

He looked startled. Then he smiled. And raised a brow. And eyed her slowly up and down. "All right, Hannah. Let's see how serious you are about playing husband and wife."

Hannah felt a shiver of expectation run down her spine as Flint took three long strides to stand directly before her. He reached behind her head, untied the ribbon holding her hair, then untangled the single braid confining her hair and thrust his fingers into it, spilling blond curls around her shoulders.

Hannah felt breathless. She looked up into Flint's gray eyes and found them focused on her face. "What are you doing?"

"You said we could kiss. And touch."

"But . . ."

He paused with his fingers caught in her hair and said, "Have you changed your mind? Are you willing to admit this is a lunatic idea?"

Hannah was frozen in indecision. She hadn't considered the possibility that Flint would want to touch so soon. If she denied him now, he might decide she wasn't serious about her offer and make himself a bed on the sofa or the kitchen floor. Then she would lose the chance to see what this part of their marriage might be like.

She swallowed noisily and said, "Go ahead."

Hannah saw surprise in his silvery gray eyes before they turned dark as storm clouds. Hannah knew the instant he slid a callused hand around to grasp her nape that she had never felt this way before. She began to tremble and wondered whether it was from fear or excitement.

She looked into Flint's eyes as he lowered his head toward hers until it was uncomfortable to do so, then let her eyelids sink closed and waited with bated breath for whatever would come next. She had a feeling of exhilaration, of possibility. Their first kiss. She wanted it to be wonderful. Was this man her Prince Charming?

Flint's lips felt soft as he pressed them lightly against hers seeking surrender. Hannah pushed back against his mouth with her own seeking something precious. Something new. Something amazing.

His arm slid around her waist and he pulled her close, so their bodies touched from breasts to hips. Hannah felt her nipples become tight buds against his chest, and noticed a strange ache in her womb. Her arms found their way around his neck, and she grasped handfuls of his hair to prolong the kiss.

Hannah's hands slid down to muscular shoulders that felt as hard as sculpted stone. She found herself wondering what it would be like to touch Flint's naked flesh. She pressed herself against him, wanting to be closer.

She suddenly felt his tongue tease her lips, and when she gasped, he slid it into her mouth to tease and touch. She could taste him! Her knees turned to mush. She clung to his shoulders to keep from sinking to the floor and leaned back to stare at him wide-eyed.

Did I ever kiss my husband like this?

Hannah didn't think so. This felt new. This felt different.

She was trembling so hard Flint must be able to feel it. Had he known what that touching of tongues would do to her?

She pushed against his chest with the flat of both hands, to put space between them, to give herself time to think, but she might as well have been pushing against a forty-ton boulder.

Hannah looked up into Flint's face and saw his gray eyes glittering with desire. She was panting for breath, and her legs threatened to buckle. She realized she wanted him. Desperately. Wanted to lie beneath him. Wanted him inside her.

The powerful feelings frightened her.

Hannah clutched Flint's shirt with both fists to keep herself upright, took a shuddering breath, and said, "That was . . . nice."

He stared at her for a moment, then threw his head back and guffawed. He gave her a quick, tight hug and then stepped back, grinning broadly, leaving her standing on wobbly legs. "Good for you, girl. Let's go to bed."

Hannah stared, too enervated to move. She wasn't sure what she'd said to amuse Flint, but she was glad he wasn't angry that she'd called a halt to his love-making. *Lovemaking.* That word suggested feelings that didn't exist between the two of them. *Seduction.* That was more to the point.

Flint crossed to the low wooden chest at the foot of the bed and began rummaging through it, finally coming out with another gray blanket. "I might be foolish enough to share the bed," he said, "but I think I'll sleep on top of the covers."

Hannah was still frozen in place as he began to ready himself for bed. She turned slightly away to give him privacy. But gazing at the fireplace, where a warm, cheery fire was burning, gave her far too much time to think.

She touched her still-damp lips. She'd liked Flint's kiss far more than she'd expected, probably because it had involved more than lips. Their bodies had been entwined, and she'd felt the warmth and the strength of him. His hands had been thrust into her hair, pulling her head back so he could claim her mouth.

Hannah shivered.

"Hey, you're getting cold. You better get under the covers," Flint said.

"Right," Hannah replied, crossing to the bed and turning down the covers. Her body was still quivering with remembered pleasure. She'd wanted to be courted, but Flint seemed to have skipped over several steps, like holding hands and taking walks, to kisses that involved not just lips, but teeth and tongues.

She sat on the edge of the bed and stared while Flint pulled off his vest and began unbuttoning his shirt. She'd told him it wasn't necessary that he leave the room while she disrobed, because he'd seen all there was to see, but she hadn't realized how discombobulating it would be to watch this almost-stranger strip down.

Hannah found herself entranced as Flint dropped

his shirt on a nearby chair, leaving him in his long john shirt. There was nothing skinny about this man. She was admiring the breadth of his shoulders when he pulled the long john shirt off over his head.

She suppressed a gasp. Everything about him looked hard as rock, from ridged abdomen to broad chest, from sinewy forearms where veins stood out, to shoulders rippling with muscle. When he looked up and caught her staring, she flushed and said, "You're beautiful."

He looked surprised, then made a face. "That's the wrong word to describe a man."

"Nevertheless, you are."

Abruptly, he grabbed his long john shirt and pulled it back on. Then he retrieved his plaid wool shirt and thrust one arm into a sleeve. He hunted for the other sleeve behind his back as he said, "I just realized I forgot to put some harness away in the barn."

A moment later he was gone.

Hannah stared at the closed bedroom door. So this was *desire*. Or was it *lust*? Whichever it was, she'd better figure out a way to control it. At least until she was sure Flint wasn't in love with his brother's fiancée.

Chapter Thirteen

Flint didn't know what had come over him. He'd kissed Hannah because he'd thought that would prove to her the danger of the two of them sleeping in the same bed. What had happened next had been totally unexpected. Especially in light of the fact that he was in love with another woman.

He stared at Ransom's closed bedroom door before he headed downstairs, buttoning his shirt along the way. He wondered if his brother was doing with Emaline what he'd been doing with Hannah. That way lay madness. He hurried downstairs and left the house through the kitchen, headed to the barn. There was enough moonlight to see his way but he lit a lantern before he closed the barn door behind him.

Most of the horses remained as they were in their stalls, dozing on three legs or lying down in the straw. He hadn't taken two steps into the barn before he was assailed by the pungent odor of manure. Another step brought the smell of fresh hay and leather.

"You awake, Buck?" he called out.

A moment later, his horse's head appeared over the top of a wooden stall door.

Flint hung the lantern on a nearby hook, then crossed to the stall and reached out to stroke Buck's neck. "Yeah, I know it's late," he said. "But I needed to talk, and you're a good listener."

The horse shook his head and snorted.

"My problem is a woman, of course. What else could it be?" He laughed at himself. "Rustlers, I suppose. I've got a hundred head of cattle missing and a pretty good idea that the man who stole them is the meanest, baddest—and second-richest—guy around.

"Patton could hide a hundred head of my stock in some arroyo on his property for months, and I'd never know it. Or hot iron my CC brand into his OOX, run those steers down to Cheyenne, and ship them east. I've got no way of proving one way or the other that he took them.

"But that's not what's worrying me tonight. Tonight it's a woman. Her name is Hannah and she's . . . different."

Maybe that was why he felt so attracted to her, almost against his will. He loved Emaline. He couldn't understand how this other woman could so quickly turn him into a stag in rut. He found it funny—more odd, really, than ha-ha funny—that he'd felt incensed at the thought of handing Hannah over to Ransom. Especially when he was perfectly happy with the thought of Ransom handing Emaline over to him.

He couldn't have them both.

What if you could have both and had to choose? Emaline, of course. No question, no hesitation, no—

Flint found himself hesitating, nonetheless. Why? What was it about Hannah McMurtry that he found so appealing? How had he let her get under his skin? Why could she make his body turn hot and hard in an instant when such a thing had never—not ever— happened with Emaline?

"It's because I've seen Hannah naked," Flint said as he shoved Buck's mane back and smoothed his hand over the horse's neck. "Even though I've laid eyes on every square inch of her, I only allowed myself to touch her enough to do what needed to be done to make her well. I wanted to touch more. A lot more. It's only because I was tempted, and resisted that temptation, that I want to do more now," he told Buck.

He stopped rubbing the horse's neck as he realized that was probably the answer he'd been seeking.

The horse shoved his nose against Flint's chest, looking for more attention. Buck lowered his head, and Flint laughed. "All right. I know what you want." He scratched behind the animal's ears while Buck hung his head low and stayed still.

"I'll tell you this," Flint said. "I'm not going to succumb to temptation. I only want Hannah so bad because I've been too long without a woman. Yes, she's damned pretty. But she doesn't have Emaline's dark beauty," he said. "Hmm. Maybe that's why I find myself so drawn to her. Hannah's so very different from Emaline."

Buck lifted his head, and Flint continued scratching, this time under the horse's chin.

"Hannah's taller than Emaline, which means she'll fit against me better in all the right places. And she has those wild, untamed blond curls, which makes me wonder, Buck, if she's anything like her hair. Emaline's hair is always combed so perfectly, every hair in its proper place, which is why I think of Emaline in terms of perfection, I suppose.

"Hannah has those forthright, almost bold blue eyes. She's not at all demure like Emaline. And Hannah's body . . ."

Flint stopped stroking his horse and let his mind's eye review Hannah's naked form, a body he'd seen in the flesh, so he knew how very flawless—and very female—it was.

Emaline was always the picture of propriety, dressed in a rigid, tightly laced corset and a dress that came up to her throat, down to her toes, and covered her arms all the way to the wrists. He could *imagine* what lay beneath the sober, well-designed cloth. But he didn't *know*.

With Hannah there was no guessing, no wondering. Emaline might be a lady. But he knew for a fact that Hannah was all woman.

That was the problem. He didn't have to imagine Hannah naked in his bed. He could remember the exact feel of the parts of her smooth, silky skin it had been necessary to touch. He'd had his hands in her hair as it tumbled over his pillow. He'd even imagined what it might be like to lie beside her but denied himself the pleasure.

That was it. All this denial was making him crave something he didn't even want. He wanted Emaline, damn it!

Buck shoved his head against Flint's chest, and he realized he'd stopped stroking the animal. He found another favorite spot, at the base of Buck's throat, and began scratching again.

Considering how long he'd been without a woman, it was no mystery that he was knotted up inside as tight as a wet rope. "I would have reacted to any female the way I reacted to Hannah tonight," he told Buck.

Buck snorted and nodded his head.

Flint laughed and rubbed Buck's jaw, then slid his hand down over his horse's muzzle. "I should be getting some shut-eye, not standing out here talking to you. Only problem is, there's a woman in my bed."

An image of Hannah standing beside his bed wearing nothing but his plaid wool shirt and his too-large gray socks rose in his mind. His body reacted violently and insistently.

Flint swore.

"She might as well have been naked," he told Buck. "Because I knew what she looked like under my clothes. Yes, *my* clothes. I could have had them off of her in two seconds flat."

He straightened Buck's forelock so it lay in the center of the horse's forehead. "If only I hadn't needed to undress her. If only I hadn't seen everything. Nipples like pink rosebuds. That slightly rounded belly."

Flint stepped back and held out his callused hands and stared at them. "A waist I could span with these two hands. And those legs of hers. Long and sleek. And strong, I bet. Strong enough to wrap around me."

Buck whinnied, and Flint realized the animal must have sensed how agitated he was in body and mind. He gripped the edge of the stall door and took a deep breath and huffed it out. That didn't really help the most obvious problem.

He was hard as a rock.

"I'd better get back inside," he said as he met Buck's steady, brown-eyed gaze. "Yeah, I know. It's crazy to spend the night in bed with her. What choice do I have? It's either a soft bed in there or a pile of scratchy hay out here. I choose the soft bed, no matter how much more agony it causes."

It was going to be sweet misery lying there on his back staring at the ceiling and wanting second best. At least he would have something to distract him from thoughts of Emaline with his brother. Flint scowled as he imagined Ransom undressing Emaline, seeing what he yearned to discover for himself.

Buck sidestepped and shook his head up and down.

"Don't get yourself all het up," Flint said in a soothing voice. "I'm taking my frustration and leaving."

He'd only moved a couple of steps toward the door when Buck's head reappeared over the stall door. Flint turned back to give his horse a consoling pat on the side of his neck. "None of this is your fault. I promise not to take it out on you like I did the other day, running you hell-bent-for-leather. Just be patient if you find me a bit distracted over the next couple of weeks."

Buck nickered.

Flint laughed at the horse—and at himself. "Yeah, we're two crazy fools, all right. Good night, Buck. See you in the morning, hopefully in a better mood than I'm in tonight."

Flint blew out the lantern and left the barn, determined to keep his hands off Hannah, no matter what.

He didn't want her. He wanted Emaline. He could wait to see whether Emaline and Ransom came to some agreement. The prize was within his grasp. He had no intention of ruining things by succumbing to the siren call of Mrs. Hannah McMurtry.

Chapter Fourteen

Hannah was already in bed, dressed in one of Flint's wool shirts, by the time he returned to the bedroom. The lantern was extinguished but she could see his silhouette in the scant moonlight. She opened her mouth to greet him, but a lump was lodged in her throat like a ragged stone.

She realized Flint was undressing when she heard him removing clothing. Cowboy boots hit the floor with two heavy *thunks*. His belt *clinked* as he unbuckled it and *clunked* as it hit the floor. She heard the soft brush of Levi's, the *whoosh* of his wool shirt dropping on the ladderback chair beside the window, and finally, the chuffing exhale as he pulled his long john shirt off over his head.

Hannah's stomach lurched when she saw the moon gleam off naked male flesh. She'd thought Flint would at least wear his long johns to bed. She told herself that stripping down to bare skin was understandable. The changeable Wyoming weather had turned sunny and warm late in the day, taking the chill out of the air. With the fire, the room felt almost toasty warm. She held her breath, waiting, but the bottoms stayed on.

Flint said nothing, so she remained silent.

Hannah felt the bed sink down and resisted rolling into the hollow in the center created by Flint's greater weight on the other side. She heard him grunt and shift as he rearranged the pillow under his head and watched him settle flat on his back.

Then all was silent.

Not quite silent. Hannah heard the whistle of the wind through a narrow slit in the wooden wall near the window.

"I'll caulk that hole tomorrow," Flint said into the darkness. "Crack's been there since spring. Didn't mind the whistle through the summer, but come winter it'll be cold as a witch's—" He stopped himself and finished, "Consider it fixed."

Hannah swallowed over the painful lump in her throat, determined to speak despite the awkwardness of the situation, since they were both awake. "I'd like to see your ranch. Could I ride out with you tomorrow?"

"It's not safe," he said flatly.

"I'm not afraid."

Flint turned his head in her direction, so she saw the gleam of two eyes in a shadowy face. "How well can you ride?" he asked. "Maybe I should be asking, 'Can you ride?' "

Hannah had a sudden image of herself and her twin dressed identically, riding in the park on identical hacks. *I have a twin! Hannah and Henrietta. And Hetty—*

"The commandant at the fort warned me that a band of renegade Sioux is on the prowl," Flint continued.

Hannah sat bolt upright. "Oh, my God."

"Is that what happened to you?" he said, sitting up beside her. "Were you attacked by Indians?"

Hannah stared at Flint, horrified by the terrible images playing out in her mind's eye. "Hetty," she gasped. "Hetty!"

"Is that someone you know?"

"My twin. My sister. Oh, no!" Hannah clasped her hands over her eyes to shut out the vision that arose, but it only became more clear. She jerked her hands away and stared at them, seeing them dripping with blood. "Hetty!" she shrieked. Then she saw the rest. "Josie! Josie, no! Help! Someone help us!"

Strong arms surrounded her and pulled her close.

Hannah struggled desperately to be free. "Let me go!"

"Hey, there. Take it easy. I've got you. You're safe," a low voice crooned.

"I have to go," Hannah cried. "I have to find them!"

"Go where? Find who?"

"My sisters! Hetty and Josie. Hetty . . ." Hannah's mouth opened wide, spilling forth a ululating wail of grief. "And Josie . . . She . . ."

Hannah's body was shaking so hard it felt like she might shatter into a million pieces. "Oh, God. Noooooooo," she wailed.

The door suddenly opened.

Hannah recoiled from the lantern-lit gargoyle face in the doorway, shrinking back against Flint's bare chest.

"What the hell's going on in here?" Ransom demanded.

"Nightmare," Flint said. "Get out. She's fine."

Ransom took another step into the room. "You sure?"

"I said get out!"

A moment later the door shut, and the darkness closed in again.

"No no no no no no," Hannah groaned, pressing herself closer to Flint, seeking succor. She couldn't get close enough. She needed to be closer, needed to escape inside him. She grabbed him around the neck and pulled his head down and pressed her mouth against his.

He pulled free and said, "Hannah, stop."

"Please," Hannah begged, burrowing closer. "Please hold me. Tighter." She shoved hard against Flint, catching him off balance, so he slid onto his back.

"Whoa," he soothed. "Easy, girl. Take it easy."

She didn't want to be soothed with words. She needed escape. She need oblivion. She pressed her body against Flint's, seeking the warmth and strength of him. Her legs slid onto either side of his hips, pressing their flesh close where his was hard and hers was soft. Her mouth reached for his again, surrendering, where no surrender was sought.

She felt his hands on either side of her head, trying to push her back. She struggled against his hold, bringing her lips back to his. When he tried to speak, she put her tongue inside his mouth to quiet his protest.

He went still.

She could taste the cinnamon from the canned-peach pie he'd eaten for dessert. She could taste the black coffee he'd drunk to wash it down. She could taste . . . him.

His hands slid to her shoulders.

Hannah fought to stay close, afraid he was going to push her away.

Instead, he slid one arm around her, while the other gripped her buttocks and held her tight along the hard ridge she could feel against her belly. His tongue came searching in her mouth. His large, callused hand thrust up under the wool shirt and stroked her bare back before moving to cup her right breast. His thumb brushed the tip, and she hissed in a breath at the pleasure that coursed through her.

Her body coiled in readiness for . . . something.

Hannah thrust her hands into Flint's hair and hung on for dear life, as her body writhed beneath his caresses. She thrust her hips against his, wanting to be closer. And closer still. Wanting to become a part of him until there was no more Hannah, no more Flint, just a single person, Hannah-and-Flint.

"Please," she begged in a guttural voice.

"Hannah."

Hannah heard her name, spoken as she'd always dreamed it would be. *Almost* as she'd dreamed it. There was something else beneath the desire. Something she didn't want to acknowledge. She shut out the doubt she heard with a grating cry of need.

The hesitation she'd felt in Flint's body disappeared as she slid her hand down to touch the iron-hard petal-soft part of him between his legs. She couldn't allow him to abandon her. She couldn't allow him to stop. She didn't want to think. She wanted to feel. She wanted to forget.

"Hannah."

Her name spoken as she'd never imagined it. Harsh. Urgent. Reckless.

Flint covered her mouth with his, his tongue intruding, seeking, demanding. His hands touching, caressing, commanding. His body throbbing and insistent.

Hannah grabbed at the escape Flint offered, as anxious as he was to rid herself of the wool shirt that kept their bare flesh apart. Buttons popped and pinged across the wooden floor. The shirt ripped and slid off her arms, leaving her bare. She gasped as Flint's rough palms claimed her breasts.

"Ahhh." Hannah had never felt anything so exquisite. She shoved at his long johns, wanting them off, wanting him inside her. Wanting to disappear inside him.

"Please. Please." She was all need. Urgent need. Unrelenting need.

His breathing was harsh and uneven as he raced to do her bidding. The rough hair on his chest brushed against her breasts, teasing her with each rise and fall of breath. He kicked once and the cloth that imprisoned his legs was gone.

He grabbed her hips and turned her onto her back, coming over her, spreading her legs roughly with his knees and impaling her in a single stroke.

Hannah gasped and surged upward to meet him. *At last. At last.* He started to withdraw, and she grasped him around the hips with her crossed legs and held on tight.

"Easy, girl," he said again. But his voice grated like a rusty hinge.

Hannah relaxed enough to let him withdraw and thrust again.

"Oh. Yes," she said.

Hannah saw fierce eyes glittering above her in a savage face. But she felt no fear. She rose to greet Flint's body with the thrust of her own, holding on to his broad shoulders, as she pursued pleasure—and forgetfulness—in frenzied abandon.

She bit Flint's shoulder to avoid crying out as her body began to spasm and convulse. He muffled his own cry against her throat as he found his own violent release, spilling his seed within her.

Then he was gone, forsaking her, lying flat on his back on the other side of the bed. Their labored breathing was loud in the silence, punctuated at odd times by the whistle from the window.

Hannah felt bereft.

She'd sought escape from the guilt she felt for abandoning her sisters and had found it in a few moments of intense, unbelievable pleasure. But her moment of madness had changed nothing. Hetty and Josie were still gone.

Her sisters had depended on her, but she hadn't redeemed her promise to return and rescue them. Their lives might be in the balance, and here she was wondering if—or when or how soon—Flint would want to repeat what they'd just done.

Hannah turned her face away, gurgling as she swallowed back the sob that threatened.

"Damn it all to hell," Flint muttered.

Hannah felt the tears overflowing her eyes and sliding down her face in warm streaks. The sob finally broke free.

When Flint reached out to her, she snapped, "Don't touch me!"

"Don't worry," he said in a ruthless voice. "What just happened was a mistake I don't intend to repeat."

Hannah turned her back on him, put her face in the pillow, and wept.

Chapter Fifteen

Emaline was standing at Ransom's open bedroom door wearing a full-length white cotton nightgown embroidered at the neck and hem with tiny pink roses when he returned from his trip across the long upstairs hallway. He hadn't wanted to go, but she'd insisted he find out what was causing Hannah to cry out so pitifully and painfully.

"Is she all right?" Emaline asked.

"Nightmare," Ransom replied curtly as he set the lantern on a chest of drawers and closed the bedroom door.

"Could she have fallen asleep that deeply so soon?" Emaline asked. "Are you sure she's all right? Flint isn't—"

Ransom rounded on her and said, "Against my better judgment I did what you asked. What happens between Flint and Hannah is their business. We have problems of our own that need to be solved."

Emaline held Ransom's sullen gaze for as long as she could before she dropped her eyes. "I wasn't trying to avoid your kiss when I sent you to see what was going on," she said in a small voice. She lifted her chin and looked him in the eye. "I really was worried about Hannah."

"Then you won't mind kissing me now," he said brusquely.

Emaline thought kissing Ransom in his current mood was a bad idea. Before she could say so, he slid a muscular arm around her waist and pulled her close, so their bodies were pressed together from chest to hip bone, the distance between their mouths growing smaller every second.

That was about how far Ransom's seduction had progressed before they'd heard Hannah's cries. Except, they'd been lying in bed.

This was infinitely safer, Emaline decided, even though her breathing seemed no less erratic. She told herself she could step away if she felt it necessary to end the embrace. She searched for the kindness she always saw in Ransom's eyes and found something far more feral and frightening.

Emaline resisted the urge to fight. Resisted the urge to flee. Ransom would never hurt her. He would never force her if she wasn't willing.

She could feel his breath against her cheek as she whispered, "I love you, Ransom."

He didn't reply in kind. He didn't say anything, simply touched his lips to the very edge of her mouth on the left side. Her mouth was slightly open because she couldn't seem to get enough air in her lungs. She heard the hitch in her breath as he slowly moved to kiss the opposite side of her mouth. Then his lips were full against her own, and she felt the supple dampness as their mouths met and melded.

Ransom had kissed her in the past, had even kissed

her quite thoroughly. But there was something different about this kiss. Something deep. Something deliberate. Something delicious.

Emaline found herself swaying toward him, letting the weight of her body lean into his, feeling her soft breasts press against his unyielding chest.

He'd pulled on his jeans to cross the house, but in his haste, the top few buttons had been left undone. Emaline reached down to nudge aside the lumpy denim, and her hand brushed his naked belly.

He hissed in a breath and speared her mouth with his tongue as his large hand caught her buttocks and relocated the hardness between his legs into the V between hers.

Emaline gasped at the curling ache she felt deep inside. The sensation traveled from her womb up through her body, creating a sting in her nose and a terrible ache in her throat.

She pulled free of the kiss and stared at Ransom. His eyes were heavy-lidded, his face taut. "What did you just do?"

He rubbed himself against her again, sending a frisson of exquisite pleasure skittering up her spine. "Are you asking me to stop?" he said in a rough voice that sounded not at all like the amiable man she knew.

Emaline bit her lip to keep herself from saying, *"Yes, I want you to stop."* Before Hannah had interrupted them with her unexplained cries, they'd been laughing and teasing one another in bed. She hadn't been the least bit frightened, because facing Ransom with their heads on separate pillows, the blankets between them, had been a sort of child's game, like spending the night with a friend.

There was nothing *friendly* about the feelings she was having now. Or the brash look in Ransom's eyes. No joking or joshing was involved. This felt deadly serious. This felt like the rest of her life was at stake.

Maybe it was.

Emaline knew she was walking a very fine line, asking Ransom to go so far and no further. She'd trusted the man with kind eyes to let her go if she asked. She wasn't so sure about the man with the wintry gaze who stared down at her now. The lover holding her in his arms looked so distant. So different.

This man was tense, his muscles bunched. His hands were tender but much more possessive. That was to be expected, since she'd told Ransom to consider them married in all but actual fact. So this was what he would be like as a husband. Tender but demanding. Possessive but gentle.

And determined. She mustn't forget that. Even though neither of them had said a word—or even moved an inch—he hadn't let go of his hold on her. Their bodies were locked together at the hips by the weight of his large hand on her behind.

She could feel the heat and the hardness of him. The insistence of his body. The demands of her own.

She hadn't expected to want him so badly. Hadn't known her body would beg her to rub herself against him like a cat. Hadn't known she'd feel like purring— or growling—as the pleasure spiraled through her body. Hadn't known that her knees would threaten to buckle, putting her on the ground, where it would be easier for him to cover her body with his own.

Her limbs felt heavy, as though she were moving underwater. She realized she was panting, that her pulse was pounding in her throat, that her chest and throat felt flushed, and that her cheeks were hot. Her eyes were so heavy-lidded she wanted to close them and surrender.

That word brought her up short. *Surrender.* If she had sex, she would get pregnant. If she got pregnant, she would die. Surrender meant death. She jerked to free herself.

But Ransom held on.

"Let me go, Ransom," she said in a brittle voice. "That's enough."

"That's not near enough, Em. We're just getting started."

He tried to kiss her again, but she turned her face aside.

"You said I could stop whenever I wanted. I want to stop."

She could feel his body throbbing against her own, feel his muscles turn to stone as he fought against his body's need to finish what he'd started. He let go of her buttocks, then let his other hand drop, and finally took a step back.

He turned away from her and took a deep breath and slowly let it out. His shoulders were rigid, his body as taut as a bow.

She felt the need to apologize and felt resentful that she did. She said the words anyway. "I'm sorry, Ransom."

"I knew what I was getting into," he said gruffly.

She reached out to touch his shoulder, but he yanked himself away and whirled on her. His blue eyes had turned to polar ice.

"Make up your mind, Em. You can't have it both

ways. Either we're done touching, or we're not. Which is it?"

"Why are you so mad?"

He made an exasperated sound. "I knew this was crazy when I agreed to it. It's my own fault. I should have kept my distance. I thought you were backing out of our agreement entirely when you sent me on that fool's errand across the house. When you let me kiss you, I guess I got carried away."

Emaline shoved a curl that had fallen free of her night braid away from her face. When it fell forward again, Ransom reached out and tucked it behind her ear. The intimate gesture felt so natural, so right. Emaline held his hand against her face and said, "I thought kissing would be safer, since we were standing up."

He smiled ruefully. And pulled his hand free. "Not hardly. I could have had you on your back in a heartbeat. Would have, if you'd been willing."

"So what do we do now?" she asked. "Do you still want to sleep in the same bed?"

He shook his head and sighed. "I don't know. I want to hold you in my arms through the night, but I can't guarantee I won't end up in the same condition I'm in right now."

Emaline flushed and said, "You mean aroused."

His lips quirked. "Yeah. Aroused. It doesn't take much. All I have to do is look at you to want you. That would normally be a healthy reaction, and it could be resolved by the two of us satisfying each other. But that won't work for us, since we can't have sex."

Emaline's blush deepened at his use of a word she'd

never used in mixed company. Or in any company, for that matter. She'd only thought it a couple of times in her own mind. But this was a grown-up relationship, and such words needed to be spoken if she and Ransom were ever to find their way to some sort of compromise that would work for both of them.

"Can we go back to bed?" Emaline said. "Things were fine before Hannah cried out. We were laughing and teasing and—"

"All that ended when you let me hold you in my arms," Ransom interrupted brusquely. He shoved a hand through his hair in agitation. "I don't think this is going to work, Emaline. I know you planned for us to spend this time together figuring things out, but I think I already have the answer I was looking for."

He turned to her, his eyes bleak. "I can't do this. I can't lie beside you and want you and never touch you. Not for a minute. Not for a night. And sure as hell not for the rest of my life."

Tears welled in Emaline's eyes and one spilled over. "Are you saying you won't marry me?"

He shook his head. "Not unless you change your mind. Do you want some time to think about it?"

"I've had my whole life to think about it. My mind is made up," she said. *And my heart is breaking.* But she didn't tell him that. He might take her in his arms again. And if he did, she might not stop him.

He cocked his hip and stood with his hands at his sides, a man without a direction to go.

So she asked the question. "What do we do now?"

"I think I take you home tomorrow."

She shook her head. "That won't work."

He frowned. "Why not?"

"You're forgetting about Aunt Betsy. I need my chaperon to confirm my whereabouts. Otherwise, my father is likely to come after you with a shotgun—and force us to marry."

His eyes narrowed. "He could try."

His response told Emaline how serious he was about not wedding a woman who wouldn't make love to him. "I guess that means you're going to have to put up with my presence for a while longer." Somehow, during the time she had left, she'd get him to change his mind.

"I don't have to sleep in the same bed with you."

"Where else can you sleep?"

"In the barn."

"It won't be very comfortable."

"It'll be a hell of a lot better than sleeping next to a woman I can't touch!"

"You can touch," she retorted. "And kiss and fondle. You just can't—"

"Put myself inside you," he finished for her with brutal frankness. "I'm not a glutton for punishment, Em. I don't enjoy being in the condition I'm in now, hurting because I can't finish what I started."

Emaline looked at him in shock. "You're hurting?"

He made a disgusted sound in his throat, as though he regretted speaking. "You had no way of knowing. It's the sort of thing women never hear about. Forget I mentioned it."

"Hurting how?" she asked, curious now to know what he was talking about. "Tell me."

"It doesn't matter."

"It matters to me."

He shot her a look of chagrin, then said, "When a

man's body is ready to plant the seeds that start a child in a woman's womb, it's painful not to finish what he started."

"Oh." She glanced down and saw the male part of him had created a hard ridge against his denim jeans. She lifted her embarrassed gaze to his face and asked, "Are you still in pain?"

"It goes away after a while."

"I'm sorry," she said. "I didn't mean to hurt you."

"Like I said, it was my fault. I knew what could happen, but I let myself get carried away anyway. I guess I thought you'd feel what I was feeling and want to make love with me."

"I *did* feel what you felt," Emaline retorted. "But I don't want to do what you wanted to do enough to die for it!"

"So you've said," he shot back. "I don't intend to repeat that mistake. Which is why I think I should sleep somewhere else."

Emaline was certain that if Ransom left her bed, whatever chance she had of changing his mind would be lost. She searched for a reason to keep him with her and said, "What will your brother think if he finds out you slept in the barn?"

Ransom looked thunderstruck.

That seemed to have made an impression, so she said, "I have a suggestion for how we can get through these upcoming weeks in the same bed."

"I'm listening."

Emaline's mind was scrambling for something to say that would convince him not to leave. "Clearly, touching and kissing is going to wreak havoc on both of us," she began.

He lifted a brow. "I didn't notice you in any pain."

She met his gaze and said, "My heart hurts. Because I want so badly to do what you want me to do and be what you want me to be. But I can't!"

He'd gathered her up in his arms and hugged her tight, his cheek pressed hard against hers.

"Em, Em, there has to be a way for us to make this work. There has to be a way for me to convince you—"

She put a hand over his lips to stop him from speaking. "For now, I think we have to treat each other like good friends. So this hug is fine, because it's meant to comfort."

As soon as she defined it that way, he let his hands drop as though she had some contagious disease and stepped back. His mouth sobered, and his face looked bleak again.

She looked up at him, pleading with her eyes for him to give them a chance, to give them the time they needed to see what life could be like if they lived it together. "There's more to a marriage than the part I'm denying you," she argued. "There's companionship and laughter. There's talking and sharing adventures. Shouldn't we try those things before we throw out the baby with the bathwater?"

"No touching?"

She shook her head.

"No kissing?"

She shook her head.

"Just companionship. And laughter."

"And talking," she said. "And sharing adventures."

He made a wry face. "I hope you know a few good jokes."

Emaline smiled with relief. "I can do better than that. I know how to tickle."

He wagged a finger at her. "That's touching."

"Oh, yes. Right. Well, I'm sure I'll think of something."

She'd better. Or this marriage was going to be over before it even got started.

Chapter Sixteen

"Are you all right?" Flint asked as he handed Hannah a cup of coffee.

"I'm fine." She took the blue-and-white-speckled metal cup from him and sat down at the kitchen table.

"You didn't sound fine last night," he said. "I don't think I've heard so much bawling since I rescued an orphaned day-old calf."

Hannah flushed. She wasn't sure how long she'd cried, but tears had still been drying on her cheeks as the sky lightened into grays and pinks outside the window. She hadn't slept well, if at all. "I wasn't crying because of what we did," she said.

He arched a skeptical brow. "No?"

"I was crying for my sisters, Hetty and Josie."

He made a sound in his throat to acknowledge what she'd said, but that didn't tell her what he was thinking.

She'd risen with the sun, anxious to find her way back to the wagon where she'd last seen her sisters. Even so, Flint had been awake and dressed before her. Hannah wished she'd had the courage to explain that she'd only been seeking escape last night when she'd begged him to put himself inside her. But he looked so forbidding she remained silent.

"There's smoked ham and biscuits for breakfast," he said, pointing to a plate on the table.

Hannah wasn't the least bit hungry, but if she was going to spend the day on horseback, as she hoped she was, she needed to eat. She picked up one of the biscuits with smoked ham stuffed inside and took a bite. The ham was salty, the biscuit stale. She chewed and swallowed and took a careful sip of hot coffee to wash it all down. The coffee was tarlike and so strong she barely managed to avoid choking.

She glanced down the hallway that led to the stairs, wondering how soon Emaline and Ransom would respond to the smell of coffee. She needed to talk to Flint, and she didn't want to do it in front of the other couple.

She kept her voice low and quiet as she said, "I was too upset last night to tell you, but I remembered what happened." She took a deep breath and said, "We were attacked by Indians."

"You and your sick husband?"

"Mr. McMurtry was already dead. Me and my two younger sisters."

"How old were your sisters?"

Hannah noticed he'd used the past tense and made sure she didn't. She refused to believe that Hetty and Josie were dead. "My twin, Henrietta—we call her Hetty—is seventeen. Josephine—she goes by Josie—is only sixteen."

"Why aren't they with your parents?"

"My parents were killed in the Great Chicago Fire. I married Mr. McMurtry and came west with him because he offered the three of us a way out of the orphanage where we lived."

"You'd have been safer back in Chicago."

Hannah thought of the hunger and cold and the beatings from Miss Birch. "It didn't seem so at the time."

"How did you escape a bunch of Sioux without being killed?" he asked.

"We were sitting in the wagon when they charged at us. Hetty aimed Mr. McMurtry's rifle at one of the Indians, who shot her with an arrow. He went crazy when I stood up beside her, I think because we're identical twins. Josie was up front on the wagon bench. She tried to fight back, but it didn't do any good. They took her with them when they drove the oxen away and left me and Hetty behind.

"I stayed with Hetty for a day. Then I left her in the wagon and went to find help."

Flint leaned his hips against a breakfront that held dishes, coffee cup in hand, and stared back at her. "How badly wounded was she?"

"The arrow was stuck too deep in her shoulder for me to get it out. She lost a lot of blood and . . ." Hannah's throat felt too raw to continue speaking, so she fell silent.

Flint shifted but remained where he was. At last he said, "Talk to me, Hannah."

"I don't—" Hannah started to say she couldn't remember all the awful details, but that wasn't the truth. Her eyes felt swollen and scratchy, and she scrubbed at them with her palms as the awful memories came flooding back. Her stomach knotted painfully.

She remembered *everything*.

Hannah covered her face with her hands. She couldn't bear to tell it all. "It was horrible." She shuddered. "Horrible."

Her blood had curdled when the band of renegades charged toward the wagon, yelling and whooping like banshees. She'd watched in awe as Josie unfurled the bullwhip at the first Indian who tried to grab her, catching him with the vicious tip and knocking him from his pony.

She heard the laughter of the Indians as Josie held them off, screaming and cracking the bullwhip for all she was worth.

Hetty had grabbed Mr. McMurtry's rifle, but she couldn't figure out how to cock it. The Indian she aimed it at, who rode up to the back of the wagon, shot an arrow into her shoulder instead.

Hannah remembered the shocked look on the marauder's face when she'd stood up to help her sister. He'd started pointing and gibbering so loudly that the other Indians had left Josie where she was and crowded around to look at the two of them together. They'd pointed from one to the other of them, and the one who'd shot Hetty screeched and flung his arms around like a crazy person.

Then Hannah heard Josie scream. She turned and saw, to her horror, that Josie had been yanked off the bench by an Indian who'd snuck up behind her on the other side of the wagon. The entire band of renegades left her and Hetty standing where they were and began cutting the oxen loose from their traces.

Hannah had eased Hetty down onto the wagon floor as she collapsed from her wound, then jumped over the tailgate to go help Josie. By the time she got to the front of the wagon, the Indians were already driving the oxen away. Josie was lying across a pinto pony in front of one of the Indians, kicking and yelling and pounding his bare thighs with her fists, as he galloped off.

Hannah ran after them for a little way, yelling for the savages to let Josie go, but they didn't even look back. She remembered screaming to her youngest sister, "Be strong, Josie! Be brave! I'll come and find you!"

She'd found Josie's glasses on the ground and picked them up. One of the lenses was cracked. She'd put them on and was startled to discover they were clear glass! She wanted Josie back, so she could ask her why she'd worn glasses when she didn't need them.

Hannah lowered her hands from her face and looked up at Flint. "How could I have forgotten about them like that? I promised I'd come back to help Hetty and to rescue Josie. I failed them both!"

Hannah thought she'd cried all the tears she had to cry, but two more pooled in her eyes and streamed down her face.

She wanted comfort. She needed it. She looked for solace, but a table—and a night of lovemaking—separated her from the one person who might have given it to her.

Instead of crossing to her, Flint headed for the stove, where he refilled his coffee cup. When he was done, he turned to her and said, "There was nothing you could have done."

"I abandoned them. I forgot about them as though they never existed!"

"You were in shock," he said. "You barely survived yourself." He moved back to the table, set down his coffee, then turned the chair across from her around and straddled it.

She reached out to him across the table. "My sisters are still out there, Flint. Josie's a captive. And Hetty . . ." Hannah's whole body was shaking like a leaf, and she couldn't make it stop.

"I'm so scared of what might have happened to them. What if Hetty—? What if Josie—?" Hannah couldn't go on. She looked beseechingly at Flint, her eyes filled with the desolation she felt.

A moment later he had her up from her chair with his arms wrapped tightly around her. "You're safe, Hannah. I've got you."

Hannah barely heard him. She was remembering again.

She'd tried removing the arrow, but the barb was caught deep in Hetty's flesh.

"Please, don't," Hetty had begged her. "Please. Don't."

Hannah knew Hetty would die if the arrow didn't come out. But she didn't know how to remove it without cutting into her sister's flesh, and she was afraid she would only make things worse if she tried.

She recalled the last conversation she'd had with Hetty, when she'd realized she would have to leave her sister behind to seek help.

"I've got to go," she told Hetty. "I have no choice."

"No. Stay with me. Till the end," Hetty begged.

"You're not going to die, Hetty. I won't let you."

"I don't mind," Hetty said. "I want to be with Clive."

"Clive is dead and gone because he was jealous and stupid. It wasn't your fault."

"Thank you for saying that, Hannah. But you and I both know that I got him killed. I've been so ashamed, Hannah. I've wanted to die. I'm ready to die."

"I'm not ready to let you go," Hannah said fiercely. "So you keep breathing, do you hear me? Fight to live, please, for my sake. I don't want to lose the other half of myself. I'm going to find help. I'll be back before you know it."

She'd left food and water, but Hetty was so weak, Hannah had wondered if her twin would even be able to lift her head to eat and drink.

She'd kissed her sister's feverish brow, aware from the heat of it how desperately wounded Hetty was. "I'm going now."

"Don't come back, Hannah," Hetty whispered. "It would be a waste of time. I won't last another day."

"Well, that gives me a day to find help. You hang on. Please, Hetty. Please hang on!"

No matter how far or how fast Hannah had walked, she hadn't seen another living soul. In the unrelenting darkness before the moon rose on the first night, she'd somehow moved off the trail. She ran out of water. She hadn't imagined she'd get so thirsty. Her food was stolen by animals during the night.

After the first day passed, Hannah had known that even if she found someone, they probably wouldn't be able to get back in time to help Hetty. Her sister had been clinging to life. Hetty had surely succumbed to her wounds. And Josie . . .

Hannah decided she wouldn't allow herself to think of what might be happening to Josie. In fact, she made up her mind not to think of either of her younger sisters, ever again. She would blot out everything. Maybe that way she could die in peace.

I forgot them on purpose, Hannah realized. She'd forgotten her sisters because she hadn't wanted to remember the horror of Hetty's death or Josie's capture.

Hannah became aware she was resting calmly in Flint's embrace. She pushed against his chest until she could lean back to look up into his face. "I want to find my twin and Mr. McMurtry and bury them. And I want to see if there's any way to find out where the Indians took Josie."

"If you left the wagon on the trail, passersby have probably buried the dead and helped themselves to whatever they found. There won't be anything left to see."

He was likely right, but she would never sleep another peaceful night until she kept her promise to return.

"If you're right, there will be graves. I can say a prayer. Or someone might have found Hetty alive and helped her. Maybe they left a note."

Or maybe she would find her twin's dead and decomposing body lying in the wagon, along with Mr. McMurtry. Hannah swallowed hard. If so, at least she would be able to give them a proper burial.

She laid her fingertips against Flint's stubbled cheek and said, "Please, Flint. I want to go back. Will you take me?"

He pulled away from her touch, and reached for his coffee cup. He took a swallow before he said, "How long did you walk after you left your wagon?"

"I don't know. A long time. A couple of days."

"Think. How many sunrises? Two? Three?"

Hannah stopped to think and was amazed at the answer she came up with. She'd never imagined so much time had passed. Maybe this was going to be a fool's errand after all. She met Flint's gaze and said, "You found me on the sixth morning."

"I presume you walked east."

"We walked toward the sun every morning for three months," she said. "So that's the direction I took."

"Did you stay on the trail?"

"At first. But I kept walking in the dark, and when the sun rose, the trail was nowhere to be seen."

"We can probably find the wagon," he said. "But I don't think you should hold out much hope of recovering the sister who was taken by renegade Indians."

"You think they killed her?" Hannah said in a voice not much louder than a whisper.

She didn't like the look that crossed Flint's face before he muttered, "If she was lucky."

Hannah's blood ran cold. But she remembered how Josie had fought and knew she would keep on fighting. "Josie will never give up," she said. "She was the one who defied Miss Birch at every turn."

"Who's Miss Birch?"

"The caretaker at the orphanage where we went after our parents died, except the word *caretaker* doesn't fit Miss Birch. She was cruel and vindictive. If not for her, we would all still be waiting in Chicago for word from our sister in—"

Hannah's eyes went wide. "I have more family! I have a sister and two brothers in Texas." The words came pouring out as the memories returned. "Miranda left with my two younger brothers, Nicholas and Harrison—Nick and Harry—to become a mail-order bride to some rancher near San Antonio. But we never heard from her again after she left. We didn't even know if she arrived safely, let alone if she married the man she went to meet."

"How many of you Wentworths are there?" Flint asked.

"Six. And someday we're all going to be together again," Hannah said.

"You know the two who came west with you are both dead," he said quietly.

"You're wrong. We survived that hellhole of an orphanage in Chicago for three years. We Wentworths are stronger than we look. We've got courage and heart and—"

"Fine."

Hannah stared at Flint, her mouth still open to argue, and realized he'd given in. "You'll help?"

"I'll help you locate your wagon. That is, whatever's left of it."

"And Josie?"

"Let's wait and see what we find when we get there."

Chapter Seventeen

Flint couldn't believe he'd let himself get talked into a wild-goose chase. Hannah had thrown herself back into his arms to thank him, and she stood within his embrace trembling, her soft, warm breasts pressed against his chest, with only a few thin layers of cloth separating them.

He didn't want a repeat of what had happened last night, so he edged his hips away. That was like closing the barn door after the horses had fled. His body had already acknowledged what his head was trying to deny.

He wanted her. Again.

Flint swore violently under his breath. Last night he'd only meant to comfort her, kissing her hair, her brow, kissing the tears from her cheeks. She was the one who'd raised her mouth to his. She was the one whose arms had circled his neck and pulled their bodies close. He'd protested. But not for long. He was a man, not a saint.

In hindsight, he realized that Hannah had been seeking oblivion. Last night, his mind had gone somewhere else, while his body took over, his little head doing the thinking for him. He'd craved her body, wanting to be inside her, needing to be as close as two people could be.

Anyone starved for water was going to take a drink if it was offered. His body had wanted a woman. He'd taken one when it was offered. That didn't make him a bad person, did it? Hannah had been an entirely willing participant. When he'd made his feeble attempt at slowing the runaway train, she'd only burrowed closer to him.

There had been nothing to keep his hand from sliding up under her shirt and closing on a soft breast, from feeling the nipple bud in response to his touch. Nothing to keep his palm from caressing her rounded belly and molding the hip bones that he could feel under velvety female flesh. Nothing to keep his mouth from tasting the salty skin at the base of her throat beneath her ear. Nothing to keep his hands from thrusting into her hair and angling her head for his kiss.

He'd wanted to taste her but hadn't been sure she would let him. He'd expected resistance, but there had been none, and he'd found a world of sweetness and honey inside her mouth.

Her hands hadn't been idle. He couldn't remember a time when he'd caught fire like that from a woman's touch. But he'd never had a woman want him like that. Never known a woman so greedy for more. Never imagined a woman so full of desire.

He remembered hearing buttons pop and ping off the wooden floor, remembered stripping the shirt down Hannah's arms and seeing her naked silhouette in the moonlight.

The rest was amazing.

Flint damned himself up one side and down the other. He'd known she was a temptation he should resist. Why hadn't he?

Logically, he knew his experiences with women had been limited to sitting on the front porch with nice girls when he was fourteen, paying for sex from camp followers during the war, and soliciting soiled doves in some saloon after that. He simply had no experience to compare with what had happened last night.

Would the same thing have happened if it had been Emaline in bed with him? Flint tried to picture her in the same situation and could not. He couldn't envision Emaline exhibiting such reckless passion.

He remembered Hannah's luminous eyes in the moonlight, remembered her open arms, willing him to pull her close. Somehow he'd lost his long john trousers and was as naked as she was. After that, all hope was lost.

"Good morning!"

Flint was ripped from his recollection by Emaline's greeting. He realized he was still holding Hannah in his arms and quickly let go of her and stepped back. He noticed he'd set down his coffee cup at some point and picked it back up again.

"Good morning, Emaline," Hannah said as the two women gave each other a quick hug.

Flint did a quick comparison of the two of them. One was immaculately turned out, her shiny brown hair tucked neatly into a bun, her dress buttoned to her throat and her wrists, falling all the way to the tips of her black, high-button shoes without a wrinkle.

The other wore scuffed brown shoes that had likely walked a thousand miles, a pair of Ransom's Levi's with ragged ends where she'd trimmed the legs to fit her, and one of his own plaid wool shirts that hung nearly to her knees. She'd gathered her blond curls into a single braid that hung down her back, but wisps had escaped to frame her face in a golden halo.

Flint felt the pulse throb in his neck and realized it wasn't Emaline who was causing the frantic beat of his heart. It was the waif he'd rescued.

Maybe that was it. Maybe it was the fact that he'd found Hannah, like a lost penny, that made her so attractive to him. Maybe it was the mystery surrounding her during the days before her memory had returned. Maybe it was the desperation he'd felt to find a woman—any woman—so he wouldn't be alone in the house when Emaline and Ransom returned to live here as a married couple.

Of course, none of those reasons explained why he was *still* attracted to Hannah when Emaline was standing in the same room with her. Standing right beside her, in fact, where the two women couldn't have been more different than a wolf and a dog.

One was feral, one domesticated. What did it say about him that he preferred the wild one?

It made no sense at all to him that two women who seemed so very different on the surface had become such fast friends. Flint glanced at Ransom over the two women's heads and saw his brother looked as disconcerted by the women's congeniality as he was.

"You two are up early," Ransom said.

"Hannah remembered what happened to her on the trail," Flint replied.

"Oh, my goodness, Hannah," Emaline said, giving Hannah another hug. "You remembered? What happened?"

Hannah glanced at Flint, and he saw the pain in her eyes that had caused him to "comfort" her and which had sent him from bed at dawn this morning.

"I'll tell you everything another time," she said to Emaline as she crossed back to the table and retrieved her coffee cup. "The long and the short of it is, Flint has agreed to help me find my way back to the wagon where I left my twin sister wounded by an arrow, and from which my youngest sister was kidnapped by Indians."

"How awful!" Emaline said. "What can we do to help?"

Flint felt his gut clench as Emaline linked her arm through Ransom's. He didn't understand his reaction to seeing the two of them together. How could he feel like he would die if Ransom married Emaline, and yet want Hannah with a physical need that was palpable? It didn't make sense. He was glad to be getting out of here. Maybe a little time away from Emaline and Ransom would help him sort it all out.

He turned to Ransom and said, "It would help if you stay here and keep an eye on things. Someone needs to find those missing cattle, and I'm not sure how long we'll be gone."

"You're taking Hannah with you?" Ransom said, arching a brow in surprise.

"I need to be there to see . . . whatever there is to see," Hannah said.

"Are you going dressed like that?" Emaline asked.

Hannah seemed to notice for the first time that she

wasn't dressed like a lady. "If I'm going to be riding horseback, this is probably as good an outfit as any."

"I have a riding skirt," Emaline said.

"I'm a lot taller than you," Hannah said. "This is fine, really."

Hannah was bigger everywhere, Flint realized. Bigger bosom. Bigger, better-for-childbearing hips. Probably a half foot taller. He'd always felt protective toward Emaline, because she was small and dainty. He realized he felt protective toward Hannah, too, but not because of her size. It was because she needed him.

Of course, Emaline had never needed to be rescued. He'd barely had a chance to get to know her before Ransom had come into the picture and stolen her heart.

He felt a spurt of resentment and shoved it down. It wasn't Ransom's fault the girl had fallen in love with him. Flint reminded himself that Ransom had his own problems with Emaline.

Flint remembered he'd told Ransom he would take Emaline with or without sex, but he wondered now if he'd been blowing smoke. He hadn't made it through one night in bed with a woman he *didn't* love without having sex. Could he possibly have spent a lifetime wanting a woman he *did* love without having her?

Which made him wonder what Ransom was going to do if Emaline didn't change her mind. More significantly, what sort of consequences would there be to their beef contract with the army if one of the Creed brothers didn't marry Emaline Simmons?

Flint took another look at his younger brother and saw the shadows under his eyes. Ransom hadn't spent an easy night. He met his brother's gaze and said, "Are you two going to be all right if we leave you here alone?" He turned to Emaline and said, "I guess what I'm really asking is if you'll be all right all alone at the house while Ransom is out riding fence."

Emaline glanced toward Ransom before she answered. "I'll be fine. After all, I'm sure there will be times in the future when it will be necessary for me to be alone at the house. I might as well get used to it now."

"You're not afraid?" Hannah asked.

Emaline smiled. "Believe it or not, I'm a good shot. So long as I have a rifle handy, I'll be fine."

"I've never even held a gun," Hannah said.

"I'll teach you what you need to know," Flint said. "Right now we'd better pack some supplies and get moving. Day's wasting."

Ransom took Flint aside and asked, "How far do you want me to go looking for those missing cattle?"

"Stay off Patton's land," Flint ordered.

"What if I see signs that that's where they've headed—or been driven?" Ransom asked.

"At least wait until I get back. I shouldn't be gone more than a few days, a week at most."

A pained expression crossed Ransom's face.

"What's wrong?" Flint asked.

"Nothing you can help with."

"Try me."

"I don't think she's going to change her mind."

The words seemed to be wrenched from his brother. Flint had no idea how to comfort him. Especially since he'd acknowledged to himself how much Ransom was being asked to give up.

"I have faith in you, Ransom. You've got a few days without another soul around. Spend as much time as you can with her. Be patient. Everything worthwhile is worth waiting for."

"Easy for you to say," Ransom said. "You and Hannah seem to be getting along fine."

"Don't believe everything you see," Flint blurted.

Ransom arched a questioning brow.

Flint wasn't about to tell his little brother how confused he felt, but he had to tell him something. So he said, "Hannah and I are two strangers forced together by circumstance. She still hasn't agreed to marry me. In the end, you and I may both find ourselves alone."

Ransom's lips quirked at the corner. "Well, big brother, at least we'll still have each other."

"Take care of yourself while I'm gone," Flint said. "No heroics over a bunch of stupid cows."

Ransom scowled. "I don't need you to take care of me anymore, Flint. I'll do what I think needs to be done."

Flint realized he'd raised his younger brother's hackles. He was used to giving orders and having Ransom follow them without complaint. This defiance was new. And disturbing. Especially since he wasn't going to be around to come to the rescue if anything went wrong.

"Be smart," Flint said. "Don't take any foolish chances."

"So now I'm a fool?" Ransom shot back.

Flint snorted in disgust. "You know what I mean."

"Yeah, unfortunately I do," Ransom said. "You don't think I can do anything right on my own."

Flint put a hand on his brother's shoulder. "Look, Ransom, I think—"

Ransom shoved away his attempt at comfort and said, "You'd better get moving. Day's wasting."

Flint had a horrible feeling of foreboding. He didn't want to leave Ransom alone while he went marching off across the prairie on some fruitless journey to find dead bodies that were probably already buried. The mood Ransom was in, he was likely to provoke Ashley Patton for the fun of it. The problem was, Ashley's hired gunslinger, Sam Tucker, was ready to put a bullet in anyone who looked at him crosswise.

Flint opened his mouth to give his brother another warning to be careful and shut it again. One more word of caution might be the spur that made Ransom do something rash.

He swallowed the warning he'd been about to give and simply said, "I'll see you when I get back."

Chapter Eighteen

"You ride better than I figured you would," Flint said grudgingly. "You must have spent a lot of time on horseback."

Hannah felt a rush of emotion as she remembered all the times she and Hetty had gone riding in Chicago's Lincoln Park—renamed after the assassinated president—along the shores of Lake Michigan. "My father loved fast horses," she said. "He owned several Thoroughbreds, and Hetty and I used to sneak away to the stables and ride them."

Flint frowned. "Stallions?"

Hannah nodded. "And yes, they always wanted to race. And yes, we had to keep them from fighting each other. But oh, how I loved to fly across the grass in the early morning with the wind off the lake in my hair!"

"Your father allowed his daughters to do something that dangerous?"

Hannah laughed, realized what she'd done, and sobered again. "Papa didn't know. But I'm not sure he would have stopped us even if he'd had an inkling what we were up to. He encouraged us to do all sorts of things that gave Mama a fright."

"Like what?" Flint asked.

"We'd drive ourselves around Chicago in a fringe-topped buggy pulled by a pair of matched chestnuts, dressed identically, of course."

"Without a chaperon?"

"We had each other for chaperons," Hannah said. "Hetty and I were pattern cards of propriety, at least in public. At home we'd race each other up the stairs and slide down the bannister. It used to drive the maids and the butler and Mama crazy."

"Maids? A butler? Sounds like your father was rich."

Hannah shrugged. "He owned a bank. It burned down in the Great Chicago Fire, and we lost everything. Our only living relative, Uncle Stephen, put the six of us in the Chicago Institute for Orphaned Children."

"Sounds like a real nice fellow," Flint said sarcastically.

"Not a nice man at all," Hannah said. "Our aunt had passed away, and Uncle Stephen swore he couldn't raise six kids by himself. Besides, he claimed that he couldn't afford to take care of us. He was unemployed, you see, because Papa's bank, where he'd worked, had burned down."

Her voice turned bitter as she added, "Two years after the fire, he opened a bank of his own."

"If he was so poor, where did he get the money to build a bank?" Flint asked.

"It does raise some questions, doesn't it?" Hannah

said with a curl of her lip. "Unfortunately, having money made no difference to Uncle Stephen. He didn't want us. We've been forced to fend for ourselves."

"By becoming brides," Flint said.

Hannah lifted her chin and looked him in the eye. "It's an honorable solution to the problem of survival."

"You were lucky you didn't die on the trail."

"Speaking of which, I can't believe how good you are at backtracking my trail. Or how many times I covered the same ground," she said with chagrin.

"It's easy to walk in circles in the dark."

"Really? It's awful to think that if I'd stopped when the sun set and waited for morning I might have found help sooner."

"Hannah," Flint began, "I don't think anything you did or didn't do would have made a difference. Not the way you've described Hetty's injuries. She needed a surgeon."

Hannah stared into the distance and saw a dust cloud that seemed to be moving closer. "Flint, what is that?"

"Riders." As he spoke, he freed his Winchester from the boot on his saddle and cradled it in his arms.

Hannah's heart shot to her throat. "Shouldn't we run?"

"Let's see who it is first."

"I'd rather run," Hannah muttered under her breath. She would have been more frightened, except Flint seemed so calm.

"I don't think it's renegade Indians this far south-east of Fort Laramie," he said. "We'll be able to see who it is in plenty of time to escape, if that becomes necessary."

He sounded sure of himself, and he was holding his rifle ready to fire, so Hannah willed her heartbeat to slow down. She wouldn't make a very good frontier wife if she jumped like a rabbit at every shadow.

The hardest thing she'd ever done was to hold her horse steady while they waited for the riders to reveal themselves. Even so, her mount sensed her nervousness and sidestepped often enough that Flint finally said, "Take it easy, Hannah."

"Who could it be, if it's not Indians?" she asked.

"Your guess is as good as mine."

She pointed and said, "Are they wearing Stetsons?"

"Looks like it," Flint agreed.

The cowboy hats meant the riders were unlikely to be Indians. Hannah let out a breath she hadn't realized she'd been holding. She followed Flint as he urged his horse forward to meet the oncoming riders.

"It's a friend of mine and his sons," he said when they were close enough to see facial features.

"Should we be meeting them like this? I mean, the way I'm dressed? And without a chaperon?"

"Holloway will take his cue from our behavior," Flint said. "If what you're wearing is okay with me, it'll be okay with him. Don't worry that he'll say anything. Out here, no man's going to insult a woman, not unless he wants every man within a hundred miles to come after him with a rope."

Nevertheless, Hannah tucked in her shirt and shoved several flyaway curls behind her ears. She was wearing a flat-brimmed hat Flint had loaned her, and she tugged it down low. Then she sat up straight and waited to meet Flint's friends.

"Howdy, Flint," a man with a windburned, deeply lined face and gray sideburns said as he pulled his mount to a halt in front of them. The hazel-eyed man was flanked by two young boys who looked similar in age to Hannah's brother Nick, which would make them nine or ten. One had black hair and blue eyes, the other had blue eyes, sandy hair, and freckles.

"Howdy, John," Flint said, putting a finger to the brim of his hat in greeting. "Josh. Jeremy."

"Hello, Mr. Creed," the boy with the dark hair replied.

A moment later the sandy-haired boy said, "Who's that with you, Mr. Creed?"

"Beat me to it, son," the older man said, turning his gaze on Hannah.

Hannah was staring at Flint *Creed* with wide eyes. It seemed unreal that she'd ended up in the home of a man with the *exact same last name* as the rancher whose advertisement for a mail-order bride her sister Miranda had answered. Could Jacob Creed from Texas and Flint Creed of the Wyoming Territory possibly be related? Before she could ask, Hannah was being introduced to the older man.

"Hannah, this is John Holloway and his two sons, Josh and Jeremy. John, this is Mrs. Hannah McMurtry. She's a widow who lost her husband on the journey west."

"Flint saved my life," Hannah interjected.

"Ma'am," Holloway said, tipping his hat to her. He

turned to Flint and asked, "Where are you two headed?"

"Hannah's wagon was attacked by renegades on the trail. I rescued her, and she's been recovering at my ranch. She had to leave a wounded twin sister behind. We're backtracking to see if we can find the wagon and any sign of Hannah's sister Hetty."

Holloway rubbed at his chin thoughtfully and said, "We were at the fort yesterday, and no one said anything about finding a girl on the trail. Sorry, ma'am."

"That doesn't mean she wasn't found," Hannah said, fighting off a feeling of panic. "Maybe whoever found her was passing through and kept moving. I had another sister, Josie, who was taken by the Indians who attacked our wagon. Have you heard anything about a white woman being captured by the Sioux?"

"Sorry to hear about your troubles, ma'am," Holloway said. He turned to the two boys and said, "You boys hear anything about a white captive at the Red Cloud Agency Camp over the past few days?"

"Soaring Eagle and Wheat Woman didn't mention anything," Josh said.

Jeremy added, "Some of the braves might have left the camp to go hunting, because they were so short of food and—"

"And attacked my wagon?" Hannah said. "I thought the Indians in the agency camps were supposed to be peaceful."

As Hannah watched, Holloway exchanged a pained look with Flint. Then the older man said, "The government confines the Sioux on a bare strip of land, then appoints a corrupt agent who steals the food and supplies they're supposed to receive. It's no wonder they run off and steal and kill."

Hannah was curious enough to ask, "Why would your sons be going to an Indian camp?"

Holloway glanced at Flint, who said, "She won't say anything."

Holloway turned to Hannah and said, "My sons are one-quarter Brulé Sioux. Soaring Eagle and Wheat Woman are their grandparents."

"Oh." Hannah was shocked. She looked again at the two boys, hunting for features that would proclaim them Indians. Their blue eyes—and Jeremy's freckles—seemed to deny the fact.

"It would cause a lot of problems for John if the truth about his kids and their mother, who's half Sioux, became known."

"I see." She turned to Holloway and said, "Your secret is safe with me."

"By the way," Holloway said, "Ashley Patton has applied for membership in the Laramie County Stock Association."

"I don't see how we can keep him out," Flint said. "He's bought up a bunch of smaller spreads. I think by now he owns more cattle and more land than anybody but you."

"I've discovered a bunch of squatters on my land who look suspiciously unlike sodbusters," Holloway said. "Wouldn't be surprised if Patton is at the bottom of it."

"I'm missing a hundred head of cattle," Flint said.

Holloway hissed in a breath. "That's a chunk of beef."

"I'm not sure yet what happened to them. Maybe they just drifted."

"With all the barbed wire you've put up?" Holloway said. "That seems unlikely."

"Yeah," Flint agreed. "Ransom is going to take a look and see what he can find out."

"Tell him to be careful," Holloway warned. "Patton is an unscrupulous son of a bitch." He turned to Hannah and said, " 'Scuse my language, ma'am."

"But he *is* a son of a bitch," Flint said.

Hannah covered her mouth to stop a laugh. "He sounds like a horrible man."

"A man worth watching, for sure," Holloway said.

"What are you three doing this far south?" Flint asked.

"We're headed to Cheyenne," Holloway said. "I need an anniversary gift for Kinyan. That's my wife," Holloway explained.

"How many years is it?" Flint asked.

"Ten."

"You're a lucky man, John."

"Don't I know it," Holloway said with a smile. "Will you be at the Association meeting next week?"

"Depends on what Hannah and I find when we reach her abandoned wagon. If there's enough of a trail, we may try to follow the Indians who took her sister captive."

That was news to Hannah, but welcome news.

"Watch yourselves," Holloway said. "There are plenty of young bucks riding around out there looking for trouble."

"They won't find me easy prey," Flint assured him. "See you later, John. Take it easy, Josh. Jeremy."

"So long, Mr. Creed," the boys said almost in unison.

"Nice meeting you, Mrs. McMurtry," the freckle-faced boy said, touching the brim of his hat.

"Nice meeting both of you, too," Hannah said.

When the Holloways had ridden beyond the point where they could hear her, Hannah asked, "Did you mean what you said?"

"What?"

"About following the Indians who took Josie? Did you mean it?"

"I wouldn't have said it if I didn't," Flint said. "But don't count on finding her, Hannah. The Sioux wouldn't have left much of a trail, and whatever little sign there was has most likely been blotted out by wind and weather. Besides, it's entirely possible those renegades came from one of the tribes in the Dakotas, where we can't follow without risking both our lives."

Hannah heard what she wanted to hear. After they found the wagon, and did whatever had to be done there, they would try to track down Josie. There was a chance she could still make good on her promise to rescue her sister.

She glanced sideways at Flint and wondered again whether her sister Miranda could possibly be married to some relative of his. "Is Creed a common name in Texas?" she asked.

"I have no idea," he replied. "Why do you ask?"

"The man my sister traveled to San Antonio to marry was named Jacob Creed. Do you know him? Could he possibly be related to you?"

Flint stared at her in surprise. "I have a brother named Jacob."

Hannah stared at him. "Really? Does he live near San Antonio?"

"Jake has a ranch a couple of hours away. But he's married and has a two-year-old daughter, Anna Mae. Last I heard, he had another child on the way."

"Do you suppose something happened to Jake's wife?" Hannah asked.

Flint frowned. "I think he would have written us about it. But maybe not."

Hannah was worried because the advertisement in the Chicago *Daily Herald* for a mail-order bride hadn't said a word about the Texas rancher having been married before or having a two-year-old daughter. Maybe they weren't one and the same person. But if they were, Jacob Creed was in for a surprise of his own, because Miranda hadn't said anything about the fact she was bringing along two little boys.

Hannah wondered if the lies Miranda and Jake had told each other had kept them from getting married. If so, where was her sister now? The only way she knew to contact Miranda was through the man Miranda had gone to Texas to marry.

What if Miranda's Jacob turned out to be Flint and Ransom's brother? How wonderful that would be! If so, there was a chance the three brothers would one day want to get back together, and Hannah would see Miranda and Nick and Harry again.

She couldn't imagine why the three brothers didn't write to each other more often. "You don't stay in touch with your brother?" she asked.

Flint shrugged. "Jake's life is in Texas. Our lives are here. Not much point."

"Have you heard whether the second child was born?"

Flint shook his head. "No, and it's strange that I haven't. Now you've got me worried."

"So your brother might be the Jacob Creed who advertised for a mail-order bride," Hannah said.

"In Chicago?" Flint snorted. "If Jake wanted another bride he could look a lot closer to home." He was silent for a moment, then said, "Except, he might have had a problem if Blackthorne wanted him gone. That English bastard sure made me and Ransom feel unwelcome."

"Who's Blackthorne?"

"Alexander Blackthorne is my stepfather, and you'll never meet a more arrogant, overbearing, merciless son of a bitch."

"Could we send a letter to your brother asking if he advertised for a mail-order bride? And whether my sister showed up in San Antonio? And whether he married her?"

"Sure. Why not? I'll post it when I go to Cheyenne for the Association meeting next week."

"Thank you, Flint." Hannah could hardly believe how easy it was going to be to reconnect with her older sister and younger brothers. *If* they'd arrived safely in Texas. And *if* it turned out that Flint's brother Jake was the same Jacob Creed who'd advertised in the Chicago *Daily Herald* for a mail-order bride.

Chapter Nineteen

Hannah was appalled at how soon they reached the abandoned wagon after leaving the Holloways. Apparently, sometime before the attack, Mr. McMurtry had taken a wrong turn and headed north on a road that led to Fort Laramie, instead of staying on the Oregon Trail to Cheyenne.

Someone had stolen the canvas cover from the wagon, and the naked wooden hoops that had supported it, called bows, looked like the rib cage of some prehistoric animal. A tumbleweed blew across the wagon tongue and caught on something that was stuck in the ground nearby. Hannah realized it was a cross.

She was off her horse an instant later, running toward the mound of earth in the shape of a body. She fell to her knees beside the grave, freeing the tumbleweed so she could see the words carved into the crude wooden cross.

REST IN PEACE

No more? Who was buried beneath that cross? Mr. McMurtry? Hetty? Both? Hannah surreptitiously put a hand to the growing child in her womb, and made a silent vow to the man she believed was buried there.

I promise to love this baby and take care of it, no matter what I have to do to make sure that he—or she—has a wonderful life.

Seeing the grave made her husband's death very real, and her own dire situation very clear. Hannah's pregnancy didn't show now, but it wouldn't be long before it did. Which meant she didn't have time to go hunting for another husband, let alone for a lengthy courtship with someone she hadn't yet met. She had a proposal from a man who wanted to marry her. She should say yes, and the sooner, the better.

The only question was whether she should tell Flint about the baby. Instinct told her to keep her secret until she was safely married. There was too great a chance Flint wouldn't want to raise some other man's child.

Hannah was smitten with guilt. Maybe after the babe was born, she would tell him it was McMurtry's child. But what if he divorced her for deceiving him? What if he threw her out?

Hannah gripped her fingers together. Why should she tell him the truth? Flint might not treat another man's child as well as he would treat a child he thought was his own. Her child's well-being was more important to her than anything else. And who would be hurt?

Only her own conscience.

Both men had blue eyes. Both men were tall. Her blond hair would be excuse enough if the child was born with red hair. And if the poor thing had Mr.

McMurtry's beaked nose, she could blame that on her father.

Hannah was a woman alone, without the means to go anywhere, assuming she had somewhere to go. She had no idea where to find the rest of her family. Even if she sent another message General Delivery to Miranda in San Antonio, she didn't have time to wait for a response that might not come.

There was no telling whether Miranda and Nick and Harry had reached their destination. No way of knowing whether Miranda was married or not. Maybe the rancher who'd advertised for a mail-order bride had decided he didn't want a ready-made family.

Hannah's throat constricted when she considered how dire Miranda's circumstances might be. Her sister didn't have only herself to worry about. She was also responsible for their two brothers.

Hannah's eyes welled with tears as she rubbed a hand over the dry dirt and stones that were mounded before her. For all she knew, Miranda and Nick and Harry might be buried somewhere between Chicago and San Antonio. She might never know what had happened to them.

Hannah glanced at Flint, who was examining the wagon. She shuddered at the thought of what he might find there. There had been no signs of life as they approached the wagon. Were Hetty's remains inside?

Hannah brushed a scalding tear from her cheek. She was done crying. Crying didn't help. She had to *do* something. She felt a comforting hand on her shoulder and shrugged it off, refusing Flint's support as she struggled to her feet.

"The wagon's empty," he said.

She was glad he'd looked, because she couldn't have done it herself. She glanced at the pitiful grave and the shallow mound of dirt above it. "Could someone have buried them both here?" she wondered aloud.

"It's possible two bodies could be under there," Flint said. "The only way to know for sure is to dig."

Hannah shuddered. "No." She turned to face him at last and asked, "Did you find any kind of note in the wagon?"

"It's empty, Hannah. Picked clean."

Hannah moaned.

"Except . . ." Flint stopped speaking and cocked his hip.

She bravely met his gaze and asked, "What did you find?"

"This." He opened his hand.

Hannah stared at the bloodstained arrowhead attached to a broken-off piece of wood. She reached for it and set it in her palm, staring at it with wonder. "Where did you find this?"

"In the bed of the wagon." He hesitated, then added, "Along with a lot of dried blood."

"What do you think it means?"

"You tell me."

Hannah felt a surge of hope. "I broke the shaft off this arrow myself when it was still in Hetty. Someone must have dug this out of her and then took her somewhere."

"Or buried her there," Flint said, gesturing to the grave.

Hannah shook her head. "The pile of dirt would be bigger."

Flint lifted a skeptical brow.

"If Hetty lived long enough for someone to dig out that arrow, she's still alive," Hannah said with certainty. "I've told you before, we Wentworths are stronger than we look."

"And took her where?" Flint asked, glancing around at the endless prairie.

"To Fort Laramie, of course."

"Holloway was there yesterday, remember? There was no report of a white woman at the fort, especially not a wounded one."

Hannah's fisted hands found her hips. "Then what happened to my sister?"

"Your guess is as good as mine. If she was rescued by white folks, I presume she'll send word once she's recovered her senses."

"Send word where?" Hannah said, suddenly realizing the futility of the situation. "Hetty doesn't know what happened to me, either. She may think I'm dead, since I never returned."

"She'll do the same thing you're doing," Flint said. "She'll look for you in the place closest to where she knew you were last, which is—"

"A place I never reached—Cheyenne," Hannah finished for him. There was nothing more she could do about Hetty until her twin sent a message about where she was. Assuming she was still alive. "What about Josie?" she asked.

"Until someone reports seeing a white woman with the Indians, there's nothing we can do."

"Nothing?" Hannah pointed to the tracks left by the oxen that had been herded away by the Indians.

"You said we could follow the trail if there was one. There it is."

Flint's lips flattened into a stubborn line. "I'm not taking you into that wilderness, Hannah. It would serve no purpose."

"We might find my sister," Hannah argued.

"Renegades reckless enough to raid this close to the fort won't leave witnesses. Your sister is—"

"No!" Hannah didn't let him finish the sentence. Josie wasn't dead. She couldn't be. "I can't believe you're scared of a few Indians," Hannah said scornfully. "I never took you for a coward."

His face tightened, and his eyes narrowed before he spoke. "You're damned right I'm scared, and I'm not too proud to admit it. One lone man and a woman are sitting ducks."

Hannah stared at Flint with disdainful eyes. What he said made perfect sense. But she couldn't believe he wasn't willing to take a little risk when the reward— finding Josie—was so enormous. "Why are you so afraid, when I'm not?"

"Maybe because I've seen the carnage these savages can wreak on human bodies—burning them over a fire like a spitted beef, skinning them alive, using them for target practice, cutting off eyelids and burying them up to their necks in an anthill. Maybe because I know this is a wild-goose chase, even if you don't."

"But Josie—"

"Is dead," he said brutally. "Dead to you, anyway. If she's found at all, she'll already be some young buck's squaw."

"Don't say that!" Hannah cried in horror.

"I'm telling you the truth, so you won't imagine some happily-ever-after fairy-tale ending for your sister. Indians can be cruel to their captives, assuming your sister lived long enough to reach whatever village up north that raiding party might have come from.

"If those bucks were from an agency camp around here, the likelihood is they raped your sister, killed her, and dumped the body. Unless we find her bones on the trail—"

"Stop it! Stop it!" Hannah pounded her fists on Flint's chest, desperate to cut off the gruesome tale he was telling.

She felt his arms surround her but she wanted no comfort from the person who'd painted such a horrible picture of Josie's fate. But his hold was inexorable, and she finally leaned her head against his pounding heart and closed her eyes, letting the sadness and loss overwhelm her.

Hannah didn't know how long they stood there, but at last she became aware of the hot sun on her back, of flies buzzing nearby, of the rush of the ever-present wind in the tall grass. She took a step away, and Flint's arms fell free.

She met his gaze with narrowed eyes and said, "I hate you for filling my mind with those awful images."

He didn't defend himself or excuse what he'd done.

"If we're not going to look for Josie," she said. "I want to go home."

"We could stop by the fort and see if any word of Hetty has come in overnight."

"She's probably halfway to California by now,"

Hannah said. She lifted her chin and said, "At least, that's where I'm going to imagine her whenever I think of her. As soon as she gets where she's going, she'll send a message to Cheyenne for me General Delivery. And when she does—"

Hannah sobbed, which cut off her speech. Flint reached for her, but she turned and ran toward her horse. She slowed before she reached the animal, so she wouldn't spook him, then mounted the chestnut and kicked him to a gallop, back in the direction from which they'd come.

She could hear Flint riding hard to catch up to her and whipped her horse with the end of the reins to stay ahead of him. She didn't want to talk to him. Especially since she was going to have to do a lot of fancy talking to make him believe she wanted to marry a man she'd all but called a coward.

She would rather not marry again, but she no longer had that choice. When Ransom and Emaline said their vows, she planned to be standing alongside them with Flint.

"Hannah, stop!" he called from behind her. "You're going to kill that horse."

Hannah pulled her mount to a quick stop and whirled to face Flint. "I see no reason to wait. Yes. My answer is yes, I'll marry you. You've got the bride you wanted," she snarled at him. "Don't expect me to love you, and we'll get along fine."

His mouth flattened to a thin line. His gray eyes turned hard as stone. A muscle worked in his jaw before he said, "Don't expect me to love you, either, and you've got a deal."

Chapter Twenty

Flint hadn't realized until Hannah responded to his proposal of marriage that he'd been cherishing a hope that he'd somehow end up with Emaline. That hope had died in a single syllable.

Yes.

It was one thing to suspect, in his heart of hearts, that Ransom would never give up Emaline. It was another thing entirely to give up hope—forever—of having her for himself. His heart hurt, physically ached in his chest, as though someone had struck him with a heavy stone.

This was what heartbreak felt like. He didn't like it.

It didn't help that Hannah had suggested he was a coward. The accusation shouldn't have bothered him like it did. Despite the label that had attached to him during the war, Flint knew he wasn't lily-livered. He was cautious. He was careful. Nevertheless, he'd suffered a blow when she'd thrown that word at him.

This was what distrust felt like. He didn't like it.

Not for the first time, Flint wondered whether

marriage to Hannah was really going to solve his problem. He might be better off suffering in silence. He swore under his breath. It was too late to change his mind now. Here in the Territory, contracts were seldom written down. A promise was a promise. When a man gave his word, he kept it, or he could forget ever doing business again.

The time to back out had come and gone. He was committed. When Ransom married Emaline, Flint would marry Hannah. That meant he had a long, cold winter to get through while living in the same house as the other couple. He'd better start figuring out how to get along with the woman who would, very shortly, be his wife.

Hannah hadn't said a word since she'd agreed to marry him. She was riding a little ahead of him, so she didn't have to look at him. It also made speaking difficult, so they'd been riding in silence.

The wind blew through the wheat-colored grass so it looked like rolling ocean waves around Hannah. She sat straight in the saddle, her shoulders squared, which made him wonder if she was really as unhappy with the prospect of wedding him as she'd seemed when she'd accepted his proposal.

He hadn't let himself think too much about her reluctance to marry him. He supposed she would have been loath to marry any man, since she was so recently widowed. At least she'd ended his torment by giving her an answer. Now that she'd said yes, he could stop agonizing and accept his fate.

He trotted his horse to catch up to her and asked, "Are you sure you don't want to go to the fort to see if there's been any word about Hetty since yesterday?"

"You told me it's a waste of time," Hannah replied.

It probably was, but at this point, he was willing to waste the time to please her. So he said, "I could use some supplies from the sutler's store."

"Then by all means, let's go to the fort."

He heard the irritation in her voice. Maybe going to Fort Laramie would only remind her of how desperate her sister's situation was. "I can wait," he said. "There's no rush. If I go another time, I can take a wagon and get everything at once. I can only buy now what I can carry on horseback."

She eyed him askance. "Could I buy a dress? Or a skirt and blouse?"

Flint hadn't given much thought to the fact that Hannah had no female clothing. Or that he would have to provide the money to purchase it. She was going to need a dress in which to get married and one she could wear to social activities, like the Laramie County Stock Association meeting next week.

"I'm not sure the sutler will have a ready-made dress, but the store has bolts of muslin and calico. I presume you can sew?"

"You'd be wrong," she said. "My mother never taught us. There was no need. A seamstress made our dresses from patterns we picked from a book. I can mend. We learned that at the orphanage. I don't think I could make a dress by myself."

"Maybe Emaline can help you," he suggested.

She made a face.

"What's wrong?"

"I don't want to be obliged to her."

"Why not?"

Hannah gave a halfhearted shrug. "I have no way to pay her back."

"She wouldn't expect payment."

"I don't know how to do anything!" she blurted.

Flint stared at her, two deep, vertical lines forming between his brows. "What do you mean?"

"I mean I can't cook pies or slaughter pigs or feed chickens or milk cows or sew clothes or knit woolen mittens or make candles or soap or do anything a frontier woman needs to know how to do."

"You can learn," Flint said.

"I don't belong out here," she muttered. "I'll make a terrible wife." She hesitated, then added very softly, "And mother."

He hissed in a breath. He'd never considered the possibility that Hannah might be pregnant. How could he have been so blind? In a quiet voice he asked, "Are you with child, Hannah?"

She turned frightened eyes on him. "Why would you think that?"

"Because of what you said about being a bad mother."

"Oh. That. Well. It's just that I'm so ignorant."

So she wasn't pregnant. He felt . . . relieved. Flint wasn't sure he was ready to assume responsibility for another man's child when he hadn't yet adjusted to the idea of being a husband. "You can learn anything you need to know," he insisted.

She shook her head. "I don't belong here."

"You're wrong about that. You have the one

quality—the only quality—that's absolutely necessary out here."

She looked up at him from beneath lowered lashes, almost seductively, and asked, "What is that?"

Flint felt a flash of heat run through him. *I find you lovely, and infinitely desirable. When I look at you, I want to hold you and put myself inside you.*

Those things were true, but he doubted they would do much to convince Hannah she belonged in Wyoming. Instead he said, "When you were seeking help for your sister, even though you were lost, you kept moving. You stayed alive. Sometimes, that's enough. You make it through one day and try to do better the next. One day at a time, Hannah. That's how we're going to build a life together."

"You make it sound possible."

"Of course it's possible," he assured her.

"Even though we don't intend to love each other?"

"Mutual respect is enough. It's plenty."

She lowered her gaze to her hands, which were knotted around the reins, and he realized he might not have her respect. He supposed he would have to earn it. That cut both ways. He would need a wife who could do all the things Hannah couldn't yet do. He would need a helpmate who could pull her share of the weight. It was up to Hannah whether she decided to accept that challenge and work to meet it.

And if she couldn't? Or wouldn't? He wasn't going to buy trouble for himself by thinking too far into the future.

Flint wasn't sure when the idea of marrying Hannah right away, today, came to him, but he mulled it over all the way to the fort before presenting it to her.

"What would you think if we got married today?"

Hannah's mouth opened in an *O* of surprise before she shut it and stared at him wide-eyed. "What would be the point of that?"

"We can start our lives now, instead of waiting a month," he said.

"I don't have anything to wear."

Flint chuckled. Trust a woman to think about the small stuff. "I'm sure one of the women at the fort will have something you can borrow."

"Don't you want your brother present? Don't you want some sort of celebration?"

"We can celebrate along with Ransom and Emaline when they get married." *If they get married.* "Ransom and I have pretty much the same friends. That way, they can have their anniversary, and we can have ours."

Hannah smiled, and the dimples he found so fascinating appeared in her cheeks.

He took that as a good sign. "You'll do it?"

"Why not?"

It never occurred to Flint to wonder why a woman would give up having a wedding day with a special dress and flowers and all the folderol that women seemed to think was so important. He was too glad she'd agreed to marry him right away.

Because he was having second thoughts about marrying her at all. Worrying about how he was going to spend his life with a woman he didn't love. Wondering if he could help her find the rest of her family and honorably be rid of her that way. Willing himself to keep his promise and make her his wife, whether he wanted to or not.

All things considered, the sooner he married Hannah McMurtry, the better.

Chapter Twenty-one

"How did you two meet?"

Hannah told the sutler's wife the story she and Flint had agreed upon. Flint had thought the truth might raise too many questions about where she'd been spending her nights.

"Flint and I met along the trail north of Cheyenne," she began. "I was traveling through on a wagon train and we had a party and Flint happened upon us and we danced together all night and . . ."

Hannah's throat was too raw with emotion to tell the rest of the lie.

Fortunately, the sutler's wife, Phileda Strauss, spoke it for her. "You fell head over ears in love," she said with a laugh, clapping her plump hands together. "And you decided to leave the wagon train and marry Flint. How romantic! He's a real good man, honey. And lucky to have found you. I suppose he couldn't wait a whole month and marry you when his brother says his vows to the colonel's daughter. He had to make you his bride right away."

Hannah nodded. She and Flint had also come up with an explanation why she had no belongings with her. Supposedly, her family had been so upset she wasn't going on to California with them that they hadn't allowed her to take anything with her. She'd been willing to come to her marriage with only the trail clothing on her back. It sounded pretty fanciful to Hannah, but Phileda had bought the story with stars of whimsy glowing in her faded, moss-green eyes.

"I'm so glad I had this dress for you to borrow," Phileda said. "I bought it off a settler's wife. They needed the money, and even though I knew it wouldn't fit me, it was so pretty I had to have it."

Phileda was easily as broad as the dress was tall, but Hannah could see why she'd been entranced by it. The ball gown, with its off-the-shoulder, short puffed sleeves, and V-shaped neckline, which was cut low enough to reveal soft mounds of feminine flesh, was made of ivory satin and decorated with seed pearls and delicate lace. It reminded Hannah of something her mother might have worn to an evening at the opera.

Phileda also loaned her a string of pearls to wear with the dress. "They're the real thing," the older woman assured her. "Brought back from some Pacific island by my seafaring father."

The sutler was busy dressing Flint in a borrowed string tie and suit coat, so they would look equally elegant at their wedding. The preacher at the fort had declared himself happy to perform the ceremony on short notice and was doing his best to get the officers' wives to organize a reception after the ceremony.

The wedding itself was planned for the end of the day, so the colonel and his officers could attend. For

their wedding night, Hannah and Flint had been offered the use of quarters that had recently been va-
cated by an officer who'd been posted back East. Flint
had argued that they didn't want to put anyone out,
but he'd been overruled by the ladies.

Everything was moving so fast, Hannah barely had
time to think, but she was relieved that they'd en-
countered no obstacles to the precipitous wedding.
She couldn't believe how close she'd come to telling
Flint that she was pregnant. Thank goodness her
common sense had overcome her conscience!

Flint wouldn't have asked unless it mattered to him.
And that could only mean he had reservations about
raising another man's child. That had settled the
matter for Hannah. She would say nothing about the
child she carried. And the sooner they were wed,
the better.

Unfortunately, there were more lies ahead.

She and Flint had already shared a marital bed, so
whether he chose to exercise his husbandly rights or
not, she would be able to claim she'd missed her
monthly courses within the next few days and announce she was pregnant at the end of the month.
When the babe was born, she would pray it was small
and pretend it was early.

Her secret would stay a secret forever.

The relief Hannah felt knowing that she had a father for her child had more than compensated for
what she'd expected would be the lack of a special
dress for her wedding or having family there to wit-
ness it. The generosity of the sutler's wife and the
people who lived at the fort, who were planning a

celebration to follow the ceremony, had come as a welcome surprise.

"You look beautiful, honey," Phileda said as she tightened the laces across the back of the elegant dress. Hannah had been surprised to discover that the gown didn't have buttons, but Phileda said the change was one she'd made herself, in what had turned out to be a fruitless hope that one day she could fit herself into the garment.

The result was that the dress fit Hannah as though it had been made for her. She admired herself in the mirror over the dresser in Phileda's upstairs bedroom. Her blue eyes sparkled like Lake Michigan in the sunlight. Her cheeks were rosy pink with exhilaration. Her hair was pulled away from her face and caught in a bow at her crown, then fell in soft curls across her shoulders.

She looked nothing like a widow, or a soon-to-be mother, for that matter. She looked like a princess on her way to the ball. This time, although she knew Flint would find the comparison fanciful, her very own Prince Charming was waiting for her at the end of a short walk across the parade ground. If, by Prince Charming, you meant a man who'd ridden up on his prancing charger and rescued you and carried you away to his castle.

Flint had actually done that.

But Hannah had learned a great deal from her first marriage. She no longer believed in the myth of Prince Charming. There were no perfect men. They were all flawed. Which is to say, they were all human. It took a great deal more than good looks and a prancing charger to make the kind of man with whom you could live happily ever after.

She'd seen what married life was like with Roland McMurtry. Her husband had been a plain man— except for his crinkly blue eyes—tall and stick thin. They'd spent their days as man and wife doing chores, with a lifetime of such labor ahead of them. Passion might have been in their future, but it had played no part during the journey west.

Mr. McMurtry had never raised his voice to her, but that was because he'd been too shy and self-effacing to carry on a conversation with her. She wondered now what he would have been like as a role model for their children. He'd never gotten angry with her, but she thought that was mostly because he was too tired at the end of the day to do more than eat his food and go to sleep.

That was the reality of marriage. Or so she'd thought.

Being with Flint was a different experience altogether. She compared her frank, lively conversations with Flint to the reticence of Mr. McMurtry. That alone made all the difference. But Flint also had breathtaking good looks. He was a gentle yet passionate lover. He owned a large, successful ranch and a warm, well-built home. He hadn't promised love, but then neither had she.

What more could a woman ask?

And yet, Hannah felt a niggling feeling of anxiety. She wanted to know what had caused the torment she'd seen in those remote gray eyes. She wanted to know how Flint would act if she disagreed with his opinion about what to do in a given situation. Clearly, he had no experience with compromise. And Flint was much more prickly and far less patient than Mr. McMurtry had ever been.

Hannah sighed. She supposed that was the price to be paid when a man was strong and self-assured. Which left her anxious about what Flint might say or do if he ever found out about her deceit.

She heard a soft sigh of sound from the officers' wives as she stepped inside the chapel and saw looks of approval on the faces of their husbands as she made her way down the aisle.

Flint was already waiting for her at the altar. He looked decidedly out of place.

Maybe it was the tie and coat, which took him out of his element, or the shave, which had left his face looking naked and vulnerable. On the other hand, he was doing a very good job of concealing his emotions. His eyes, like impenetrable gray stone, gave away nothing.

Hannah felt so much remorse for what she was about to do that she almost turned and ran. Almost. She had to think of the tiny being inside her, who deserved a better life than she could give it on her own, who deserved to be loved. And would be, if she had anything to say about it.

Hannah made herself take the last few steps to join Flint at the altar. When he reached out to her, she set her hand in his, feeling the warmth and the strength of it.

He turned to face the altar and said, "We're ready, Reverend Scofield."

"Dearly beloved," the preacher began.

Hannah didn't hear any more of this wedding ceremony than she had of her first. She was too busy worrying her lower lip with her teeth, feeling guilty. Just not guilty enough to stop what was happening.

Flint's voice sounded strained when he said, "I do." Her voice was no louder when she responded in kind. She was surprised when Flint put a plain gold ring on her finger. She had no ring to give him in return.

Then it was all over and Reverend Scofield was telling Flint he could kiss his blushing bride, as though it were the first time their lips would touch, when this man had already, and quite thoroughly, made love to her.

Hannah held her breath, waiting. She felt the brush of Flint's soft lips on the edge of her mouth and glanced up as he stepped back in time to catch the look of pain in his eyes. *Pain?* This was different from the *torment* she'd caught flashes of in the brief time she'd known him.

Hannah felt a spurt of panic. Flint was the one who'd suggested the sudden wedding. Was he regretting it already? What had that look meant?

"Are you all right?" she asked, searching his eyes, which were shuttered again, showing no signs of the suffering she'd seen.

"I'm fine," he said curtly. "Let's go say hello to everyone."

Hannah felt her heart sink. She didn't understand why he'd pressed her to marry, and marry so quickly, if he didn't want her for his wife. Why had he done it?

The answer was niggling in her mind, out of reach. Before she could find it, he put a hand to her elbow and ushered her toward the ladies who'd gathered in the aisle to wish them well.

Phileda had a hanky pressed to her mouth and tears brimming in her eyes. "Honey, you're the most beautiful bride I've ever seen."

"No one's as beautiful as Emaline," Flint said.

Phileda looked taken aback.

Hannah glanced at her new husband. There it was. It had been staring her in the face all the time! Flint hadn't wanted to marry her. He'd wanted to marry Emaline Simmons.

But Emaline was engaged to his brother.

Hannah stared at Flint with eyes opened wide to the truth.

His jaw was taut, his lips pressed flat, as though he regretted what he'd said. But it was too late to take it back.

No wonder he's in pain, Hannah thought. *He's married to a woman he not only doesn't love, but one he can never love.*

It was as simple—and as complicated—as that. Flint was marrying a substitute, because his brother had laid claim to Emaline Simmons.

Hannah's heart wasn't broken. After all, she wasn't in love with Flint, either. But she felt justified in keeping her secret. Especially since it seemed Flint had at least one dreadful secret of his own.

Phileda tutted and said, "Surely the bride is always the prettiest lady in the room on her wedding day."

Flint turned wary eyes in Hannah's direction and said, "You're certainly right about that, Mrs. Strauss. You look lovely, Hannah. I'm a very lucky man."

Hannah smiled at him, but the smile never reached her eyes. He was lucky, all right. Lucky she didn't reveal this sham of a marriage to his friends and neighbors. This was all playacting and, by God, she could do it as well as he could.

"Thank, you, Flint," she replied. "You look very handsome yourself."

She couldn't wait to get him alone. She would demand he tell her the truth. Had she guessed right? Was he in love with his brother's fiancée? She would forbid him the use of her body as a proxy for the woman he couldn't have.

Hannah pulled herself up short. Who was she to be making demands? Who was she to be criticizing Flint for marrying under false pretenses? What if he became suspicious in return, when she announced so quickly that she was pregnant? Especially if she got on her high horse and denied him his marital rights?

No, she'd made this hellish marriage bed. Now she was going to have to lie in it.

Chapter Twenty-two

How could he have been so stupid as to compare his bride—unfavorably—to another woman on his wedding day? Flint wondered. On the other hand, he'd never claimed to be in love with Hannah, and she'd certainly made no bones about the fact that she didn't intend to love him.

"Congratulations, Flint."

Flint turned to find himself facing the fort commander, who had his hand outstretched. Flint took it, managed a smile, and said, "Thank you, Colonel."

"What's your brother going to think about this?" Simmons asked.

"I'm sure Ransom will be happy for me, sir. After all, he's going to have a bride of his own by the end of the month."

The colonel cleared his throat and said, "About that. I've had some disturbing reports that I wondered if you can explain to me."

Flint's heart skipped a beat. He'd never indicated by word or deed that he had feelings for Emaline. How on earth could the colonel have found him out?

His stomach clenched as he had another thought. It

was that accusation from the war, that label of *coward*. He knew exactly who to blame for that rumor. But there was no excuse that would suffice for a soldier not following orders. No excuse that could explain withdrawing when he'd been commanded—by a leader who'd then retreated behind the lines—to hold an untenable position.

Luckily, he was too surprised to speak.

The colonel had his mind on something else entirely. "I've heard there's some chance the Double C won't have enough stock to supply the fort with beef if you were to get that yearlong contract."

Flint gritted his teeth to keep from uttering an oath. He had a pretty good idea who was responsible for putting that kind of doubt in the colonel's mind, but he wasn't about to make an accusation when he had no proof. Instead, he said, "We've had a few cows stray, but we're rounding them up."

The colonel tugged on his mustache and said, "Ashley Patton has been making a pretty good argument that he's a more reliable supplier. After all, he has five times the cattle you do."

"Which creates a big problem for him," Flint pointed out.

"How so?" Simmons asked.

"You may not know this, Colonel, since you're from back East, but out here, a single steer requires from twenty acres of the best land to thirty acres of the worst. Despite how many settlers he's bought out, Patton still has too many cattle grazing on too little land. He can supply beef, all right. But they're going to be scrawny critters compared to the fattened cattle you'll be getting if you buy from the Double C."

"Hmm." The colonel straightened the other side of his mustache, apparently deep in thought. "I had no idea it takes so much pasture to support a single cow. No wonder everyone out here is so land hungry."

Since Flint was as guilty as every other rancher in the Territory of claiming and controlling as much land as he could hold with a Winchester, he let that comment pass. Instead he said, "Over the past year, Patton's been able to buy out a lot of folks who underestimated this land. My brother and I have been here nine long years. We've learned what it takes to raise a calf into a prime piece of beef. The Double C deserves to be considered for that contract."

"I'm getting some pressure from Patton to be fair," the colonel explained. "It's understandable, when my daughter is marrying one of the partners in the ranch I've been favoring."

Maybe marrying one of the partners, Flint thought. Even more reason for him to encourage the colonel to look at the merits of the Double C's claim to be able to supply the very best beef to the fort.

"Send someone to check out the average weight of the cattle Patton has been shipping to eastern markets from Cheyenne," he suggested. "Compare it to our numbers last year. I think you'll have all the evidence you need that our beef is better."

The colonel smiled. "By George, I'll do it. And congratulations again, Flint. I hear the music starting. I presume you and your bride will be sharing the first dance."

"Of course." Flint realized he was going to have to dance with Hannah. He should have thought more carefully about that story they'd made up about how they'd met. It had been Hannah's idea, really, but he'd gone along. Now they were going to have to dance together for the first time and act as though it was something they'd already done for an entire evening.

He found Hannah in a circle of well-wishers, mostly women, and said, "May I have this dance, Mrs. Creed?"

She blushed prettily when he addressed her with her married name, as a new bride might be expected to do.

Except she was a widow and had already been through all this before. He was the one feeling out of sorts. He was the one who had gotten married for the first time. He was the one feeling the weight of the lifetime of responsibility he'd taken on. She held out her hand and said, "I would love to dance."

There was something strange about her voice, something low and sultry that skittered down his spine and settled in his loins. Flint's body felt hot. He stuck a finger under his collar, which suddenly felt tight. Then he reached out to take Hannah's hand and draw her onto the dance floor.

The fiddler played a slow, melodic waltz. Flint slid his arm around Hannah's waist and felt nothing beneath his palm but warm silk, and beneath that, a flesh-and-blood female. Instead of keeping her gaze averted, Hannah looked up into his eyes. She was taller than Emaline, so her face was closer, and he had the sensation of falling into those two deep blue pools.

He shouldn't have been surprised when she moved with him as though they'd been dancing together their entire lives. He saw the sheen of perspiration above her bowed upper lip and wondered if she was nervous. He could feel her breath on his face.

He admired the fine arch of her brows and the length of her dark eyelashes as they brushed her cheeks when she lowered her gaze. He smiled faintly at the spattering of freckles across her nose and said, "Well, we did it."

She raised her eyes to meet his and managed a wobbly smile. "I'm trying to look happy. Am I succeeding?"

"Let me see if I can help." He lowered his head and kissed her lightly on the lips. And felt a sizzle shoot down his spine.

The crowd around them applauded, and there were even a few hoots of laughter.

Hannah blushed rosily and ducked her head shyly.

He grinned in an attempt to hide how stunned he was by how much he wanted her. He had to swallow before he could speak. When he did, his voice was hoarse. "There. Now you look like a bride."

And he was acting like an idiotic groom.

It was obviously doing him no harm with either Hannah or the officers and their wives standing around them on the dance floor. It dawned on Flint that he'd made vows to this woman. He was pretending affection for her right now, but the wedding had been no sham. They were well and truly married.

First and foremost he felt regret. That he hadn't tried harder to wrest Emaline from his brother before Ransom had captured her heart. That he'd been so desperate to avoid the pain of losing Emaline that he'd agreed to marry the first woman who came along.

He felt sorry it was Hannah he'd found. Because if things had been different, he would have been proud to marry a woman like her. This just felt wrong.

Not that he wasn't grateful for all the things Hannah was. But she wasn't Emaline.

Flint realized he'd been woolgathering, and the music had stopped.

"Flint?" Hannah said.

He let his hands drop and took a step back and bowed to her. She curtseyed to him.

The crowd applauded, and he made himself smile at the sea of faces as he took Hannah's hand in his own and moved toward the table where refreshments had been laid out.

"I'm not thirsty," Hannah said. "Can we go outside and get some air?"

"Sure." Flint didn't know why he hadn't thought of it himself. They worked their way through the crowd to the door and out onto the front porch, which was lit by several lanterns that had attracted both moths and mosquitos. Hannah led him down the stairs and out onto the moonlit quadrangle.

When they stopped, she turned to him and said, "This was a mistake."

"Maybe so," Flint agreed. "But it's a little late to do anything about it."

Her chin was quivering, but she didn't cry. "I could leave. I could go . . ." Her voice drifted off.

"Where?" he said, knowing she had very few options. "You're safer staying with me, Hannah. Besides, you're my wife now. You belong with me."

She shook her head. "You don't want me."

He shouldn't have been surprised to hear her say it. He hadn't exactly been playing the part of the happy bridegroom. But the facts hadn't changed. "I need a wife." That was true, but so much less than the truth. "And you need a husband."

She grimaced. "What are we going to do?"

"We're going to excuse ourselves and go to bed and get a good night's sleep. Tomorrow we're going to ride back to the ranch and start the rest of our lives."

"I didn't think the wedding would feel so real," she said quietly. "It seemed profane to be making vows like that when we feel as we do toward one another."

"Yeah. I know."

"Is there any chance we'll ever be happy together?"

He snorted and shook his head. "Hell, Hannah. How can I know that? We have as much chance as any other two strangers who marry out of necessity. We can always hope for the best."

"Will you promise me something?"

Flint's stomach was knotted, and his throat felt raw. He didn't know when he'd had a more uncomfortable conversation. "What?" he asked at last.

"Promise you'll help me keep searching for my sisters."

"Hannah—"

"I feel so lonely, Flint. I've grown up in this enormous, crazy, loving family, and now I'm all alone." She looked up at him with her heart in her eyes. "I don't think I can bear a life of loneliness."

"You have me, Hannah." The words were out of

his mouth before he could stop them. Her response came just as quickly.

"Do I?"

"I'm your husband," he said. "For better or worse."

"In sickness and in health."

"As long as we both shall live," he finished.

She sighed. "I'm tired, Flint."

"Come on, Mrs. Creed. Let's go say good night and get some sleep."

Flint had the fleeting thought as they left the parade ground that sleep should be the last thing on his mind on his wedding night.

Chapter Twenty-three

"I'm not worried." Emaline said the words aloud because the truth was, she was trembling in her high-button shoes. Ransom had promised he would return before dark. The sun was long gone from the sky, and he was still out there somewhere on the prairie.

She continued the soliloquy because she found the sound of her own voice comforting in the awful silence of the empty house. "Ransom is fine. He got busy and forgot how late it was. He'll show up any minute and hug me and kiss me and apologize profusely for being tardy."

Emaline had kept herself busy throughout the day sweeping floors, dusting furniture, making beds, even doing laundry and hanging sheets out to dry on a rope she found strung between two lodgepole pines behind the house. She'd made a stew for supper out of dried beef and fresh vegetables from the garden out back. She'd felt very much like a wife. She'd also felt very much alone.

Her aunt had been a constant presence in her life, and Emaline hadn't realized how much she would miss sitting down to a cup of tea in the late afternoon, exchanging gossip and discussing the day with another woman. She found herself praying that things worked out between Flint and Hannah. Even if Flint ended up building another house for the other couple, it would likely be close enough that she and Hannah could visit often.

"Where are you, Ransom?"

Emaline was shocked at the anger she heard in her voice. She never got angry. Well, hardly ever. There was no reason to get angry when her father and her aunt catered to her every whim. If she wanted something, she asked for it, and usually, she got it. Before today, Ransom had been as accommodating as her father and her aunt. When he promised her something, he delivered.

So where was he? Something must have happened to him. Something bad.

Emaline put her hand to her mouth and realized she was about to chew on a fingernail. She knew better. Ladies didn't do such things. And she'd been raised to be a lady.

So why hadn't she married one of the gentlemen she'd met back East in Virginia, before her father had been posted to this godforsaken place? Wyoming was vast and dangerous. So many things could kill a man here. A Virginia gentlemen would never have stayed out in his tobacco fields so late that he missed supper.

"Where are you, Ransom?" This time her voice sounded plaintive. And alarmed.

Emaline stared out the kitchen window at the barn and the corral down the hill, where the wind carried the smell of manure away from the house toward the river below. She eyed the bunkhouse. It was empty. She'd already checked to be sure.

Ransom had told her that Cookie—a lot of ranch cooks were apparently called Cookie—who prepared the cowboys' meals during the roundup, would be staying out on the range with the cook wagon, since the cowhands would be doing some sort of fall roundup over the next week, counting cattle or some such thing.

Emaline stomped her foot and said, "You promised, Ransom! You said you would be here. How am I supposed to trust you if the first time you leave me alone in the house you don't come back when you said you would?"

The worst part was, Emaline had no idea where to go hunting for him. The only thing she could do was wait.

She sat down at the dining room table, which she had set for dinner with the only thing available, mismatched plates and forks and metal cups. She planned to replace those items with china and glass and a set of genuine silverware when Aunt Betsy returned from Denver.

She would have a linen tablecloth, too, she decided. Not that the pine table wasn't beautifully crafted, but the finish left something to be desired. It was a long table, built to seat eight. She'd put herself at the opposite end of the table from Ransom, as her father did when she hosted a dinner with him.

The expanse of the table loomed large. It was meant for a large family, which she and Ransom would never have. The space separating them from each other at the table reminded Emaline of the space separating them from each other in bed last night.

Ransom wanted a *real* wife. That was the exact word he'd used. *Real*.

"A wife is more than a bed partner," she said aloud. "A wife is a helpmate. A wife supports her husband. She isn't only a brood mare."

But that was obviously one of the main functions of a wife in the West, where the population was scarce. Men needed sons to help them labor on their spreads, to help them herd and brand and round up their cattle. Most of all, they needed sons to carry on after them when they were gone.

They needed daughters to help their wives do myriad tasks around the house, from gardening to canning, from soap and candle making to cooking, cleaning, sewing, and laundry.

Thanks to her aunt Betsy, Emaline was proficient at all of those tasks. Of course, she'd done more observing and supervising than actual work. She even knew how to wring a chicken's neck, although she'd done it only once.

Emaline had lit every lantern she could find downstairs, hoping to keep her fears at bay. The shadows created by the flickering lights left her feeling skittish. She paced from the kitchen to the dining room to the parlor, then back to the kitchen. She kept glancing out the kitchen window. She figured Ransom would return to the house from that direction, since he'd need to put his horse away in the barn for the night.

She was keeping a pot of coffee hot on the stove, but it had been on the fire so long she was sure it must have burned down to sludge by now. She poured herself a cup and sat down at the kitchen table. "I'm going to drink this cup of coffee and when I'm done, Ransom will walk through that door and beg pardon for being so late."

Emaline had to sip the coffee, it was so hot. It did taste like tar, though it wasn't nearly as thick. She took her time, holding the coffee cup in both hands. Nevertheless, when she drank the dregs, Ransom had still not returned.

She slammed the tin cup on the kitchen table and stood in a rush of skirts. "This is intolerable! I won't stand for it!"

There was no one to hear her outburst. No one to placate her. No one to soothe her fears.

"What am I supposed to do, Ransom? I haven't the slightest idea which way to ride to find you. I have no idea where you went today. It would be ridiculous for me to go haring off in the dark after you. You're probably sitting around a campfire somewhere with those cowhands of yours exchanging stories, having a grand old time, forgetting all about me," she finished petulantly.

Telling herself nothing was wrong did nothing to quench the growing terror clawing at her innards. She kept imagining the worst. From the little she'd seen during her stay in the Territory, the worst could be pretty bad.

"Don't be hurt," she whispered past an aching throat. "You can be late, darling. I'll understand. But please, please don't be hurt."

This land was unforgiving. If Ransom had been

thrown by his horse and knocked unconscious, some wild beast might have decided he would make a tasty dinner. If he'd been ambushed by renegades, he might have become a pincushion for their arrows. Squatters might have put a bloody hole in his chest with a shotgun blast. He might have been caught and crushed in a stampede of cattle.

"You have a wonderful imagination, Emaline," she chided herself. "But it's getting you nowhere. You need to *do* something."

But what? What could she do?

It was the feeling of helplessness, Emaline decided, that left her so discombobulated. She sat down again at the kitchen table and made herself wait. Any minute, Ransom would walk through that door. She would hug him and kiss him and promise to do anything he wanted, if only he would promise never to be late coming home for supper again.

Emaline snorted, an inelegant sound, but the only one that fit her mood. She was wondering what she could use to bribe Ransom, to ensure he was never late again. She was ready to promise him anything, even that she would make love to him and get pregnant and die in childbirth, if he would promise to get home every day on time.

The snort became a chortle. She was the most laughable creature on the planet. A fool for love.

Emaline had known in her heart she loved Ransom. But the depth of her fear for him, and the lengths to which she was willing to go to make sure he was safe, brought home to her how necessary he was to her happiness. Her unwillingness to make love to him seemed beyond ridiculous now. What if he never came back? What if she never had a chance to experience that closeness with him? How great was the risk, really? For heaven's sake, she might be barren!

Emaline made up her mind, then and there, that if Ransom came back—no, *when* he came back—she was going to lie with him, and damn the consequences.

It was a long night. Emaline changed her mind about making love to that *stupid, inconsiderate man* at least a dozen times. By the time dawn came, she'd been through every emotion, from frustration to fury to forgiveness and back again a hundred times. Her eyes were gritty from fatigue. Her heart lay heavy in her chest.

No one had come during the night.

Emaline made her weary way upstairs and changed into a split riding skirt and blouse, put on a riding hat and boots, and headed out to the barn to saddle her horse. She knew she was probably on a fool's errand, that Ransom would likely return to the ranch house while she was gone and be frantic at her absence.

"So let him worry for a change," she muttered as she tightened the cinch on the saddle.

The one thing Ransom had said he was going to do for sure was ride fence—that is, ride along the length of the barbed-wire fence that provided a boundary for the Double C—checking for posts downed by cattle rubbing against them or barbed wire cut by interlopers. She headed away from the house in the same direction she'd seen Ransom take when he'd left the previous morning.

Since she didn't know the land, Emaline stayed

close to the fence. She'd brought a rifle for protection, which she carried in a boot attached to her saddle. She'd been tempted to carry it in her arms, but she knew she'd get tired holding it, and as flat as the terrain was, she should be able to see danger coming in time to retrieve it.

At least, that was what she'd thought, until she came to a rise expecting to see more flat land ahead of her and instead faced a cliff and a deep gully that ran about fifty yards in either direction. Anyone could have been hiding there.

If she'd been galloping her horse, as she'd been tempted to do, they might have gone flying off into space when they reached that spot. Except, knowing her mount, Concho would have stopped dead, and she would have gone flying over the gelding's head all by herself.

Was that what had happened to Ransom?

Emaline couldn't believe he would make a mistake like that. Besides, after almost ten years on the range, he must know this land like the back of his hand. Which was all the more reason for concern. There was no reason she could think of, except an accident, for him not to have returned last night. She wished she knew where Ransom's cowhands were working. If she could find them, they could help her search for him.

Emaline lifted the canteen that hung off her saddle to have a drink and realized it was empty. "Emaline, you simpleton! What were you thinking? You'd better hope you find Ransom soon, or you're going to get awfully thirsty."

She'd been so tired this morning, and so focused on

getting on the trail, that she hadn't even thought to fill her canteen.

"That sort of mistake is what kills people out here," she muttered. "You'd better look sharp, missy, or you might be the one whose body people have to go hunting."

Emaline felt discouraged. The lack of water meant she was going to have to curtail her search sooner than she otherwise would have. Naturally, today the sun was hot as blazes. Wyoming was high desert, and she would dehydrate quickly.

Her stomach made a gurgling sound, reminding her that she hadn't eaten since lunch yesterday. She'd been too anxious about Ransom to eat supper last night and too anxious to get on the trail to eat breakfast this morning, although she'd fed the stock.

Of course, she'd brought nothing with her to eat, either.

Emaline huffed out a breath in disgust. Living together was supposed to prove how well suited she and Ransom were for each other. That she could be a helpmate and friend to him. That their lives together could be wonderful, even if they never had children. It wasn't supposed to be full of disappointment and dread.

Emaline's mount snorted and sidestepped, and she automatically reached out to pat his neck and say soothing words to calm him, at the same time looking ahead to see what might have upset the gelding.

She didn't have far to look. Vultures were flying overhead in the distance. She nearly gagged when she caught a whiff of what her horse must have perceived a few moments before.

Emaline was a soldier's daughter. As a child, she'd been close enough to a battleground to know that smell. It was the stench of decaying flesh.

She kicked her mount into a gallop, even though the looming vultures overhead told her what she would find when she got where she was going. She rode pell-mell, heedless of the danger, not caring if she was thrown, desperate to find out what had brought out those scavengers in the sky.

Maybe it's what's left of a calf some wolves have brought down. Maybe it's a horse that stumbled and broke a leg and had to be shot. Maybe it's some wanderer who lost his way and died of thirst. Please, please, God, let it not be the man I love.

Emaline prepared herself to see death. The vultures were there for a reason. She drew hope from the fact they were still soaring overhead, rather than feasting on some carcass below. That suggested whatever carrion they'd found might not yet be dead.

Except, it didn't explain the rotten smell.

Emaline came over a rise and yanked her horse to a halt. She dropped the knotted reins over the saddle horn and put both hands to her mouth to shut off the scream of horror that rose in her throat. She closed her eyes to shut out the awful sight, but it was already branded there forever.

Dead men lay sprawled around the black ashes of a campfire. Had she seen three? Or four? The cook wagon was turned on its side, and the mules that had drawn it were gone.

Emaline was afraid to move another step. Was Ransom down there among the dead? She raised her eyes to the vultures. Why weren't they feasting on the carcasses? What was keeping them at bay? She made herself look again at the dead men sprawled on the ground.

And saw one move.

Chapter Twenty-four

Emaline sat still as death. She stared, horrified, at the shocking carnage below her. In order to reach the body that had shown signs of life, she was going to have to walk past every putrid corpse down there. And she needed to do it *now*.

Whatever wounds the lone survivor had suffered were severe enough that he hadn't been able to drag himself out of the searing sun into the shade provided by the overturned wagon. He must be conscious and able to move, though, because otherwise the vultures would already be feasting.

"Ransom isn't down there," she told herself. "Those men are his cowhands. Ransom wouldn't be with them. He left by himself yesterday and said nothing about joining up with anyone."

So why hadn't he come home last night?

Emaline's body began to tremble. She was afraid to look too closely at the dead bodies, afraid she would recognize Ransom. But staying put wasn't going to change what she found.

She kneed her horse, but instead of moving forward the gelding sidled away. "Come on, Concho," she muttered, giving the gelding a nudge with her heels to get him moving. The horse snorted and turned to eye her over his shoulder, but at last moved down the hill toward the awful scene in the valley below.

Emaline knew her mount was feeling her own anxiety. Whatever had happened here had occurred sometime yesterday, early enough that the relentless sun in a cloudless sky had done its work, drying the blood to an ugly brown and hastening the decomposition of the bodies. The menacing vultures had used that stink of death to discover the carcasses.

Emaline ground-tied her horse about ten feet from the nearest body, knowing Concho was trained not to stray so long as the reins dragged on the ground. She put a hand over her mouth and nose, but that did little to protect her from the awful smell. The buzzing swarm of flies laying their eggs in open wounds made her skin crawl. She forced herself to stop and look at each face as she passed three dead bodies on her way to the one nearest the wagon, the one that had moved. She studied throats looking for pulses and glanced at glazed, wide-open eyes to make certain none of the victims were still alive.

She didn't recognize anyone. She presumed the dead were Flint and Ransom's cowhands because she recognized the cook wagon, which had the Double C brand burned into its wooden side.

She had an awful feeling in her gut that Ransom hadn't heeded Flint's warning to stay away from Patton. Or maybe Patton hadn't needed any excuse to do this. She'd never liked the man. He had so much, yet he was greedy for so much more. She would make sure her father brought down the might of the whole

Second Cavalry on the wealthy rancher if it turned out he was responsible for this massacre.

Emaline tiptoed past the dead men as though they were only asleep and might wake if she made too much noise. She knew their souls had fled their earthly forms, but she nearly jumped out of her skin when the wind caused a red scarf around the neck of one man to flap. She screamed and jumped sideways, causing Concho to snort and rear his head and back away.

She froze where she was and turned to her horse. If the gelding panicked and ran, she was going to be in a great deal of trouble. "Easy, boy," she said. "Everything's okay."

The horse's head was up, his ears forward, his nostrils flared, as he stared at her. She stayed where she was until the animal relaxed, shivered his hide to dislocate the flies that had gathered on his neck and shoulders, and dropped his head to crop grass again.

Her scream had an unintended result. When she turned back, she discovered that the wounded man had rolled completely over onto his back. She could see his face now.

It was Ransom.

Emaline forgot her fear and ran to his side, dropping to her knees beside him. His eyes were closed, and it was impossible to tell by looking whether he was still breathing. "Ransom?"

She expected him to make some sound, to raise his hand, to sigh or speak or do *something* to prove he was still alive. But he lay unmoving. She stared at the two small, ragged spots of dried blood on his shirt, one near his heart, the other on his collar near his throat. She glanced at the short grass around him, which was crusted with an ocean of dried blood. Was she too late? Had he already bled to death?

She delicately put two fingers to the spot where Ransom's carotid should be, near one of the wounds, and felt for a pulse. She let out the breath she'd been holding when she found it, slow and thready. He was alive!

Now what? Even if she managed to get him back to the ranch house, who was going to remove the bullets? She had a sudden thought. Maybe the bullet in his chest had gone all the way through. He groaned when she pushed him onto his side to look, and she said, "I'm sorry, sweetheart. I have to see something."

Emaline took one look at Ransom's back, then lowered him to the ground, closed her eyes, and said a prayer.

Whoever had shot Ransom must have been standing close. The bullet in his chest had gone all the way through his body. The hole in back was larger than the one in front, but neither wound was bleeding anymore. It looked like the weight of his body as he lay on his stomach had eventually stopped the bleeding in his chest.

If she had brought food and water, she could stay right here and nurse Ransom. But she hadn't even brought supplies for herself, let alone for an injured man. She stared at the cook wagon, wondering if there was anything left inside that she could use. She jumped up and went to search.

Emaline cried out in delight when she discovered that several inches of water remained in a hollow in the overturned water barrel. And she found enough food for several men for several days in the wagon, including dried beans, flour, a slab of bacon, canned peaches, canned tomatoes, dried apples, and lard. At least they wouldn't go hungry.

She also found medical supplies in the cook wagon, since Cookie was also responsible for providing first aid to injured cowhands. She looked through the box and found clean cloths for bandages, a small bottle of whiskey, a folding knife, a needle and thread, and sticking plasters. Emaline took a deep breath and let it out. She had everything she needed to treat Ransom's wounds.

She found a tin cup and dipped it into the barrel and came up with half a cup of water, which she drank. Then she filled it with another half cup of liquid and carried it to Ransom.

She knelt down and held his head up and pressed the cup against his lips. "Drink," she ordered.

Emaline didn't know what she was going to do if Ransom wasn't able to drink by himself, but he opened his lips wide enough for her to spill water into his mouth. He coughed and spit the liquid back out and groaned. She realized the water must have gone down the wrong way. She lifted his head a little higher and waited for him to stop coughing.

He turned his head away, but she put the cup to his lips again and said, "Drink some more."

"Hurts," he croaked.

"Do as you're told!" she ordered, terrified that the terrible wound at his throat was making it impossible for him to swallow. "You can't get well if you don't eat and drink. As soon as you finish this water, I'm going to sew you up. Then I'm going to make you something to eat. Then we're going to settle in here and wait for Flint and Hannah to return."

Emaline realized as she was speaking that Flint had said they might be gone several days. It could be as much as a week if Flint and Hannah's journey took longer than they'd expected, before they were found. She glanced toward the water barrel, wondering if it held enough water for two people for a week. Then she glanced at Ransom and wondered whether he would still be alive in a week.

She swallowed back her fear and said, "When Flint doesn't find us at the house, he'll come looking for us. Maybe by the time he finds us, I'll have you well enough to ride out of here."

She continued talking because it kept her worry at bay. She eased Ransom back down flat, then hesitated, unsure what to do next. She made a list in her head.

First, treat Ransom's wounds.

Second, make a shelter near the wagon to get him out of the sun and drag him under it.

Third, move the dead bodies away from the wagon, stack them together, and cover them with the tarpaulin from the wagon so they won't attract vultures or scavengers, and so they can be buried later.

Fourth, make a meal for Ransom and feed him and herself.

Fifth, unsaddle her horse and stake him out close to the wagon, where he can eat grass, but where she can shoot any predators that threaten them during the night.

Sixth, wait for help to come.

Making a mental list was something Emaline had

learned from her military father. It helped her to organize her thoughts, and she was able to function in an emergency like this by doing each item in order as it came up.

Unfortunately, she also made a list of all the things that could possibly go wrong. Emaline was on the seventh item when she realized she was procrastinating, afraid to get started on the first item on her list of things to do.

She needed to treat Ransom's wounds and make sure he survived until help could come. She trotted back to the wagon and collected the medicine box and carried it to where Ransom lay. She wet one of the cloths and used it to wipe the dirt from his dear face, which was shadowed with dark beard, to postpone what came next.

She leaned down and softly kissed his lips and heard him make a humming sound. Any sound at all was welcome, since at any moment she expected him to give up the ghost.

Emaline opened the folding knife and used it to cut Ransom's shirt off his body, first the stitches in the chambray sleeves, then the buttons, then the fabric, before carefully separating the cloth from his skin. She used water to soak the cloth where it had attached itself with dried blood to his chest wound, blocking out his moan of pain as she pried it away.

She knew enough to disinfect the wound with whiskey. She knew she was hurting him because, although he made no further sound, Ransom writhed beneath her ministrations. She planned to sew the gaping hole back together, but her hands were shaking too much to thread the needle. She set down both needle and thread and took a swig of the whiskey, which made her eyes water.

She snickered, because now her hands were no longer shaking, but she could no longer see because of the tears in her eyes. She scrubbed them with the backs of her hands, huffed out a breath, then picked up the needle and threaded it.

Emaline had never set stitches in human flesh, but she'd done more than her share of samplers. She decided to do a cross-stitch to pull the flaps of skin together and close the bullet hole. She started on what seemed to be the more threatening wound, the one near his heart.

The bullet had obviously missed his heart because he was still alive. She deduced that it had also missed his lung, because although his breathing was shallow, it wasn't labored. Blood seemed to be clotted in the chest wound, and she didn't want to do anything to start it bleeding again.

"I'm going to stitch you up," she explained. "I know this will hurt, sweetheart, but it has to be done."

Emaline realized she was using words of endearment that she'd never before spoken to Ransom. Why had she waited so long? She saw Ransom's mouth moving, but no sound was coming out.

"I'm sorry, darling," she said, her voice tender with love. "I can't understand you. I'm going to start now."

Emaline plucked up her courage and stuck the needle into Ransom's flesh. He made a grunting sound, but he didn't move, which seemed like a bad sign. He must be very weak.

She worked as fast as she could, knowing she was causing pain with every stitch. She tied off the thread when she finished sewing up his chest wound and surveyed her work. The hole was closed, and the only new blood showed in the needle pricks where she'd made her stitches. She brushed a strand of hair that had fallen out of her bun away from her face with the back of her hand and examined the wound on his neck.

His skin was mottled brown with blood, but when she looked more closely, she realized the bullet had merely grazed him, taking out a small chunk of flesh. Other than cleaning the bullet's furrow with whiskey and putting a sticking plaster on the wound, she left it alone.

She still had to stitch the large, through-and-through wound on his back.

"I don't want to put you on your stomach," she told Ransom, "so I'm going to lean you on your side and use Cookie's pillow to hold you up." She suited word to deed, dismayed by how little help she was getting from Ransom, whose body was almost a dead-weight.

"This is the last thing I have to do," she said. "Then you can rest."

He made a sound, not quite a groan, almost a moan.

She soaked the shirt off his back and doused the larger gunshot wound with whiskey. Her hands were steady this time when she threaded the needle, and she made short work of sewing up the wound. When she was done, she dropped her hands to her lap and felt her shoulders sag as the trembling began again.

Tears of relief welled in her eyes, threatening to become a waterfall, and she blinked them back.

She didn't have the luxury of feeling sorry for Ransom or herself. She had work to do. The sun would soon be down, and she'd only done the first item on her list. It would be a race to get everything finished before dark.

She rolled Ransom onto his back on Cookie's blanket, then pulled it across the slippery grass until she reached the rectangle of shade created by the bottom of the wagon and the wheels. She'd already pulled Cookie's sleeping pallet out of the wagon and rolled it out on the ground. She pulled Ransom onto it, arranging him as carefully as she could.

She was horrified when she turned to see a vulture perched on the farthest body, pecking out an eye. She lurched toward it, screaming like a banshee and waving her hands frantically to scare it away.

The bird took flight. But so did her horse.

"Concho! Stop! Come back!"

Emaline watched in horror as the gelding wheeled and galloped away in fright. By the time Concho calmed down he would be long gone. She wondered whether the gelding would be able to find his way back to the barn at the Double C. A saddled horse with no rider would be an immediate clue to Flint that something was desperately wrong.

She realized almost as soon as she felt that flash of hope that it was unlikely Concho would go back to the Double C, since he'd only been stabled there for a day. Would the gelding return to the fort, where he was usually stabled? Her father would have the whole

Second Cavalry out looking for her if that happened. It was possible. But not probable.

Most likely, Concho would simply wander. If that happened, what were the chances her saddled horse would be found by some rancher? Even if he was, how would that person know the horse belonged to her? They'd certainly have no idea where to come looking for her.

"You stupid, stupid girl," Emaline muttered. "You should have staked Concho first. You saw he was skittish around all those dead bodies, and what did you do? You scared the dickens out of him and sent him racing across the prairie."

Her situation had been dire before. Now it wasn't only Ransom's life at risk. Flint didn't expect to be gone for more than a week, but as she very well knew, accidents could happen. He could easily be gone for longer. If help didn't come before the scant water in the barrel ran out, she would die, too.

Chapter Twenty-five

Flint was feeling grumpy. Who'd have thought, when Hannah said she was tired, that she'd meant it. As soon as she got into bed, she turned her back on him and went to sleep. He lay there wide awake, frustrated and feeling sorry for himself.

In the morning, she'd woken up looking delightfully tousled, delectable, in fact, but she got out of bed almost the instant she woke up. She dressed herself and then chided him for being a slugabed. A *slugabed*!

He hadn't slept a wink. He'd spent the night feeling deprived and depraved, because he'd had visions of undressing and seducing the woman who slept soundly beside him.

Some honeymoon he was having. He couldn't get back to the Double C fast enough.

He wasn't in the mood to talk, and they were halfway home before Hannah said anything other than, "I hope we're home in time to have supper with Emaline."

He had no intention of sitting down to supper. He was going to ride out and find his brother and then spend every minute he could on the range until Ransom and Emaline tied the knot.

The second half of the ride was as silent as the first, which gave Flint too much time to think.

No one had held a gun to his head to make him marry Hannah. He'd done it of his own free will. She was his wife, like it or not. He didn't think it was necessary for them to love each other, but his life with Hannah was going to be a lot easier if he made an effort to get along with her. So maybe he shouldn't go running off the instant they got home.

"What are you thinking?" she asked.

He glanced at her in surprise and blurted, "That I'm going to have to learn how to be a good husband."

She smiled at him, revealing those two entrancing dimples, and he felt his heart skip a beat.

"I think I have far more to learn than you do," she said. "At least you know how to survive out here."

"It's my job to keep you safe."

"You won't always be around," she said. "I think I'd like to have those shooting lessons sooner, rather than later."

"That can be arranged." Flint was so busy watching the play of the sun on Hannah's golden hair, which hung down her back in that solitary braid, and listening to the litany of things she wanted to learn, that they were home before he knew it.

He was torn between staying and going, and compromised somewhere in-between. "I'll help you put away the supplies and have something to eat before I head out to find Ransom." Which was a good idea, since he'd skipped breakfast.

"How do you know Ransom isn't at the house with Emaline?" Hannah asked.

The thought of Ransom and Emaline together in the house didn't give Flint the same sick feeling in the pit of his stomach that it usually did. He wondered why not. He still considered Emaline a lost love. The difference was, she was truly *lost*. What had once been a possibility could never happen now except in his dreams.

"It's awfully quiet," Hannah said, looking around as they rode up to the back of the house.

"Cookie and the boys are working the fall roundup. Ransom's likely with them."

"I can already see the advantages of having another woman in the house," she said. "It must get awfully lonely for women in the Territory when their men are gone all day."

"I suppose it does." Flint had never thought much about loneliness because he'd always had Ransom to talk to during the long winter nights. And although they often went their separate ways in the morning, he knew he'd see his brother at the end of the day for supper.

Flint sensed something was wrong the instant they entered the kitchen. He set a hand on the stove and said, "There's been no fire here today."

Hannah walked down the hallway leading to the staircase calling, "Emaline? Are you up there?"

When she turned back, Flint was right behind her.

"Wait here," he said tersely.

"What's wrong?"

"Do as I say!" He ran up the stairs, taking them two at a time. The bed in Ransom's room was made up. Either it hadn't been slept in, or Emaline had gotten up early to make it. He checked the pitcher of water that usually sat on the sideboard. It was empty. And bone dry.

He checked his bedroom, just in case, but it was as he and Hannah had left it. He ran back downstairs, told Hannah, "Don't move!" and quickly searched the downstairs rooms. They were all neat and untouched and vacant.

Flint didn't know why he had such a feeling of foreboding. It was entirely possible Ransom had decided to take Emaline with him this morning, that she'd felt abandoned and had wanted company for the day. But there was no residual smell of bacon or coffee. Could Ransom possibly have taken her out to the roundup last night?

Flint didn't think his brother would subject Emaline to the hardships of a camp on the prairie. But maybe Emaline had talked him into letting her spend a night at the roundup. Anything was possible.

"Where do you think Emaline is?" Hannah asked.

"I don't know. I better ride out and see if I can find the two of them."

"I want to come along," Hannah said.

"It might be dangerous."

"What is it you think is wrong?"

"That's the problem. I don't know that anything *is* wrong. It's a feeling I have. And I've learned to listen to my gut."

"I know what you mean," Hannah said. "When I walked in, I thought the same thing, but everything's in perfect order. Wouldn't things be awry if there was a problem?"

"Not necessarily," Flint said.

"Which means Ransom and Emaline might be in trouble wherever they are," Hannah concluded. "I want to come and help."

Flint debated whether Hannah would be safer if she stayed at home or came with him. She was defenseless here alone. At least if she was with him, he could protect her. On the other hand, she might not need protection if she stayed at the house.

She met his gaze and said, "Please. I don't want to stay here alone."

That settled it. "All right. Let's grab something to eat, make sure we have water and food for the trail, and then go."

"Do you really want to stop and eat?" Hannah asked. "If something's wrong—"

"If things go haywire out there it could be a long time before we have another chance to eat. Better to stoke up now."

Flint wasn't any hungrier now than he had been yesterday before the wedding or at the reception afterward or at breakfast this morning. But his growling stomach was telling him he needed sustenance. He'd learned during the war to eat when he had the chance, because the next chance might not come for a good long while.

He forced himself to sit down and swallow the leftover stew that he and Hannah found sitting in a pot on the cold stove. It looked like it had been there overnight.

"I wonder why Emaline cooked this if they weren't going to eat it," Hannah mused.

"Maybe something happened to draw them both

away from the house." Flint was remembering how he'd warned Ransom to stay away from Ashley Patton. And how Ransom's neck hairs had hackled at the idea of obeying orders from his older brother.

"I hope to hell he didn't do something foolish," Flint muttered.

"What?" Hannah said.

"Nothing." He rose abruptly from his chair, leaving his stew half-eaten. "Let's get out of here. I've got a bad feeling Ransom's in trouble."

"And Emaline?" Hannah said.

Flint's stomach knotted. If Ransom was in trouble, Emaline was, too.

He grabbed Hannah's arm and pulled her along behind him. "Come on," he said. "The sooner we get on the trail, the sooner we can find out what's happened to the two of them."

Flint had enough common sense left to know that he might have created a mountain out of a molehill. It was entirely possible he would find Emaline and Ransom enjoying supper at Cookie's campfire. He was going to feel pretty ridiculous if he did.

On the other hand, Ransom was a young man with something to prove, and Sam Tucker was a fast gun who enjoyed showing off. Flint didn't want to think what might have happened if the two of them had met up on the prairie. That was a gunfight waiting to happen.

He was impatient to be gone, but he made sure that he and Hannah both had full canteens, enough food for three days, and bedrolls tied behind their saddles. He didn't want them to end up in a situation where they needed rescuing themselves.

"Which way should we go?" Hannah asked.

Flint knew the decision he made now could be important, especially if Ransom and Emaline were in trouble. "I sent Cookie and the hands to round up cattle on the northeast corner of the ranch. If Ransom and Emaline are with the hands, they're fine."

Hannah frowned. "Then why are we in such a big hurry?"

Flint sighed. "I'm concerned that Ransom might have decided to ride fence along the border I share with Ashley Patton and ran into Patton's hired gun. I think we should go there."

Hannah was worrying her lower lip with her teeth. Her eyes looked frightened. "You're scaring me."

"Maybe you should stay home."

She shook her head. "I'd be more afraid to stay at the house by myself. I presume you don't intend to get into any gunfights."

Flint snorted. It wasn't a question, so there was no need for a response, but he could tell from the look on Hannah's face that she thought he wouldn't fare well if he did. He didn't wear a Colt .45 because he'd had enough of killing men during the war. Hannah didn't know that. Neither did Ashley Patton or Sam Tucker.

But woe betide the man who made the mistake of thinking he wouldn't defend himself . . . and those he loved.

Chapter Twenty-six

"What're you doin' here, Creed?"

"Looking for my brother. Have you seen him?"

Hannah stared at the Colt .45 in Sam Tucker's hand. Ashley Patton's gunman sat on horseback on the other side of a wrought-iron gate. Tucker hadn't waited for Flint to make an overt threat. He'd simply pulled the Peacemaker from his holster the instant he saw the two of them and held it on them the entire time as they approached.

Hannah had never had a gun aimed at her, and she was finding it hard to catch her breath. Her heart kept trying to pound its way out of her chest. There was so little distance between them now, Tucker couldn't miss. She would have been happy to turn around and come back another time, but Flint kept riding, so she kicked her mount and remained by his side.

Flint didn't seem the least bit intimidated by the gunman. Hannah wondered why not. There wasn't another soul around.

Patton's sprawling ranch house sat on a majestic

rise a quarter of a mile away. She wondered if the sound of a gunshot down here would carry all the way up there. It seemed to Hannah that Tucker could shoot them both dead and bury them, and no one would be the wiser.

She eyed Flint askance and whispered, "I'm scared, Flint. Why aren't you?"

"Tucker is a bully and a backshooter. He doesn't have the guts to pull the trigger when I'm staring him in the eye."

Hannah wasn't reassured. She figured there was always a first time for everything. Her heart fluttered like a frightened bird as they closed the distance to the man with the gun.

When they reached the fancy gate, which had an arch at the top with the OOX brand in the center and was flanked on both sides by a whitewashed split rail fence, Tucker said, "You can turn around now and go home."

"I asked you a question," Flint said. "Have you seen Ransom?"

"That's for me to know, and you to find out," the gunman said.

"Is Patton at home?" Flint asked.

"What's it to you?"

"Go get your boss."

"What if he don't wanta talk to you?"

Flint leaned over in the saddle to release the latch that held the iron gate closed, and a deafening gunshot reverberated in Hannah's ear.

She pulled the reins taut to keep her horse from bolting but then sat frozen in fear. Her overworked heart had jumped to her throat, preventing speech. It took her a second to realize she hadn't been shot. She slanted her gaze toward Flint, expecting at any moment to see him topple from the saddle. Instead, she saw his hand gripping the stock of his Winchester.

He had the rifle halfway out of the boot when Tucker said, "That was me, callin' my boss. Put it back, or I'll blow your head off."

Hannah gasped, found her voice, and said, "That would be murder!"

"No, missy," Tucker said with a crooked, toothy grin. "That would be self-defense."

"Let's go, Flint," Hannah begged. Tucker was clearly hoping to provoke Flint so he would have an excuse to shoot him. Actually, it didn't look like he needed much of an excuse.

Flint eased his hand off his Winchester, sat back in the saddle, and stared daggers at Patton's hired man. "I always figured you were crazy, Tucker."

The gunslinger kept the .45 aimed at Flint and smirked. "Trespassin' is a shootin' offense."

In the distance, Hannah saw a rider loping his horse down the hill. She pointed and said, "Flint, look! Is that him?"

"Yeah," Flint said through tight jaws. "That's Patton."

Tucker's lip curled. "The boss can tell you hisself he ain't seen nothin', ain't done nothin', and don't know nothin'."

It seemed strange to Hannah that Tucker had his boss denying knowledge of doing Ransom harm when Patton hadn't been accused of anything yet.

Hannah watched a muscle work in Flint's cheek, but he remained silent, apparently waiting for Patton to arrive.

When the rancher pulled his horse to a stop beside his hired man, Flint said sarcastically, "Appreciate your range hospitality, Patton. I don't usually get greeted with a bullet."

Patton seemed unperturbed as he replied, "It's a long way up to the house. I asked Tucker to fire a shot to let me know if I had company. Sorry if the noise bothered you."

Hannah found herself being examined like a prime piece of horseflesh Patton was considering buying, before he said, "Who's this?"

"Mrs. Hannah McMurtry," Flint said curtly.

"Why haven't I met you before, Mrs. McMurtry?" Patton said.

Hannah glanced at Flint, wondering if he realized the mistake he'd made. She watched him flush, turn to her with a look of regret, resettle himself in the saddle, and say, "I mean, Mrs. Hannah Creed."

Patton smiled, an expression that never reached his eyes, touched the brim of his hat with a forefinger, and said, "I see congratulations are in order. Welcome to the Territory, Mrs. Creed. This is rather sudden, isn't it? I hadn't heard we had such a lovely lady in the neighborhood. Where did you and Flint meet?"

Hannah opened her mouth to answer, but Creed interjected, "Where's my brother? What have you done to him?"

"I have no idea where Ransom is," Patton replied with a bluntness equal to Flint's.

"You threatened him."

"I threatened to take Emaline from him, if I could," Patton replied easily.

"So where is she?" Flint snarled.

For the first time, Patton looked surprised. "At home with her father, I expect."

"You know damned well she was traveling with Ransom."

"No, I didn't know that," Patton said. "Where were they headed?"

Hannah saw the trap Flint had set for himself. If he said Ransom had gone to Denver with Emaline, why was Flint looking for him on the range? "When I left the house, Ransom and Emaline were there. Now they're both gone. I have to wonder why you're keeping me away from your place. Do you have Emaline up there?"

"I do not."

"How do I know you're telling the truth?"

"Are you accusing me of lying?"

Hannah heard the menace in Patton's voice and wondered if Flint was going to provoke him into a gunfight, especially when Tucker had never holstered his weapon.

Flint glanced at her, seemed to reconsider, and said, "I suppose it's possible they've gone to the fall roundup."

"You haven't looked there yet?" Patton said.

"No," Flint admitted.

Patton eyed the setting sun and said, "Guess you'll have to wait till tomorrow morning to find out, unless you want your new bride spending the night under the stars."

Flint eyed the sun, which had dropped almost to the horizon, and said, "Let's go, Hannah."

Hannah kneed her horse to stay beside him as he rode away, but she couldn't help glancing over her shoulder to see what Tucker was doing.

He still had his gun out, pointed at Flint's back.

Hannah couldn't quite breathe right, knowing a gun was aimed at her back, but Flint appeared to be right. Tucker was mostly bark and no bite. At least, to a man's face.

"Where to now?" Hannah asked.

"Home."

"Not to the roundup?"

"It's a four-hour ride from here in the dark."

"Why are you so sure Patton's involved?"

"Patton threatened Ransom to my face at my brother's engagement party. He meant what he said. He wants Ransom out of the way so he can have Emaline. Not to mention the fact that Ransom and I are all that stands between him and owning most of the land along this stretch of the Laramie River."

"He can't get away with killing people willy-nilly, can he?" Hannah asked skeptically.

"He can do whatever he wants. There's no law out here on the prairie, Hannah."

"What about the army?"

"The army's here to keep the Indians under control. They don't have authority in civil matters."

"So who keeps the peace?"

Flint patted the stock of his rifle. "There's a sheriff in Cheyenne, but out here, it's every man for himself."

Hannah stared at Flint wide-eyed. She'd known the West was unsettled. She'd seen how the wagon master's word was law on the trail. She'd observed for herself that only the strong survived. But she'd never imagined an influential rancher like Ashley Patton would take such terrible advantage of those weaker than himself. "Why don't the smaller ranchers band together to help each other?"

"That's exactly what we did when we created the Laramie County Stock Association," Flint said. "The problem is, Patton has been able to convince folks he's one of the good guys. He's planning to join the Association."

"Can't you keep him out?"

"Not unless we can catch him in the act. And that's hard to do with the distance between spreads here in the Territory."

"How can one man intimidate so many others?"

"It's one thing to face a man in a fair fight, but Patton's mad dog has no conscience. If Tucker's threats don't work, he rustles a man's cattle or burns him out or buries him."

"Has Patton attacked the Double C?" Hannah asked.

"Over the past month, a hefty percentage of our herd has gone missing. Ransom and I are sure it's Patton and his man Tucker, but we have no proof. I warned Ransom to leave Patton alone until I got back. I hope to hell he didn't decide to confront that son of a bitch."

Hannah heard the bitterness in Flint's voice. And the anger. "What are you going to do?"

"You and I are going home and get a good night's

sleep. It's possible Ransom and Emaline returned to the house while we were gone. If so, all's well that ends well. If not, we leave early tomorrow morning for the roundup."

"And if Ransom and Emaline aren't there?"

"I'll be making another visit to Ashley Patton."

Chapter Twenty-seven

Emaline debated whether to build a fire. On the one hand, it would keep four-legged predators at a distance. On the other, it might attract predators of the two-legged variety. In the end, she had no choice. After the sun went down, the windswept prairie was surprisingly cold. Besides, she wanted to make soup for Ransom, and she needed coffee to stay awake.

Not that there was much she could do for him, now that his wounds had been sewed up. He was unconscious, restless, and feverish. She used a wet cloth to soothe his forehead and cheeks and chest, and she talked to him, because that seemed to calm him.

"I don't expect help to come right away," she told him. "We might be here a day or so on our own. Eventually, Flint will check in with the roundup, and he'll find us. We have to hang on until then."

It had dawned on Emaline that Ransom's injuries were going to be difficult to explain to her father. The two of them were supposed to be shopping in Denver. Papa was going to know that she'd deceived him. He was going to know that she and Ransom had snuck away on their own. He was going to be angry with Aunt Betsy for letting it happen, which wasn't fair to her aunt.

Emaline would gladly accept whatever punishment her father meted out, if she and Ransom survived. Not that the punishment would be severe. Her father was as lenient with her as he was rigid in disciplining his troops.

That was probably why she'd felt free to forgo her aunt's supervision. She was used to doing what she wanted without paying the consequences. Only, this time, she'd been caught, and the price for her disobedience might be Ransom's life.

Emaline was aware of the terrible danger they were in. Other than a shovel, a folding knife, and the fire, she was utterly defenseless. She didn't think the Indians would come back, but there were other drifters on the plains, both of the two-legged and four-legged variety.

She'd never imagined her life being cut short by anything except pregnancy. While she knew there were dangers for a man on the range, she'd never imagined anything bad happening to Ransom. She'd thought the two of them would have the rest of their lives to love each other, especially if she didn't get pregnant.

She'd also been certain that making love was not necessary to living happily ever after, certain that she was right and Ransom was wrong. Oh, how the mighty had fallen. She wasn't sorry for sneaking away with Ransom, but she would forever regret not making love to him.

Emaline sighed. How foolish she'd been. If he lived . . . She sobbed and forced the sound back down. Self-pity was an emotion she couldn't afford. She had to stay strong. She had to take care of Ransom.

Was he unconscious? Or was he merely sleeping? She rested her hand against his cheek, which was fiery hot, and leaned close to listen. His breathing was slow and even. He'd only taken a couple of swallows of the soup she'd made for him, but she'd been glad to get even those few drops of liquid down his throat.

His wounds were grievous, and he'd lost a lot of blood. Maybe too much. She'd already done everything she knew to nurse him. Besides, she'd seen enough wounded men in military hospitals to know that the fever was far more likely to kill him than the wound itself.

She wet the cloth again and used it to cool Ransom's fevered brow, but it felt like she was fighting a losing battle.

"You're not going to die, sweetheart," she said, as though speaking the words could make them true. "You're going to live. Of course, the wedding will have to be postponed until you've recovered your strength, but that shouldn't be a problem."

Or maybe, when he found out what she'd done, her father would insist—at the point of a gun—that Ransom wed her, healthy or not.

Emaline shivered and pulled Cookie's blanket tighter around her shoulders. The warmth of the day had fled. It was getting colder. Please, God, no more freakishly frigid weather. All she needed was for it to snow.

Ransom's hand moved restlessly, and she took it in

her own and continued, "I want to make love to you, darling. I'd give anything now for a chance to grow a precious life inside me and deliver a son or daughter into your hands. If I die in childbirth . . ."

Emaline shivered. She knew she would die. There was no "if" about it. Her mother had endured long enough to deliver her and then bled and bled until she was as white as parchment and as cold as ice. There was no reason to believe she would be any more capable of living herself, although she could hope to give Ransom the gift of a living child to love after she was gone.

Because she loved him, she would have his child. If only God gave her the chance.

Emaline knew if she didn't think happier thoughts, she would go crazy with fear. Shadows loomed large beyond the campfire. She thought she saw glowing eyes in the darkness. Wolves? She was sitting here as though she'd spent a great many nights out-of-doors, when the truth was, this was the very first. Even when she'd followed her father to the battlefield during the War Between the States, he'd made sure she at least had a tent over her head.

She brushed a stray curl off Ransom's forehead and said, "Do you remember the first time you kissed me?"

Emaline smiled as she leaned over and tenderly kissed Ransom's cheek. "Shall I tell you what I was thinking? What I was feeling?"

To Emaline's surprise, Ransom made a grunting sound. Could he be aware of what she was saying? Had he heard what she'd said about bearing his child? Had it given him a reason to fight harder to live?

She'd been acquainted with Ransom for exactly one hour before he'd requested permission from her father to court her. She'd been giddy with excitement, even though there were plenty of other beaux who'd taken her for a ride in her buggy, who'd shared dinner with her family, and who'd strutted before her like preening cocks, before Ransom had come into the picture.

The hardest part of their courtship was how little time Ransom had to pursue it. He was busy on the range, and the only day he was willing to take off was Sunday. She had church with her father in the morning, which left only Sunday afternoons for them to get to know each other, under the watchful eye of Aunt Betsy. Emaline had lived for those Sunday afternoons.

"I wondered for three long months what it would be like to kiss you," Emaline said, smiling as she recalled all the times when she'd thought Ransom might kiss her but hadn't.

Emaline remembered that momentous spring day in every detail. They'd taken along a picnic of ham sandwiches and deviled eggs and pickles, with iced tea to drink. The two of them had left her aunt taking a nap on a blanket in the shade of a cottonwood and walked away hand in hand along the river.

They had passed a bend that took them out of her aunt's sight when Ransom stopped and took both her hands in his, gripping them almost too tightly.

"I thought you might break my fingers," Emaline recalled. "Then you laughed at yourself and raised my hands to your lips and kissed them, one at a time."

Emaline smiled. "You were so gentle. And I was so disappointed! I thought you'd chickened out again." She shivered as she remembered what came next. "Then you lifted my hands to rest on your shoulders, and you set your hands at my waist. If I'd taken a deep breath, our bodies would have touched."

Ransom made another sound, a moan, and Emaline leaned down to brush her lips against his, then kept her face close as she said, "Your lips were so soft when they touched mine. I could feel you trembling. I was trembling, too. Then you slid an arm around my waist and pulled me close so I could feel you everywhere."

She hadn't expected his tongue to touch her lips. She'd been so surprised, she'd opened her mouth to protest. Before she could, his tongue had touched hers and withdrawn, surprising her with how good it felt. She'd gasped, and as she did, his mouth had captured hers again, his tongue making another foray that she'd welcomed and then returned.

He'd broken the kiss to look into her eyes, speaking without words.

Emaline had seen his desire, and for the very first time in her life, she'd felt it in return.

She'd been surprisingly innocent when they'd shared that first kiss. Over the following months, Ransom had introduced her to other kisses on her neck and ears and fingertips. He'd introduced her to other touches on her breasts and belly and made her want to touch him in return.

She'd pleaded her innocence as an excuse for not doing more, an excuse for not giving him the ultimate pleasure, and he'd accepted her reasons for not wanting to go further. She'd kept mute about her unwillingness to make love even after they were married. That had been far too intimate a conversation to have with a man to whom she was not yet engaged.

Their occasional escapes from Aunt Betsy's eagle eye hadn't allowed for undressing, but Ransom had touched her and kissed her and given her pleasure she'd never imagined in her wildest dreams.

"Emaline?"

"You're awake!" Emaline could see the shine of Ransom's eyes in the moonlight. "How are you feeling?"

"Rotten." He cleared his throat and continued, "But I suppose this is better than being dead. How did you get here?"

"I came looking for you when you didn't come home. And saw the vultures."

He made an anguished sound in his throat. "Is anyone else alive?"

"No. Only you. Who would do something like this, Ransom?"

"A dozen or so renegade Indians. Every damned one of them had a brand-new rifle."

"How do you know they were new?"

"We shot a couple of them and got a good look at their weapons."

"There were no Indians, or rifles either, by the time I got here. Do you think someone at the fort is selling rifles to the Indians?"

"I didn't think of that," he said. "I thought they were given the rifles in exchange for attacking us."

"That would be stupid," Emaline said. "Whoever gave a bunch of savages brand-new rifles would never be able to control where they used them after they attacked you."

"Whoever gave them those guns is probably counting on more attacks—on ranchers who can't defend themselves against Indians with rifles," Ransom said. "The fewer settlers left out here, the more land men like Ashley Patton will be able to gobble up."

"You think Mr. Patton gave guns to the Indians?" Emaline said, aghast. "My father will have something to say about—"

"I can't prove it," Ransom interrupted.

"We have to warn folks," Emaline said anxiously. "We have to get word to my father."

"Fine. Let's go. Why are we still here, by the way? I would have thought you'd rig up some way to get me home."

Emaline dropped her chin to her chest in shame. "I didn't tie my horse, and he bolted. I don't have any way to get you out of here."

He tried to sit up, groaned, and lay back down. "I'm sorry."

"For what?"

"I can't get up."

"Don't be foolish!" she snapped. "You're lucky to be alive. Lie down and be still, so you don't rip out those stitches. I had enough trouble getting them in the first time. I don't want to have to do it again."

She saw a shadow of his charming smile, the one that had won her heart the first time she'd seen it, before he said, "When did you get so bossy?"

She heard a sound in the distance that kept her from

answering. Hoofbeats. Lots of them. That meant more than one man on horseback. She met Ransom's anxious gaze and knew he'd heard the same thing. In the next few moments, their fate would be decided.

Were they going to be rescued? Or were they going to die?

Chapter Twenty-eight

Flint lay beside Hannah in his bed and stared at the ceiling. This was his first night in his home with his wife. He ought to be holding her in his arms. He should have made love to her. She'd pleaded fatigue again, turned over, and promptly fell asleep.

Flint slipped out of bed, careful not to wake Hannah. There was plenty of moonlight from the bare window to see without a lantern. He crossed around the bed and pulled the covers up over her shoulders. After he did it, he realized it was a strange thing to have done, when he hardly knew the woman.

Except the night had turned cold, and they hadn't lit a fire in the fireplace before they'd gone to bed. It wasn't that he cared for her, it was simply that he'd spent a lot of time and effort nursing her back to health, and he didn't want her to get sick.

He grabbed his jeans, shirt, socks, and boots and left the room. It was dark in the hallway, but he knew where he was going. He found the rail along the wooden stairs and avoided the creaks as he headed down to the kitchen. He lit a lantern to provide more light than the moon gave him and got dressed.

He wanted a cup of coffee and felt the half-full pot on the stove, which was still a little warm. He opened a lid on the stove, added wood and coal to the remaining embers, and waited for the coffee to heat up.

Flint chewed his lower lip. What the hell had happened to Ransom and Emaline? He couldn't imagine any scenario where Ransom would have agreed to take a woman as delicate as Emaline Simmons out to spend the night on the prairie. Which meant one or both of them was in trouble.

The only question was how much?

There was always the possibility they'd had an argument, and Ransom had returned Emaline to her father before joining the roundup. But when Flint had checked, Emaline's clothes and personal effects were still in Ransom's room. Again, if the argument had been serious enough, she might have taken off without her things, expecting to retrieve them later.

He didn't think it was a case of foul play here at the ranch, because the house was neat and clean, feed had been left out for the chickens and pigs, and the cow had been milked.

Flint felt like a man trying to scratch his ear with his elbow. Helpless. Frustrated. Wanting to give up, but so irritated by the itch that he had to do something.

He poured himself a cup of steaming coffee and sat down at the kitchen table, knowing that if he drank it, he wouldn't be able to sleep. Hell, he wasn't going to sleep anyway. Not until he knew what had happened to his brother.

And Emaline. Beautiful Emaline. Perfect Emaline.

He told himself he had no business worrying about the colonel's daughter. He had a wife of his own. Emaline was Ransom's problem.

Which still left Ransom for him to worry about.

Flint left the cup of hot coffee sitting on the table and retrieved his flat-brimmed hat and shearling coat from the antler rack beside the kitchen door. He stopped himself right there, turned and dropped his coat and hat on the table, grabbed the lantern, and headed to the room off the parlor that he and Ransom used as an office.

There was no sense leaving Hannah ignorant of where he was going. There had been enough confusion and misunderstanding already. He wrote:

Gone to check at the roundup for Ransom and Emaline. Wait here. Back for supper.

Flint

Hopefully she'd do as he asked and stay home until he got back.

Flint set the note on the kitchen table where Hannah would be sure to see it, then took a big gulp of coffee that burned his tongue. He put on his coat and hat and blew out the lantern. He had his hand on the back door when he heard a female gasp.

Flint turned and made out Hannah's face in the moonlight. "It's me," he said.

Her eyes were large and luminous. Her hair was tousled, curls falling down around her shoulders. She looked like a woman who'd just gotten out of bed after making love to her man.

That last part, of course, was his imagination at work. They hadn't so much as hugged since their wedding.

She was dressed in an open-throated nightgown she'd borrowed from Emaline, which was too short for her and revealed her bare feet. She'd thrown a shawl over her shoulders for warmth.

He didn't want to desire her. But he did. He resisted the urge to take the few steps that separated them, pull her into his arms, and kiss her until they were both panting with need.

"I woke up and you were gone," she said in a wary voice. She lifted her chin and said, "I thought you might have been mad at me because I didn't want to . . ." Her voice drifted off. "I'm not ignoring your needs, Flint. I really have been tired."

And sleep is a good way of avoiding my attentions in bed. He realized he was being unreasonable. Of course she was tired, the way he'd been dragging her around the countryside. He was surprised she'd said anything at all about the lack of touching between them. But she must have been as aware as he was that they'd been husband and wife for two days—and two nights—and hadn't consummated the marriage.

He wanted to go to her but made himself stay where he was. This wasn't the time. The moon was going to be up barely long enough for him to see his way to the roundup camp. He didn't have time to dally here, even if the temptation to bed Hannah was enormous.

To his surprise, she took the few steps to close the distance between them, so her entire face was lit by the moonlight coming in through the window over the copper sink. "Where are you going?" she asked.

He pointed to the table. "I left a note."

She glanced over her shoulder, then back at him, and asked, "What does it say?"

"I'm going out to the roundup to see if Ransom and Emaline are there."

"You couldn't wait till morning?"

Instead of explaining, he simply shook his head.

She reached out and pulled the two sides of his shearling coat together and began attaching the leather thongs over the horn buttons.

He didn't know why he stood there, like a bump on a log, doing nothing. He could damn well close his own coat, if he wanted it closed. But he would have felt churlish stopping her, so he stood there like a six-year-old and let her finish, his fists clenched at his sides, to keep him from reaching out to her.

When she was done, she flattened the collar over his shoulders, smoothing it with her palms, looking him in the eye the entire time. "Be careful out there. I don't want to lose another husband."

He'd forgotten she was a widow. Amazing how the idea of another man making love to her could slip his mind. He quashed the image of a naked Hannah in the throes of lovemaking with a faceless man. "You need to stay at the house," he said, his voice harsh with the sexual frustration he was feeling. "I don't want to have to worry about you, too."

She tilted her head and smiled up at him. "You'd worry about me?"

"You're my wife," he said curtly. He wasn't about to go through the trouble of finding another one. Besides, where would he find another one with dimples like hers?

Her smile disappeared, along with the dimples, and he felt like a wretch. He didn't want to leave her feeling unhappy. He brushed his knuckles against her cheek, then caught her by the nape, leaned down, and brushed her lips with his.

And felt his whole body shudder with need.

He took her into his arms after all, pulling her tight against him. But she'd buttoned the damned coat, and he couldn't feel her body next to his the way he wanted. He thrust her from him, tore at the thongs until he was free of the coat, shoved it off his shoulders, and threw it aside as he took her back in his arms.

He felt hungry, and she was sustenance. He could feel her unrestrained breasts soft against his chest. He could feel her breath against his cheek. He caught her buttocks with both hands and pressed her close, as his body came alive.

He slid his tongue into her mouth, and felt her hands grasp his hair, holding tight, returning his intrusion with her tongue, thrust for thrust.

Flint wasn't thinking, he simply knew he had to have her. He reached for the hem of her nightgown and pulled it off over her head. He quivered with expectation when he saw her naked.

Her body was silvery in the moonlight, lush and shapely. He caught her by the waist with one hand and palmed a breast in the other, leaning down to suckle it.

Her knees buckled, and he thought she'd swooned. He glanced at her face and saw her eyes were heavy-lidded, her mouth open to gasp needed air. Her hands were busy at his waist, unbuttoning his jeans and shoving at them. A moment later she had his long johns down and her insistent hands were gripping his naked buttocks, pulling him close.

Flint didn't need more invitation than that.

He lifted her, and she wrapped her legs around his hips. He turned and pressed her against the back door, thrusting upward as she reached down to help him find his way home.

He made a guttural sound at the warmth and tightness and wetness of her. She bit his neck, but the pain felt good, and he buried his face in her hair and lost himself in a deluge of sensation. He emptied himself inside her with a primal cry of pleasure and satisfaction.

It took a few moments to realize where he was. And what he'd done. Never had he been so inconsiderate of a woman as to have sex with her standing up, braced against a wooden door. And this woman was his *wife*.

He blurted, "I'm sorry."

"I'm not."

When Hannah spoke, he leaned back to look at her face, at the sheen of sweat on her skin, at the glazed eyes, at the panting mouth, and realized no apology was necessary.

She glanced up at him almost shyly and said, "That was . . . nice."

Flint chuckled. "Nice. Yeah. It was, wasn't it?" He eased her legs down to the floor, quickly rearranged his own clothes, then found her nightgown and straightened it out.

"I don't want you to catch a chill." She raised her

arms like a child as he slipped the garment over her head.

She grinned and said, "I'm feeling pretty warm at the moment."

He picked her up in his arms, not yet ready to let her go, but knowing he needed to leave. "You should go back to bed."

"You don't have to carry me."

"The floor's cold, and you're barefoot." It made a better excuse than saying he wanted to feel her warmth next to him. That he was grateful for the pleasure she'd given him and didn't know how to thank her for it. And that he was feeling flustered, because a man shouldn't have to thank his wife for having sex.

Or should he? Emaline certainly wasn't offering it to Ransom as part of the marriage bargain. And Flint couldn't, in his wildest dreams, fathom Emaline accepting the sort of spontaneous, against-the-door romp he'd just enjoyed, and enjoyed heartily, with his wife.

He glanced down at the woman in his arms, feeling torn between his months-in-the-making love for Emaline and his very confused, brand-new—but very strong—feelings for Hannah. "Let's get you back to bed," he said. "If I don't get moving, I'll lose the moonlight."

"Put me down, Flint. I can walk. And you'll be gone that much sooner."

He ignored her request and headed back up the dark staircase. He carried her all the way to the bedroom and laid her on the bed and pulled the covers all the way to her neck. "Don't leave the house until I get back, Hannah. I mean it."

She caught his hand and held it to her cheek. "Don't worry about me, Flint. I'll be waiting right here."

As Flint headed back downstairs, he felt worried down to his bones. About Ransom. About Emaline. And about Hannah, who'd given him that totally unexpected gift of lovemaking in the kitchen. It felt like a betrayal of his supposed love for Emaline to have been so satisfied by his wife.

He was a married man. He'd better start rearranging his feelings to suit the reality of his situation.

As Flint mounted his horse and rode off into the darkness, he found himself pondering whether it was really possible to tell your heart where it should love. His heart and mind and soul had fixed on Emaline long months ago. What kind of man did it make him if he could so easily transfer his affections to a woman he hadn't even known existed a week ago?

Of course, the whole point of marrying Hannah had been to give himself the means to avoid coveting his brother's bride. Hannah was holding up her part of the bargain. Maybe it would be for the best if he made an effort to care a little less about Emaline.

The moment Flint had that thought, he felt a sharp pang of loss. He hated giving up or giving in. It wasn't in his nature. Besides, who would be hurt if he continued loving Emaline in secret?

No one but him.

Hannah would never know. He would take care of her and respect her and make babies with her. They

would have a good life together. He just wasn't sure
he could—or ever would—fall in love with her, the
way he had with Emaline Simmons. Hannah was
welcome to his mind and body. But Emaline would
always possess his heart and soul.

Chapter Twenty-nine

Flint felt reassured when he saw the fire in the distance. Then the whistling wind changed direction, and he caught the smell of death. His stomach knotted. A body, or bodies, had been left unburied. And that meant there had been some sort of disaster.

His horse sidestepped, and he urged Buck forward at a walk, pulling his Winchester from the boot and cocking it, the sound ominous in the silent night. He approached from downwind, not wanting to alert any horses that might be at the camp to his presence, in case those he found there were enemies, rather than friends.

He heard voices carried on the wind. A man's. And a woman's. So Emaline was here and alive. He listened hard to the man's voice, hoping it was Ransom's. But the sound was distorted by distance, and he couldn't tell who it was.

Flint debated whether to dismount, so he could approach more quietly, but decided there was too much advantage to staying on horseback. He kept Buck at a walk and closed the distance until he could hear the conversation taking place. Unfortunately the man's face was in too much shadow to be identified.

Flint could see at least three men on horseback besides the faceless man on foot by the fire. Emaline was standing across from him, her arms folded over her chest.

"You need to come with me, Miss Simmons. You can't spend the night out here all alone," the man said.

So the woman was Emaline. But alone? Where were the Double C cowhands? Where was Ransom?

"I'm not alone," Emaline replied. "Ransom is here."

"Along with a lot of dead bodies."

Flint's heart lurched. *A lot of dead bodies?*

"Ransom isn't dead," Emaline said.

"He will be soon," the man replied. "I've seen wounds like his in the war. If the hole in his chest doesn't get him, the fever will."

"You could help me get him home," Emaline said.

"It would kill him for sure to put him on a horse."

"There's a wagon."

"Turned over, with no mules to pull it. Leave him," the man urged. "I'll take you wherever you want to go."

"I'm staying right here until Flint shows up."

"Flint's not going to get here anytime soon. At least come back to my ranch."

"I'm not going anywhere with you, Mr. Patton."

Flint's blood froze in his veins. Ashley Patton must have come here right after Flint had spoken with him this evening. Was he responsible for the death and destruction? Had the rancher known what he would find here? Had he suspected this was where Emaline might be? Why else would Patton come out to the Double C camp in the middle of the night?

Flint stayed beyond the reach of the light from the campfire and called out, "Patton."

Patton's head jerked around. "Creed? Is that you?"

"My Winchester's cocked and ready. All of you, keep your guns holstered," he ordered.

"Flint?" Emaline said. "Thank God you came!"

"Patton, take your men and get out of here," Flint said. "I'll take care of Miss Simmons and my brother."

"Your brother's a dead man," Patton said. "And I'm wondering what the colonel is going to say when I tell him you've got his daughter all alone at your house."

"You're forgetting my wife," Flint said.

Patton looked thunderstruck. He swore under his breath. He turned and said, "Let's go, boys."

"Before you leave," Flint said, "how about a little help righting Cookie's wagon."

Patton glanced at Emaline, scowled, then said, "Sure. Why not?"

Flint held his rifle in the crook of his arm while Patton, Tucker, and the two cowhands with them levered Cookie's wagon back onto its wheels.

"Unsaddle two of your horses and harness them to the wagon," Flint instructed. "Then empty out the back of that wagon and lift Ransom—carefully—into it."

Flint knew the only thing keeping Patton compliant was Emaline's presence. Patton needed her good opinion, because he hoped to convince her to marry him once Ransom was dead. He couldn't afford to do anything that might cause her to reject him as a suitor.

While Patton didn't do the work himself, he stood by without complaint as Tucker and his two henchmen emptied the wagon. He watched silently as Emaline arranged a pallet for Ransom inside. He stood aside as one of the cowboys slid his hands under Ransom's arms and the other took his feet. They carried him over to the wagon and settled him on the pallet inside.

When they were done, one of the cowboys said plaintively, "What are we supposed to do now? Walk back?"

"That's up to your boss," Flint said. "You can ride double or hoof it home. I don't give a damn, so long as you're off my land by morning. If you're still here, I'll figure you're trespassers here to rustle my cattle, and I'll shoot you where you stand."

"Stealin' horses is a hangin' offense," Tucker said with a sneer.

Flint met Patton's eyes and said, "I'll tell the members of the Association how you helped me out by loaning me a couple of horses when I needed them." The threat was there, that if Patton didn't agree to "loan" the horses, Flint would also pass along that message at the Association meeting next week.

"I'll return your horses and saddles after I get Ransom home. Now get the hell off my land."

"What about Miss Simmons?" Patton asked.

Emaline scooted off the tailgate of the cook wagon, faced Patton, and said, "I'm going with Flint and Ransom."

"I'm sure your father will be interested to hear about this," Patton said.

"Feel free to tell him," Emaline replied scornfully.

"I'm sure he'll thank you for lending me assistance—after Flint held a rifle on you and forced you to help."

Patton turned and mounted up. Tucker mounted his horse as well. For a moment, Flint thought Patton would make the two cowboys walk home. He must have thought better of it, because he held out a hand, and one of the cowboys put a foot in Patton's empty stirrup and settled on the horse behind him. Tucker followed suit with the other cowboy.

Flint sat on Buck, rifle in hand, until their silhouettes passed over a rise in the distance and disappeared from sight. Then he nudged his horse into the firelight and dismounted.

A moment later, Emaline was in his arms.

She clutched his waist, sobbing. "I was so afraid he would make me go with him. I didn't know what to do."

Flint rocked her and crooned, "It's all right, Emaline. Everything's going to be all right."

But so many things about this were all wrong.

When her sobs subsided, Flint caught her shoulders and pushed her away. "How is Ransom, really?"

"The wound in his chest is bad, but I sewed it up."

"*You* sewed it up?"

"Of course!"

"I didn't know you'd done any nursing."

"I haven't," she admitted. "Those are the first stitches I've set in flesh. But it had to be done. So I did it."

Flint stared at her. The "delicate" lady he couldn't imagine spending a night on the prairie with a bunch of cowhands had not only been camped out here on her own, but her presence of mind and willingness to do the hard thing had probably saved his brother's life.

"How is he?" Flint asked.

"There's a shallow crease at his neck that bled a lot, but it's nothing. The wound in his chest is bad. And the fever . . ." She met his gaze and said, "He's so hot. I've been trying to cool him with a wet cloth, but it doesn't seem to be doing much good."

He watched her blink back the tears that brimmed in her eyes. She brushed at a strand of hair that had come out of her bun, and he realized it was the first time he'd seen her less than perfectly put together. It only made her more human. And his feelings more conflicted.

At least Ransom was still alive. But for how long?

"We'd better get started home," he said.

"I'll ride in back with Ransom."

Flint tied Buck's reins to the back of the cook wagon, made sure Emaline was settled comfortably, then climbed onto the bench, took up the reins, and set the horses in motion. Once they were moving, he asked, "How did you end up at the camp alone, Emaline? What happened to everyone?"

"I went looking for Ransom this morning, since he didn't come home for supper last night," she explained. "When I got here, everyone but Ransom was dead. He was conscious long enough to tell me they were attacked by renegade Indians with brand-new rifles."

"Did he speculate on where they got them?" Flint asked.

"He thought Ashley Patton might be responsible.

That he gave guns to the Indians so they could attack the smaller spreads."

"It makes a crazy sort of sense. Patton's enough of a greenhorn to think he can control a bunch of savages."

"Then you think Patton's responsible, too?" Emaline asked.

"Nobody else I know is greedy enough to do something that stupid."

"What happens now?" Emaline said.

"You do your best to nurse Ransom back to health."

"What are you going to do?"

"Find a way to prove Ashley Patton sold guns to the Indians, and make sure the full force of the law comes down on his head."

Chapter Thirty

Hannah fell fast asleep after Flint put her back to bed, but woke up when the first gray light came through the bedroom window. She stretched like a cat, aware of her body in a way she never had been before. The sex had been surprising, fierce and frenzied. She still marveled at the raw intensity of what had passed between them.

She'd only gone downstairs hunting Flint because she'd felt guilty for falling asleep—again—as soon as her head hit the pillow, thereby avoiding her brand-new husband's attentions.

It was the pregnancy, of course.

Hannah wasn't as tired these days as she had been in the very beginning, but she had nowhere near the stamina she'd had before a life had begun growing inside her. When she'd woken up and found Flint gone from bed, she'd suspected he was going to the roundup camp to find his brother. And Emaline.

She despised herself for feeling jealous of the other woman, but that did nothing to make the feeling go away. She'd run downstairs hoping he hadn't left yet and wishing there was something, anything, she could do to end her husband's infatuation with his brother's fiancée.

She'd buttoned Flint's coat because it gave her an excuse to close the distance between them. She'd wanted to tell him that she was his wife now, that he had to forget about Emaline. But how could she accuse him of loving another woman, when she was guilty of hiding her pregnancy by another man?

She hadn't expected what came next. The first kiss was hesitant and tender. The second sent the blood thrumming through her veins. By the time his coat came off, she was lost in a rush of sensations that left her reeling. Her breasts were exquisitely sensitive to his touch. His mouth and hands brought delightful torment wherever they roamed.

Hannah still couldn't believe her wanton behavior. She'd shimmied out of her nightgown as Flint pulled it off over her head and stood proudly before her husband, not flinching as his gaze roamed her naked body. She forgot about everything except the heat in his eyes and the brush of his callused hands over her willing flesh.

Hannah shivered at the memory of how good it had felt to thrust her fingers through Flint's hair and pull his head down to hers for a kiss. How salty the skin at his shoulder had tasted. How her body had moved with his once they were joined. How she'd exulted in his passion and felt exalted by his pleasure.

Hannah shivered. The gray light in the bedroom window was turning pink and yellow, telling her that dawn wasn't far off. She should get up and get dressed. If Flint did find Ransom and Emaline, he would likely bring them home with him. If she was going to be compared to the other woman, she wanted to look her best.

Hannah wished she had something feminine to wear, but since that wasn't an option, she settled for tying her hair away from her face with one of Emaline's ribbons and letting the golden curls fall on her shoulders. She pulled on jeans and tucked in a borrowed blouse, then grabbed a shawl and tied it in a knot to hold it in place before heading downstairs.

Hannah had barely made it to the kitchen when she heard a wagon rolling up to the back of the house. She hurried to the kitchen door and opened it to find Flint pulling the cook wagon to a stop.

She ran outside and asked, "Where are Ransom and Emaline?"

"In the wagon," he said tersely. "Ransom's been shot."

"Oh, no!" Hannah hurried to the back of the wagon and looked over the tailgate. She saw a bedraggled Emaline sitting beside Ransom, who lay unmoving, his eyes closed. "How is he?" she asked.

"Burning up with fever," Emaline replied.

Flint appeared at the back of the wagon, opened the tailgate, and said, "Come on out of there, Emaline." He turned to Hannah and said, "I'll need you to hold the kitchen door open for me." He caught Emaline at the waist when she reached the back of the wagon and lifted her to the ground, then said, "Go upstairs and turn down Ransom's bed."

Flint used the pallet under Ransom's body to pull him far enough out of the wagon that he could slide his arms under his brother's shoulders and knees, then hefted him into his arms. Hannah found it ominous that Ransom didn't move or make a sound when Flint picked him up.

She ran in front of Flint to open the kitchen door, then stood back as he carried Ransom over the threshold.

"Bring a pitcher of water upstairs," he said. "Emaline will need it to sponge Ransom's body. We have to get this fever down."

Hannah saw the fear in his eyes as he walked past her with his brother's lifeless body in his arms. Hannah closed the door, then filled a pitcher with water at the kitchen pump and hurried upstairs after him.

She found Emaline sitting on the bed beside Ransom weeping. Flint stood with his back to Hannah, his hands resting on Emaline's shoulders, his face close to hers.

Hannah stopped by the door, telling herself to pull her claws back in, that Emaline probably needed comforting. She tamped down the savage jealousy she felt and asked, "Is he dead?"

Flint let go of Emaline's shoulders as though he'd been caught embracing her, turned to Hannah and said, "No. I was just . . . offering comfort."

Hannah felt a flare of fury. Emaline might have been seeking comfort, but Flint had wanted more than that. The look of regret in his eyes told Hannah how much he wished he hadn't married her. He might not want his brother to die, but if he did, Flint was already saddled with an unwanted and unwelcome wife.

Hannah bit the inside of her cheek to keep herself from saying something she would be sorry for later, swallowed over the knot of anger in her throat, and said, "Are you all right, Emaline? Is there anything I can do for you?"

Emaline swiped at her eyes with a lace hanky and said, "I'm fine. It's silly to cry now. I'm just so relieved that we're here, and that Ransom is still alive."

Hannah set the pitcher of water on the table beside Emaline. She took a good look at Ransom and saw a man who had one foot in the grave. She placed her hand on his forehand and found it fiery hot. She'd dealt with fever at the orphanage in Chicago. It was relentless. And it killed without mercy.

"You should get him out of these filthy clothes," she said to Emaline. "You can cool him down while you wash him up. I'll be glad to help. In fact, I can take care of Ransom while you clean yourself up."

Emaline looked down and seemed surprised to discover that her white blouse and tan riding skirt were stained with dirt and dried blood.

"Hannah's right," Flint said. "You need to take care of yourself first, Emaline. I'll undress Ransom while you wash up."

Hannah realized Flint had solved the problem of having either of the two women undress his brother. But he was only postponing the inevitable, unless he wanted to nurse Ransom himself.

"Come on, Emaline," Hannah said, eyeing Flint over her shoulder as she helped the other woman to her feet. "You can dress in my room. It sounds like you've had quite an adventure. I want to hear all about it."

Hannah found Emaline reticent about discussing the events of the previous evening. "You mean you stitched his wounds yourself?" she said, amazed at

Emaline's courage in the face of such adversity. "Where did you find the nerve?"

"It was either that or watch him bleed to death," Emaline replied as she scrubbed at her face and arms with a wet washcloth. "You would have done the same thing."

"I can barely mend clothes," Hannah said. "I can't imagine sticking a needle through someone's flesh."

Emaline shuddered. "I hope I never have to do it again." She swiped once more at her chest, then threw the washcloth into the bowl next to the pitcher and began dressing herself.

"Wait," Hannah said. "You must be tired. Did you sleep at all last night?"

Emaline shook her head.

"Why don't you lie down in my bed for a while and rest? Flint and I will watch over Ransom. I promise to come get you if anything changes."

"I want to be with him," Emaline said, continuing to dress. "I need to be with him."

Hannah didn't want to like Emaline. She certainly didn't want to admire her. But she wondered if she would have done so well if she'd found herself in the same situation. Clearly, Emaline needed rest. She crossed to the other woman and caught her hands, stopping her from buttoning the blouse she'd put on. Hannah slid it back off Emaline's shoulders, leaving her in her chemise and underdrawers.

"Lie down, Emaline. If you're still awake at the end of five minutes, I promise I'll let you go to Ransom. Otherwise, I'll call you if there's any change in his condition."

Emaline was clearly torn. And clearly exhausted.

She glanced at the bed, then toward the door. "You promise you'll come get me?"

Hannah crossed her heart with a finger. "Cross my heart and hope to die, stick a needle in my eye."

Emaline smiled. Her eyes were watery with tears. "Thank you, Hannah."

Hannah quickly pulled down the covers so Emaline could crawl under them. She covered her up and said, "Rest. Try not to worry. I'll be back in five minutes to check on you."

Emaline closed her eyes and sighed as her body sank into the mattress. "Oh, I almost forgot. Best wishes on your marriage, Hannah. Flint told me the two of you tied the knot."

Emaline's eyes remained closed. Obviously, she didn't expect a response. Hannah was glad, because she wasn't sure what to say. She wondered what else Flint had discussed with Emaline on that long drive back from the roundup camp. She waited to see how restless Emaline would be, but within two minutes, the other woman was lightly snoring.

Hannah turned and left the room. She had a vested interest in making sure that Ransom Creed survived. She wanted Emaline married to Flint's brother. Then maybe Flint could stop pining for his brother's woman.

Chapter Thirty-one

Over the next three days, Hannah, Flint, and Emaline took turns nursing Ransom, whose fever raged. Hannah shared Flint's bed with Emaline, while he stayed in the room with his brother. On the third night, it was touch and go, and Hannah thought for sure Ransom would die. She tried to offer Flint comfort, but he kept his distance. He looked grim and said nothing.

On the fourth morning, the fever broke, and Ransom woke up long enough to speak to Emaline, who collapsed in tears. Hannah had to take her out of the room while Flint reassured his anxious brother that Emaline was only tired.

Hannah ushered Emaline downstairs to the kitchen and poured her a cup of coffee, patting her shoulder and agreeing with her that it had been a long four days and surely now that the fever had broken Ransom would recover.

She was pouring herself a cup of coffee when someone began pounding on the back door. Hannah shared a worried look with Emaline before she crossed to the door and cautiously opened it.

Emaline's father stood there in an impressive blue military uniform with a lot of gold buttons across his chest. A man with a clerical collar, the same preacher who'd married Hannah and Flint, stood beside him.

"Let me in," the colonel said.

Hannah stood back, responding automatically to the authority in the colonel's voice, and the colonel and the cleric stepped into the kitchen.

When Emaline saw her father, she jumped up and threw herself into his open arms, sobbing and speaking incoherently. He patted her shoulder awkwardly and spoke softly to her, but Hannah could see his eyes blazed with anger and his mouth flattened to a thin, uncompromising line.

"Where's Ransom?" the colonel asked his daughter.

"In bed. He was shot, Father. His fever broke this morning, and he's finally conscious."

"Good," the colonel said. "Take me to him." He put an arm around Emaline's shoulder, urging her toward the hallway, and gestured for Hannah to precede them. He turned to the preacher and said, "Come along, Reverend Scofield."

Hannah led the way up the stairs and then down the hall to Ransom's room. The bedroom door was open, and Flint sat on his brother's bed talking quietly with him. "Flint, we have company," she said to give him some warning.

Flint rose abruptly and turned, hands fisted, ready to fight. He stiffened when he saw the colonel. Hannah watched him grit his teeth when he caught sight of the preacher standing behind him in the doorway.

"Hello, Colonel," Flint said.

Hannah noticed the colonel didn't offer his hand. Instead he said, "I understand from Mr. Patton that my daughter and your brother spent the night together. If I had my way, I'd finish the job those renegade Indians started, but my late wife's sister, whom I located in Denver, tells me my daughter loves that scoundrel."

"I do love him, Father!" Emaline cried.

"Don't interrupt me, Emaline," the colonel said doggedly. "Under the circumstances, I see no reason to delay their wedding three more weeks."

"I presume Mr. Patton also told you that my brother was shot and near death when he and Emaline spent the night together," Flint said through tight jaws.

"That's beside the point," the colonel said.

"Ransom's too sick to go through any kind of ceremony," Flint objected. "Especially a shotgun wedding."

"I'm fine," a hoarse voice interjected. "I'll be happy to marry Emaline right now, Colonel."

"I see you're still kicking," the colonel said, eyeing Ransom dubiously. "Mr. Patton seemed to think the issue was in doubt. I brought along Reverend Scofield, just in case. It seems he'll be of some use after all."

"You don't have to do this, Ransom," Flint said.

Ransom reached a feeble hand toward Emaline, and she hurried to his side and grasped it. "I want to marry Emaline," Ransom said. "The sooner the better."

Hannah felt guilty because she was glad the colonel had shown up. Glad that he was insisting Emaline and Ransom marry. The sooner they were wed, the sooner Flint would have to let go of his dream of a life with the other woman.

Guilt that she was feeling so glad, when Emaline would be robbed of her lovely wedding, prompted her to ask, "Emaline, do you want to change into something prettier?"

Emaline shook her head. "I'd be happy to marry Ransom barefoot and wearing a shift."

The colonel harrumphed. "That won't be necessary, my dear. Well, Reverend Scofield. Get to it."

The preacher was carrying a prayer book, which he opened, and Hannah listened to him speak the words she'd heard so recently herself.

"Dearly beloved, we are gathered here . . ."

Hannah glanced at Flint and saw his eyes were riveted on Emaline. A muscle worked in his jaw, and his mouth became a thin line. His gaze skipped to his brother as Ransom spoke the words that would bind him to Emaline forever.

Hannah felt her heart squeeze. Why did she care so much what Flint felt for Emaline? Theirs was merely a marriage of convenience. Flint needed a wife. She needed a father for her child. When had her feelings gotten engaged? When had she started wanting him to desire her and her alone?

Maybe she was simply being a dog in the manger. She hadn't insisted that Flint love her, but she didn't want him loving Emaline, either.

Their wedding should have been sufficient to take Emaline out of the picture. But she had caught that yearning look on Flint's face once too often. Perhaps this ceremony would kill his feelings for Emaline Simmons, soon to be Emaline Creed, once and for all.

Or maybe not.

Hannah felt sick to her stomach. Maybe it was the sausage she'd eaten for breakfast. Maybe it was morning sickness. All she knew was that if she didn't get out of this room right now, she was going to embarrass herself.

She bolted for her bedroom, yanked the chamber pot out from under the bed, dropped to her knees, and promptly lost the contents of her stomach in the porcelain bowl.

She felt her hair being pulled back from her face as she vomited. When she was done, someone handed her a wet cloth, which she used to wipe her mouth. That same hand pushed the chamber pot back under the bed.

A moment later she was being lifted into Flint's lap as he sat down on the bed. She leaned her head against his chest and closed her eyes as she fought against further nausea and tears. "Thank you," she whispered.

"You should have told me you were sick."

"I'm not sick."

"Then what the hell was that?" he demanded.

"I'm pregnant."

Hannah knew she'd made a mistake the instant the words were out of her mouth. Every muscle in Flint's body tensed. They hadn't been married long enough for her to know for certain she was pregnant if Flint was the father. Certainly not long enough for her to have morning sickness.

It didn't taken long for Flint to figure out that he wasn't the proud papa of her child. "I see," he said. He sounded upset.

She was glad! Glad he wouldn't have the satisfaction of being the one to impregnate her. Glad, glad, glad she was going to bear another man's child! It was only fair, since he seemed so determined to love another woman.

Tit for tat. Pain for pain. Hurt for hurt.

"I asked you if you were pregnant," he said. "You told me you weren't."

"I . . ." Hannah almost said she hadn't known. But the time for lying was over. His arms had dropped from around her waist, so she slid off his lap onto the bed, then looked him in the eye as she admitted, "I lied."

"Why?"

"I was afraid you wouldn't marry me."

He gritted his teeth. But said nothing.

Which suggested she'd been right on the mark. She felt sick at heart and so angry she could spit. So she told him, "The baby is due the middle of January."

He did the math and said, "You were three-and-a-half months along, and you didn't think to mention it to me?"

"It was none of your business."

"None of my business? I'm going to be the father of McMurtry's kid, and it's none of my business?"

Hannah raised a brow in surprise. So he was still willing to be the child's father? Even though he wasn't the one who'd set the seed? Then she replayed what he'd said.

Flint had called the child "McMurtry's kid." Not his. Not hers. Not theirs. *McMurtry's.* Hannah felt sick to her stomach again. And sick at heart.

Then he said, "That explains why you've been so tired."

She nodded. "It's not as bad now as it was a month ago."

"You should have told me."

"Why? What would you have done differently?"

"I would have taken better care of you," he said. "I wouldn't have let you go riding all over the country-side on a wild-goose chase."

"You couldn't have stopped me," Hannah said.

"I could. And I will. From now on, you'll take better care of yourself."

"I'm not one of your cowhands that you can order around," she retorted. "And I can take care of myself."

"Which is why you were puking your guts up a minute ago," he snapped back.

"I can't help getting morning sickness."

"You can stay in bed until you're sure you're not going to be sick. If I'm not mistaken, you were up today at the crack of dawn taking care of Ransom."

"Emaline was exhausted, and you were dead to the world. He wanted water."

His lips twisted and he said, "From now on, you think of yourself first. I don't want this pregnancy killing you."

Of course not, Hannah thought bitterly. *Then you'd be put to the trouble of raising "McMurtry's kid" on your own.*

"Emaline and I will take care of Ransom," he continued.

Hannah seethed. So, while she was cooking and cleaning, Flint was going to be spending his time with Emaline. She felt helpless and hopeless.

"We should get back," she said curtly. "You'll want to congratulate your brother on his wedding."

Flint helped her to her feet and said, "We'll go together. We can share our happy news with them."

Hannah stopped. "I think we should keep this to ourselves."

Flint snorted. "You're not going to be able to keep it a secret much longer, Hannah. Might as well get it over with."

Hannah realized he was right. "All right. Fine."

"Maybe seeing you get through your pregnancy and deliver a healthy child will give Emaline the courage to do the same."

Hannah bit her cheek, which was already feeling sore, to keep from screaming. It seemed every syllable out of Flint's mouth had something to do with Emaline.

"I give up," she muttered.

"What's that?" Flint asked.

"Nothing," Hannah said. "Let's go wish the newlyweds well."

She left the room without looking at Flint again. She would be far better off if she stopped feeling anything for him. Otherwise she was going to be in for a lot of heartbreak. It appeared his gaze was going to remain firmly fixed on his lodestar, even after she was a married woman.

Hannah was no fool. She'd learned some hard lessons in that Chicago orphanage. Life wasn't fair. You could give up. Or you could choose to fight. The problem was, where Flint Creed was concerned, Hannah hadn't yet made up her mind which option she wanted to pursue.

Chapter Thirty-two

Emaline waited patiently for Ransom to recover from his wounds. She said nothing about her change of heart, nothing about her willingness to bear him a child. There seemed no reason to broach the subject before he was well enough to do something about it.

But that hesitation gave her a great deal of time to think. She was troubled by several of the conclusions she reached.

Emaline remembered how astonished she'd been when Ransom had so readily agreed to marry her without further discussion of her ban on sex. It made her wonder if he'd done the same sort of soul-searching when he'd thought he might die that she had done. Perhaps he'd also decided that being together, no matter what the terms, was more important than anything else.

That was the conclusion that gave her the most solace.

She was also forced to admit that his decision to marry her could have been made simply because he hadn't wanted to risk the dangerous confrontation between Flint and her father that would have resulted if he'd refused.

Emaline was tormented by her memory of Ransom's face when he'd spoken his vows. His eyes had looked haunted, his mouth pinched. His voice had sounded brusque.

At the time, she'd attributed all those things to pain from his injuries. When she appraised his behavior toward her since their wedding, she wasn't so sure.

Ransom was as courteous and kind and thoughtful as he had ever been while he was courting her. But a chasm existed between them now that hadn't been there before their wedding. Emaline had struggled to understand what had put it there and concluded that Ransom had felt himself obliged to marry her. His hand had been forced by her father's sudden appearance with a preacher in tow.

She'd responded to that thought with a surge of rancor. If Ransom hadn't wanted to marry her, he should have said so then and there! Her heart had dropped to her toes, and she'd spent the rest of the day hiding her tears from Hannah. She knew Ransom had loved her once upon a time. But did he still?

Emaline wanted to ask Ransom for the truth, but she kept putting it off, telling herself it wasn't fair to confront her husband before he was completely recovered.

To her dismay, it had taken six weeks before Ransom was on his feet again and another six weeks beyond that before he was well enough to spend an entire day on the range.

Three months seemed like forever.

Of course, the longer she delayed, the more uncertain she was about whether she should admit she was willing to consummate their marriage. She desperately wanted a long life with Ransom, and pregnancy would surely cut that life short. So maybe she should let the moment pass. Then she would think of closing that growing chasm between them by making love with her husband and change her mind again.

It was Ransom's strange behavior that finally convinced her she had to get off the fence.

During his recovery they'd slept in the same bed, but Ransom had made no effort—none—to consummate their marriage. To her consternation, the kisses and hugs and touches had also disappeared. The more she delayed, the more worried Emaline became that it was too late.

Her husband seemed to have fallen out of love with her.

She was terribly afraid that if she approached Ransom and told him she wanted to make love with him, that she was ready to have his child, he would reject her offer.

So she said nothing. And he said nothing. And the chasm grew deeper.

Weeks passed with no change in Ransom's behavior, until finally, Emaline decided that if Ransom wasn't going to reach out to her, she was going to have to seduce her husband. She was frightened, but determined. This morning, she'd made up her mind that, come hail or high water, tonight was the night.

Thanksgiving was a mere three weeks away. She wanted lovemaking with her husband, and the reconciliation between them she hoped it would cause, to be one of the things for which they could both be truly thankful.

She might have looked outwardly calm that evening, as she sat on the sofa in the parlor instructing Hannah how to knit booties for her baby, but a herd of wild mustangs was stampeding in her stomach.

She was half listening as Flint and Ransom sat in wing chairs before a roaring fire arguing over how best to deal with Ashley Patton. Because Flint was needed at the ranch, he'd missed the Laramie County Stock Association meeting the day they voted on Patton's membership. The blackguard had been unanimously approved.

Over the past three months, the renegade Sioux had wreaked devastation on the smaller spreads with their brand-new '73 Winchesters, and Patton had bought out several of the homesteaders at rock-bottom prices. The wealthy rancher was becoming a juggernaut that threatened to swallow everything in the Territory.

Her father had sent his soldiers out to hunt down the renegade Indians, but they attacked at random and then disappeared. Ransom seemed certain Patton was providing a refuge for the band of Sioux on his ranch and wanted to go hunting for it. Flint had argued that they had enough problems without giving Patton's gunslinger an excuse to shoot them for rustlers.

Once Ransom's life was no longer in danger, Flint had traveled to Cheyenne and hired a new cook and enough cowhands to finish the roundup, but he'd never located the hundred head of missing cattle.

When the roundup was done, it turned out another hundred and fifty steers were gone. The army needed twelve hundred beeves on the hoof over the next twelve months. Flint and Ransom didn't have the cattle necessary to meet the contract.

It had gone to Ashley Patton.

"Oh, I messed up again," Hannah said.

The frustration in her voice caught Emaline's attention and she helped Hannah unravel the yarn to undo the mistake. "Take your time," she said. "You're doing fine."

"I'll never be as fast or as good as you are."

Emaline smiled. "It won't take you long to catch up to me. You're already better than I was when I first started."

Hannah was resting her arms on her pregnant belly, which protruded from her thin frame beneath a blousy wool dress. Emaline had helped Hannah sew two warm dresses that could be altered as her size increased. They'd already had to take out the seams twice.

"Oh!" Hannah said. She put her hand to her belly, drawing the cloth down tight, then looked up at Emaline and smiled. "She kicked me."

Emaline couldn't help being intrigued as she watched Hannah's baby grow inside her. If Hannah had figured correctly, she was now a week shy of being seven months pregnant. She was already huge. Emaline was fascinated when she saw Hannah's stomach change shape as the baby moved, showing what appeared to be a bulge from a tiny hand or foot. "May I touch?" she asked.

"Of course."

Emaline reached over and tentatively set her hand on Hannah's belly. And promptly had it kicked. She drew her hand back and laughed. "Oh, my goodness." She returned her hand to the same spot and waited to see what the baby would do next. It had apparently settled, because she didn't feel anything more.

She removed her hand and said, "He must have decided to take a nap."

"She," Hannah corrected.

Emaline cocked her head and asked, "What makes you so sure it's a girl, Hannah?"

Hannah shrugged. "I just know."

Emaline thought it was more a case of Hannah *wanting* a girl and *wishing* for one. No one could predict the sex of a baby before it was born. "You want a girl?"

Hannah nodded. "I have two younger brothers. Boys are no fun. With girls you can do their hair and dress them in pretty clothes."

"And a girl can become the apple of her father's eye," Emaline said. "I certainly was."

That is, before she'd embarrassed her father so badly he'd felt it necessary to marry her off. He'd offered to hold a reception for her and Ransom at the fort, once Ransom was fully recovered, but Emaline had declined. She hadn't wanted to give the gossips anything more to chew on.

"What does it feel like when the baby moves?" she asked Hannah.

"In the beginning, it's sort of like a butterfly's wings.

Lately, she's been kicking my bladder, so I need to use the chamber pot or make a trip to the necessary."

Emaline saw Flint glance over his shoulder at Hannah when she wasn't looking. He did that a lot lately, which was interesting, because Emaline had also noticed that Hannah had stopped talking to him at the kitchen table. She wondered what had happened between the couple to cause Flint's wife to give him the silent treatment.

She didn't ask, because she didn't want Hannah asking about her relationship with Ransom. In Emaline's case, all she did was talk to Ransom, since nothing had been happening between the two of them in bed.

She missed Ransom's kisses. She missed the yearning that had been in his eyes before they were wed. She hoped the very special spark that had once existed between them could be relighted, or she was going to be totally humiliated in bed tonight.

Hannah yawned, and Flint immediately said, "Time for bed, Hannah."

She made a face of disgust that Flint couldn't see and replied without looking at him, "I'm not done knitting."

"You need your rest."

"I'm comfortable where I am."

"Flint is right," Emaline said, playing peacemaker. "I'll help you again tomorrow."

Hannah glared at Emaline and said, "I know when I'm tired. And I'm not tired!"

Flint had risen from his chair and crossed to the couch. "The fact that you're so irritable is proof you're exhausted."

Emaline watched Hannah close her eyes and grit her teeth. She waited for an outburst that never came. Hannah set the knitting in the basket beside her, rose, and pressed her hands to the small of her back.

"Are you all right?" Flint asked.

Hannah ignored the question and headed for the stairs. By now, Ransom was also on his feet.

"I guess we should all get some shut-eye," he said. "With that early snowfall, Flint and I need to get hay out to the cattle tomorrow."

Hannah turned on the three of them, her eyes narrowed, her hands balled into fists at her widened waist, and said, "I wish all of you would stop treating me like an invalid. I'm pregnant, for heaven's sake! It's the most natural thing in the world. Women have been having babies for centuries. I'm perfectly fine. Or I would be, if all of you would stop pestering me!"

Hannah burst into angry tears and turned and tried running up the stairs. Except she stumbled after the third one and fell to one knee. Flint was beside her a moment later to help her up. She slapped his hand away and said, "Leave me the hell alone!"

Emaline was shocked by the profanity. Apparently, so was Flint, because he stayed where he was as Hannah pulled herself to her feet and stumbled up the stairs alone.

He glanced once at Ransom, his face troubled, then turned and followed Hannah up the stairs.

Emaline huffed out a sigh. This wasn't a very propitious beginning for what she'd hoped would be a romantic evening with her husband. She glanced at Ransom to see how he'd reacted to the turbulent scene between the other couple.

"Why is she so mad at him?" Ransom asked.

Emaline shrugged. "I don't know. Why aren't you attracted to me anymore?"

That was not what Emaline had planned to say, and apparently not what Ransom had been expecting, either. Caught off-guard, his stark expression revealed how upset he was by the question.

"What makes you think I'm not attracted to you?"

"You never touch me. You never kiss me. You act as though my father cut your manhood away when he forced you to marry me."

That was plain speaking. She was surprised to hear the anger in her voice. She was pretty sure this was not the way to seduce a man. She should act winsome and willing. She shouldn't be accusing her husband of failing in his duties to his wife. Especially since she was the one who'd set the ground rules he'd been following.

Emaline blurted, "I want you to make love to me."

There. She'd said it. She lifted her chin and stared at Ransom, whose jaw had dropped. "You don't have to act so surprised."

"You said sex was off-limits. You said you were scared of dying," he accused.

"I've changed my mind."

She expected him to stride across the room and take her in his arms and ravish her. He stayed where he was. He looked wary and unsure.

"What are you saying, Emaline?"

"I don't think I could be much plainer. I'm saying I want to make love to you. I want you to make love to me."

"Despite the consequences?" he said doubtfully.

"*Because* of the consequences."

He took a hesitant step toward her, then visibly stopped himself. "So you don't believe anymore that you're going to die if you get pregnant?"

She pursed her lips. Why couldn't he understand? It was all so very simple. "Yes, I'll probably die," she said matter-of-factly. "But I want to make love to you anyway. I don't want to live my life without having that experience with you. If I can, I want to give you a baby."

His brow furrowed. "You believe you're going to die if you do this, but you want to do it anyway?"

She nodded.

He shook his head. "No. Not on your life. Not for all the cows in Texas."

Emaline held out her hands in supplication. "Why not? I want you, Ransom. I need you."

He looked pained, but he stood his ground. "I'm not going to be responsible for killing you, Emaline."

"You won't."

He shot her a disgusted look.

"I want us to have a baby," she said.

"If I believed that, Emaline—that you want *both of us* to have a baby—I'd have you off your feet and on your back in two seconds flat."

Emaline felt breathless. "Believe it."

But he didn't look convinced. "When did this change of heart occur?"

"When you were hurt," she admitted. "When I thought I was going to lose you, I realized I wanted to experience—"

"So this is about having sex?" he interrupted.

"It's about making love," she said. "Ever since that awful wedding, I've felt you pulling away from me, Ransom. I want us to be close again."

"Through sex," he said flatly.

"Why can't you understand?" she wailed.

"Explain it to me, Emaline."

She noticed he hadn't even used the shortened form of her name, putting him one more step away from her. She reached out to him again. "I love you, Ransom. I want you to make love to me."

"Even though you believe making love to me is a death sentence? No thanks." He turned to leave.

"Please, stop," she begged. "Please, listen to me."

He paused with his rigid back to her. She could see his hands were balled into fists. She closed the distance between them and put a hand on his shoulder. He stiffened.

"Please, Ransom. Turn around and look at me."

He hesitated so long, Emaline was afraid she'd lost him forever. Then he turned and looked at her with tortured eyes. In a voice raw with emotion, he said, "You're killing me, Emaline. Lying beside you night after night and not touching you is killing me. I don't know how much longer I can stand it. But I'll be damned before I make love to you when you're lying beneath me like some virgin sacrifice."

Emaline stared up at him. "Lying beside you without touching you is killing me, too," she said quietly. "It's killing my soul. You're the other half of me, Ransom. I can't live without your love. I can't live without your touch. I want you and I need you."

"Em." Her name seemed wrenched from somewhere deep inside him. That single word held a world of agony and unfulfilled desire.

Emaline swallowed over the hard knot in her throat and said, "I can't help my fear of dying. It's real. But the fear of losing you is greater by far. Please don't turn me away. Please make love to me."

Ransom pulled her into his arms and held her tight. "I love you, Em. So much I can't bear the thought of losing you. I want to make love to you, but I'm afraid."

Emaline's brow cleared. "Darling," she said, brushing a stray curl off his forehead. "Maybe if we face our fears together, we can overcome them."

She watched him search her face, looking to see whether she meant what she was saying. "Do you believe I love you and need you?" she asked.

Apparently he did, because he scooped her into his arms and headed for the buffalo hide in front of the fireplace.

Chapter Thirty-three

Flint had been aware all evening of the tension between Ransom and Emaline. That had caused him to focus on the situation in his own marriage, which was strained. He'd been content to let well enough alone, hoping his relationship with Hannah would improve with time.

It hadn't. He felt no closer to his wife now than he had on the day he'd married her. Truthfully, he felt more distanced from her. He'd thought they were getting along well together. Then something had changed. He wasn't sure what had happened, but tonight he'd finally come to the conclusion that the only way to find out was to ask.

He closed the bedroom door, turned to Hannah, and said, "I want to know why you've been giving me the cold shoulder."

"I don't know what you mean," she replied.

"You know exactly what I mean."

She flushed, her cheeks turning dark in the lamplight, so he knew she knew what he meant. Since the day Ransom and Emaline had returned from the roundup camp, his wife had shut him out of her life.

Hannah spoke to him if he asked her a question, but she confined her give-and-take conversation to Emaline and Ransom.

He hadn't even noticed at first, because he usually spoke with Ransom at the supper table about business matters, while the two women talked about the soap making or candle making or laundry or cooking that had occupied their day. After supper, he and Ransom sat planning their next workday in chairs perpendicular to the stone fireplace, while their wives read or talked or worked on some sewing or knitting or crocheting project on the sofa across from them.

In addition, Flint had been distracted by his concern for Ransom. Over the past couple of months, he'd come to realize his brother was terribly unhappy. Since the two women were sitting so close, it was impossible to ask Ransom what was wrong. Flint had figured his brother's discontent was probably caused by the unresolved personal issues in his forced marriage to Emaline.

He gave Ransom plenty of openings to discuss the matter when they rode out together in the mornings, but Ransom hadn't picked up his cue, and Flint wasn't about to offer advice that hadn't been requested. However, thinking about Ransom's troubles with Emaline had caused Flint to mull over—to compare, actually—his own relationship with his wife.

That was when he'd noticed that although Hannah was talking plenty, she wasn't speaking to him.

"I want an answer, Hannah. Did I do something wrong? If so, tell me, so I can apologize, and we can get on with our lives."

Her chin took on a mulish tilt, and for a moment he

thought she wasn't going to answer. She sat down near the foot of the bed, gripped the bedpost with one hand to steady her front-heavy pregnant body, and said, "Are you sure you want to know?"

That sounded foreboding. Did he want to know? Was he opening a can of worms? Was he going to create more problems than he already had? Surely not knowing was worse than knowing. He was pretty good at solving problems when he knew what the problem was.

"Just tell me, Hannah. Why aren't you talking to me?"

She caught her lower lip in her teeth, then let it go, took a deep breath, and said, "I don't see the point in getting to know you any better."

Flint felt like she'd slapped him. He was shocked. And hurt. He kept his face impassive, unwilling to give Hannah the satisfaction of seeing how deep her words had cut. He realized he still didn't know how she'd come to that decision. "Can you tell me why?"

"You're never going to love me the way you love Emaline."

Flint hissed in a breath. How did she know? How long had she known? He'd thought his secret was safe. He'd been so careful to hide his feelings. He felt a jolt of horror, wondering if his brother had divined his feelings for Emaline, wondering if that was why Ransom was so unhappy. There was no way he could ask.

"What makes you think I have feelings—"

"Don't bother lying," she interrupted. "I'm not blind. I can see what's right in front of my nose."

"Emaline is married to my brother."

She snorted. "Yes, she is. So what?"

"I would never—"

"You covet your brother's wife."

He'd thought those words, but he'd never heard them spoken aloud. Put that way, it sounded truly awful. Literally sinful. He felt the heat on his throat rising up to become a guilty flush on his face. He would never, ever act on his feelings, but he hadn't been able to banish them.

Hannah took a deep breath and said, "You can't help who you love, Flint. But I don't want to get burned." She met his troubled gaze, and said, "So I'm keeping my distance from you."

That was plain speaking. Flint had no idea how to reply.

She asked, "Is there anything else? If not, I'm tired and I want to go to bed."

"How long is this shutout going to continue?"

She glared at him. "How long do you plan on being in love with another woman?"

"I met her long before I knew you."

"And fell in love with her?"

He nodded.

"And stayed in love with her? Even though she chose your brother?"

"It wasn't something I could control," he argued. "It just happened."

"And you still love her?" she asked.

He wasn't going to say he had no feelings for Emaline, because that would be a lie. But he wasn't going to admit he did, either, not to his wife's face. "Isn't there some way we can work this out?" he asked instead.

"It's your problem," she said. "You solve it. Now, if you don't mind, I'm going to bed."

"I do mind," he said, taking a step toward her. "There's more to being a wife than cooking and cleaning and sewing, Hannah."

She stared at him in disbelief. "Like what?"

"Like kissing and touching."

"In case you haven't noticed, I'm pregnant."

"So?"

She glanced at him warily. "You can't like the way I look."

"Why not?"

"I'm ugly."

"You're beautiful. And desirable."

"I don't believe you."

"I've always wanted you. Never doubt that, Hannah."

"But you don't love me," she said flatly.

"Do you love me?" he countered.

She hesitated, then said, "Even if I did, I wouldn't be fool enough to admit it."

"So you don't?" he pressed.

"My feelings are my business," she said stubbornly.

"So, where does that leave us? I don't love you, and you won't admit to loving me," he said. "Does that mean we can't take comfort from one another? Or that we can't give each other pleasure?"

"No, I don't think we can."

"We can try," he insisted. "If you're physically uncomfortable, we can stop." He didn't know why he was trying to convince Hannah to make love. Especially when she'd just called him on his feelings for Emaline.

"I'm not the woman you want," she said flatly.

"You're wrong about that." His emotional commitment to Emaline had done nothing to quench his physical attraction to Hannah. He'd kept his distance from his wife ever since the night he'd brought Ransom home, in deference to her pregnancy. But maybe, in hindsight, that had been a mistake. It seemed Hannah had gotten the wrong idea.

"I've never wanted Emaline the way I want you."

"You're lying."

He shook his head. "No, Hannah. I wouldn't lie about something like that. If I didn't desire you, why would I want to make love to you?"

She looked confused and unhappy. "All right," she said at last. "I'm willing to try. But turn out the lamps."

He shook his head again. "I want to see you. I want to see how your body has changed with the baby growing inside you."

"You won't like it," she said.

He smiled. "Let me be the judge of that."

"I don't want to be judged at all," she retorted.

"Okay. Fine. I won't tell you how beautiful I find you."

She glared at him, obviously not believing a word he said. She scooted off the bed and began unbuttoning the voluminous dress she was wearing. When she had the buttons down the front undone, she slipped it off her shoulders and let it drop to the floor, leaving her wearing a large white flannel shift. She removed her shoes and stockings, then reached under the shift and pulled off a pair of underdrawers. Finally, she pulled the shift off over her head.

She stood before him with her feet apart, her blond hair barely covering her enlarged breasts, her hands balled into defiant fists at her sides, her pregnant belly distended, gloriously naked.

Flint gasped.

She moaned and stooped down to grab the shift. "I warned you!"

He had his arms around her a moment later. He eased the flannel garment from her clutch and let it fall back to the floor. "Hannah, don't. I was gasping with disbelief because you're so beautiful."

She looked at him, her eyes swimming in tears, and said, "You're just saying that."

He laughed and grabbed her naked buttocks in his hands and pressed her rounded abdomen against the fly in his jeans. "Feel that?"

Her eyes went wide.

"That happened the instant I saw you naked. Is that the response of a man who doesn't like what he sees?"

Her head turned down, and he put a hand under her chin to lift her face so he could see into her eyes. "This hasn't ever happened to me with Emaline. Not once."

She searched his face, and he could see she was trying to determine whether he was telling the truth. He met her gaze and said, "Only you do this to me, Hannah. Only you."

"Don't tease me, Flint. I'm vulnerable. I can be hurt."

He lowered his head and touched his lips to hers. His hand slid down to her belly. He was astonished to find that it was hard, rather than soft.

Then the baby kicked him.

He let go and stared at her belly, amazed and amused, then met her gaze and asked, "Was that what I thought it was?"

She smiled and nodded. "She's active at night."

"She?"

"It's a girl. Her name is Lauren," she added.

"Lauren. That's pretty. What if it's a boy?"

"Then you can name him."

Flint was intrigued by the idea. He'd had mixed feelings when he'd learned he would be raising another man's child. Disappointment was uppermost, because he couldn't start on his own family until McMurtry's kid was born. He was surprised Hannah was going to let him name the child if it was a boy.

"How about Douglas?" he announced. After a good friend who'd died in the war. "Or maybe Russ." He'd had a good hunting dog named Russ. "Or Jesse." He had a sibling named Jesse, a sister with a boy's name, who'd disappeared during the war.

"Thank goodness it's a girl," she said with a laugh. "Sounds like you can't make up your mind."

"I'll think about it," he said. "Just in case." He dropped to his knees, put his mouth next to her belly, and said, "Hey, you in there. Don't be kicking your mom."

He felt Hannah's hand on his head, felt her fingers threading tenderly through his hair. He kissed her belly, then stood and picked her up and carried her to bed.

Flint revered Hannah's pregnant body. He found satisfaction in the way she clung to him and arched her body toward his. He felt exhilarated by her sighs and moans of pleasure. He marveled at the fullness of her breasts, admired the roundness of her belly, and at last, found his way home.

As he lay oxygen-starved beside her afterward, Flint wondered whether it was possible to learn to love a woman. Unfortunately, that wasn't all he needed to do. He also needed to fall out of love with a woman. Surely there was a way to accomplish both.

He figured he had about two months—until Mc-Murtry's kid was born—to figure it all out.

Chapter Thirty-four

"Are you all right?" Ransom asked.

Emaline rolled onto her side on the buffalo hide rug and threaded her fingers into the dark V of curls on Ransom's chest. "I never imagined sex would be like that. It's not just pleasurable, it's uplifting. What I felt was so . . . unexpected."

Emaline was hard-pressed to come up with superlatives. Ransom had been gentle at first. She was the one who'd become demanding. She was the one who'd bitten and scratched. She was the one who'd lifted her hips in time with his thrusts. She was the one who'd clasped her legs around his thighs at the ultimate moment as he set his seed in her womb.

"Glad to hear you approve," he said, sitting up and grinning down at her.

Emaline rolled onto her back, reached her hands up over her head, and stretched, arching her back like the cat that got the cream. "When can we do it again?" she asked.

He laughed. "I'm ready."

Emaline glanced at him and blushed. He certainly was. She sat up, amazed at how unashamed she felt to be naked with him. She crossed her legs and said, "I think we already made a baby."

"I hope you're right," he said with a smile. "I can't wait to be a father."

"I know you'll be a wonderful father," she said, smiling back at him.

"And you'll be a wonderful mother."

Emaline's smile disappeared as she ducked her head. She wanted to believe she could survive a pregnancy, but she'd heard so many horror stories from her aunt that she found it hard to believe. "I hope I get the chance," she said quietly.

A furrow appeared between Ransom's brows. "Does that mean you're thinking you have nine months left to live?"

She shrugged.

He pulled her onto her feet and into his embrace and hugged her. Hard. "You can't give up like that, Emaline. I won't allow it."

She hugged him back, hoping against hope that he was right.

"I can't help being scared, Ransom."

He let her go and looked into her eyes and said, "Do you think I'm not scared, too? I know pregnancy has risks, but they can be managed. I plan to take very good care of you. I don't intend to let anything happen to you."

"You can't help the fact that I have narrow hips. You can't change the way I'm made."

He huffed out a frustrated breath, then turned abruptly and went hunting for his clothes, which he'd dropped willy-nilly around the parlor. He didn't look at her as he dressed.

Emaline realized that while it had felt perfectly natural to be standing naked together, it was very uncomfortable to be a naked female in a room with a fully clothed male. She began pulling on her own things, hurrying to catch up with Ransom.

When she finally got her blouse on, he was standing with his hip cocked, something she'd noticed both brothers did when they were anxious or uncomfortable, waiting for her to finish buttoning her skirt. Her fingers kept fumbling with the last button, until finally he took a step closer and said, "Let me do it."

He did up the button, then took her by the shoulders with both hands and said sternly, "Look at me, Emaline."

"You sound like my father," she said petulantly.

"But I'm not, as you very well know. I'm your husband. You're mine to love and cherish and protect. I'm making a rule that—"

"I hate rules!"

"You will never, ever again mention childbirth and dying in the same breath," he continued as though she hadn't interrupted.

"But—"

He kissed her to stop any further objection, then wrapped his arms around her and pulled her close, so she could feel his need. But they were fully dressed now, and he slowly withdrew his tongue from her mouth and said, "As much as I want to make love to you again on that rug, I think we'd better get to bed. I'm going to need all my strength tomorrow."

"I thought you said you were completely well," she said.

"I am. But we're short a cowhand and there are a

lot of hungry steers out on the range. Flint and I are going to be running hay all day tomorrow."

"I wish I could help."

"It helps to know you'll be waiting here with a hot meal when I get home."

"So you married me for my cooking?" she teased.

"And other things," he said as he kissed her beneath her ear. He looked deep into her eyes as he laid a hand on her belly and said, "I hope there's a child growing in there, Em. I pray for the day we'll have sons and daughters, lots of them, playing around us. And I mean *us*. I have no intention of raising those brats alone."

Emaline was surprised into laughter. "Brats? I would never raise a child who wasn't courteous and kind and thoughtful. Why, if a child of mine ever—"

He kissed her again to cut her off and said, "Exactly! I'm going to need you to teach our kids all those manners. Start planning to stick around for the long haul. Do you hear me?"

Emaline had never loved Ransom as much as she did at that moment. He was going to make a wonderful father. But she knew what was likely to happen if she got pregnant, even if he wasn't willing to accept it yet. "Ransom, it's not something I can control," she said quietly.

"Oh, yes, you can," he insisted. "*Believe* you're going to live, and you *will* live."

"It doesn't work like that."

"A lot of times, it does," Ransom said. "Out here, Emaline it's about survival of the fittest. You're healthy. You decide you're going to live through this pregnancy, and you will."

He put a finger to her temple. "Sometimes, more times than you can imagine, you can survive against the odds. Think about my gunshot wounds. They should have killed me, but they didn't. I had a very good reason to stay alive. You, Em. You were the reason I fought so hard to live. Now I need you to start thinking like a survivor."

"But—"

Ransom kissed her again. Thoroughly. When he finally let her go, her legs felt like wet noodles. She clung to him, leaning her head against his chest, where she could hear his heart beating as hard as her own.

"Ransom, I don't believe—"

He captured her mouth, the kiss almost savage. When he let her go, he said, "That isn't what I want to hear, Em."

Emaline sighed. "All right. Fine. I'll imagine a future with a dozen children sitting around us at the table."

He grinned and said, "That sounds a little ambitious. But if you're willing, so am I."

She laughed at his silliness. A dozen children. He was going to be lucky to get one. She sobered and said, "I'll try, Ransom. I promise to try."

He took her in his arms and held her close. "That's all I ask, Em. I want children, I won't deny it. I know there's peril. I'm not denying that, either. But you can do this. I know it."

She hugged him back, because she knew there was no sense arguing with him anymore. He'd only kiss her again. She would keep her promise to think positive. She would also write a letter to her child, in case she didn't survive its birth.

It was a comfort to know that Hannah would be nearby. At least her motherless child would have an aunt to provide the kind of female guidance she'd had from Aunt Betsy.

"Let's go to bed," she said at last.

He surprised her again by lifting her in his arms and heading for the front door.

"Ransom, where are you going?"

"I never got to carry my bride over the threshold."

Emaline laughed. "Don't be ridiculous. We've been married three months. And it's freezing outside!"

"Indulge me, Em. Will you get the door?"

She leaned down and opened the door and a swirl of snow blew into the house. Ransom stepped out onto the covered front porch, and she pulled the door closed. The moon was half hidden by snow clouds, leaving the porch full of shadows. She shivered in his arms as the wind whipped stinging snowflakes against her nose and cheeks.

Ransom lifted her a little higher, kissed her mouth, and said, "I love you, Em, now and forever."

For a cowboy, it was poetry. She kissed the edge of his mouth and said, "And I love you, Ransom. I'll spend the rest of my life loving you."

It wasn't until she finished speaking, that Emaline noticed the difference between what he'd vowed and what she'd sworn. *Forever* was a great deal longer than *the rest of my life*. But it was too late to make the change without pointing out the difference.

She shivered again and clung to him, feeling the desperation of her situation. If she was pregnant, she was going to have to hide her fear from Ransom. She was going to have to cope with it on her own.

At last she said, "Take me inside, Ransom. It's cold."

She leaned over and unlatched the door, and he carried her across the threshold. As soon as she was inside, he set her down and turned to close the door behind him.

She looked at him and saw that his shoulders and hair and eyelashes were covered with snowflakes and began brushing them off. He did the same for her.

A moment later she was in his arms, being hugged so tight she couldn't breathe.

"Don't leave me, Em," he said in a harsh voice. "Don't ever leave me."

There it was. The plea he would have made on her deathbed, stated at the start of her pregnancy. What should she say in reply? She said the only thing she could. What she'd promised him she would say. "I'm here, Ransom, and I'm not going anywhere."

Chapter Thirty-five

Flint surveyed the hide of the OOX cow on his land and saw what he thought was the CC brand barely visible beyond the OO on the cow's brown hide.

"I told you he stole those missing cattle," Ransom said. "Let's skin it, and find out for sure."

"Then we're the thieves," Flint said.

"Not if it turns out to be our cow."

The only way to know for sure that the brand had been changed was to kill the cow, skin it, and check the hide on the inside for the original brand. The cow had a broken leg, so it needed to be put down, but Flint didn't want to give Ashley Patton an excuse to accuse them of rustling by skinning it.

"We're still losing stock," Ransom pointed out. "It's got to be Patton. We should do something about it."

"Like what?" Flint asked. The renegade Indians had disappeared, probably to some Sioux camp in the Dakota Territory, where they could snuggle down in their buffalo robes and ride out the bitter winter.

Ransom shot his brother a disdainful look that Flint recognized. *Coward,* it said.

It's caution! Flint wanted to snap back. But the insult hadn't been spoken, so there was no way to refute it.

Then his brother said, "I defended you, you know. When they said you were yellow, I denied it. I was there, Flint. I saw how hopeless our situation was, how the odds were stacked against us when General Sheridan counterattacked.

"But there were a lot of battles like Cedar Creek in the war, from beginning to end," Ransom continued. "Why did you back away, run away, I should say, on that particular day, Major Creed? I've always wondered, but I've never asked."

Flint's belly was knotted with tension. He kept his hands easy on the reins, but inside, his blood ran cold. He'd never expected his own brother to confront him. How should he answer? What could he answer?

"We'd be dead now if I hadn't," he said at last.

"True. But it would have been an honorable death."

"Are you saying you're sorry to be alive?" Flint asked.

Ransom shrugged. "It wasn't my call. I would have stayed if you'd ordered it. All of us would. We'd have followed you to hell, we had so much trust in you. When you said retreat, we thought the order had come to retreat.

"It was only later we learned the truth. That there had been no such order. So why did we run, Major Creed?"

It was ominous, Flint thought, that Ransom kept using his rank to address him. Ominous that his brother was asking now, nearly a decade after the war had ended.

"The war is done. Does it really matter?" Flint asked.

"It does to me. Because I see how you're reacting to this threat from Patton by backing away, by not confronting him, by letting him get away with murdering a lot of innocent settlers."

Flint had opened his mouth to comment, but Ransom kept talking. "We're supposed to help our neighbors," he said, "but we've stood aside and let Patton mow them down, one by one. All that's left are the three big ranches—Holloway's, Grayhawk's, and ours—and the smaller ranches that border the three of us to the west and south. Patton has title, legal and by right of possession, to everything else."

Flint understood his brother's need to attack Patton. But he could see no way to do it without putting themselves in the wrong. It was another no-win situation, like the Battle of Cedar Creek.

General Jubal Early had addressed the ranks three days after that fateful battle in the Shenandoah Valley, near Strasburg, Virginia, to chastise them for their behavior during General Sheridan's afternoon counterattack. Flint had never forgotten Early's condemnation of the Army of the Valley. It was seared in his mind, especially because of the labels that had been attached to him in the aftermath.

General Early had accused officers like Flint, when they saw the ranks thinned by those who'd left it to "disgracefully" plunder the Union camps they'd vanquished that morning, of yielding to "needless" panic and fleeing the field in confusion.

Standing there listening to his commander, Flint had felt the humiliation of being spanked like a naughty child for something he hadn't done—plundering—and the frustration of knowing he was guilty of retreating, but *not* of retreating in "needless" panic.

His men had made an orderly withdrawal, fighting all the way. The panic he'd felt at the time was not at all "needless." Sheridan's counterattack had been devastating, causing nearly three thousand casualties.

"We never panicked and ran, like the troops to our left and right flanks," Flint told his brother. "We made an orderly retreat."

"We were supposed to stay and fight."

"You saw how thin the line was. It would have been suicide. I made sure we got out of there alive. That was the best I could do. Next time, you be the leader," Flint said in a harsh voice.

"Fine." A moment later, Ransom pulled his rifle from the boot and shot the injured steer in the head. He quickly dismounted, pulled a knife from a sheath at his belt, and cut into the hide surrounding the brand on the animal's flank. He flayed the skin around the cut, freed the square from the rest of the hide, and held it up for Flint to see.

The CC brand was clearly revealed.

"I say we take this to the Association meeting this month, make our accusation, and let the chips fall where they may," Ransom said.

"That's not enough."

"It's plenty," Ransom argued.

"It would be our word against his."

"We can't be the only ones losing stock. Patton's cows would have to be bearing triplets for his herd to grow this big this fast. Surely there are other brands that don't fit so conveniently under the OOX. I say the Association ought to take a ride through his herd and take a good close look."

"You do that, and Patton's going to come gunning for you."

"He already has, and I'm still alive and kicking."

"Barely," Flint muttered.

"Are you with me or not?" Ransom demanded.

Flint sighed. Here was proof that one cow, at least, had seen a running iron. Then he had an idea. "I'm with you," he said. "But I have a suggestion."

"Fine, so long as it doesn't mean we have to keep running from Patton."

"There is someone who has the right to legally skin Patton's cows."

"Who's that?"

"Colonel Simmons. I'd be willing to bet that a few of our cows have ended up in the fort's monthly beef supply. I say we have the colonel take a look at some of those skins when the beef is slaughtered."

"Surely Patton wouldn't be stupid enough to send our beef to the fort," Ransom said.

"He gets paid by the pound, and our cows are a lot fatter than his. He's greedy enough to try and arrogant enough to think he can get away with it."

Ransom grinned. "You may be right."

"I'll send a letter to the colonel, along with this hide, and he can start investigating with Patton being none the wiser."

"Maybe he'll rescind the contract with Patton, and we'll have another crack at it," Ransom said.

"That would be nice," Flint said. "We might as well butcher that cow and take home the meat, seeing as how she's ours."

As the two men worked together cutting up the beef into portions they could carry in tarps tied to the back of their saddles, Ransom said, "I see Hannah is speaking to you again."

Flint grimaced. "You noticed that?" To deflect the need for further explanation he said, "How are things going with you and Emaline?"

"Better," Ransom said. "She's still convinced she's going to die in childbirth, but she's ready to make the great sacrifice."

Flint stared at his brother. "Holy shit."

"No shit," Ransom replied. "I'm doing my best to convince her life doesn't end with childbirth."

"Maybe when Hannah gives birth she'll see it's not as bad as she thinks."

"You sound pretty sure Hannah isn't going to have any trouble," Ransom said.

"Her mother bore six children. And you've seen Hannah's hips. They're the right shape for bearing kids."

"Yeah," Ransom said glumly. "Emaline's a lot smaller and a lot narrower through the hips."

"At least Emaline's willing to try," Flint said. "You have to be glad for that."

"I am," Ransom agreed. "But I feel like I'm taking fate in my hands every time I make love to my wife."

"You could stop making love to her," Flint pointed out.

"I love her, Flint. I want her constantly. I restrain myself as long as I can, but I'm not a monk. And she's . . . responsive," he said.

It should have been an extraordinarily uncomfortable conversation. After all, Ransom was discussing making love to the woman Flint supposedly loved. The strange thing was, Flint realized he wasn't feeling envious of his brother. Or jealous.

Only last night Hannah had accused him of loving Emaline, and he hadn't denied it. At the same time, he'd told her that he'd never had carnal thoughts about Emaline. Which didn't make sense. What man didn't desire the woman he loved?

He remembered telling Ransom that he'd take Emaline even if she didn't want children, when he desperately wanted children of his own. What kind of love was that?

It was hard for Flint to admit that he'd been acting like an ass, but when he looked at the cold, hard facts, the truth was right there staring him in the face. When Emaline had chosen Ransom so soon after he'd met her, he'd put her on a pedestal, like some untouchable goddess. He'd coveted and desired the beautiful goddess—but not the flesh-and-blood woman.

Flint felt thunderstruck. He wasn't in love with Emaline. He wasn't in lust with her. She was simply his sister-in-law, who might die in childbirth and leave his brother heartbroken.

When had the change occurred? When had he stopped dreaming about Emaline and started wanting and wishing for Hannah instead?

Flint realized the change had begun when Hannah started avoiding him. He'd realized that he wanted her to notice him. That he wanted her to want him. That he wanted her to love him.

Did that mean that he loved her? Flint examined the idea and realized he might. He just might. And when had *that* happened?

He couldn't wait to get home. He wanted to talk with his wife. He wanted to watch her eyes when she spoke to him, to see if her feelings could be found there. He'd already asked her if she loved him, and she'd said . . . What had she said?

Even if I did, I wouldn't be fool enough to admit it. So did she love him? Or didn't she?

Then he remembered how their conversation had started. She'd accused him of being in love with Emaline. And he hadn't denied it. Would she believe him a day later if he told her his feelings had changed? Probably not.

So what should he do?

Flint knew the answer even before he asked himself the question. Hannah had made her assumption based on how he'd been looking at Emaline. Well, he would simply have to start looking at Hannah that way instead. Would that be enough?

He had two months before McMurtry's kid arrived and took up a great deal of her time and attention. It might behoove him to start right now convincing Hannah his feelings for her had changed.

Chapter Thirty-six

Hannah had been looking forward to Thanksgiving Day because it was the first time since the Great Chicago Fire that she would celebrate the holiday by eating turkey. Flint and Ransom had gone hunting and brought home a large tom. Both Emaline and her aunt Betsy had helped Hannah pluck it and stuff it and cook it. Emaline's father had come to the ranch as well, to help eat it.

Besides turkey and stuffing, the table was filled with more food than the six of them could possibly eat. Which was what a Thanksgiving table should look like, Hannah thought with a smile, as she perused the stuffed turkey, honey-laden sweet potatoes, mashed potatoes, pickled green beans, corn relish, deviled eggs, biscuits with blackberry jam, and pumpkin pie.

Hannah had made the soda biscuits herself. She'd found the instructions in a Confederate Receipt Book, a thin manual she'd discovered in one of Flint's cupboards, which also contained directions for how to make candles and soap, which had been a blessing.

In addition, she'd found remedies for common ailments such as dysentery (table salt in vinegar, corked

in a bottle after the foam is discharged, then a spoonful in a gill of boiling water), chills (hoarhound boiled
in water and served in tea), croup (cold water applied
to the neck and chest with a sponge or towel), and
sore throat, scarlet fever, or diphtheria (a cup of fresh
milk, two teaspoonfuls of pulverized charcoal, and
ten drops of spirits of turpentine, gargled frequently).

Hannah was grateful her mother had insisted that
she learn to read and write proficiently, so she could
make use of all that information. She'd already mem-
orized many of the culinary receipts, including the
one for soda biscuits: one quart of sour milk, one tea-
spoonful of soda, one of salt, a hunk of butter the size
of an egg, and flour enough to make them roll out.
Her biscuits were perfect, if she did say so herself.

"Will you say grace, Colonel?" Flint said.

Flint sat at the head of the table, the colonel to his
right, Hannah to his left. Ransom sat at the opposite
end of the table with Aunt Betsy to his right and Emaline to his left.

"Shall we hold hands, Father?" Emaline said as she
reached for her father's hand.

"Yes, child."

Hannah was taken back to her childhood, when
her father had said grace at Thanksgiving and the six
Wentworth children had held hands around the table.
"We should each say something we're thankful for,"
she said. That had been the custom in her family.

She saw a flicker of approval in the colonel's eyes
before he said, "Grace first, I think." He bowed his
had and said, "Dear Lord, make us truly thankful for
the blessings of family and friends on this beautiful
Thanksgiving Day."

Everyone joined in to say, "Amen."

The colonel released the hands he was holding, turned to Emaline and said, "You go first, my dear."

Emaline blushed, then said to Ransom, "I'm thankful because I expect to give you a son or daughter in nine months."

"Em! Are you sure?"

"As sure as a woman can be," she said, blushing at the need to acknowledge in front of everyone that she'd missed her courses.

Ransom jumped out of his chair and pulled Emaline into his arms and gave her a crushing hug, then released her and laughed as he looked down at her flat belly. "I'm going to squash you both, I'm so happy!"

"I hoped you would be," she said.

Hannah glanced at Emaline's father, whose face had gone stark white. His eyes looked pained, rather than happy. But Emaline saw none of that. By the time she turned back around, her father had a happy smile on his face and was on his feet, as was everyone else at the table. He put his hands on her shoulders and leaned over to kiss her brow. "I'm happy for you, my dear." He shook Ransom's hand and said, "Congratulations, son."

Ransom's face flushed at the salutation. "Thank you, Colonel. I promise to take good care of them both."

"I know you will."

"Oh, dearie," Aunt Betsy said, weeping as though Emaline were already on her deathbed. "You're going to be a mother." She put a lace handkerchief to her mouth and sobbed once into it as Emaline hurried around the table to hug her.

Hannah watched as Flint crossed and shook his brother's hand, slapped him on the back, and said, "I'm happy for you, little brother."

Hannah was the last to hug Emaline, who'd returned to her place at the table after reseating her aunt. Her sister-in-law was trembling like a leaf. "What's wrong?" she whispered in Emaline's ear.

"Nothing that won't correct itself in nine months," she whispered back.

Hannah looked into Emaline's eyes. What she saw was fear, quickly masked. Emaline smiled at her and said, loud enough for everyone to hear, "Thank you for the kind words, Hannah."

Hannah recalled the discussion she'd had the first day she'd met Emaline, and realized the other woman believed her pregnancy was a death sentence. She hugged Emaline again and whispered, "You're going to be fine, Em." It was the first time she'd used Ransom's nickname for Emaline. "I simply refuse to raise my daughter without a playmate."

Emaline giggled. "Oh, Hannah, you are so funny."

"What did you say to her?" Ransom asked.

"Yeah, let us in on the joke," Flint said.

"It's something only a pregnant woman would understand," Hannah said, exchanging a smile with Emaline.

It took a little while for everyone to find their seats again. Right away Ransom said, "I'm next. I'm thankful that in nine months I'm going to be a father."

Everyone laughed.

"Your turn, Aunt Betsy," Emaline said.

"I'm thankful you've found your young man, dearie, and that the two of you seem to be so happy," Aunt Betsy said.

Emaline blushed, and Ransom lifted his eyebrows comically.

Everyone laughed again.

"Now you, Hannah," Ransom said.

She looked at Flint and said, "I'm thankful that Flint found me on the prairie and made me his wife." She put a hand on her large belly, all the while keeping her eyes on his, and said, "And that he's willing to be a father to my baby."

Aunt Betsy made a gurgling sound in her throat and put the hanky to her tear-filled eyes, but she said nothing.

"Your turn, Flint," Ransom said.

"Let the colonel go first," Flint said, never taking his eyes off Hannah.

The colonel cleared his throat and said, "I'm thankful my daughter has found such a good man to be her husband. And that she's making me a grandfather."

Everyone laughed.

"Now you, Flint," Ransom said.

Flint reached into the pocket of the vest he was wearing and pulled out a folded paper. He met Hannah's gaze and said, "I'm thankful I found a wife to love, and that she's going to make me a father without waiting nine whole months."

Everyone laughed again.

Hannah laughed with everyone else, but she felt a hand squeeze her heart. *A wife to love.* How could he speak those words when he loved someone else? And how dare he joke about becoming the father of a child he never called anything but "McMurtry's kid"! She stared—would have glared if she'd dared—back at him, willing him to lower his eyes in guilt and shame.

But he didn't. He kept looking at her, and Hannah realized there was something in them she hadn't seen before. Tenderness, maybe? Something more? Something *else*?

"I wanted to go last, because I have a gift for my wife," Flint said.

"But it isn't my birthday yet," Hannah said.

"When is your birthday?" Emaline asked.

"I was born on Christmas Day."

"Then it's perfect that I have a gift for you now," Flint said. "So I won't have to give you two on Christmas."

Despite her misgivings about Flint's strange behavior, Hannah was curious. "What is it?"

Flint passed an envelope to Hannah.

When she saw the return address, tears sprang to her eyes. She turned to Flint and said, "How did you get this? You haven't left the ranch for months!"

"I sent a letter to my brother, Jake, with one of my cowhands who was headed to Cheyenne. John Holloway picked up this letter for me when it came to General Delivery in Cheyenne and brought it out here."

Hannah noticed the envelope was still sealed. "You didn't read it?"

He shook his head. "It wasn't addressed to me."

Hannah hurriedly opened the envelope and pulled out the letter inside. There was writing on both sides in a tiny, looping hand she recognized very well. It read:

Dear Hannah,

I was so relieved to get your husband's letter.

I am married to Flint's brother, Jake, so we're sisters-in-law now, as well as sisters!

I've been desperately trying to find you and Hetty and Josie for months, but there was no word of your whereabouts once you left the orphanage and headed out onto the Oregon Trail.

It seems we still have two missing sisters that need to be found. I'll send the Pinkerton detectives I've hired off to the Wyoming Territory, now that I know where to start the search.

You're probably wondering where I got the money to hire Pinkertons. It wasn't from my husband. It was our inheritance. We're rich! Father's money didn't burn up with his bank. Uncle Stephen tried to steal it. He's disappeared and taken a lot of it with him, but he'll turn up sooner or later. I have the Pinkertons looking for him, too. There's still plenty of money, if you need some.

Nick is so tall you won't recognize him, and Harry hasn't had the sniffles once since we got here. Both are fine and growing like weeds. I'm also a stepmother to Jake's two-year-old daughter, Anna Mae.

I hope one day all of us Wentworths will be together again. I was sorry to hear about the loss of your first husband, but at least you'll have a little one to remember him by. Since you're in the family way, now is not the time for you to be traveling here, but we can write.

Promise you'll stay in touch. I'll let you know if the Pinkertons come up with any information about Hetty or Josie.

Best wishes on your marriage. Jake says Flint is a good man.

All my love,
Miranda

Hannah met Flint's gaze over the top of the paper, but she couldn't see much through the film of tears. "She says she's married to your brother. She says my two younger brothers are fine."

"That's wonderful news," Emaline said.

Hannah never took her eyes from Flint's as she continued, "She also says I'm rich. She says my father's money didn't burn up with his bank. My uncle Stephen tried to steal it. She says there's plenty if I need some."

"I don't need or want your money," Flint said.

"We could use it to buy more steers," she said. "So we can get the beef contract with the fort."

"About that," the colonel interjected. He turned to Flint and said, "I got your note about the beef and had the butcher save the brands."

"And?" Ransom said.

"You were right," the colonel said, looking from one brother to the other. "Of the hundred head of beef we got last month, six had original CC brands changed to OOX."

"I knew it!" Ransom said, pumping a fist in the air.

Emaline's father turned to Flint and said, "However, I'm not sure what I can do about it."

"You can cancel Patton's contract," Flint said.

The colonel shook his head. "He delivered the proper number of beeves. They all had OOX brands, at least, on the outside of their hides."

"You must be able to do something," Ransom said.

"I can point out the discrepancy to the Inspector General," the colonel said.

"So Ashley Patton's going to get away with rustling our cattle and selling them to the army, and there's nothing we can do about it?" Ransom said.

"I'll make the hides available as evidence if you want to take Patton to court. Or you can confront him yourselves with the hides at the next Laramie County Stock Association meeting," the colonel said.

"He's going to say someone else stuck his brand on there to blacken his name—like us. Especially if we're only talking about six cows," Flint said in disgust.

"It wasn't only your brand we found on those cows," the colonel said.

"What do you mean?"

"There were quite a few steers that had been re-branded from smaller spreads Patton has bought. Unfortunately, there's no way to know whether he stole the cows from those settlers or branded the cattle after they sold out. What's interesting is that I also had one cow with MacDougall's Bar 7 brand, two with Beaumont's Diamond B brand, two with Grayhawk's Flying Eagle brand, and four with Holloway's Triple Fork brand."

"That's fifteen stolen cattle!" Ransom said.

"Fifteen percent of what he delivered," Flint added.

"How could Patton have believed he'd get away with flagrantly delivering so much stolen beef?"

The colonel raised a brow and stared at Flint. "You tell me."

Hannah saw Flint flush.

Ransom was also staring at Flint as he said, "It's because not one of the big ranches has confronted him. Patton thinks we're all afraid of him, or at least, of his hired gun."

"I'll be glad to keep checking brands over the life of the contract," the colonel said. "That's all I can do."

"Meanwhile, we're still losing cows," Ransom said to Flint.

"There's nothing we can do about it today," Flint said.

"There's one other thing," the colonel said. "About those brand-new Winchesters."

"What about them?" Flint asked.

"One of the bucks from the Red Cloud Agency Camp tried trading one to the agent for extra supplies. He was questioned closely about where he got it. He said he'd traded for it, but word was that a white man was giving them away to any Indian willing to attack the local ranches. That is, all the ranches except the OOX."

"That bastard," Ransom muttered. He looked up and met Emaline's eyes and then Hannah's and said, "Sorry for the language. But he is."

"Unfortunately," the colonel continued, "one Indian's testimony won't hold up in a court of law. However, I also sent an inquiry to the New Haven Arms Company in Connecticut, where the rifles were produced, asking whether Ashley Patton had placed a large order for the brand-new '73 model."

"And?" Ransom asked eagerly.

"He did."

"Got him!" Ransom said, smacking his fist in his palm.

"It isn't that simple," the colonel said. "There's still no proof he gave those guns to the Sioux. He could always argue they were stolen from him."

"So he's going to get away with that, too?" Ransom said.

"Not exactly," the colonel said. "I can't cancel his current contract with the army. I can assure you that he won't be getting another."

"That's something at least," Ransom said.

"If you don't mind sharing your information from the New Haven Arms Company, that's more evidence Ransom and I can use to eject Patton from the Laramie County Stock Association," Flint said.

"Glad to," the colonel said.

"That's not going to be much consolation for the havoc that man has wreaked," Ransom said. "We should do something."

"We can't take the law into our own hands," Flint said.

"Why not? He does."

Seeing the argument escalating, Hannah said to Flint, "Our food is getting cold. Why don't you cut the turkey?"

"She's as good at changing the subject as you are," Ransom muttered.

"Watch what you say about my wife," Flint retorted.

Both men rose, and Hannah rushed to Flint's side as Emaline moved to Ransom's.

"Stop it! Both of you," Hannah said.

"She's right, Ransom," Emaline said. "It's Thanksgiving. Sit down right now. Or else."

"Or else what?" he snapped at Emaline.

"Or else I might throw up all over you and this delicious table full of food."

Everyone laughed. And sat back down to eat.

But the tension never left the room. Hannah looked from one brother to the other. A showdown was coming. She only hoped both brothers survived it.

Chapter Thirty-seven

"I understand wives can attend the Laramie County Stock Association meetings," Hannah said as she cleared the last of the breakfast dishes from the table.

"Where did you hear that?" Flint asked warily.

"Emaline told me. She heard it from Wilhelmina Beaumont and Bessie MacDougall. I'd like to go."

Flint took a sip of coffee to give himself time to formulate a response to her request. The two women Hannah had mentioned were the wives of Hoot Beaumont and Warren MacDougal, ranchers with large spreads south of John Holloway's Triple Fork, just north of Cheyenne. It was the end of the second week of December, and Hannah was a short month away from her due date. "I'm not sure you should be traveling this close—"

"I might be the size of a walrus," she interrupted, "but I'm feeling perfectly fine."

The weather had been cold but dry, so he couldn't use that as an excuse to leave Hannah at home. If it turned bitter cold or a blizzard struck, they could always take refuge at one of the ranches along the way, and finish their journey to Hoot Beaumont's place, where the holiday meeting of the Association was being held, when the weather improved.

However, the meeting itself might become dangerous, since Flint and Ransom intended to accuse Patton to his face of rustling and giving rifles to the Sioux. "Wives don't actually attend the meetings," he pointed out. "They gather in one room, while the men gather in another."

"I have a pretty good idea what's going to happen at that meeting," Hannah said, eyeing him over her shoulder as she washed up the last of the dishes. "I want to go."

Flint grimaced. Of course she did. "You're eight months pregnant, Hannah."

"I'm pregnant, I'm not an invalid," Hannah replied, turning away from the sink and drying her hands on her apron. "I'm perfectly capable of riding in a buckboard."

"Ransom and I can travel faster on horseback."

"Emaline's coming, too."

"Since when?" Flint asked.

Emaline appeared in the kitchen doorway with Ransom on her heels. "Since I talked Ransom into it," she said with a smile. "We never did get to Cheyenne. I thought we could combine the trip to Hoot and Wilhelmina's ranch with a trip to Cheyenne to do some Christmas shopping. We can all have supper and spend the night at a hotel in town."

Flint glanced at his brother and said, "You went along with this harebrained idea?"

"Didn't seem too crazy to me," Ransom said. "We have no way of knowing how long this good weather will last. Might as well take advantage of it to get some shopping done."

"And I want to send off a letter to Miranda," Hannah said. She sat her ungainly bulk down on the chair next to Flint, put her hand on his, looked into his eyes, and said, "Please, Flint?"

Maybe he could have said no if she'd made it a demand. But there was no way he could deny her when she was asking him so prettily. Besides, he needed some paint to dress up the cradle he'd made as a Christmas gift for her, which he could pick up in Cheyenne.

"All right, fine. You can go."

"Yes!" She rose immediately, kissed him on the cheek, and then waddled like a duck toward the stairs.

Emaline followed after her and turned to call back, "We'll be ready to go in the shake of a lamb's tail."

"You realize this is a bad idea," Flint said to his brother.

Ransom shrugged. "They'll be with everyone else's wives. I don't expect they'll be in any danger."

"Not at the meeting. What about after? We'll still have to get from Hoot's ranch to Cheyenne. Then we'll be in town overnight. If Patton gets mad enough, it could mean a lot of trouble for us."

"Better to face that trouble in town, where we'll have witnesses, than out here at the ranch," Ransom said.

Flint knew his brother was right. If they were going to be ambushed, it wasn't going to happen in town. It was the trip home that was worrying him. "You don't think it's crazy to take two pregnant women on a two- or three-day trip each way in the middle of December?"

Ransom grinned. "Crazy as a loon, but I wasn't going to tell my wife no, and it looks like you couldn't say no to yours, either."

Flint smiled. "No, I couldn't."

"We're ready," Hannah announced as she came waddling back into the kitchen with Emaline right behind her.

"That was fast," Flint said.

The two women exchanged a conspiratorial look that told Flint they'd been planning to make the trip all along. He should have felt resentful at being manipulated. But the delighted smile on Hannah's face, and the appearance of her dimples, kept him from regretting his decision. It felt good to make her happy. He wasn't going to examine his feelings for his wife any more closely than that.

Since the weather stayed clear, they ended up camping their first night on the road. They rose early the next morning to finish their journey, and the rest of the trip to Hoot Beaumont's ranch was filled with lively chatter from the women.

Flint's mind was only half on what Hannah and Emaline were saying. The other half was focused on how and when he should accuse Ashley Patton of being a cattle thief as well as selling guns to the Indians.

The other ranchers hadn't yet seen the evidence Flint possessed. He had a letter from Colonel Simmons documenting how many cows with doctored brands had been butchered at the fort. He also had the colonel's written response from the New Haven Arms Company regarding Patton's order for a dozen Winchester '73s.

"Flint, we have a problem," Ransom said.

Flint was surprised to discover how far ahead of the buckboard he'd ridden. He stopped Buck and asked, "Are the women all right?"

"Hannah's having labor pains."

"Damn! I was a fool to let her come." He reacted with anger because that kept him from revealing to his brother how terrified he felt. "Are we sure it's the real thing?" he said as he turned his horse back toward the wagon.

Ransom shrugged. "I don't know any more about this than you do. Em's scared."

"How's Hannah?"

"I'm fine," Hannah answered. She placed a hand on her belly and said, "I'm not sure it's labor pains, Flint. I just mentioned to Em that I had some twinges."

Flint felt sick to his stomach. If this was labor, it was bad news. Babies who weren't fully formed didn't often survive. "You sure about the date you got pregnant?" he asked bluntly.

Hannah glared at him. "I know what day I got married. I guess I know when I got pregnant!"

Flint stared at her. He couldn't believe what he seemed to be saying. She'd gotten pregnant on her wedding night? How could she know she hadn't gotten pregnant after that? Unless she hadn't had sex after that. It hardly seemed possible, but it wasn't something he could—or would—ever ask her about.

Instead he said, "How hard are the contractions?"

"Not very," Hannah replied.

"So maybe it isn't labor," he said. But if it was, they were going to need help. "Let's get where we're going. Maybe one of the ladies at the meeting can tell us more."

And deliver the baby if that became necessary.

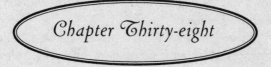
"False labor," Wilhelmina Beaumont announced.

Flint had never heard two more comforting words. "Thank God. Is Hannah all right?"

"Your wife's fine, Flint. She's resting in my bedroom," Wilhelmina said. "We'll do our quilting upstairs today and keep Hannah company. Don't worry. She'll be fine."

"Is it safe for her to travel on to Cheyenne after the meeting?" Flint asked. "We were planning to spend the night there."

"What twinges she had have stopped," Wilhelmina said. "So I don't see why not. That's a strong girl you have there."

"May I talk to her?"

"Sure. We'll all finish up our coffee and tea cakes down here and give you a little privacy before we head upstairs."

Flint took the stairs to Hoot Beaumont's bedroom two at a time. When he got to the door, he was strangely nervous. He knocked softly, and Hannah called, "Come in."

He opened the door and found her sitting up in an

enormous bed with a fancy canopy set on four carved posts. She was wearing one of Wilhelmina's voluminous nightgowns and was sitting upright with several pillows stacked behind her. A cheery fire crackled in a river rock fireplace.

"I'm sorry to be so much trouble," she said, her eyelids dropping so her lashes sat on her freckled cheeks. She looked bashful and vulnerable. "I really thought it was labor."

"I'm glad it wasn't," Flint said. "Wilhelmina says you'll be well enough to travel to Cheyenne after the meeting is done."

She lifted her gaze to his timidly, and Flint felt his heart take an unexpected leap. "I wanted to be downstairs to hear how things went," she said.

"I'll tell you everything later," he replied.

"Why are you standing so far away?"

Flint realized he was still poised right inside the door. He closed the distance to the bed and sat down beside Hannah. She reached out her hand, and he took it. His heart began to romp in his chest. "I was worried about you," he admitted.

She smiled. "I was worried about the baby. I'm glad to know she's going to be staying put for a while longer."

"It made me realize I should probably send you somewhere to stay this last month where there's a doctor to deliver the baby, either to town or the fort."

She shook her head. "Our daughter is going to be born at home. You're going to deliver her."

Flint felt sweat break out on his forehead. It wasn't heat from the fire, because where he sat, the air was chilly. "I don't know squat about delivering babies, Hannah."

"I'll find out everything we need to know before I leave here today. I'm sure the ladies can tell me all the important things. Emaline can help, too."

Flint wondered how much help Emaline would be, considering her fear of childbirth. He hadn't minded nursing Hannah when she was a stranger. Now that he was falling in love with her—or maybe already had fallen in love with her—he was terrified of doing the wrong thing and causing harm.

"What if something goes wrong?" he asked.

"Then a doctor wouldn't be much use, would he?"

"Hannah, I don't want to lose you."

She closed her eyes, leaned back against the pillows, and sighed. "I know. That would be difficult for you, I'm sure."

He knew what she was thinking, that if she died, he would no longer have a wife as a buffer between himself and Emaline. He felt his heart squeeze. He wanted to tell her that that wasn't why he would miss her, but he didn't think she would believe him. So he remained silent. How could he prove his feelings had changed?

Only by loving her.

He leaned over and kissed her softly on the mouth. If only he could convince her he loved her. If only she could learn to love him in return. Life would be so . . . He wasn't sure what word would properly fill in that blank. Wonderful? Happy? Satisfying? Special? All of the above.

"Get some rest, Hannah. If you're not feeling well later, we can always stay here for the night."

She opened her eyes, sat up straight, and smiled at

him. "I'm already feeling better. The only reason I'm in bed is because Wilhelmina insisted on it."

The smile, which showed no signs of the twin dimples that appeared when she was truly happy, made his gut wrench because he knew it was meant only to soothe his worries. She didn't want to be a bother. He wanted her to know she was no bother at all. That for her, he would carry the world on his shoulders. All she had to do was ask.

But Hannah wasn't asking for anything from him. Especially not his love.

"Wilhelmina is worth listening to, Hannah. She's borne and raised a bunch of healthy kids."

Hannah pursed her lips. "All right. I'll stay here and rest. Promise me you'll come get me when you're done, and that we'll go to Cheyenne tonight, so I can mail my letter to Miranda."

"Only if you're feeling—"

"I'm fine!" she snapped. She huffed out a breath and said, "Really, I am. I hate all this fuss. I want to be downstairs with the other ladies."

She wasn't fine, or she wouldn't be so irritable. She must be more tired than she was letting on. Thank goodness she would be able to rest this afternoon. "They're all going to be up here in a minute," he said, "so you'll have plenty of company. I've got to go, Hannah."

He rose and glanced down at her. She looked flushed and beautiful and very desirable lying in that big bed. He felt himself becoming aroused and turned away so she wouldn't see.

"Flint," she called after him.

He turned to look at her over his shoulder. "What?"

"Don't get yourself killed."

He chuckled. "I'll do my best to stay alive. See you later, Hannah."

He supposed it was a good thing that she didn't want to have to find another husband. It meant she wasn't going anywhere before he had a chance to woo her properly.

Flint hurried down the stairs and joined the ranchers who'd congregated in the parlor. The women were bidding their husbands good-bye and heading toward the stairs. He perched on the arm of the chair where Ransom was sitting, waiting for all the ladies to vacate the room. When they were gone, twelve men remained, including Ashley Patton.

Because Sam Tucker wasn't a member, he wasn't allowed to attend Association meetings. But Flint had seen Tucker's horse tied up near Hoot Beaumont's bunkhouse, which meant the gunslinger was close by. Flint figured there wasn't much risk of physical harm from Patton or his gunman at Hoot's house. The danger would come after they left, somewhere between here and Cheyenne.

Ransom held the saddlebags that contained the double-branded pieces of hide from cows slaughtered at the fort, a letter from Colonel Simmons confirming that he'd collected the strips of hide, and the colonel's letter from the New Haven Arms Company regarding Ashley Patton's recent purchase of Winchester '73s.

"What you got there, Ransom?" Hoot asked as the men settled around the parlor in wing chairs and sofas and an upright piano bench.

"Evidence," Ransom replied. He handed the saddlebags to Flint, who would present their case to the Association.

There was an immediate hubbub among the gathered men, who turned to one another to speculate on what Ransom had meant. Flint found Patton staring straight at him, his lips pressed flat, his eyes narrowed.

"Why don't you call the meeting to order, Hoot," Flint said. "Then I can make my case."

"This isn't a courtroom," Patton said.

"Hoot?" Flint said.

"I call the December meeting of the Laramie County Stock Association to order. Warren, will you read the minutes from the previous meeting?"

"I move that we waive the reading of the minutes," one of the members interjected, "and hear what Flint has to say."

After the majority voted to waive the minutes, Hoot said, "Don't have any old business to take care of, which leads me to ask if there's any new business. Flint?"

Flint fumbled at the buckle on the side of the saddlebags but finally got it open. He reached inside to collect the two letters, which he set on the coffee table in front of him. Then he unbuckled the other side and pulled out numerous squares of cowhide. He stood and draped the saddlebags over the arm of the chair where he'd been sitting. He handed half the squares to Ransom, then fanned out the rest of them, skin side out, so the gathered men could see what the brands on each of the hides had originally been.

"These are all brands from steers belonging to Association members in this room." Then he turned the hides over to reveal the OOX brand on the other side. "These steers were delivered by Ashley Patton to Fort Laramie for slaughter, as part of his contract to supply beef to the fort."

Ransom held up the rest of the hides, turning them to show the incriminating hot-iron brands.

The men rose almost as one and gathered around Flint and Ransom, claiming the strips of hide that held their brands.

When they were done, John Holloway held four. Hoot Beaumont held two. Warren MacDougall held one. Jim Grayhawk held two. And Flint and Ransom were left with the last six.

"This appears to be pretty damning evidence," Hoot said as eleven men turned to confront Patton.

"It might be, if I were responsible," Patton said. "These two boys have had it out for me ever since I moved into the neighborhood. They've got the best water, and they're determined not to share it."

That was news to Flint. There had never been any question of Patton using the Laramie River to water his beef. He realized it was a red herring to take focus away from the rustled cattle. Instead of commenting on the accusation, he said, "Are you suggesting we changed these brands?"

"Who else?" Patton said.

"To what purpose?" Flint demanded.

"To give me a bad name," Patton retorted. "To paint me as a thief."

Ransom said, "You *are* a thief. A liar and a thief."

"Those are strong words," Hoot said.

"How else do you explain all these changed brands?" Ransom argued.

Hoot's lined face looked harried. "What other evidence do you have that Ashley is responsible?" he asked Flint.

"I have this letter from Colonel Simmons, confirming that these brands came from cattle delivered by Patton under his contract with the fort," Flint said, picking up one of the letters from the table and handing it to Hoot.

"Why would I take the chance of delivering stolen beef to the fort?" Patton asked.

"Because you thought no one would check," Flint said. "And that even if someone did, he wouldn't dare confront you."

Patton's face was flushed. His gaze darted around the room looking for support from other ranchers, but Flint could see he wasn't getting it.

"You're all making a big mistake," the accused man said.

"You're the one who made the mistake, Patton," Flint said.

"What's that other letter," Hoot asked, pointing to the paper on the table.

"More proof that Patton isn't the good guy he pretends to be," Flint said.

"What does it say?" one of the ranchers asked.

Flint read the letter aloud. It confirmed that Ashley Patton had bought a dozen brand-new Winchester '73s from the New Haven Arms Company.

"So what?" Patton said.

"You only have a half-dozen cowhands," Flint pointed out. "Most of whom have their own rifles. Why did you need a dozen Winchesters? More to the point, where are they now?"

"At my ranch," Patton blustered. "I need them for defense against the Sioux."

"I think you gave them to the Sioux," Flint accused. "I think you're the source of those brand-new rifles the Sioux have been using to raid the ranches around here."

"That's a bald-faced lie!" Patton said. "Another example of Creed producing false evidence. The son of a bitch is too lily-livered to face me on his own. He doctored those brands so you'd help him push me off land he wants for himself," Patton snarled.

Flint's face turned white at the insult. He didn't bother answering because the indictment was so obviously without merit.

Then Patton added, "Which is exactly what you'd expect from a coward like Major Creed, who took his men and ran at the Battle of Cedar Creek."

Flint felt all eyes focus on him.

"That's a lie!" Ransom retorted. "Flint didn't run, he retreated."

"Without orders to do so," Patton said.

Ransom said nothing to that.

Flint wished his brother hadn't come to his rescue. Ransom had only put meat on the bone Patton had thrown to the ranchers. He met the eyes of each of the other men, one at a time, and said, "You all know me. I've been a friend and neighbor for nine years. You know what the war was like. Nothing is that cut and dried."

He saw men look away and realized that whatever he said, it probably wouldn't be enough to counter that ugly word. *Coward.* Nevertheless, he tried.

"It's a well-known fact that Jubal Early chastised

his officers after the Battle of Cedar Creek for running," Flint said. "When faced with overwhelming odds after the soldiers on both my flanks had fled in panic, I made an orderly retreat with my men."

"You ran," Patton said flatly. "Like the lying yellow belly you are."

Flint found it interesting that he was now a *lying* coward. But he saw the allegation was finding surprisingly fertile ground.

"I was there," Ransom said. "Fighting alongside my brother. It happened just like Flint said."

"I'm not a coward. Or a liar. Or a thief," Flint began, his gaze moving from one man to another in the parlor. "Consider how difficult it would have been for me to ensure that fifteen steers with this variety of altered brands ended up among the one hundred cattle delivered to the fort last month," he argued in his defense. "Besides, if I were the one stealing cows, why wouldn't they have my brand on them?"

"I see your point," John Holloway interjected. He turned to the other men and said, "Flint would have had to spend a lot of time stealing and branding other men's cattle in order to get this many to show up in the group that Patton cut out to send to the fort. What motive would he have to do that?"

"I told you, he wants all the land along the Laramie River for himself," Patton said.

"You're the one burning out—and then buying out—small ranchers," Flint said coldly. "Not me."

Flint saw the agreement with his point in the nodding heads of the Association members.

Patton scowled and searched the eyes of the gathered men. "You're taking the word of a coward over mine?"

"I haven't known you for nine years," John Holloway said. "I'd ride the river with Flint any day."

Flint felt a weight shift off his shoulders. At least one of his neighbors wasn't going to ostracize him for what had happened during the war.

"Me, too," Warren MacDougall said.

"And me," Jim Grayhawk added.

"I don't have to stand for this," Patton retorted. "I could buy and sell every one of you here!" Instead of winning him friends, that statement seemed to have the opposite effect. Patton put his hands on his hips and said, "Why would I need to steal your cattle?"

"Because you can," someone muttered.

"Who said that?" Patton demanded.

"Whoever said it hit the mark," Hoot said. "Do I have a motion to rescind Ashley Patton's membership in the Laramie County Stock Association?"

"I so move," Warren MacDougall said.

"Second?" Hoot asked.

"I second," John Holloway said.

"All in favor?" Hoot said.

Not every hand went up. Ritter Gordon and Willis Smithson both abstained.

"All opposed?" Hoot said.

Ashley Patton didn't bother raising his hand, but it was clear from his red face and blazing eyes that he was definitely opposed. "You'll all pay for this," he said through tight jaws.

"I suggest you stop rustling our cattle," Hoot said. "We string up cattle rustlers out here in the Territory. You might want to tell your hired dog to put his tail between his legs and head for wherever he came from, because he's not welcome here any longer. Neither are you."

"I'm not going anywhere," Patton said. "Neither is Tucker." He headed for the door, grabbing his Stetson from a table full of them, and his wool coat from a rack near the door, before stalking out. He never looked back.

Hoot glanced around the room and said, "Well, boys, you heard the man. We can count on trouble. Keep a sharp lookout, and send for help if you need it."

"You take special care, Flint," Hoot said as he shook Flint's hand. The other men crowded around to wish him well and offer their support.

Flint wanted to say thank you to his neighbors, but his throat was too swollen with emotion to speak.

Chapter Thirty-nine

Ashley Patton had left the Association meeting early and angry, and Flint had a feeling of foreboding as he headed south to Cheyenne from Hoot Beaumont's ranch. He rode beside Hannah, who was driving the buckboard. Emaline sat beside her, with Ransom riding alongside his wife. The brothers had agreed in advance to flank the wagon to protect the women in case there were gunshots from ambush.

Flint's eyes were constantly moving, scouting the horizon for signs of movement, and he knew Ransom was doing the same. To complicate matters, the temperature had dropped twenty degrees since they'd left Hoot's ranch house. What looked like snow clouds had moved in, and the wind had picked up.

Flint leaned over and tucked the blanket around Hannah's legs. "Are you warm enough?"

She shivered and said, "Warm as any iceberg at the North Pole." She glanced at him and said, "Don't worry so much."

"Does it show?"

"You're hovering like a concerned husband."

"I want to keep you safe."

"I know," she said, glancing toward Emaline.

Flint felt frustrated enough to say, "Look at me, Hannah."

Her head swiveled back, and she raised her left brow in question. "What is it?"

He rode closer to her side, so he could speak quietly and not be overheard by the other couple, who were engaged in a conversation of their own. "I care about you, Hannah."

"I know. I heard you."

"But you don't believe me," he said flatly.

She nodded her head slightly toward Emaline and said quietly, "This isn't the time to be discussing this."

"This is the perfect time."

She looked confused. "I don't understand."

"No, you don't," he muttered. Then he blurted, "I love you, Hannah."

His comment surprised a trill of laughter out of her. She slipped the reins into one hand so she could cover her mouth with the other.

Flint had known it was too soon, but he'd said the words anyway. He hadn't been able to contain them, because he wanted Hannah to know. The feelings were new, but they were strong. And they were real.

Hannah had responded with laughter. Amused laughter? Disdainful laughter? Disbelieving laughter? All three, probably, Flint thought with a sinking heart.

"What's so funny?" Emaline asked, turning to Hannah.

"Yeah, let us in on the joke," Ransom said.

Flint held his breath, wondering if she would repeat

what he'd said. She glanced at him, sobered, and said, "You wouldn't get it."

"I thought it might have something to do with this crazy weather," Emaline said. "Can you believe it's starting to snow?"

"The way my day has been going, yes, I can," Flint replied. His eyes searched the horizon, which was quickly becoming obscured by falling snow. The snow would make waiting in ambush a lot less comfortable for Sam Tucker. With any luck, if he was out there, he'd give up and go home.

"Maybe we'll be snowed in and have to stay in Cheyenne for a whole week," Emaline said. "I would love to shop and shop and shop."

"If the snow gets that deep, we need to be at the ranch to drop hay for the cattle," Ransom said.

Emaline made a face. "We never did have a honeymoon."

"I'm sorry, Em. I'll make it up to you, I promise."

She laughed. "Yes, you will."

Flint watched the couple exchange a happy, conspiratorial look that he envied. He made the distinction in his mind between appreciating what Ransom had with Emaline and wishing he had the same thing with Hannah.

Flint was so disturbed and distracted that he almost missed the flash of gunfire to his right. "Ambush!"

Hannah slapped the reins hard against the horses' backs and yelled "Giddyap!" The team's gait went from a trot to a gallop in a few steps, sending the buckboard careening along the bumpy, snow-slick road, while Flint and Ransom spurred their mounts to stay next to it.

The gunshot had reverberated in Flint's ear a second before he felt the tug on his sleeve. He clenched his teeth at the pain in his biceps and saw blood spurt from his torn coat sleeve.

"You're hit!" Hannah cried.

"Don't stop!" Flint said. "Let's get the hell out of here."

They kept up the hectic pace for another half mile, till the knoll disappeared behind them.

"Slow them down, Hannah," Flint said.

"How badly are you hurt?" she asked as she tugged on the reins.

"It's a flesh wound," Flint replied.

As Hannah stopped the buckboard and began tearing at her petticoat to get a piece of cloth to tie up Flint's wound, Ransom glanced behind them and asked, "Do you think Tucker will follow us?"

It was a foregone conclusion that Sam Tucker had been the man at the other end of the rifle. Patton didn't do his own dirty work, and Flint and Ransom had no other enemies.

"He's already headed to Cheyenne," Flint said as he eased his coat off. "He'd have to be a fool to try riding all the way back to Patton's ranch in this weather."

He turned his horse so his injured arm was presented to Hannah, who sat waiting with a strip of cloth in her hand.

She tore his shirt away from the wound, examined it, and said, "You were lucky. The bullet only grazed you."

Flint hissed and said, "Take it easy," as she tied the cloth tightly around it.

"If you don't like my nursing, you can see a doctor when we get to Cheyenne."

"You're prickly."

Her eyes met his as she said, "I don't fancy becoming a widow twice in the same year!"

He realized all the blood had fled from her face. "Hey. I'm fine." He reached out a hand to support her, because it looked like she might faint, and she shoved it away.

"You need to do something about that man!" she snapped.

"What do you suggest?" he said, shivering in the cold.

"For a start, put your coat back on before you freeze to death."

He grinned and then grimaced as he eased his shearling coat back on over his injured arm. He surveyed the ragged hole in his coat sleeve and said, "That son of a bitch has a lot to answer for."

"What are you going to do?" Ransom asked.

"Confront Tucker," Flint replied.

"Is that a good idea?" Emaline asked anxiously.

"When you're attacked by a rabid dog, you put it down," Flint said.

He glanced at Hannah, whose face looked drained of blood again. But she said nothing.

"Won't that be dangerous?" Emaline persisted.

"Not as dangerous as leaving Tucker on the loose to ambush us again," Flint said.

The rest of their trip to Cheyenne was uneventful. Hannah insisted they stop by the doctor's office first. Once the doctor confirmed there wasn't even enough damage to require stitches, they checked into the Western Winds Hotel on Main Street.

"I'm looking forward to dinner in the restaurant," Emaline said.

"I hope you'll excuse me," Hannah said. "I'm tired. I think I'll go to bed."

Flint was alarmed, because he'd overheard Emaline raving about the restaurant's steak dinners and Hannah agreeing it would be wonderful to eat somewhere with a fine linen tablecloth and fancy silverware. He perused her carefully, noting her flushed face and mussed hair, and said, "I think I'll stay in the room with Hannah and have the hotel send up some dinner for both of us."

"You don't have to do that," Hannah protested.

Emaline hugged Hannah in the hallway in front of their room and said, "We can always have dinner tomorrow, if you're feeling better."

"We're going home tomorrow," Hannah said.

Emaline smiled, glanced at Ransom, and said, "Maybe. Maybe not."

Flint exchanged a look with Ransom, who shrugged and said, "She wants to shop."

Emaline giggled.

Hannah waved and said, "I'll see you tomorrow."

Flint followed her into their room, closed the door behind him, and said, "I wish you had let the doctor take a look at you when he took care of my arm."

"Why? I'm fine."

"If you're so fine, why aren't we having dinner downstairs with Ransom and Emaline?"

She turned back to him, looked at him with stark eyes, and asked, "Why did you say it?"

He didn't have to ask what she meant. He'd been wondering the same thing himself ever since he'd said those three fateful words, *I love you,* which she'd dismissed as a joke or an insult or a flat-out lie.

"I wanted you to know," he said at last.

She crossed her arms protectively over her breasts, above her burgeoning belly, and asked, "When did this change of heart occur?"

How could he tell her what he didn't know himself? He shrugged. "I don't know."

Her mouth tightened. "Because it hasn't happened. For some reason you've decided to lie to me about this. It isn't necessary, Flint." She unfolded her arms, looked down, and placed her hands on her enlarged belly, caressing it as she said, "I have a child to love. That's all the love I will ever need."

Flint winced. "I wasn't lying."

Tears brimmed in her eyes. "Please. Don't."

Flint stared at his wife. He'd made a terrible mistake. He shouldn't have said the words, not when she wasn't ready to hear them. He wasn't sure where to go from here. How did you prove to a woman that you loved her, when she was certain you didn't?

She looked him in the eye and said, "I'd rather be alone."

She didn't even want him in the same room with her. He felt hurt, but he knew he had a great many fences to mend. Better not to try and do it all in one day.

"I'll have some supper sent up to you."

"Where are you going?" she asked as he opened the door.

"I think I'll take a walk."

The door wasn't quite closed when he heard her say, "Be careful, Flint. Don't make me a widow again."

He took surprising comfort from the fact that he would have the rest of his life—however long it lasted, considering the threat from Ashley Patton—to convince his wife that he loved her.

Chapter Forty

"I expected Cheyenne to be a collection of shacks and saloons," Hannah said to Flint. "It's so much more than that."

They were strolling the weathered wooden board-walk along Main Street in Cheyenne, Hannah's arm looped through Flint's, headed for Taylor's Dry Goods, where Flint and Ransom had an account, to buy Christmas gifts.

"Cheyenne sprang up seven years ago, when the Union Pacific railroad came through," Flint explained. "When gold was discovered in the Black Hills this past July, it became the stepping off point for miners headed north to the Dakotas. There's even a Cheyenne to Deadwood stage."

So why couldn't you find a bride in Cheyenne? Hannah wondered. Then she took a second look at the people swarming past one another like ants head-ing home with a fallen grasshopper and realized there were easily ten men for every woman. At the moment, she and Emaline, who was keeping pace with Ran-som behind her, were the only two females on the street.

"Where are all the women?" Hannah asked Flint.

He pointed across the street. Hannah followed his finger to a female face peeping at her from a second-story curtained window above one of the many saloons, from which the sounds of a tinkly piano and a screeching violin spilled onto the street.

"Oh," she said, her face pinkening with embarrassment. "I meant—"

"The decent women are at home with their kids or shopping for supplies or working with their husbands. I'm not quite sure how many folks live in town, but I expect the population will grow with all the business from prospectors," he said.

The sun had come out to sparkle on the thin layer of snow, which was rapidly being muddied by wagons and men on horseback. Hannah lifted her face and felt it bathed in surprising warmth.

"Thanks for agreeing to this, Flint," Emaline said.

Flint glanced over his shoulder and said, "I don't think Hannah could handle another trip to Cheyenne later this month."

"Speak for yourself," Hannah said with a smile.

Flint glanced at her bulk, and she laughed and ducked her head. "Okay, so maybe you're right," she said. "I'm glad we have a chance to shop. I haven't shopped since . . ." Her voice trailed off.

Hannah hadn't gone shopping since the week before the Great Chicago Fire, when her mother had taken her and her twin to Marshall Field's to buy matching dresses, whose design they had first seen in *Harper's Bazaar*.

She and Hetty had each ended up with a paisley-striped, heavy linen sheath in the new princess style.

Hannah could remember the dress as if it were yesterday. It had an upstanding white lace collar, while the
lapels, the velvet bow at the neck, the buttons down
the front, and the trimming on the pockets and long
sleeves were all made of dark pink velvet.

Hannah tried to avoid thinking about her parents—
or her siblings—because when she did, she missed
them, especially her mother, who would have been
excited about this grandchild. Her mother probably
would have been appalled at Hannah's first husband
but perhaps more pleased with the second. She definitely would have wondered at a daughter who'd
loved pretty things spending most of her days dressed
in a man's wool shirt and Levi's, or a shapeless piece
of muslin, instead of a Marshall Field's ready-made
dress in the latest fashion.

"Penny for your thoughts."

Hannah turned to Flint and said, "I was thinking
about my mother." She sighed. "And missing her."

He didn't say anything, and Hannah realized Flint
had no idea how to express sympathy. Not that she
needed his pity. Or wanted it. Not to mention the love
he was offering.

Hannah glanced askance at her husband. She
couldn't understand why Flint had said he loved her.
The words were a painful reminder of the fact she'd
twice married strangers for whom she'd felt nothing.
She was especially suspicious of Flint's proclamation
of love, because it had come out of nowhere.

One day he was in love with Emaline and making
no effort to deny it. The next he was supposedly in

love with her. Only an idiot would believe that sort of turnaround.

Hannah was no fool.

The problem was, she was softhearted. Or soft-headed. Because somehow she'd developed feelings for Flint. She hadn't known they existed—hadn't even admitted them to herself—until Flint had asked her straight-out whether she loved him.

She'd started to say no and realized that wasn't the truth. She had feelings for Flint, but she didn't know how to define them, because she wasn't sure how it felt to be "in love."

On the Oregon Trail, she'd asked herself whether a person could make herself fall in love. She'd never imagined someone could fall in love without even try-ing. That was what she was afraid had happened with Flint.

She'd taken one look at the tall, handsome, fairy-tale Prince Charming, with his thick black hair and silvery gray eyes, with his strong nose and chiseled cheeks and chin, and had fallen for him like some stupid fairy-tale princess. Hannah wanted to give her love to a man who deserved it, not one who seemed to have stolen it while she wasn't watching.

She'd desperately wanted Prince Charming to love her back, to no avail. She had some inkling now of how Mr. McMurtry must have felt, loving her and getting nothing in return. It hurt.

Mostly, Hannah felt terribly confused, which Flint had made worse with his declaration of love. She didn't believe he was telling the truth. But why would he lie about something so important? Hannah tried to imagine what could be going through his head.

Maybe he hoped to talk himself out of loving Emaline by professing love for Hannah. Maybe he hoped to make Hannah more willing to lie with him. Hannah snorted. Soon she would be too big to lie with him, so what would be the point?

Maybe Flint wanted her to feel cared for during these last months of her pregnancy. If so, she was grateful. Hannah had a lot of doubts about how good a mother she would be and what kind of father Flint would be and whether a tiny, fragile baby could survive the rugged life into which it would be born.

Hannah was torn from her reflection when Flint jerked on her arm. She turned and saw he'd been jostled by another man.

"Watch your step," Flint said to the man.

The cowboy's coat was open, and Hannah saw he had a Colt .45 belted at his waist.

"Or what, yellow belly?" the cowboy said.

Hannah watched the blood leave Flint's face. She waited to see how he would react to the insult.

"I don't know you, do I?" he said.

The cowboy sneered. "We ain't met, but I heard about you at Goldie's Saloon last night. You're the major who ran at Cedar Creek." He glanced over Flint's shoulder and said, "And that's your chicken-shit brother."

Hannah had never seen anyone move as fast as Ransom.

"Why you—" Ransom never finished what he had to say, he simply threw a punch that landed on the cowboy's jaw, knocking him backward. The man reached for his Colt, but Flint was there before him, pulling it from the man's holster and holding it aimed at his chest.

"That's enough," he said.

Ransom apparently didn't hear Flint, because he threw another punch that knocked the cowboy off his feet.

"I mean it, Ransom," Flint said. "Cut it out."

"You gonna let him get away with that?" Ransom snarled at Flint.

"I'm not going to beat him to death for it," Flint said quietly. He turned to the cowboy and said, "Keep your opinions to yourself."

"Or what?" the cowboy said, smirking as he swiped blood from his lip and struggled to his feet. "I ain't scared of no lily-livered coward."

Flint said, "I'll leave your gun with the sheriff. You can pick it up when you leave town."

Hannah saw Ransom's knuckles were bloody where they'd hit the bones in the cowboy's face.

"We better make a stop at the doc's office and get those hands wrapped up," Flint said.

Ransom glared at Flint and said, "I'll go by myself. Come on, Emaline."

Ransom stalked off, and Emaline hurried after him, glancing over her shoulder with a worried look on her face.

Flint tucked the gun in his belt, took Hannah's arm, and continued on his way, his jaw rigid, his eyes focused straight ahead.

"What was that all about?" Hannah asked. "What did he mean about Cedar Creek?"

"I was one of the soldiers who retreated at Cedar Creek during the war. Yesterday, at the Association meeting, Patton accused me of being a coward. Ransom admitted he was one of the soldiers under my command."

He shook his head and said, "I was surprised when the members of the Association didn't condemn me. I should have known that wouldn't hold true for folks who don't know me. It doesn't take a mental giant to figure out that Patton or Tucker or both spent some time slandering me at the saloons in town last night."

"Then maybe we should go," Hannah said. "Leave town."

He stopped and turned to her and said, "I didn't run then. I'm not running now."

"But you don't wear a gun!"

His lip curled, and he glanced down at the gun at his waist. "Maybe I'll hang on to this one until we leave town."

What Hannah saw in her mind's eye was Clive and Joe killing each other in a senseless showdown. "I don't feel like shopping anymore. I want to go home."

"I'd oblige you, but I don't intend to make another trip back to Cheyenne before Christmas. If you want Christmas presents, I have to get them now."

Hannah saw the mulish look on his face and realized he couldn't leave town without giving credence to the cowboy's accusations. "Fine. Let's get this over with."

Hannah marched across the street at the corner and entered Taylor's Dry Goods, determined to do her shopping as quickly as possible and dodge another confrontation.

Unfortunately, word had spread beyond the cowboys in the saloon. The other customers in the store

were eyeing Flint with disdain and edging around
corners to avoid getting near him. The man at the
counter waited on everyone else before him. When
Flint finally set his can of paint on the counter, the
merchant said, "That'll be cash."

"I have a monthly account with you, Curtis," Flint
replied.

"There's a lot of bad stuff being said about you,
Flint. Might be you and Ransom won't be around to
pay that bill at the end of the month."

Hannah saw a muscle work in Flint's jaw, but he
didn't argue. He simply took out some coins and laid
them on the counter.

Hannah felt sick to her stomach. Her breakfast was
threatening to come back up. Whatever Flint had
done in the past, she owed him her life. And he was
her husband. Besides, Wentworths were born with
guts and gumption. She wasn't the kind to run, either.

So Hannah took her time shopping. Flint stood by
the door, paint can in hand, waiting patiently. Hannah asked about patterns, about ribbons, about fabric and buttons. She asked about men's gloves. About
ready-made men's shirts. She inquired about knitting
needles and yarn. She was aware the entire time of the
whispers behind hands and the looks of contempt
being aimed at Flint. She kept swallowing her gorge,
unwilling to give in to the urge to vomit.

At last she crossed to Flint and said, "I want to buy
something for you, and I don't want you to see it.
Would you mind stepping outside for a moment?"

He gave her a handful of coins and said, "If you
need more, shout."

Once he was gone, Hannah went to the counter

with her purchases. While they were being wrapped, Hannah said to the man Flint had called Curtis, "I'm disappointed in your behavior toward my husband."

Curtis lifted his eyebrows in surprise. "Have you heard what's being said about Flint? He ran. Cowards don't last long out here."

"Flint's already lasted nine years," Hannah replied. "I don't think that would have happened if he was a man afraid to face danger. After Flint deals with whoever has been spreading these lies, I'll expect you to extend him an apology."

Curtis stood with his mouth gaping as Hannah paid him and collected her purchases. "Good day, Mr. Taylor. It was nice meeting you." Then she turned and walked out the door. The bell rang as it closed behind her.

She looked up into Flint's stony face and realized he must have endured a lot of ugly stares while he'd been waiting for her. She handed him her package—several handkerchiefs she intended to monogram with his initials—which was wrapped in brown paper and tied with string. "I'm ready now. Can we go home?"

"I thought Ransom would be here by now. He and Emaline still have to shop."

Hannah frowned. "What do you suppose happened to them?"

Flint stared down the street toward the doctor's office and said, "Maybe I better find out."

"I'll come with you," Hannah said.

"I think you should go back to the hotel and wait for me."

"All by myself?" Hannah wasn't the least bit afraid to walk down Main Street on her own, but she didn't want Flint walking Main Street by himself with a gun in his belt. That seemed like an invitation to a gunfight.

Flint huffed out a breath. "Fine. Let's go put these things in the buckboard at the livery. Then we'll go find out what's happened to Ransom and Emaline."

Chapter Forty-one

When they arrived at the livery, Flint went to his saddlebags and took out the gun and holster he kept there. He saw Hannah's eyes go wide when he set the cowboy's Colt aside and buckled on his own gunbelt.

"What are you doing?" she asked.

"Making sure we get out of town without any more trouble."

"By putting on a gun? I don't want you to fight."

"I don't want to fight, either, Hannah. I may not have a choice."

"You always have a choice. People get killed in gunfights."

Flint saw the worry in Hannah's eyes. But Ashley Patton and his henchman had sown ugly seeds that had grown into noxious weeds overnight. Flint didn't want a confrontation, but the more he backed down, the more likely it was to happen. And it was clear that, if challenged, Ransom wasn't going to give an inch.

"I'd be happier if you went back to the hotel to wait for me," Flint said.

Hannah put a hand on her bulk and said, "No one's going to shoot with a pregnant woman around."

Flint flushed. Now his wife was offering to let him hide behind her skirts. Her heart might be in the right place, but he felt humiliated by her lack of confidence in him. How could she love a man she didn't respect?

He felt her hand on his arm, and when he met her gaze he saw the apology there. At least she didn't say anything to make it worse.

"Come on," he said. "Let's go find Ransom and Emaline."

They started at the doctor's office. It was empty. No doctor. No Ransom and Emaline.

"Where do you suppose they went?" Hannah asked.

"Let's go by the sheriff's office. I want to turn in this Colt. He can tell us if there's been a ruckus anywhere in town."

That was also a dead end. The sheriff was out of town, but his deputy took the Colt and told Flint the town was quiet as Sunday morning, even though it was Wednesday.

"Maybe we missed them at the dry goods store," Flint said as they left the sheriff's office.

They headed back to Taylor's. Flint took a look inside while Hannah waited on the boardwalk. He stepped back out and shook his head. Flint's stomach churned. There was no reason to believe Ransom was in trouble, but his gut was telling him otherwise. "Maybe they're waiting for us at the livery."

They hadn't taken three steps when Hannah cried, "Flint, look!"

Flint followed Hannah's pointing finger to where Ransom stood, legs spread wide, in the middle of the street, which was suddenly barren of people. He was faced off against Sam Tucker, who stood twenty feet away from him. Emaline was backed up against a wooden church nearby, her eyes wide with fright, one hand clamped over her mouth, the other held protectively over her unborn child.

Flint grabbed Hannah's arm, dragged her into the nearest alley, and snarled, "Don't move. I mean it, Hannah!"

Then he headed down the boardwalk toward his brother, his bootsteps loud on the wood planking, his spurs jingling in the silence. Ransom had either provoked this gunfight or been provoked into it. Flint's heart was caught in his throat. Ransom didn't stand much of a chance drawing against the gunfighter.

Even so, Flint could do—would do—nothing to stop the showdown. Live or die, Ransom had to fight his own battles.

But Flint knew too much about men like Sam Tucker to believe the gunman would leave the results to chance. Somewhere out there, Flint knew, Tucker had another gunman hidden, waiting for his chance to kill Ransom—either backshoot him, or shoot him from ambush, or provoke another gunfight right after the shoot-out—when Ransom, if he was still alive, would be at a disadvantage.

Flint didn't intend to let that happen.

He would have given anything to have his rifle right now. Chances were, that secreted gunman was watching the street from behind closed curtains in an up-stairs window or was concealed in one of the dark alleys between wooden buildings. Flint stood in the frozen shadows beneath an overhanging porch, his glance flicking from point to point along the street looking for anything out of place, searching for trouble.

Suddenly, to his utter disbelief, he saw his wife marching down the street toward Ransom. He didn't dare yell at her and distract his brother. Tucker might take advantage of the moment to draw his gun.

However, he'd mistaken the matter. It was Tucker who was distracted. His eyes goggled at the sight of a hugely pregnant woman in his line of fire.

"Hey!" he shouted, keeping his hands away from his body and jerking his chin in Hannah's direction. "What's she doin' here?"

Flint watched as Ransom hesitated, then turned and spotted Hannah.

"Get out of the street!" Ransom yelled, keeping his hands still, not giving Tucker an excuse to draw.

To Flint's horror, Emaline joined the fray.

"Hannah's right," she said, stepping off the board-walk into the street. "This is ridiculous. Both of you stop it right now!"

Flint watched Ransom's face flush and his eyes nar-row into angry slits as the two pregnant women ap-proached him arm in arm.

Ransom shot a helpless look at Tucker, who smirked and said, "Figures a fraidy-cat like you would hide behind a couple of skirts."

Flint watched as Ransom spoke angrily to the

women, urging them to get out of the way. His efforts were futile. The two women stopped right between the men with guns, obstructing their line of fire, and didn't move another inch. Two stubborn chins rose in defiance.

Flint had stepped into the street in a vain attempt to intercept Hannah, and his gaze was focused on Tucker, so he missed the moment when Ashley Patton appeared at the entrance to an alley across the street. But he heard his name called.

"Flint!"

Flint realized Hannah and Emaline had played right into Patton's hands. Flint couldn't shoot while they were at risk, and Ransom didn't dare take his eyes off Tucker or the two women to watch for an ambush himself.

The wealthy rancher stayed in the shadows as he called out, "You're in my way, Creed. Time to move on."

"I'm not going anywhere," Flint said.

"Then say good-bye to your brother."

Flint looked for a way Ransom could escape the trap Patton had set, but his brother had no way out. Sooner or later, Tucker was going to find a moment to shoot, and Ransom was going to die.

Flint stood his ground and said, "Too many sets of eyes watching for you to get away with this, Patton."

"We'll see about that. Your brother called out my man. I'm only here to make sure it's a fair fight."

Flint heard Tucker say to Ransom, "What do you say, boy? You ready to finish this?"

"Better go get those women out of there," Patton said. "Otherwise, somebody's wife is liable to get hurt."

"You wouldn't dare," Flint said.

Patton said, "Wouldn't I? Accidents happen all the time."

Flint's heart jumped to his throat and his stomach churned. Patton was a man who'd dared a great deal over the past year. Killing and burning and stealing with impunity. Still, Flint wondered if he was bluffing. No one was going to shoot a woman in the West. That was an invitation to a hanging.

But Patton was pushing for a confrontation. Why?

Because he has another gunman hidden somewhere to ambush me. He isn't worried about Ransom. He's sure Tucker will take care of him. He wants me dead, too, and he knows I'm too cautious to get drawn into a gunfight like my brother.

Which meant the instant Flint went for his gun, he was going to be a dead man, and Patton was going to come out of the situation smelling like a rose.

Flint kept Patton talking as he began searching each darkened corner for that other gunman. "You're done around here, Patton. No decent person will have anything to do with you now that the Association has thrown you out. Word will get around, and you'll find yourself unwelcome in the Territory. You should leave now, while you still can."

"You Creeds talk big," Patton said through tight jaws. "When you've got your women to protect you."

"Flint, look out!" Hannah cried.

To Flint's horror, Hannah was running straight for

him, all the while pointing to a spot behind him to his left.

Everything happened at once.

Flint drew his Colt and dove for Hannah. First and foremost, he wanted her safe. He ignored her cry of outrage, shoving her down and putting his body between her and the danger as he searched for the gunman she'd spotted.

Flint found him in the next alley over. He shot at the same time as the gunman. The sound was deafening, but not loud enough to keep him from hearing Hannah cry out in fear as a bullet blasted past his head.

The gunman missed. He didn't.

Flint heard Emaline scream and turned his attention to the confrontation in the street.

Tucker was down. Ransom was still standing.

"You goddamn son of a bitch! How the hell did you beat him to the draw?"

When Flint heard Patton swear, he realized the threat wasn't over. He rose and saw that Patton's gun was aimed at Ransom's back.

"Patton!" he shouted.

The wealthy rancher turned to confront Flint, his face a mask of fury. "You're a dead man, Creed. You and your brother both!"

Flint's reflexes were so heightened, he saw everything in slow motion. Patton took hours to aim his gun, took aeons to finally fire.

Flint bolted left the instant he saw a flash of gunfire. In that same moment, he thumbed back the hammer on his Colt and fired.

Patton's bullet missed.

Flint's did not.

He saw Patton's eyes widen in surprise, saw the look of agony contort his mouth, saw him stumble forward.

Even so, the miscreant's gun came up, and he shot twice more. His first bullet went wide, shattering a picture window in a nearby saloon. The second kicked up the dirt at Flint's feet.

Flint's own gun had not been silent. Both of his bullets found a home in Patton's chest. He watched as a look of stunned disbelief crossed Patton's face before he dropped to his knees and fell forward.

Flint stood frozen for an instant, before his body began to tremble. He knew it was only the aftereffects of adrenaline coursing through his bloodstream. His hand was visibly shaking as he returned his gun to the holster.

Flint met his brother's gaze and saw the thanks there. He could feel his heart pumping hard and took a deep breath and huffed it out, trying to settle himself down. He felt dazed, unable to believe both he and his brother—and their two silly wives—had escaped unscathed.

He turned and found Hannah still in a heap on the ground. He helped her to her feet and said in a voice made harsh by leftover fear, "Don't ever do anything like that again."

She dusted off the back of her skirt and replied pertly, "I trust it will never be necessary to do it again." Then she took a look at his face and said, "You're white as a ghost."

"A ghost is what I nearly was," he shot back.

She placed her hand tenderly against his cheek and said, "What you were was amazing."

Flint realized he was smiling. He took her into his arms and hugged her tight. "So were you."

"You're squashing me," she said breathlessly.

He held on tight, his heart thundering with relief, now that the worst was over and they were all alive and well. "That's the price you have to pay when you decide to put your life on the line for somebody."

"Oh," she said in a small voice.

She looked up at him, her face flushed, and he realized, *She hasn't said she loved me, but would a woman risk her life for a man she didn't care for at least a little?* Maybe there was hope for him yet.

She winced, and he asked anxiously, "Are you all right?"

"I'm not hurt," she protested when he began to search her body for some sign of injury.

He shook her and said, "What were you thinking, Hannah? What possessed you to put yourself in the middle of a gunfight?"

"I know I shouldn't have done it," Hannah said. "It was foolish. And I can see, in hindsight, that it was completely unnecessary. But I didn't want to lose you."

Flint was stunned into silence. It was the closest she'd ever come to saying she cared for him. He wanted to pursue the conversation, but Emaline marched over and announced, "Ransom is furious with me!"

She glanced at Ransom's stiff back as he spoke with the deputy sheriff, who'd arrived to hear explanations and collect the dead.

Hannah winced again.

Flint frowned. "Something's wrong, Hannah. What is it?"

Emaline took one look at Hannah, met Flint's gaze with large, anxious eyes, and croaked, "I think she's in labor."

"Hannah? Is that true?" Flint asked anxiously.

"Of course not!" Hannah replied. "If it's anything at all, it's false labor again. Let's get the buckboard and go home."

Flint didn't know whether to believe her or not. Her forehead and the space above her upper lip were dotted with sweat. Her whole body looked tense. But that was hardly surprising, considering what they'd just been through. "Don't lie to me about this, Hannah."

"I'm okay. Really." She attempted a smile but it was cut short by a wince. "Please," she said. "Can we go home?"

She was clearly more afraid of one of Patton's cronies coming after them than she was of labor, if that's what was going on with her. He thought of taking her to the doctor anyway, then remembered he wasn't in his office. Besides, the sooner they were out of Cheyenne, the better.

"Are you all right, Emaline?" Flint asked.

She nodded. "But Ransom is mad at me."

"He'll get over it," Flint said. Patton was dead, but there would be other Pattons in the future. Before that next confrontation arrived, he was going to have a long, hard talk with his wife. He could fight his own battles. If Hannah really cared for him, she would trust him to take care of them both.

"Come on," he said. "Let's collect Ransom and get the hell out of here."

Chapter Forty-two

Hannah was in labor. Not false labor, the real thing. The twinges she'd felt in Cheyenne had gone away. But this morning, on their last day of travel before reaching home, she knew the baby had decided to come early. Contractions had started in earnest.

She was surprised, because she'd thought when labor started, it would mean constant pain. The pain came at regular intervals, but it didn't last long, maybe ten seconds, and the contractions were far apart, only three in an entire hour.

At least, that was true in the beginning. As they drew closer to home, the pains were longer, stronger, and they came more often. Hannah had said nothing, because she knew from her mother's experience that the time from the beginning of labor to birth was likely to be as much as twelve hours. That was plenty of time to arrive home before the child was born.

The weather was beautiful, sunny and surprisingly warm, considering that the ground was still patched with snow. It had been necessary for Hannah to drive the buckboard because she didn't want to ask for any special favors, thereby revealing her delicate condition.

She had to keep her labor secret until they'd passed by all their nearest neighbors' ranches. Otherwise, she was sure Flint would have insisted they stop somewhere until the baby came. Hannah intended to give birth at home. She wanted this baby to be a part of Flint's life from its very first breath.

Assuming it had a first breath.

She hadn't allowed herself to focus on the fact that the baby was coming three-and-a-half weeks early. Flint had made it clear that his family would start with the *next* child. Mr. McMurtry's child was welcome in his home, but it would be "McMurtry's kid."

Hannah couldn't allow that to happen.

She wanted Flint to acknowledge this baby as his own. She wanted him invested in the child's survival from the very beginning.

Hannah did her best to keep from wincing as she felt another labor pain begin and held her breath until it was over. They weren't far from home now. She decided to wait until they arrived to announce that she was in labor.

She wished Flint wasn't so angry with her. He hadn't spoken another word of rebuke for her venture into the street to break up Ransom's gunfight, but his lips had been pressed into a flat line for most of the journey.

Ransom, on the other hand, had been chastising Emaline without relief every hour of the way.

"Please," Hannah said, bracing herself as a hard contraction kept going . . . and going. "Stop. That's enough."

Her plea caused Ransom to turn on her and snap, "You two could have been killed!"

"But we weren't," Hannah replied, her rigid shoulders slumping as the contraction finally ended. "Can't you leave it at that?"

"No," Ransom said. "Not when my sister-in-law and my wife—two pregnant women—felt it necessary to come to my rescue in front of the whole town." He turned cold blue eyes on Hannah and demanded, "What were you thinking?"

"I was thinking it would be better if you didn't get yourself killed!" she snapped as another contraction came right on the heels of the one that had finished. It was too soon. Too soon! "I was thinking it was stupid to get yourself into a gunfight that might leave your wife a widow and your brother alone to run a ranch too big for one person to manage. I was thinking you're an idiot to take that kind of chance!"

Ransom's jaw dropped.

Flint's mouth curved with the hint of a smile. "I have to agree."

"*Et tu, Brute?*" Ransom said.

"What?" Hannah gasped.

"It's Shakespeare," Emaline explained. "My idiot husband doesn't appreciate his brother siding with you."

"Idiot husband?" Ransom protested.

"I don't agree with what you did, either," Flint said, speaking to Hannah at last. "I think you were every bit as foolish as Ransom."

"Foolish?" Ransom interjected. "Now I'm a *foolish* idiot?"

"Yes," Flint said, a hard edge to his voice. "Because

you played right into Patton's hand. Another gunman was waiting to see if you survived your showdown with Tucker, so he could put a bullet into you, if need be. If I hadn't gotten there when I did, things might have ended very differently."

"I can take care of myself," Ransom flared.

"You can't think only of yourself anymore," Flint argued. "You have a wife and a baby on the way."

Ransom glanced at Hannah, and she saw the blame in his eyes for her interference. "I'd do it again," she said. "I'd rather have people think you're hiding behind skirts than have you dead."

"I wouldn't be dead," Ransom argued. "I'm a good shot. And Flint had Patton covered."

"Only because we showed up in the nick of—" Hannah stopped in mid-speech, dropped the reins, grabbed her belly, and moaned.

"What's wrong?" Flint asked, angling his horse closer to the buckboard.

"Oh, my goodness," Emaline said as she picked up the reins Hannah had dropped.

"What's going on?" Ransom said.

"I think this time she really is in labor!" Emaline cried.

"Are you, Hannah?" Flint demanded.

Hannah didn't answer because the contraction hurt so much it robbed her of speech. She waited endlessly for it to pass. Then she met Flint's gaze and gasped, "Yes. I am."

Flint swore, using epithets Hannah had never heard. At last he said, "How close together are they?"

Hannah went rigid again, and Flint had his answer without her having to say a word.

She glanced at Flint and saw the look of stark terror in his eyes before his gaze shifted to Ransom.

"Don't look at me," she heard Ransom say. "It's your baby."

"Not mine. McMurtry's," Flint corrected.

Hannah didn't contradict him because she was concentrating on the horses' rumps in front of her, watching them plod, willing them to get where they were going before this baby was born. Flint's attitude toward the child she was carrying convinced her she'd done the right thing. Once he delivered this baby, once he held the tiny being in his large hands, he couldn't help but love it as though it were his own flesh and blood.

The contraction finally ended, and Hannah let out a long, soughing breath of air.

"It's another five minutes to the house, Hannah," Flint said. "Take it easy, if you can."

Hannah smiled ruefully. "I don't seem to have much control of the situation. The baby's making all the decisions."

"Scoot over, Emaline. You, too, Hannah," Flint said as he maneuvered from his saddle onto the buckboard's bench seat next to Hannah. He tied his horse's reins on an iron ring, then took the buckboard reins from Emaline. "I don't know what you thought you were doing, Hannah. Why the hell didn't you say something sooner?"

"I wanted this baby to be born at home," she replied.

"Hang on," he said to both women. Then he lashed the horses from a walk to a fast trot. "Are you okay with this?" he asked Hannah as the buckboard bumped and heaved over the rutted road.

She replied by grabbing her stomach to protect the baby inside from being jolted. Another contraction attacked her, causing her to wince and moan.

Emaline's arm came around her shoulders to steady her. "What can I do, Hannah?" she asked. "How can I help?"

In the grip of an excruciating contraction, Hannah said nothing. She clutched Flint's forearm with one hand and grasped Emaline's hand with the other, then closed her eyes and held on for dear life.

The contraction seemed endless. Hannah was counting the seconds. By the time she got to thirty, she thought she would go mad. When would it end? How much longer? She was in agony.

She sobbed when the contraction ended and opened her eyes to discover that the wagon was stopped at the kitchen door of the ranch house. Emaline climbed down off the buckboard on her own, while Ransom ran to open the back door. Flint was already on the ground and reaching for Hannah.

She slid gratefully into his arms and leaned her head against his chest as he carried her inside and up the stairs.

"Set some water to boil," she heard him tell Ransom. Then he turned to Emaline and said, "Get me some clean sheets, some newspaper, twine, and a pair of scissors. Have Ransom bring that water up when it's hot."

Hannah was in the middle of another contraction by the time he reached their bedroom door. The guttural groan that erupted from her mouth sounded like the death throes of a wounded animal.

"Easy, Hannah. Easy, girl. I've got you. You're all right. It'll all be over soon."

Hannah didn't recognize the words Flint spoke, just the tone of his comforting voice. He promised it would all be over soon. She prayed it would, because she wasn't sure how much more of this agony she could bear.

Flint tried to set her down on the bed, but she clung to him, in the clutches of yet another unending contraction. By the time she went limp, Ransom was at the door asking, "What else can I do?"

"Pull down the covers," Flint said. "And put a match to that wood in the fireplace."

By then Emaline had arrived with some of the supplies Flint had asked her to retrieve, and he ordered, "Spread the sheets with newspaper."

As soon as she was done, Flint laid Hannah down and adjusted a pillow under her head. He spread the clean sheet and used it to cover her.

"I'll undress her," Emaline volunteered.

Hannah saw the fear in her eyes and said, "I can undress myself."

"I'll help her," Flint said. "Leave us alone."

"You sure, Flint?" Ransom asked.

"I'm sure."

A moment later, the door was shut, and they were alone.

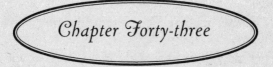

Chapter Forty-three

"You're cold," Flint said when he saw Hannah shiver.

"The fire will warm me up."

Quickly and efficiently, Flint got Hannah out of her coat and boots. He left her socks on, because he could still see his breath in the bedroom. By the time he was done, she was in the grip of another contraction. She clung tightly to his hands until it passed.

He could see the torment in her eyes as she met his gaze. His heart was beating so hard he thought she must be able to hear it. "Are you all right?" he asked as she relaxed her hands and let out a *whoosh* of air.

Despite the cold, sweat had popped out on Hannah's forehead. "Labor is well named," she muttered.

Flint couldn't believe he was going to have to deliver McMurtry's baby. What if something went wrong and the child died? Would Hannah blame him for the loss of the last thing tying her to her first husband? He'd often wondered whether Hannah had loved McMurtry, but he'd never asked because he was afraid of the answer. Maybe she was still in love with a ghost. Maybe that was why she'd never said she loved him.

"Let's get you out of those clothes and into a nightgown."

"I can do it myself," she said, ducking her head shyly. "I'm enormous."

Flint met her gaze solemnly and said, "Yes, you are. Enormously beautiful."

She looked up at him in surprise. "What?"

He laid his hands on her pregnant stomach, so he felt the next contraction begin. Her hands grabbed his wrists, and he watched with awe as her body struggled in an effort to expel the child inside her. When the contraction ended, he swallowed past the sudden knot in his throat and said, "That was amazing."

"I'm glad you think so," she said irritably.

He resisted the urge to smile. "Let's get you more comfortable."

"I don't think that's possible," she shot back.

He went to the clothes chest and looked in the two drawers Hannah used until he found one of her nightgowns. He returned to the bed and undid the buttons on her dress, then pulled it off over her head. He drew the nightgown down over her head and waited while she shimmied out of her underclothes. Before he could even throw the clothing aside, she was caught by another shuddering contraction.

"Let me know when you have to push," he told Hannah.

Hannah wasn't speaking. She was grunting, animalistic, guttural sounds that seemed to come from her very core, as the contraction went on . . . and on . . . and on.

Flint was afraid to count the seconds. Toward the end of labor, he knew the contractions were longer and closer together. Hannah seemed racked with pain, and he had no laudanum to ease it.

"I wish you'd said something sooner, Hannah. The baby's early. We could have used a doctor."

Hannah exhaled noisily when the contraction ended and then gulped air into her heaving lungs. "It's too late now, Flint." She looked up at him and said, "I trust you."

Those three words didn't have quite the same effect as *I love you,* but they were a step in the right direction. Flint didn't want to fail her, but he was going to be in trouble if something went wrong with the delivery, or if the child wasn't able to survive on its own once it was born.

"Are you sure about the date you got pregnant?" he asked.

"Good God almighty! Why would you ask me something as stupid as that?" Then she gasped and grabbed her belly and began making those raw, grating sounds again in her throat.

Flint had asked because he was wishing for a full-term baby, rather than a child whose lungs might not be fully developed or one who might be too frail to live outside the womb.

"I have to push!" she cried.

Flint wasn't ready. "Get that hot water up here!" he yelled. "Where the hell are those scissors? Get me that twine!"

The door burst open and Emaline stood there,

white-faced, scissors and twine in hand. "The water's not boiling yet," she said in a small voice.

"Set those things down on the chest and get over here," Flint snarled.

"But—"

"Move, Emaline!"

Emaline dropped what she carried on the chest and hurried to his side, then stood frozen with her hands wrapped around her elbows.

"Sit down beside Hannah. Hold her hands. Talk to her."

"But—"

"Do what I say!"

Emaline sank onto the bed beside Hannah, but Flint was too busy to notice whether she'd followed his instructions.

"Fliiiiinnnnnnt!" Hannah cried.

"It's all right, sweetheart," Flint said. His insides cramped as tears of pain slipped from the corners of her eyes. "Scream all you want," he croaked past a throat knotted with emotion. "It won't bother me."

"It's bothering me," Emaline muttered. "Look at me, Hannah. Look at me!"

Flint couldn't afford to pay attention to Emaline. He made sure both Hannah's feet were flat on the bed and lifted the sheet that had covered her for modesty's sake to see whether the baby's head had crowned.

Flint realized that Hannah had stopped screaming and shot a look at her to see what was wrong. He saw that the two women were speaking to each other in hushed tones. "What the hell is going on, Hannah?"

"Shut up, Flint," Hannah snapped. "Shut the hell up!"

Then she was writhing on the bed and wailing like someone had died.

"Push, Hannah. Damn it! Push!" he ordered.

"I aaaaaammmmm!"

"The head is out, Hannah," Flint said.

"What did you say?"

Flint turned and saw Ransom standing in the doorway holding a pot of steaming water and looking stunned. "Set that down and bring me those scissors and the twine from the chest," Flint ordered.

"I have to push again!" Hannah cried.

Flint saw the shoulders slide out and then the rest of the baby slipped out easy as butter. He turned the baby over and saw it wasn't breathing. He opened the baby's mouth and slid out a wad of mucus, but still the child didn't cry.

"Give me the damn scissors and twine!" he said to Ransom. He cut the cord and tied it off, then took the baby in his hands and turned his back on Hannah, so she couldn't see it.

"Flint? What's wrong?" Hannah said, pushing herself upright.

"Don't get up," Emaline warned. "You still have to deliver the afterbirth."

"What's wrong?" Hannah insisted.

"She's not breathing," Ransom said.

"It's a girl?" Emaline said.

It's a dead baby, Flint thought. And then, *Like hell it is!* He checked the child's mouth again and found more mucus, which he removed. Then he put his mouth over the baby's mouth and nose and breathed air into its lungs. He watched the chest expand and then deflate. And nothing.

Breathe, kid. Damn it, breathe! I'll do anything, God. I'll be a perfect husband. A perfect father. Please, do not let this baby die.

He put his mouth over the tiny girl's mouth and nose and gently, carefully, breathed air from his lungs into hers again. "Come on, sweetie," he begged. "Breathe. You can do it."

The baby coughed. And then gave a feeble wail.

Flint's eyes closed in hosanna.

He heard Hannah laugh and say, "Lauren! Is that any way to greet your father on your birthday?" Then she said, "Oh!"

Emaline said, "That's the afterbirth." She wrapped it in newspaper and set it aside to be taken out and buried.

Flint rose and realized he hadn't thought far enough ahead to have a blanket in which to wrap the baby.

"Get one of my long john shirts out of the top drawer," he instructed Ransom.

"I have clothes for the baby," Hannah protested.

"You can dress her when you're up and about. Right now she's going to turn into an icicle if I don't get her wrapped up snug and warm."

Ransom spread the shirt open in his arms so Flint could lay the little girl—Lauren, he amended—in it and wrap her up like a papoose. Flint smiled as he met his brother's eyes and said, "I have a little girl." He took the bundled child in his arms, then turned to Hannah and said, "We have a little girl."

Chapter Forty-four

Hannah felt like her prayers had been answered. She would treasure Flint's words for the rest of her life: *We have a little girl.* "May I hold her?"

"Lauren, your mama wants to hold you," Flint said, laying the tiny child in Hannah's arms.

"Did you check?" Hannah asked anxiously. "Does she have all her fingers and toes?"

"Ten of each," Flint assured her. "And your blue eyes."

Hannah unfolded the long john shirt long enough to check for herself. Then she beamed up at Flint. "She's beautiful."

"And redheaded," Flint said.

Hannah smiled as her fingers smoothed over the amazing mass of red curls on the baby's head. "Mr. McMurtry had the most beautiful red curls." She glanced at Flint and saw his lips had pressed flat. "You'll be the only father Lauren will ever know, Flint." She lifted her chin and continued, "But I'm glad she'll have her red curls to remind her of the father who rescued me from that awful orphanage and then died bringing me and my sisters west on the Oregon Trail."

"Hannah!" Emaline said.

"What?" Hannah cried, afraid something had gone terribly wrong.

"You're not bleeding! I mean, not excessively," she corrected. "It looks like you've come through the delivery with flying colors. You're going to be fine."

"Of course I am," Hannah said. "And so will you, Emaline, when you deliver your baby." She grinned mischievously and said, "Especially now that we know what good midwives Flint and Ransom are."

"Oh, no, you don't!" Flint said. "The next baby born around here is going to have a doctor in attendance."

"I second that," Ransom said.

"You won't get an argument from me," Emaline said. "Although, this was lovely, wasn't it? All four of us here to see Lauren born. It's a story she can tell her grandchildren, how her father and mother and aunt and uncle were all there for her birth."

Lauren began to root around, and Hannah realized the baby wanted to nurse. She turned to Emaline and said, "If you and Ransom will excuse us, I'd like to be alone with my husband and our daughter."

"Of course, Hannah," Emaline said, looping her arm through Ransom's. "I'll be up later with some supper. Come on, Ransom."

When the door had closed behind them, Hannah opened the tie at the front of her nightgown and lowered it so the baby could find her breast.

Without a word, Flint crossed and sat beside the

two of them on the bed, watching with as much fascination as Hannah felt herself. The baby's nose brushed Hannah's breast once or twice before she found the nipple. She latched on and began to suck.

Hannah laughed, giddy at the thought of holding her child in her arms and having it nurse at her breast. She looked up and met Flint's gaze. She couldn't keep the smile of satisfaction and pride off her face. "We have a daughter, Flint. Our first child."

He reached out and brushed the baby's cheek with his finger. "She's so soft. And everything about her is so tiny—eyelashes, fingernails, fingers, and toes."

He looked worried, so Hannah said. "We'll take very good care of her, and she'll grow fast. You watch and see."

The wrinkles on his brow were still there, so Hannah asked, "Is something wrong, Flint?"

"I'm not sure I want any more children, Hannah," he said. "Lauren's enough for me."

"What are you saying? I can't count the number of times you've told me you want a big family."

"I do. But . . . What if something goes wrong during one of those births? I couldn't bear to lose you, Hannah. I don't know exactly when it happened, but somewhere along the line, I realized my joy in life comes from seeing you happy. It makes me want to do whatever it takes to keep those dimples showing the rest of our lives."

Hannah laughed and felt the dimples her husband found so enchanting appear in her cheeks. Her heart was soaring. Here was the proof of what she'd been unwilling to believe. Flint did love her. He loved her enough to consider her happiness first and foremost.

He loved her enough to give up having children of his own blood to hold the land after he was gone.

"I'll make a deal with you," she said.

He took her hand in his and pressed it against his cheek, then kissed her palm. "Anything. Ask me anything, Hannah."

"After we have a brood of six, if you don't want any more, then we won't have any more."

He laughed. "Six? Only six?"

Hannah laughed with him. Life was good. Life was perfect. Except . . . "One more thing," she said.

"I told you, Hannah. Anything."

"Someday, I want to go to Texas to see my sister and brothers. Maybe after the Pinkertons find Hetty and Josie, we can all be together again."

"Done," he said, kissing her lips.

Hannah was distracted by the kiss, so that when Flint released her lips at last, it took her a moment to remember what else she wanted. "One last thing."

He smiled. "I'm listening."

"About those six kids . . ."

"What?"

"I think I should warn you. Twins run in my family."

Flint laughed and kissed her again. "I can't wait."

Hannah wondered how long she had to wait before they could start on the next baby. Next time, she wanted a boy, a son for Flint. After that, twin girls. Then maybe twin boys. Oh, my. She was going to be awfully busy over the next few years loving her husband and her six wonderful children.

"What has you smiling like the Cheshire cat?" Flint asked.

"I'm in love," Hannah said.

Flint sat frozen in place. "What?"

"I love you, Flint. I'm *in love* with you, too. Head over ears. Crazy like a loon. Silly as a goose." She paused and glanced at him. "Now you're grinning like the Cheshire cat."

"You bet I am! Ransom! Emaline! Get in here!"

"Flint, have you gone crazy?" Hannah said.

The two came on the run and the door opened with a bang. "What's wrong? Is she bleeding?" Emaline asked.

"Is the baby all right?" Ransom said.

"My wife is in love with me. We're going to have six kids and live happily ever after."

Hannah laughed and shrugged. "I'm married to a crazy man."

"Oh, Hannah, I'm so happy for you both," Emaline said, crossing to give her a hug.

Ransom shook his brother's hand. "Congratulations. Looks like being a father has sent you over the bend."

Flint laughed and said, "Just you wait. You'll see. You are looking at a deliriously happy man."

"Delirious, for sure," Ransom said, chuckling.

As Hannah watched, Emaline hugged Flint. She tensed for the barest instant but saw nothing on his face but joy at the birth of their daughter.

Then Emaline turned back to her and said, "I've got supper cooking on the stove. How would you feel if we bring everything up here and have a picnic?"

"Sounds wonderful," Hannah said. She was a little sore, but now that labor was done, she felt exhilarated. She thought she could have danced a jig, but she was too happy sitting right where she was, holding her newborn daughter in her arms.

When they were gone, Flint crossed and sat beside her. He brushed a knuckle against her cheek, then tucked a stray curl behind her ear. "I love you, Hannah. You've made me a very happy man."

"And I love you, Flint. I never dreamed . . ." Hannah's throat was clogged with emotion, and tears blurred her eyes.

She'd never dreamed when she left the orphanage and married a stranger that she would someday find her Prince Charming. Flint wasn't perfect. No man was perfect. But he loved her and he loved Lauren and with a lot of hard work, they would live happily ever after.

"Whatever your dreams, Hannah," Flint said in the silence, "I want to make them come true."

Hannah smiled through her tears, kissed him with all the love she felt, and said, "You already have."

Epilogue

The knock on the kitchen door startled Hannah. She exchanged a glance with Emaline, who was nursing her newborn daughter at the kitchen table across from her, and said, "Are we expecting company?"

Emaline shook her head.

Hannah rose with her eight-month-old baby in her arms and headed for the door. She glanced back at Emaline and said, "I wonder who it could be."

Emaline laughed. "Open the door and find out."

Hannah decided to lay her wriggling daughter on the pallet in the corner, where she'd created a safe place for Lauren to crawl and play. Then Hannah smoothed her apron, tucked a stray curl behind her ear, and headed for the door.

When she opened it, she found a short man with dark eyes and a thick black mustache standing before her. His black vest and trousers were covered with dust, and a rim of sweat had left a dirty stain inside the collar of his white shirt, which was open at the throat. Despite the warm September weather, he had on a black overcoat that came all the way to his knees.

He was holding a black bowler hat in one hand and a cracked leather briefcase in the other.

"May I help you?" Hannah asked.

"No, madam. But I believe I may be of assistance to you."

Hannah's heart leapt to her throat. "Are you a Pinkerton?"

"I am an employee of the Pinkerton Detective Agency, madam." His lips curved beneath the mustache as he repeated the Pinkerton motto, "We never sleep."

"Come in. Come in," she urged. "Let me take your coat. Would you like a cup of coffee?"

Hannah had completely forgotten that Emaline was nursing her baby at the kitchen table. When she turned and saw her she said, "Oh, Em, I'm sorry."

"No problem," she said as she rose and quickly turned her back to the stranger. "I'll excuse myself and be back as soon as I lay Jesse down for a nap."

Hannah saw that Lauren had crawled off the quilt and she abandoned the Pinkerton to retrieve the baby and put her back in the middle of the colorful cloth square. When she turned to him again he was standing exactly where she'd left him. "I'm so sorry." She gestured toward the kitchen table and said, "Won't you please sit down?"

"Thank you, madam. I believe I will."

As he seated himself, still wearing his coat, Hannah hurried to pour him a cup of coffee. "My husband and his brother aren't at home. If you would like to wait and speak to them, they should be back shortly."

"My business is with you."

Hannah's heart climbed to her throat and threatened to choke her with excitement. She set the coffee on the table in front of her visitor and asked breathlessly, "Have you found them?"

The Pinkerton sighed. "I wish I had good news for you, madam."

Hannah's knees turned to jelly at such an ominous beginning. She sank into the nearest chair and said, "Please tell me it isn't bad news."

"You must decide that for yourself," he said as he unbuckled the briefcase on his lap and pulled out a folder full of papers. "As you know," he began, "the Pinkertons were employed last year to search for three missing Wentworth girls. Our search had stalled when your husband contacted your sister, Mrs. Miranda Wentworth Creed, at which point, our investigation began again, focusing on the other two missing girls.

"As far as your twin goes, we Pinkertons have posted copies of a line drawing—created from the daguerreotype of you taken by one of my colleagues this past January—with the authorities in every city and town in the Wyoming and Montana Territories. We have also shown the drawing to any and all individuals to whom we have made inquiries about your sister.

"I am here to report that several persons in the mining city of Butte, in the Montana Territory, have admitted to seeing the woman in that drawing."

"Then Hetty is in Butte?"

"Not any longer," the Pinkerton said. "It seems she was there briefly and moved on. We haven't yet determined where. One identification in particular, by a Chinese gentleman named Bao—rhymes with cow—

proved, beyond a doubt, that your sister is alive. Or at least, was alive and well in the fall of last year."

"That's nearly a year ago! You haven't found anyone who's seen her since?" Hannah asked.

The Pinkerton shook his head. "I am sorry, madam. We have done our very best. We must presume she is somewhere in the Montana Territory, but the land is a vast forested wilderness. Finding her will take time."

Hannah didn't understand how her twin could simply disappear. But if the Pinkertons couldn't find her, she really must have fallen off the end of the earth. "What about Josie?" she asked.

"Ah," he said. "We had better luck there."

"You know where she is?" Hannah asked, her fisted hand pressed against her racketing heart to keep it from bursting from her chest.

"Not exactly."

"Then what, exactly?" Hannah asked, unable to keep the exasperation from her voice.

"We know she was held captive in an Oglala Sioux village in the Dakota Territory. We also know she was 'bought' by an Englishman."

"Did you say my sixteen-year-old sister was *bought*?"

"I am afraid so, madam. But that was a good thing, we believe. A young Englishman was traveling the American West looking for adventure. He discovered your sister among the Indians and traded a gold watch for her person. That is how we know his name. It was inscribed in the watch, which we recovered."

"You know his name? Who is he?" Hannah asked.

"Marcus St. John Wharton. It seems he's a British lord. The Duke of Blackthorne, to be precise."

Hannah felt as though she might faint. *Blackthorne. Oh, God. Could this Duke of Blackthorne possibly be related to the English Blackthorne who'd married Flint's mother?* "Where is Josie now?"

"The duke took her with him. He's still traveling as far as we know. But we've located his country home in England, Blackthorne Abbey, south of London in the county of Kent. When he returns, presumably with your sister in tow, a Pinkerton will be waiting."

The kitchen door opened, letting in a whirlwind of dust and two tired, sweaty cowmen.

Flint drew up short and demanded, "Who are you?"

The Pinkerton detective rose and extended his hand. Instead of giving his name he said, "I'm a Pinkerton."

"He brought news about Hetty and Josie," Hannah said. "They're both still alive. But both still lost."

"Da da da da da," Lauren called as she crawled rapidly in Flint's direction.

Flint took two steps, swept the little girl up into his arms, and gave her a smacking kiss. "How is daddy's little girl?"

Lauren put her arms around his neck, laid her head on his shoulder, and held on tight. Flint reached an arm out to circle Hannah and pulled her close, kissed her lips, and said, "It's good to be home."

"Where are my two girls?" Ransom asked.

Emaline arrived at the kitchen door in time to hear his question and said, "I just put Jesse down for a nap."

Ransom gave Emaline a gentle hug and a kiss. "How are you feeling?"

"Ransom, I'm fine," she said. "You worry too much."

Hannah saw the flash of concern come and go from Ransom's eyes. Emaline had safely delivered their daughter, but it had been a long and difficult delivery, and Emaline hadn't bounced back from it as quickly as Hannah had from the birth of Lauren.

Hannah was amused to see that Emaline was now the one soothing Ransom's anxiety as she put her hands to his cheeks, looked into his eyes, and said, "I swear to you I'm completely recovered. Jesse is growing like a weed, and I'm already looking forward to having the next one."

Ransom groaned. "Do you really think that's a good idea?"

Emaline laughed and hugged him and said, "We have to keep up with your brother. Hannah is pregn—" She cut herself off and stared at Hannah in dismay. "Oh, my goodness, Hannah. I didn't mean to spoil your surprise!"

"Hannah is pregnant?" Ransom said.

Flint looked at her and asked, "Hannah, is it true?"

She smiled, setting free the dimples that confirmed her happiness. "Yes, I am."

"Are you sure?" Flint said.

She could understand his doubt. She'd gotten pregnant on the first try with Mr. McMurtry. But she and Flint had made love for months without starting a babe in her womb. Every time her courses had come, she'd despaired of ever giving Flint a child of his own blood. He'd told her it didn't matter, that he loved Lauren, and if she was all they ever had, he would still be the happiest man on earth.

But Hannah could see the hope and joy in his

eyes as she confirmed, "Yes, Flint, I'm pregnant. With your son."

She saw the sudden sheen of tears in his eyes as he said, "You can't know it's a son."

"I was right about Lauren, wasn't I? I'm right about this, too. I'm carrying your son, Flint. He'll be born in the spring."

She saw Flint's smile broaden as he leaned down and whispered, "I love you, Hannah."

Lauren said, "Da da da da da."

Flint laughed and kissed his daughter and said, "I love you, too, little bit."

Hannah glanced at Ransom holding Emaline in his arms, then looked at Lauren and Flint and thought how lucky they all were.

Then she glanced at the Pinkerton, who she'd completely forgotten was still in the room. And felt her elation dim.

She fought against the feeling of sadness, reaching for the utter joy that had been hers only moments ago. She turned in Flint's arms to face the Pinkerton and said, "Find them. Please. Find them."

The Pinkerton rose, rebuckled his briefcase, and said, "We will, madam." He winked and added, "Pinkertons never sleep. I can let myself out. I see you are otherwise occupied."

Hannah turned back to the comfort of her husband's embrace.

"It'll be all right, Hannah," he said in her ear.

"I love you, Flint," she replied.

She felt his smile against her cheek. Life was good. And it was only going to get better. "Oh, no," she said.

"What?" Flint asked anxiously.

"We were supposed to go visit Miranda at Christmas. Do you think it will still be all right for me to travel?"

Flint laughed. "No problem," he said. "Miranda and Jake and the kids can come see us."

Hannah made a face. "Didn't I mention it? Miranda's pregnant, too." She hadn't mentioned it because she hadn't wanted Flint to feel bad that both his brothers had sired children when he hadn't.

Flint chuckled and shook his head. "Maybe this is a sign, Hannah."

"What do you mean?"

"Maybe we're not supposed to get together until we can *all* get together."

Hannah's eyes went wide. "Do you really think so?"

Flint kissed her instead of answering with words. He allowed her to hope. He allowed her to dream. Hannah chose to hope and dream that one day soon the Wentworths would all be together again.

Letter to Readers

Dear Reader,

I hope you enjoyed Hannah's story. It was great fun to write. If you're wondering what happened to Hetty, watch for *Montana Bride,* coming soon! I haven't forgotten Josie. She'll have her own story in *Blackthorne's Bride,* which will take us all from England back to Texas, where the Mail-Order Bride series began.

If you're looking for something to read in the meanwhile, check out my Bitter Creek books connected to the Mail-Order Bride series: *The Cowboy, The Texan,* and *The Loner.* If you want to read about Kinyan Holloway, her husband, John, and her sons, Josh and Jeremy, they're featured in *Colter's Wife.* The historical Grayhawks are also featured in my modern-day Bitter Creek series, including *A Stranger's Game* and *Shattered.*

The Blackthornes were introduced in my Regency-era Captive Hearts series, *Captive, After the Kiss, The Bodyguard,* and *The Bridegroom.* So you see, there's plenty to read while you're waiting for the next book.

If you'd like to contact me directly, you can do so through my website, www.joanjohnston.com. I always enjoy hearing from you!

Take care and happy reading,

Joan Johnston

Did Wyoming Bride
steal your heart?

You won't want to miss
the adventures
of the other Wentworth sisters
as they seek love in the Wild West!

Read on for a sneak peek at

Montana Bride,

the story of Hannah's twin sister,
Hetty Wentworth.

Chapter One

"Don't you dare strike that child!" Henrietta Wentworth set her plate of hardtack and beans aside and rose from her seat on a fallen log beside the campfire.

"He's my son. I'll hit him if I want." Mrs. Lucille Templeton had grabbed her seven-year-old son, Griffin, by the arm as he tried to escape after "accidentally" dropping the plate of beans he was bringing her into her lap.

"Look at my dress!" Mrs. Templeton wailed, staring down at a green-velvet-trimmed traveling dress that was clearly ruined. She tightened her grip until the boy grimaced and said, "This fiendish brat spilled that plate on purpose. He deserves the whipping he's going to get."

Hetty balled her fists and took three steps to put herself toe-to-toe with Mrs. Templeton. "You will beat that child over my dead body. Let him go."

"Hah!" Mrs. Templeton snorted. Nevertheless, she loosened her grip, and Griffin jerked free and fled. He disappeared behind the Conestoga wagon in which they'd all been traveling from Cheyenne, in the Wyoming Territory, to Butte, in the Montana Territory, where Mrs. Templeton was destined to become a mail-order bride.

The hodgepodge Templeton family included the widow Templeton, her nine-year-old daughter Grace, and her seven-year-old son Griffin. Hetty had trouble imagining how Mrs. Templeton had produced a daughter as kind as Grace, although she had no doubt how she'd spawned a hellion like Griffin.

Nevertheless, not one of the three Templetons looked like any of the others or seemed anywhere near their professed ages. Mrs. Templeton, with her dyed blond hair, mud-brown eyes, and substantial figure, looked considerably older than twenty-five.

Grace was plump, had flyaway red hair and green eyes, and was already sprouting small buds on her chest, which told Hetty she was more likely twelve or thirteen than the nine she professed to be.

Her brother, Griffin, was a skinny sprout with bright blue eyes and tangled black hair that made Hetty itch to take a brush to it. She figured he'd last seen the age of seven three or four years ago, which would make him ten or eleven.

No less odd was the short, slender, but very strong young Chinese man who was their guide, protector, and driver, Mr. Lin Bao, who said he'd come to America ten years ago to work on the transcontinental railroad. Hetty had learned that the Chinese put their family name first, so Mr. Lin's first name was Bao, which he'd told her rhymed with cow. Bao now worked for the man who would become Mrs. Templeton's husband, Mr. Karl Norwood.

"If I'd had my way, Miss High-and-Mighty," Mrs. Templeton muttered as she lifted her skirts to dump beans from its folds, "we would have left you to rot in that wagon where we found you."

Hetty had no doubt of that. She'd never met a lazier, meaner, or more selfish person in her life than Lucille Templeton. It was appalling to think that she owed this woman her life.

Mrs. Templeton had forced Mr. Lin to stop near the apparently abandoned Conestoga wagon because she'd wanted to scavenge whatever remained inside. Instead, she'd discovered Hetty, dehydrated, weak from loss of blood, and with an infected wound from an arrow in her shoulder. If not for Mrs. Templeton's avarice, Hetty would be dead.

Although, honestly, it was Mr. Lin's doctoring that had kept her alive. He'd used mysterious medicines from the Orient to bring her back to life over the past seven weeks as they'd traveled north. Mrs. Templeton claimed to be a nurse, but she didn't seem to know much about caring for anyone. Hetty shot a quick look at the young Chinaman, who was still sitting quietly beside the fire smoking a long, curved white clay pipe.

"If it had been up to you, Lucy," a young female voice accused, "you *would* have left Hetty in that wagon to die."

Hetty hadn't seen Grace approaching from the opposite side of the campfire, but she'd seen the girl defend her brother from their mother's slaps often enough to know that where Griffin was, Grace was never far behind.

"I'll take care of this, Grace," Hetty said, knowing that Mrs. Templeton was still angry enough to lash out at her daughter.

Her warning came too late. Mrs. Templeton reached out her arm like a lizard's tongue, grabbed a handful of Grace's tumbled red curls, and yanked hard. "You're the one to blame for this. I should never have brought the two of you along."

Grace shot a fearful look in Hetty's direction.

Hetty couldn't imagine having a mother who wished she'd left her children behind. A mother who felt free to slap faces and yank hair. A mother who considered her children a nuisance. No wonder Grace looked so scared.

Hetty's heart went out to the girl. Hetty's own wonderful, loving parents had been lost three years ago, in the Great Chicago Fire, when Mrs. O'Leary's cow kicked over a lantern and burned down most of the city, including the Wentworth family mansion and her father's bank.

Overnight, Hetty had gone from being the pampered daughter of wealthy parents to being an orphan stuck living in the Chicago Institute for Orphaned Children. Her uncle Stephen had left Hetty and her three sisters and two brothers at the orphanage even after they'd begged him to rescue them from the cruelty of the headmistress, Miss Iris Birch.

Miss Birch, like Mrs. Templeton, seemed to find joy in brutality against those weaker than herself. Every infraction at the Institute had been punished with three—"You're lucky it's only three!" Miss Birch was fond of saying—vicious strokes of a birch rod.

Hetty forced her thoughts away from her five siblings, who were all lost . . . or dead . . . but certainly gone. She couldn't do anything to help them. But she could help Grace.

"What I said about Griffin goes for Grace, too," Hetty said. "Let go of her."

Mrs. Templeton twisted Grace's hair until the girl whimpered and stood on tiptoes to avoid the pain. "This is my kid. I'll do with her as I like."

"Not while I'm here, you won't." Hetty obeyed a sudden impulse, and her balled fist struck Mrs. Templeton in the nose.

"Ow!" Mrs. Templeton released Grace and grabbed her bloodied nose. "You'll pay for that."

Instead of running like Griffin had, Grace stood and watched with anxious eyes. "Please, Lucy," the girl pleaded. "I'm sorry. Griffin's sorry."

"Shut up, you ungrateful whelp!" Mrs. Templeton said.

That was another strange thing about the Templeton family. Hetty couldn't imagine calling her own mother by her first name, yet both children called their mother Lucy. Nor could she imagine any mother calling her daughter an "ungrateful whelp."

Hetty should have known better than to think Mrs. Templeton wouldn't strike back. A moment later she felt nails claw their way across her face, narrowly missing her left eye. One of the scratches across her brow bled into her eye, blurring Hetty's vision on that side. She almost missed seeing Mrs. Templeton bend to pick up a long, heavy dead branch.

"Lucy, don't!" Grace cried. And then, to Hetty, "Look out!"

Hetty ducked as Mrs. Templeton swung the unwieldy weapon, but she lost her balance and fell backward onto the ground. Hetty made the mistake of trying to push herself upright with her injured shoulder and yelped in pain. Even after seven weeks, it wasn't healed enough to support her. She was stuck on the ground like a sitting duck.

Mrs. Templeton must have realized Hetty's predicament, because she uttered a shout of triumph. However, the weight of the swinging branch as it continued in its arc pulled her sideways. Instead of letting go of the branch to regain her balance, she held on, and her momentum forced her several steps backward.

Hetty heard Mr. Lin yelling something behind her, but she was too busy trying to avoid being brained by the tree branch to pay attention. She heard Mrs. Templeton cry out and wondered if Grace had somehow intervened to save her.

Hetty looked up in time to see Mrs. Templeton's arms flailing as she tripped backward over a large stone. She finally let go of the branch, which flew several feet upward before it began falling, falling, disappearing from sight before ever hitting the ground.

Hetty struggled to her feet, recognizing at last what Mr. Lin had been shouting. "Be careful!" she cried. "The cliff!"

She got one last look at Mrs. Templeton's face in the firelight—a ghoulish mask of fury—before the woman fell backward out of sight.

Her shrill scream seemed to go on endlessly. Then it stopped.

Hetty dashed with Grace toward the edge of the hundred-foot rock cliff that had been visible in the daylight when they'd camped, but which had disappeared beyond the light of the campfire after dark. She felt sick with grief and regret. She'd only wanted to protect Grace and Griffin. Instead she'd made them orphans. She couldn't do anything right. Mr. Lin should have let her die.

"Careful," Hetty gasped as she put a hand across Grace's waist to keep the girl away from the edge.

Grace kept repeating, "Oh, no. Oh, no. Oh, no."

"What happened?" Griffin called out. "Did the witch hurt herself?"

Grace turned on her brother as he appeared in the light of the campfire and said, "The witch is *dead*."

Hetty stared at the two children, dismayed to hear what they were calling their mother. "What's wrong with you?" she asked Grace. "Your mother has just died a ghastly death."

"She wasn't our mom!" Griffin retorted.

"Griffin," Grace warned. "Don't say another word."

"There's no reason to lie anymore. Lucy's dead. We're DOOMED."

Hetty remembered her twin sister Hannah using that precise term, DOOMED, when their eldest sister Miranda had turned eighteen and could no longer remain at the orphanage. Miranda was the one who'd protected them from Miss Birch's terrible punishments. Without her, they would certainly suffer under the iron discipline of the horrible headmistress.

In the end, Miranda had stolen away, along with their two younger brothers, Nick and Harry, to become a mail-order bride in Texas. At least, Hetty hoped that was what had happened. The three sisters left behind—Hetty, her identical twin sister Hannah, and Josie—had never heard from Miranda again.

When Miranda failed to contact them, they'd taken desperate measures to escape Miss Birch. Hannah had followed Miranda's lead and become the mail-order bride of an Irishman, Mr. McMurtry. Hannah, Hetty, and Josie had journeyed west with him to the Wyoming Territory.

That trip had ended in disaster, with Hannah's husband dead of cholera and their sixteen-year-old sister, Josie, taken captive by the Sioux, who'd attacked their wagon and wounded Hetty. Hetty's widowed twin, Hannah, had disappeared after leaving Hetty in the wagon—wounded and dying—to go for help.

By the time Hetty had come to her senses, after weeks and weeks of being nursed back to health by Mr. Lin, they'd been closer to Butte than Cheyenne. She'd been forced to continue the journey to the Montana Territory. Once she got to Butte, Hetty hoped to find some way to get back to Cheyenne, locate Hannah, if she was still alive, and begin a search for Josie.

Hetty realized she must have been in shock to get so lost in her thoughts at such a dire moment. She shook her head and focused on what Griffin had blurted.

She wasn't our mom!

That explained so many things that had seemed strange about Mrs. Templeton's behavior toward her supposed children. About Griffin's pranks, which often had Mrs. Templeton as their victim. About Grace's wariness around her pretend mother. About the disparities in ages and appearances of the entire fake family.

Hetty turned to Grace and Griffin, who were now standing beside each other. She crossed her arms over her chest because she could feel her body beginning to tremble. Mrs. Templeton was dead on the rocks at the bottom of the cliff. Hetty was at least partly responsible for someone dying. Again.

She forced her mind away from the memories of the calamity she'd caused on the journey west. There was nothing she could do to change the past. She closed her eyes to shut out the awful vision of the man she loved dying in her arms. When she opened them again, she said to the two children, "Is there something you'd like to tell me?"

"Mrs. Templeton worked upstairs at the saloon where we were living," Griffin said. "Before our mom died, she used to work there, and some of the ladies made sure we had a place to sleep and food to eat. But Grace was getting older, and they wanted her to—"

"Griffin, that's enough," Grace interrupted.

"Anyway," Griffin continued, "Mr. Norwood's advertisement for a mail-order bride said he'd give preference to a widow with children, so Grace went to Lucy with this crazy idea that we could all get out of that place if Lucy became this guy Norwood's mail-order bride."

"And Mrs. Templeton went along?" Hetty said.

Griffin snorted. "Yeah, as soon as Grace agreed to pay her, she did."

"You *paid* her and she treated you that badly?" Hetty said, appalled.

"Why do you think I dumped those beans in her lap?" Griffin said. "Lucy wrote back to Norwood that she was twenty-five, so we had to pretend to be younger, too. I'm nine and a half, not seven."

Hetty turned to Grace and asked, "How old are you?"

"Thirteen."

Hetty glanced at Mr. Lin, who was listening to this

confession, wondering what he was thinking. His dark eyes remained inscrutable.

"We're DOOMED all right," Grace said.

Hetty watched tears pool in Grace's eyes before they slid onto her freckled cheeks. Her heart went out to the two children.

Grace glanced at her brother and said, "I can always get work at a saloon in Butte."

Griffin's eyes narrowed and his mouth flattened to a hard line. "Not that kind of work. Not if I have anything to say about it."

"What other choice do we have?" Grace said quietly.

It took Hetty a moment to realize what kind of work Grace was considering. At seventeen, Hetty was still naive enough, even after meeting a girl at the orphanage who'd taken a lover, to be shocked. "There must be a better alternative," she said.

"Not unless we go to some orphanage," Griffin said bitterly. "We ended up in one right after our mother died, but we ran away and have been hiding out at the saloon ever since. I'm never going back. I'll starve first."

Hetty shuddered. Grace working in a brothel? Grace and Griffin at the mercy of a cruel headmistress like Miss Iris Birch? "There has to be a way for the two of you to avoid either of those choices."

"There is way," Mr. Lin said.

Hetty, Grace, and Griffin all turned to find the Chinaman tapping out the contents of his long clay pipe.

"What do you suggest?" Hetty asked.

"I think *you* be mail-order bride," Mr. Lin said.

"Two kids be your kids. Mr. Norwood get bride, kids get home, you get husband help you look for sisters." He smiled and said, "Work out happy for everybody. Okay?"

Hetty stared at Mr. Lin for a moment in astonishment, then glanced at the two children, who were staring back at her with hopeful eyes. Hetty wanted to help, truly she did. But she'd caused so much pain and suffering, she wasn't worthy to become someone's wife. She'd had her one chance at love, and she'd utterly destroyed it. She didn't deserve another.

Besides, the deception would never work. She could never pass for twenty-five. She knew nothing about being a mother or a nurse. And she was a virgin.

Then she thought of the occupation Grace might be forced to join if she refused. And pictured mischievous Griffin in an orphanage, with a cruel headmistress like Miss Iris Birch.

Hetty looked from one young worried face to the other and said, "Okay. I'll do it. I'll become Mr. Norwood's mail-order bride."